Kinney's Quarry

by

Verlin Darrow

The Wild Rose Press, Inc.
PO Box 708
Adams Basin, NY 14410-0708
Visit us at www.thewildrosepress.com

Publishing History
First Edition, 2025
Trade Paperback ISBN 978-1-5092-6037-9
Digital ISBN 978-1-5092-6038-6

Published in the United States of America

Dedication

To my wife Lusijah. She liked this one.

Chapter 1

The situation wasn't what Kinney had been told. For one thing, the target wasn't asleep in his house despite the late hour. The older, gray-haired man slouched in a green Adirondack chair on his front porch, sipping a murky brown drink. He'd rolled up the sleeves of his white dress shirt in defiance of the early April chill.

He could've been an executive in a blue collar company. Trucking? Construction? He would've worked his way up. The hard lines around his dark eyes, slightly downturned mouth, and weathered, olive skin lent him a permanently tired look, as though he'd depleted his internal resources years before.

A muscle-bound bodyguard in a tight black T-shirt and desert camouflage fatigue pants stood at parade rest a few feet past the target, his hands clasped behind him—not a helpful stance against the likes of Kinney. It also let Kinney know that the guy was likely to fight military-style. When Kinney had trained with an elite black-ops Marine unit—as an outsider who didn't wear a uniform, salute, or even deign to say sir—the martial arts instructor had insisted on going by the book—until Kinney kicked his ass in about thirty seconds when they sparred.

A mission-style porch light dangled on a heavy black chain from the slatted wooden ceiling, casting short shadows, rendering both men more three-dimensional to Kinney's eye.

The target stared off into the dark on a line adjacent to where Kinney stooped behind a tall hedge. He'd cut a small hole with a pocket knife at eye level to reconnoiter. When he'd first positioned himself behind it, one of the spiky mini-branches had scratched his forehead, drawing a bit of blood.

To his credit, the brawny bodyguard's eyes scanned continuously. He probably had a headache by now since the near empty liquor bottle on the teak end table beside his employer suggested a prolonged drinking session. When Kinney had suffered similarly stultifying duty protecting a nuclear scientist on Gibraltar, his head had ached for days.

Next to the bottle on the table, a black cylindrical speaker softly played bossa nova music. It wasn't the sort of thing anyone would tap their feet to. In fact, it was one of Kinney's least favorite genres. He liked foot tapping and even snapped his fingers on occasion.

The other small detail Barber had failed to mention was the Rottweiler that suddenly appeared behind Kinney, announcing its presence with a low-pitched snarl. When Kinney whirled to face it, the muscular dog stared Kinney in the face from fifteen feet away, foam forming at the corners of its mouth as it decided what to do.

Kinney had taken the precaution of rubbing the scent of a dog in heat on his black jeans—just in case the intel had been incomplete. God knows where his partner Reed got it. Poorly trained guard dogs either tried to mate with his leg—an awkward moment for both of them—or simply became too confused to serve as an effective deterrent.

This dog was not poorly trained. After another long moment of staring, the Rottweiler charged.

Kinney surprised the dog by mimicking its charge, quickly closing the ground between them. His roundhouse-kick to the side of the Rottweiler's head landed well before the dog could react.

Dogs were trained—both by humans and evolution—to expect certain responses when they attacked. Kinney liked to color outside the lines. Whatever was expected, he did something else if he could. Most of the time, this approach worked out well.

Hoping the loud thud of the kick hadn't been audible over the music from the porch, Kinney bent over and sprayed a cocktail of butorphanol, diazepam, and several other strong tranquilizers into the stunned dog's nostrils. He was rewarded with gasps of foul-smelling breath. First problem solved.

Now that Kinney couldn't slip into the Spanish-style mansion and surprise the target in bed, he decided to simply stride up the flagstone walkway to the porch and play it by ear.

The man in the chair saw him first. "Howard, take care of this," he growled to his bodyguard.

Howard swaggered forward, each loud step on the wooden porch announcing he meant business. His posture and fierce scowl further communicated that whoever stood before him should quake with fear. He cracked his knuckles melodramatically and morphed his scowl into a sneer. On his broad face, the expression was almost lost under a sharp hawk-like nose that widened at the bottom. His blue-black stubble couldn't quite hide all his acne scars, and his brow sported several vertical scars as well. The man had boxed.

"Who the hell are you?" the seated older man asked Kinney, his voice booming now. "And how the fuck did you get into the compound?"

Kinney beat his chest, tilted his head back, and roared like a lion. "Nothing can stop the mighty Kong!" he added as Howard the bodyguard stomped down the porch steps.

Howard paused a moment on the walkway in front of Kinney, clearly puzzled. Was this guy a threat or just a crazy person?

Kinney snap-kicked him in the gut. Surprisingly, the man didn't go down. When Kinney kicked someone, they almost always did.

Howard doubled over from a second kick in exactly the same spot before he could react to the first. Then Kinney swept the bodyguard's legs out from under him and the man fell hard, his Glock flying loose from its hip holster. Kinney kicked it while it was still in midair and it landed in a flower bed beside the porch. Howard had the good sense to stay down. He wouldn't even have seen any of the moves—just three blurry arcs of a black-clad limb.

Kinney climbed the three stairs and approached the man in the chair.

"I'll pay you a lot not to kill me," the man said, his voice quavering. "I've got three kids. I go to church."

Close-up, it was clear the target was quite drunk. The ashen-faced man tried to shape his hands in prayer as if to demonstrate his devotion. Instead, Kinney noticed that the asymmetrical formation cast a shadow puppet onto the floor beside him. For a moment, he tried to discern what animal it most resembled. He settled on an alligator.

"Good for you," Kinney said, resisting the urge to point out the incidental portrait.

Sometimes he wished he didn't notice so many odd details while on the job. Kinney knew he might become sufficiently distracted someday to end up dead. On the other hand, he'd been on the job long enough that things like the shadows livened up boring assignments.

Reaching into his back pocket with his free hand, Kinney pulled out a sheaf of papers and passed them to the man.

"Here you go. You've been served. Don't run. Don't hide. I'll find you."

Kinney held his phone up and took a photo of the man holding the subpoena. Kinney had never acted as a process server before, but if a witness to a major terrorist act couldn't be approached by ordinary means, someone had to do it.

Howard charged up the steps behind Kinney, launching himself as if he were a human projectile. Kinney stepped to the side and punched his would-be tackler in the kidney as he flew by.

"Olé!" he cried, swirling an imaginary cape.

Chapter 2

Giving up lethal missions had been hard at first. The adrenaline rush had been addictive and the withdrawal tough to endure. Pretty much everything seemed flat and uninteresting for months after Kinney recuperated from getting shot in Cambodia.

Even his near-death experience on an operating table had felt anticlimactic soon after his surgery. So he'd seen a light. So he'd drifted toward it and met someone who told him some things. So what? Eight months later, the net effect of what was usually the most profound event in a survivor's life was simply that Kinney didn't want to kill anyone anymore. He felt the same otherwise.

Barber wasn't happy about his decision. "You're our most valuable asset, Kinney," the agency's director told him. "We can't afford to lose you." His desk chair squeaked as he rolled forward until his gut hit his desk, which he ignored.

They sat in Barber's office—a sterile, forbidding environment designed by his draconian wife. Whenever Kinney saw her, he lavished sarcastic compliments on her decorating taste. If she were his boss, she'd have sent him on a suicide mission by now.

Almost everything was either silver, gray, or black. All the surfaces were metallic. The sepia tinted windows rendered the outside world almost colorless, as though an apocalyptic event had obscured the sun. The only feature Kinney liked was the painting on the wall behind Barber's desk. Kinney enjoyed making shapes out of the abstract splotches of blue, green, and black. That day, he saw a woman's torso and an elongated skull. He knew he was probably flunking some sort of Rorschach test because he usually saw at least one image of a woman's nude body.

"Flattery will get you nowhere," Kinney responded. "I don't care how valuable you say I am. I've literally seen the light."

"I have no idea what that means."

Barber's tone was studiously neutral, as was his expression. He worked hard to be a black box. His words came out, and it was up to his listeners to make meaning out of them without any of the usual cues to guide them.

Square-faced, in his late fifties with deeply etched wrinkles to prove it, Barber's most prominent feature was a pronounced jet-black widow's peak. The close-cropped intrusion onto his high, flat forehead almost seemed to have a mind of its own. Kinney could swear it sat lower on Barber's face than it had when he'd met him nine years earlier.

As usual, Kinney's boss wore a black suit with markedly padded shoulders and a white dress shirt buttoned at the neck, sans tie. Kinney once likened the overall effect to an autistic man-in-black poised to discredit a UFO sighting.

"Why not use me on nonlethal missions?" Kinney suggested. "We've got lots of those, right?"

"Sure," Barber conceded, nodding. "But I've got plenty of people capable of that kind of work."

He paused and looked down through his horn-rimmed glasses at Kinney. Given his agent's height, he only managed this by jacking up his chair before each meeting with him.

"Not everyone has morals as flexible as yours," Barber continued. "It's hard to find agents who are willing to kill but aren't loose cannons."

"You cut me to the quick. That's Shakespeare by the way."

"No, it isn't. The phrase predates his plays. You're not the only one who attended high school, Kinney."

"Here's my point," Kinney said. "I take pride in being both loose and cannon-like. If I'm not those, what am I?"

"Do we really need to do this, Kinney?" Barber rolled his chair back a foot or two. This time there was no squeak. The omission distracted Kinney for a moment. "Can we stay on topic for once?" Barber continued. "Listen to me, I need you to reconsider. Your country needs you to reconsider."

Kinney leaned back, pursed his lips, and looked off to the left at a supposedly inspirational quote hanging on the wall while he pretended to reconsider. The quote: "Overpower. Overtake. Overcome." Kinney knew this had been plagiarized from a tennis player.

"Nope. No killing," he finally told Barber.

So now Kinney and his partner Reed Bolt worked domestic nonlethal missions. In Reed's case, these more mundane assignments were involuntary. He'd taken out the wrong guy at an airport in Cairo—a very wrong guy, according to Barber.

In the past six months, Kinney had beaten up a mob enforcer—which had been fun—he and Reed had kidnapped a rogue Secret Service agent from a ferry in the Florida keys, and they'd protected an extremely nervous young lady from an unnamed threat—unnamed to Kinney and Reed, anyway. Barber enjoyed withholding information.

Barber was, in fact, something of a prick. Kinney tolerated him because he couldn't imagine doing anything else for a living. Although the adrenaline rushes were much milder than before, how could he give them up entirely? And for all his cynicism, he was a patriot at heart.

When Kinney mentioned to his sister how alive he felt when he was in danger, she told him that being addicted to anything required strict sobriety. Laura didn't know exactly what Kinney did, but she wasn't stupid. Who got shot in Cambodia? Kindergarten teachers?

Since Kinney wasn't aware of a twelve-step group for thrill-seeking government agents, he figured he didn't have a problem in need of a solution, and he certainly wasn't going to take the junior executive job Laura's husband offered him.

****

After a mission, however routine, the agency gave its agents three days off. Typically, Kinney played golf, which he was determined to master—an unlikely outcome after years of concerted effort. He wasn't terrible, but not being terrible didn't come close to meeting Kinney's standards.

Kinney and Reed's days off overlapped after he'd served the man on the porch. His partner had journeyed to eastern Washington to abduct a white supremacist who Barber wanted to "talk to."

The two agents met at a golf course in Aptos, California—down the road from Santa Cruz where Reed had been a member since he was a kid.

Neither man liked to practice, warm up, or conform to golf traditions. They sat on the wide redwood deck behind the clubhouse and drank beer while they waited for their ten a.m. tee time. It was sunny, about sixty degrees, with a slight breeze coming off the Monterey Bay. A stray dog scoured the deck's planking for culinary debris. Kinney tried to lure the disheveled terrier to their table, but he couldn't compete with shreds of hash browns.

The ninth hole stretched out in front of them. The course was in great shape for spring—the end of the rainy season. The undulating green across an asphalt path from the two men was currently confounding a young player, who swore creatively, stringing together unrelated obscenities. Kinney's favorite was "Eat fuck, you pissbrain!" It wasn't clear if the pissbrain was the ball, the hole, friction, or the golfer himself.

Reed wore olive cargo shorts and an orange and yellow tie-dyed sweatshirt. His black cap read "Rated R" in white lettering.

Reed was dazzlingly handsome, with green eyes, a slightly aquiline nose, and a squarish jaw. On its own, his jaw inspired trust, which could be a dangerous assumption depending on whether Reed decided you grazed on the good guy or the bad guy side of the fence. Even taller than Kinney and more muscular, his shoulders extended out much farther than his waist, creating an inverted triangle.

Kinney wore brown corduroy jeans and an unzipped navy windbreaker over a Hawaiian shirt that sported bikini-clad surfers riding enormous waves on the backs of purple sea turtles. He wasn't unhandsome, with his liquid brown eyes and chiseled cheekbones, but when he was with Reed, the contrast wasn't flattering. On the other hand, when on the move, Kinney embodied a cat-like grace that Reed couldn't match.

"You win," Reed said.

"How's that?"

"Your outfit is even more inappropriate than mine."

Kinney smiled. "Thanks. I work at it. How'd it go on your mission?"

Reed grimaced. "It was pretty routine until the guy's wife came at me with a straight razor. It was like a scene in a 1930s movie. I mean, who has a straight razor these days? What about you?"

"As usual, the intelligence was for shit," Kinney told him.

"What was the deal? A moat filled with alligators? Armed Navy SEALs?"

"A Rottweiler and a bodyguard."

"Well, those are better than my guesses. So, any problems?" Reed took a swig from his beer bottle.

"No, not really. Fido didn't find me as attractive as some dogs do."

"Bummer."

"Are we paired up with anyone today?" Kinney asked, gazing across the expansive putting green to the first tee box.

"Yeah, another twosome. Fred said they're titans of industry, whatever that means."

"I think it means we won't like them."

When the duo climbed into one of the new silver golf carts that werc lincd up beside the clubhouse, both nearly fell out after sliding on the slick vinyl bench seat.

"Whoa," Kinney said. "If we can't even sit down without screwing up, how's it going to go out on the course?"

"You know how it'll go. I'll kick your ass as usual—even after I give you more strokes than you deserve."

Then the cart didn't want to go anywhere. They had to switch to another one that had been properly charged. This time they sat down so carefully that both looked as though they were recovering from major surgery.

They met the other twosome on the first tee. The starter was off somewhere—probably hiding in the bathroom. He usually found an excuse to avoid Kinney and Reed ever since the latter had told him a joke so dirty that the retired minister couldn't sleep for days.

"John Molton," said the older of the two men waiting for them, extending his hand to Reed, who introduced himself as Alphonse. "I sure hope you don't mind us joining you."

Most golfers the two agents were matched with were visibly alarmed to meet yahoos in eccentric clothes. Molton ignored their appearance, gazing almost lovingly into Reed's eyes, which Kinney found weird. Was the guy gay? A Buddhist? He glanced at Reed, who broke eye contact to raise his eyebrows at his partner.

Otherwise, as advertised, Molton did look as though he belonged in a suit on the top floor of a corporate headquarters. Some people couldn't look casual in their casual clothes. The man's red polo shirt and khaki pants were both pressed, and his saddle-style black and white golf shoes appeared to be brand new.

A slight gap in Molton's front teeth drew Kinney's gaze away from the man's regular features and deep-set brown eyes. All in all, Molton's oval face beamed insincere goodwill the way a politician's did.

"No worries," Reed responded. "It's a busy day here."

"The starter told us you know the course. It's our first time at Seaview. Maybe you could be our guide." He raised his eyebrows in anticipation of consent.

"Guide, huh? Sure."

The other man introduced himself as Chet. A bit younger than Molton, he projected confidence. His gaze was penetrating, as though he were employing an x-ray device from behind his pupils. Lean in body and face, Kinney thought that if Chet were a dog, he'd be a greyhound. In lieu of handshakes, the man nodded as amiably as he could manage.

Kinney told the men his name was Jasper.

"That's an interesting name," Molton said. "I don't think I've heard it before."

"My mom liked rocks." Kinney shrugged to demonstrate he didn't think this explained his mother's whimsy.

"Ah." Molton nodded and seemed satisfied.

Chet suggested they bet.

"No, thanks," Kinney told him. "The last thing I need is more pressure. I get over the ball and tense up as it is." He demonstrated this by shaking his driver as though he'd suddenly been stricken by a neurological disorder.

"Come on. We'll use handicaps," Molton cajoled.

"I'm in," Reed told him.

Kinney shook his head and rooted in his pocket for a ball and a tee, tucking his driver under his other arm. The other three agreed on the amount of the bet and the ground rules while Kinney teed up. He couldn't help but smile. He'd never seen Reed lose money playing golf.

After a forgettable first hole—everyone had a bogey—the foursome encountered another group waiting in their carts beside the next tee box. It was a bad sign that the course was already backed-up. Usually it didn't slow down until the par three sixth hole.

"This could be a five hour round," Reed told Kinney. "It's all these old men that play on weekdays and only hit the ball a hundred yards. Then they stand around telling corny jokes. They should have a test you have to pass in order to play."

In fact, the other foursome must've averaged eighty years old. One of them was so stooped he looked as if he'd topple onto the dashboard of his golf cart if the wind picked up.

"I'm not sure I'd make the cut if there was a test," Kinney told Reed.

Chet drove the other cart up alongside Kinney and Reed's on the asphalt path leading to the logjam. Tall oaks formed a canopy over them, filtering the sunlight. The moist, tangy bay breeze threatened to muss Reed's hair. He patted it down with some urgency.

"So what do you two fellas do?" John asked from the passenger seat. He peered at them intently, as though he might earn a more substantial commission by upselling them a condo if they worked in lucrative fields.

Reed enjoyed concocting ridiculous professions, so Kinney let him answer.

"We raise weasels for scientific research."

"I've never heard of that," John said, wincing as though not knowing something was physically painful.

"The thing is, they share so much DNA with us that some scientists think we descended from them," Kinney added.

Chet was onto them. "Good one. John and I have a penguin ranch ourselves. Good eating."

"Now, seriously," John said. "You two seem like ex-military. Am I right?"

"I was," Reed said. "Jasper here would've gotten kicked out the first week. He's a loose cannon."

"Thank you," Kinney said. "*Someone* gets me."

"The reason I asked," John said, "is that our company is always on the lookout for a certain type of employee."

"Yeah, like who?" Reed asked.

"Let's just say, capable men who don't shirk from delicate assignments."

"It's not an accident we got paired up, is it?" Kinney asked.

"No. The grapevine says you boys might be unhappy in your current positions. And you both have some very useful skills."

They had to tee off at that point. Kinney and Reed mulled over what they'd heard while Reed outdrove everyone by forty yards and then won the hole with a downhill twelve foot putt. While the group waited on the closely mown next tee for the green to clear, Kinney strode forward and invaded John's personal space while he spoke.

"John, there's no way for someone to know anything about us. Who the hell are you?" His menacing tone fell out of him naturally.

"I'm the guy willing to pay you a lot more than Barber does." Molton smiled a decidedly creepy smile as he backed away, holding up his hands in front of him as though that could ward off the likes of Kinney.

Reed spoke up in a contrasting casual tone. "You know, Barber would probably have you killed if he heard you say his name."

"Probably," Chet interjected, once again attempting and failing to sound friendly. Kinney thought the "probably" conveyed a mixed message. On the surface, Chet was agreeing with Reed. On another level, he made it clear he wasn't worried about Barber, when any sane person would be.

"What makes you think we won't take you out right here?" Reed asked, crouching into a coiled athletic stance.

"Well," John answered hurriedly, "my understanding is that Kinney here doesn't kill anyone anymore, and if I were you, I wouldn't take the chance I might kill the wrong man again. I could be one of the good guys, couldn't I?" He pointed at his sternum as he finished, as though that was where he resided in his body.

Reed stood up straight and glared at John.

"You've got to have a man in the agency," Kinney pronounced. "That's the only way you could know all that. How long do you think he'll last now that we know about him?"

"Fore!" a golfer called as his ball bounced off the back of the last green and stopped a few yards in front of them. All four men stared at the ball for a moment.

"Let me worry about our mole," Molton finally said. "And I'll tell you all you want to know once we get you under contract. Think about it." He turned to Chet. "Give them cards."

The younger man frowned at John for some reason, handed the two agents business cards, and then the two men climbed back into their cart. Chet backed up and took off toward the clubhouse, almost colliding with the doddering golfer hunting for his errant shot.

The cards read, "Molton Enterprises," with a San Jose phone number underneath that.

"They owe me twenty bucks," Reed said. "I don't like those guys."

"I told you we wouldn't."

Chapter 3

After the round—golf was too sacred to be derailed—Reed drove them to the agency's office in downtown San Jose to report. During the forty-minute trip on Highway 17, over a pass in the Santa Cruz Mountains, the two agents speculated about their encounter. Kinney usually preferred to watch the redwood forest flash by and peek back at the spectacular views of the Monterey Bay coastline. Not that day.

Kinney told his partner that Molton must've known they'd tell Barber about the encounter. What were the odds that two veteran agents would simply abandon their posts for more money? Beyond that, they failed to reach any conclusions, although Reed's suggestion that Molton and Chet might have been sent by Barber to test them had some traction for a few miles as they reached the summit and began their descent into the Santa Clara valley.

"Hmm, interesting," was their boss's response to Kinney's story once he made them wait a half hour. The two agents had played hangman in the hallway, sitting with their backs against the wall. Waiting in the waiting room felt too much like waiting. Kinney stumped Reed with "jazzy" and "vow." Reed came up with several misspelled words and one he invented—gorgonzolalike.

"You've had time to think about it," Barber continued, gazing at the two agents with his usual mask of frozen features. "What's your take, Kinney?"

Kinney and Reed sat in front of Barber's desk, forced to look up at him. Reed tried elevating his butt off his chair but couldn't hold the pose very long.

Barber wore his usual black suit—what most of the agency referred to as his uniform—and his hair must've been cut and razor trimmed within the last twenty-four hours. A whiff of spicy aftershave drifted across the desk. Reed sniffed ostentatiously and scrunched his nose.

"He wants us to think we have a bad apple somewhere high up the chain of command," Kinney replied. "Someone who knows about Reed and me."

Reed chimed in. "I don't like those guys."

Barber ignored him. Since he mostly ignored him after Reed's faux pas in Cairo, Kinney's partner felt free to pretty much say whatever he wanted.

"So you don't think he believes you'll sign up with him," Barber said.

"No, I don't," Kinney answered. "Certainly not both of us. Why approach us together? That doesn't make sense."

Barber pondered for a moment. "If this John Molton character is savvy enough to find out about you two, he probably knows we'd look at it the way we're looking at it."

"That makes sense," Reed said. "Way to go, Chief." He started to high five his boss and then thought better of it. There was a limit.

"Then what's he up to?" Kinney asked.

"Clearly, he wants us to know your covers are

blown." Barber paused again, looking down at his tidy desktop. "What *are* your covers these days?"

"I switched from a career in consulting to another career in consulting," Reed told him.

"And what do you consult about?" A hint of frustration leaked out of Barber's pursed mouth. He shoved his glasses up onto his widow's peak. Not for the first time, Kinney wondered if he actually needed glasses.

"Honestly, I don't remember," Reed said. "It's something obscure in both cases. I've got a business card in my car if you want to see."

Barber let out a deep breath. "What about you, Kinney?"

"I retired early because of a hefty inheritance."

"Okay, good enough. So we've got men out there who know about you both, aren't afraid to demonstrate that, and want us to think there's a mole in our organization. It's puzzling. Their asset is much more valuable if we're not aware of him, so whatever they're up to with you two has to be even more important than that."

"Maybe they think the agency will scuttle an operation if we're blown," Kinney suggested. "Or they might have a plan in place that we'd be likely to disrupt."

"Maybe," Barber conceded. "But you two don't do anything important anymore." His mask slipped on a grander scale for a moment, and he frowned at them.

"That hurts," Reed told him, narrowing his eyes and tightening his mouth in an unsuccessful attempt to look hurt.

"Could the source be an ex-employee—someone

you fired or something?" Kinney asked.

"I'll look into that. Whoever it is, he must be expendable or they wouldn't have told us any of this."

"Why do we keep using a male pronoun?" Kinney asked. "It could be a woman."

"Good point," Barber told him. "Are either of you pillow talkers?"

"Say what?" Reed said.

"Have you talked to lovers about yourself—about your work?"

"Of course not," the two agents answered in unison.

"We're not idiots," Reed added.

Barber stared him down, raising his eyebrows. Reed studied the abstract painting over his boss's shoulder.

"So how can we use you in this situation?" Barber mused. "Could we have you sign up with Molton's organization, Kinney? Would that be credible?"

"I doubt it," Kinney said. "The other guy with him was sharp. He must know how unlikely that would be even if Molton doesn't."

"What if I fired you because your cover was blown? What if you were standing in an unemployment line somewhere?"

"You know, that might be what they want. They've probably reasoned we wouldn't be useful to the agency if people know about us," Kinney replied.

Reed chimed in. "What do you usually do with blown agents?"

"We don't have them. I run a tight ship, but I suppose I'd assign them to desk duty—running missions remotely."

"We wouldn't stay if you did that to us," Kinney told him. He knew he could speak for both of them.

"Okay," Barber said, almost breaking into a smile. "I think we're onto something here. If we keep all of this in the room, and role-play some big scene where you two quit because I've reassigned you, maybe you can go undercover, Kinney."

"What about me?" Reed asked.

"Enjoy your unemployment, Reed. You've earned it."

Chapter 4

Kinney and Reed trudged out of Barber's office, their shoulders slumped. Kinney's face reflected convincing dejection. Reed looked constipated. No one even glanced at them. They headed to the nearest tech guy's office, where Reed surrendered his business card from Molton. Kinney hung onto his.

"Barber wants you to look into these people," Reed told Henry Cutler.

Like their boss, Cutler always wore the same clothes to work—in his case, a yellow T-shirt and forest green sweatpants. Nobody knew if he had duplicates or just frequently washed his clothes. They were always spotless. The tech guys were the only office employees allowed to wear casual clothes.

"Look hard," Kinney directed. "When you get something, we'll be sitting in the bullpen with all the other dweebs. At least for now."

"I *thought* something was going on," Henry said, although his eyes pretty much never strayed from his monitor. "What happened?"

"We got demoted," Kinney told him, trying to sound bitter.

"No more fieldwork for us. Fuck Barber!" Reed added.

"Sorry, guys. I'll get right on this."

Kinney and Reed trudged past a row of manned

desks to the break room. Kinney attempted defiant sadness; Reed tried for the stage of grief where you were angry. Again, no one seemed to notice.

The break room was empty. They sat and nursed coffees. The room had obviously been designed to be uninviting. It was even more sterile than Barber's office. Sound echoed off the bare walls and yellowed linoleum tiles. The table wobbled, and the chair cushions were lumpy. Kinney was convinced Barber had even found a way to pump in odious odors to discourage long breaks. That day, the room smelled like burnt tires.

"It's good we got to practice on Henry," Kinney said. "He's all about numbers, not people, so no harm done."

"What do you mean? No harm? We did great. My 'Fuck Barber!' was inspired."

"It was over the top. We've got to keep our behavior believable, Reed."

"Actually," his partner told him, "I say that all the time to these guys when you're not around."

"Great, Reed. I'll bet that's really boosted your career path."

"Speaking of my career, do you think Barber will take me back eventually—or even let me live? I don't mind playing golf every day, and I've got some money stashed away, but I'm not ready to find out if there's an afterlife."

"You really think he'd have you killed?"

"Well, I know a lot and I do say 'Fuck Barber' a lot. What do you think?"

"We're not in the KGB, for Chrissakes," Kinney said. "People retire. People move on."

"Who?"

"Porter, for one."

"He got killed in Bulgaria—remember?"

"No, I didn't know that. I just haven't seen him around for a while. What about Rodriguez?"

"He's working in the basement now, doing God knows what. You know he slept with a Belarusian operative, right?"

"Oh yeah, I forgot. Anyway, you may get put to pasture, Reed, but I'm sure it's not the kind you tell kids about when their golden retriever keels over."

"I guess you're right. So what now?"

"I don't know. You want to sit at a desk awhile before we stomp out?"

"Hell, no."

"Me neither," Kinney told him. "So how do you want to play it?"

"We could go back to Barber and make a scene—leave the door open and yell a lot. You could try a few 'Fuck yous' of your own," Reed suggested. "Insubordination is a great way to get fired."

"And you know that from personal experience?"

Reed hung his head. "Maybe."

"I like that idea," Kinney told him. "Let's finish our coffees first. Do we need to come up with a script or rehearse?"

"Naw. Pretend you're on a mission using a fake identity and that fake guy's really mad at someone."

"When you put it that way, it sounds like a piece of cake," Kinney agreed. "If I can fool spies and terrorists, I can fool the guys in the office."

"Sure. It'll be fun."

"By the way, Reed, I'll need your help when I go

undercover. We're still partners as far as I'm concerned."

Reed's smile split his face. "I'm glad to hear that, bro."

****

Ten minutes later they strode back to Barber's office.

"Hey, asshole!" Reed called before they even got there.

Barber's door was closed. Kinney ran forward and thrust it open.

Maria Bagatsing, a junior agent, sat across the desk from Barber, who suddenly stood, hands on his hips.

"Get out of here!"

"Fuck you, Barber!" Reed shouted.

"Sorry, Maria," Kinney told her. A slight Filipina, she shrank away from the two agents even while she remained sitting.

"Yeah, sorry Maria," Reed echoed. "Hang around if you want to see how to quit in style. Otherwise, you might want to go tell everyone in the bullpen to hide under their desks cuz the shit's gonna fly."

"This is outrageous!" Barber shouted. He was a very bad actor.

Maria scurried away. Thankfully, she was sufficiently flustered to leave the door open.

"I don't care if our covers *are* blown," Kinney said in as loud a voice as he believed to be credible. "We're not working at desks—not for you or anyone else. You can take your new assignments and shove them up your ass."

"Hey, guys," Barber whispered, "tone it down a bit, please."

"After all we've done for this agency, this is how you reward us?" Reed said. "I spit on you!"

"You better not," Barber whispered.

Kinney swept his arm across the desktop, knocking various items onto the gray carpet, notably a framed family photo. He glanced out the door after that and saw several faces peering in.

"Hey!" Barber said, not acting at all for a moment. "That's it! Get out!" He thrust his arm toward the door. Returning to his unconvincing performance, he added, "You're both fired!"

Reed picked up the chair Maria had been sitting on and started to hurl it at Barber. Kinney grabbed his arm and said, "He's not worth it, Reed. Let's get out of here." He remembered the line from a cop movie he'd seen.

Begrudgingly, his partner dropped the chair, nearly hitting Kinney's foot. They both pivoted and stormed out of the room, through the crowd of co-workers, and down onto a busy San Jose street.

Someone had just power washed the sidewalk. The wet cement smelled musty. The two men each stood in shallow puddles.

"Good touch with the chair," Kinney said.

"Thanks. I liked your desk move."

"Maybe we should blow off the mission and become actors," Kinney joked.

Reed shook his head. "You're not good-looking enough."

"Sure I am."

"No way. Let's take a poll," Reed suggested.

He called to a thirty-ish woman who held a purple clipboard in one hand and a stainless steel thermos in the other.

"Excuse me, miss," Reed said. "Could you settle an argument we're having?"

"Sure."

Kinney figured she was peddling a petition for a cause of some kind. Her alert eyes marked her as someone unlikely to care what the public thought about a new brand of toothpaste.

Solidly built, with small ears peeking through the blond hair that cascaded down to her shoulders, she stood erect the way yoga instructors did—straight but not stiff. Those impressive blue eyes peered at Reed from a tanned face devoid of makeup. One eye was a bit lower than the other. Its accompanying light brown eyebrow compensated by being more substantial than its counterpart. A weathered brown leather messenger's bag was slung over her shoulder. It looked like it might slip off if she even cleared her throat.

Reed turned to Kinney. "See? She wouldn't have even stopped if I wasn't so handsome."

The woman smiled radiantly. Her smile transformed her from a mildly attractive woman into an enchanting creature—at least to Kinney's eyes.

"You're quite a character," she told Reed in a friendly tone.

A loud bus careened past them, interrupting the conversation for a moment.

"Thanks," Reed replied. "Here's the thing. I say I could be an actor, but my friend couldn't because he's not good-looking enough. He disagrees. What do you think?"

"Hmm, let me see." She studied Kinney's face first, squinting slightly and crinkling her lightly freckled nose. "I like the ruggedness of your friend's face. He looks like a guy who'd win a fight, which could come in handy now that the country's going to hell. And his eye color is interesting—brown with a hint of green. I wouldn't have thought those two could blend like that."

Kinney smiled.

"I like his smile, too. It seems genuine. And he's got great teeth. Do you whiten them?" she asked Kinney.

"They're a gift from my mother's side of the family. I don't believe in altering one's appearance except as a disguise when I commit crimes."

The woman laughed—a melodic ripple of sound.

"I didn't know you had a mother, Kinney," Reed said.

"Everyone has a mother." Kinney was annoyed by his partner's inane interruption. He flashed a look to Reed that displayed this.

"Mine died when I was two," the woman said. Her tone was curiously neutral.

"I'm sorry," Kinney said. He couldn't imagine what that was like.

"Thank you. I ended up with a great stepmom, so it worked out. I like your voice. Is that a trace of a Texas accent?"

"Yes. I escaped in my teens."

"I'm from Shreveport originally," the woman told him.

"I wouldn't have guessed. How did you get rid of your drawl?"

"I took acting classes in college. Being a woman with a Southern accent would've been two strikes

29

against me in my career."

"Let me guess," Kinney said. "You're a lawyer working for a political campaign on your lunch hour."

"Please. A lawyer? Insulting a volunteer poll-taker isn't in your best interests." She grinned. Apparently she wasn't actually offended.

"Sorry."

"I work in law enforcement," the woman told him. She held her features still as she watched Kinney to see what he made of this.

"He was only kidding about committing crimes," Reed told her hurriedly. "Anyway, what about me? You've gotten bogged down with Kinney."

The woman turned to him and tilted her head to the side as she surveyed his face. "You, on the other hand, seem to be one of those pretty boys who expect women to fall all over you if you just look at them. Your features are hideously regular. Your hair looks like it's been superglued in place. And your long eyelashes belong on a thirteen-year-old girl. Your voice drips with ego. It's like every word has a subtext of 'Look at me. Look how great I am.' If either of you were to commit crimes, it would be you, and you'd never expect to be caught. But you would be."

"Go ahead," Kinney told her. "Don't sugarcoat it."

"Butch Cassidy," she said, smiling again.

"What?" Reed asked.

"It's from a movie," Kinney told him. "It's one of my favorites—two wisecracking outlaws." He was growing more intrigued by the minute. Was the woman a fellow film buff?

"It's one of my favorites, too," the woman said. "My name's Georgia. Here, let me give you my phone number. Call me sometime."

"I just might," Kinney told her, handing over his phone for her to put the number in.

"Listen, I gotta go," she said when she was done. "I hope I've been helpful." She turned to look at Reed. "I may have been a bit harsh with you," she told him. "My ex was a pretty boy."

Reed nodded his acknowledgement. Once she was a few steps away, he turned to his partner. "See? She says I'm better-looking."

"That was your takeaway?"

"Rugged versus pretty boy—which is better?" Reed asked.

Kinney just shook his head. "Let's get out of here and start getting down and out," he suggested. "You know, like guys with poor coping skills flaming out of promising careers. I say we get drunk somewhere highly visible in case Molton's people are watching us."

"They are," Reed told him. "Three o'clock on the bench and one o'clock looking in her purse. She's been rooting around in there since before I accosted that astute poll-taker."

"It was an N of one, Reed—not a significant sample."

"I selected her because it was obvious she represented the entire female demographic."

"Why's that?" Kinney asked.

"Her hair, of course. It was parted on the right. Don't you know anything about women?"

"No, I don't. My dating history can attest to that."

Chapter 5

Kinney was almost too hungover the next morning to function. And the next morning. And the next. He made a point of staggering to his mailbox in boxers and a stained pajama top.

After the initial night of excess, replete with a very brief bar fight—one pulled punch—Kinney was on his own. Reed ostensibly took off to stay with his brother in Seattle while he actually hid out in a vacant condo a friend owned in Fremont.

Kinney called John Molton after a week. And after a sober evening at home. It was the first morning he felt like himself. Being down and out wasn't fun.

"Thanks a lot for getting me canned, John. I really appreciate that."

"As I understand it, you canned yourself when you didn't like your reassignment."

"You don't have to show off anymore. I don't care what you know about the agency."

"So you're ready to hear my proposition?" Molton asked.

"Yes."

"What about your partner?"

"He's looking into real estate. He's under the mistaken impression he's charming."

"That's fine. Can you meet me for lunch?" he asked.

"How do I know you won't kidnap and torture me for information?" Kinney wasn't worried about this. He just wanted to hear how Molton responded.

"There are several reasons. One, we don't need to. We know all we need to know already. Two, if we wanted to, we've had plenty of opportunities. And three, you pick the restaurant—somewhere you'll feel safe."

"Okay. How about Casa Lulu's?"

"In Campbell?" Molton sounded surprised by Kinney's choice.

"Yes," Kinney said.

"Why so far?"

"Obviously, I don't want to be seen with you. Make sure you're not followed. I will."

"I assure you, Barber and his people don't know who I am." Kinney could picture Molton's smarmy face as he said this.

"Don't be so sure," he replied. "He would've sent agents to the golf course after you met us. Did anyone see your car? Are you in the agency's database and you don't know it? Barber's got massive resources and a very generous budget. My phone is probably tapped, by the way, so only call on the burner I'm using if you need to."

"Fine. Shall we say 12:30?"

"Sure. See you then."

Kinney could hardly wait to find out what Molton considered so important about him that it trumped maintaining secrecy about the mole. Surely, there were other competent operatives he could hire.

At a quarter to noon, Kinney picked up a tail a couple of blocks out of his driveway. He was curious to see who it was. It could be someone Barber sent to maintain the fiction of Kinney's disgrace or it could be Molton's man. He drove around the block, back into his driveway, and hurried into the house. An observer might believe he'd forgotten something.

Exiting through a sliding glass door to his patio, Kinney made his way around the back of both his condo complex and an adjoining home, which enabled him to sneak up on the compact sedan parked several houses down the quiet Scotts Valley street. He climbed into the passenger seat.

"You should lock the doors, Gil."

The agent whirled in his seat to face him. His face reflected surprise, not alarm. "There's no need for this, Kinney. I'm here to keep an eye on you. That's all."

Saunders' black plastic glasses and shaggy Amish-style beard disguised his capabilities. It helped that he usually wore a red plaid London cabbie's cap. Saunders had told Kinney once that these were the things people remembered while he was on a mission. All he had to do was change them and no one recognized him.

"Who sent you?" Kinney asked, although he already knew the answer.

"Barber, of course. What do you think happens when someone leaves the agency—when someone says 'fuck you' to the bossman?"

"I don't know. You tell me. Do you know anybody else who left?" Kinney was still curious about Reed's fate. He'd reassured his partner about what Barber might do to him, but he wasn't at all sure about this.

"Well, not personally, but there's Porter," Saunders said.

"He's dead."

"Oh, yeah. What are you going to do, Kinney?"

"Let's get out of the car and fight."

"What?" Saunders' eyebrows shot up, and his mouth formed an O.

"You heard me."

"Why would we do that?" Saunders asked, still genuinely puzzled.

"I've got my reasons. No weapons. Hand to hand."

"I can't beat you. I don't know anybody who can."

"Try." Kinney lashed out and punched the air an inch short of Saunders' nose. The agent flinched and then nodded his head.

Kinney figured that Molton had someone watching the house. Beating up a fellow agent could cement his status as a disgruntled former employee, and he'd told Molton he'd make sure he wasn't followed. Also, Kinney didn't like Saunders because he'd eaten the last piece of flan at the agency's Christmas party.

Kinney told Saunders to lay his gun down on the floor mat and climb out. His fellow agent had demonstrated his good sense by not to trying to pull it out during their conversation. Then Kinney clambered out himself.

Saunders took off sprinting down the sidewalk, his slightly tubby frame moving faster than Kinney would've imagined. Kinney caught him two driveways down and grabbed his arm.

"Look, Saunders, it won't be too bad, but you've got to try. If you run again or just stand there, I'm going to be very unhappy. We don't want that, do we?"

"No."

A moment later, Saunders lashed out with his free fist to the side of Kinney's knee, which suddenly wasn't there anymore. Whirling, once again more athletically than Kinney expected, the agent chopped at Kinney's throat.

Kinney lowered his chin and took the blow, which stung. The sensation triggered his training, and he blocked the next punch with a high kick—nothing an opponent would expect. Saunders' counter move was dependent on Kinney blocking with his arm, which rendered Saunders vulnerable to a straight right to his exposed gut.

An involuntary exhalation exploded out of Saunders, and the agent fought not to double over, which he knew would be the end.

Once again surprising Kinney, Saunders did a backflip, landing on his feet a yard away. If Kinney hadn't been entranced by the maneuver, he could've easily taken him out while Saunders was in the air.

"Wow," Kinney said. "I'm impressed."

"Thanks," Saunders gasped. "Why don't we call it a draw?"

"Why don't I show you why being on the gymnastics team in school doesn't help much in a fight?"

Recognizing that surprise had been the only reason he'd survived so far, Saunders launched himself, seeking to bury his shoulder in Kinney's hip. Kinney was familiar with the move, having used it himself once or twice for fun, but it was easy enough to turn to the side, cup his hand, and clap it onto Saunders' ear, stunning him. A knee to the chin finished him. Saunders went down and stayed down.

"You'll be fine," he whispered to the unconscious agent. "Just put some ice on it."

****

Molton was prompt. Kinney had left early enough to nab the table in the back corner of Casa Lulu's despite the fight. His back was against the wall and a soft drink sat in front of him on the bright yellow vinyl tablecloth.

There wasn't any Lulu at Casa Lulu, but Carmen—the owner of the Mexican restaurant—was a big fan of anything festive-looking. Some of the brightly colored paintings and folk art lining the high shelves obviously hailed from Africa and Asia. Staying slightly more consistent with a Latin American theme, a red piglet piñata hung over the bar next to a cobalt blue burro. An indeterminate green shape bumped into the burro when a rotating fan by the register sent air its way.

Kinney had once made the mistake of pointing out these decorating incongruities. Carmen's response had been brief and to the point.

"Shut the hell up, Kinney."

"Yes, ma'am."

He suspected that the restaurant owner could take out some of the agency's junior agents. The gang tattoos on her neck and her confident swagger attested to that.

Molton didn't spy Kinney at first, giving Kinney another opportunity to survey who he was dealing with. The man's dark pinstriped suit didn't fit him as well as it probably had before he'd gained some weight. Even unbuttoned, the fabric hugged his gut. His bright white shirt and red knit tie completed the Wall Street look.

Molton's cheeks were subtly indented, as though his body had compensated for the weight he'd gained below his neck by subtracting something from his face.

A series of vertical wrinkles creased the space between his eyes. Kinney wondered what you had to do to get those. Could someone move their eyes toward one another somehow? Maybe you just had to frown a lot.

Molton's baseline expression, or at least the one he demonstrated while searching for someone in a restaurant, was a pronounced smirk. Kinney couldn't imagine any woman who would find that attractive.

Once Molton joined Kinney and they'd ordered, the older man got right to it. The titan of industry didn't even look at the chips and salsa. Kinney respected his self-discipline.

"You're the only man for this job, Kinney. We've gone to a lot of trouble to set this up, and now that you're available, we want to pay you more money than you've ever seen for just a week of your time. If it works out, we can make things permanent."

Kinney nodded. He wasn't sure how a man in his fictional position ought to respond. Molton waited.

"Tell me more," Kinney tried.

Molton seemed satisfied with that. He continued in his inauthentic salesman voice, leaning forward in an effort to create a positive connection. Kinney half expected Molton to mention the accessories he'd throw in if Kinney bought a top of the line Lexus.

"You've got a prior relationship with the target," Molton told him. "You can get close. You can make it look like an accident."

Kinney shook his head. "You know I don't kill people anymore."

"Let me ask you this. What would happen if the West African Brotherhood, Qamar Mawt, or any other number of organizations found out who you are?"

"I don't think they can touch me on American soil." Kinney paused for a moment. He wasn't sure about that. "What would happen if I strangle you in the men's room before you have a chance to tell anyone about me?" He smiled in what he hoped was a terrifying way. Who would be happy to kill someone?

Molton thrust up his hands. "I'm just a representative of a corporation. Do you think I'd be here if I was the only one who knew about you?"

"Well, there's Chet. Other than him…"

"Look around. That's Chet at the bar," Molton said. "He's armed. And there's more where he came from, I assure you. You won't stand a chance if you attack me."

Kinney turned to look at the slim, slightly younger man. Molton's colleague wore a straw hipster fedora with a floral headband, a teal fleece pullover, and well-worn jeans. He'd glued on bushy sideburns as well.

"Seriously? That's the worst disguise I've ever seen."

Kinney waved to Chet, who ducked his head and stuffed a tortilla chip into his mouth.

"His disguise worked on you," Molton asserted. "You didn't notice him, did you?"

Kinney would be damned if he'd admit it. "So you're extorting me to go back to killing? Is that what you're saying?"

"Essentially."

"Are you sure you know who you're dealing with? Have you been planning on a long life? If I go back to killing, you're going to be way up on my hit list, Molton. In the long run, it doesn't matter how you threaten me. I won't forget this."

"Oh, I doubt I'll be in danger, Kinney. Remember, I know all about you—and your sister and your young niece—a beautiful girl I've chatted with on her way home from school."

It was all Kinney could do to not tear Molton apart and stuff the pieces into Chet's chip-filled mouth.

The older man leaned back as far as he could. "Take it easy, Kinney. Chet's pretty good with a gun, and I know your family will be fine because I know you'll do this job for us."

Kinney unclenched his hands and took several deep breaths. What had begun as just another assignment was now personal. He needed to control himself. "It doesn't look like I have a choice," he told Molton, his voice deceptively calm.

"No, you don't."

More deep breathing allowed Kinney to stay on task. "So who is this guy I know? Who's the target?"

"Brigadier Wilbur Pope."

Kinney leaned back and frowned. "The head of the armed forces in Guyana? Why do you care about him? That northeast corner of South America has got to be one of the least important places in the world."

"Then why were you there in 2019? Why did you save his son's life? Why does he still send you lavish Christmas gifts?"

"Okay. You've made your point. He's a good guy, though—trying to do right in a crime-ridden country with corrupt cops."

Now Kinney had another personal goal in the mix. Besides keeping his family safe, he needed to insure the brigadier stayed alive. He couldn't begin to imagine how Pope's kids would manage without him. Their mother was an alcoholic with a gambling problem, and Pope's son was still traumatized from having been kidnapped. Thanks to Kinney, those kidnappers were no longer a threat, but there were others.

"Think about it, Kinney," Molton said, pointing to his own head. "Why does Guyana even need an army? What idiot would want to invade a swamp like that and inherit all its problems? What do you think the brigadier's real role is?"

"Tell me."

"Never mind. I've said too much already. We need him gone. End of story. Yours is not to reason why."

"Gone, huh? So an extraction would be okay with you? What if I dump him in the middle of Australia? What could he do there?" Kinney asked.

"He could come back. History repeats itself, doesn't it? Look at Napoleon. Exile is no guarantee."

Molton had a point. "So let's get back to why me? I mean, I understand it would be easier for me. The man trusts me. But any competent assassin can take out a public figure like Pope."

"Believe me, we've tried." Molton looked off into the distance, his eyes unfocused. "Our first man missed from long-range, and since then it's been hard to even get a glimpse of the guy. We had a servant in his house. He's dead. A driver, too. It's such a small country that everyone's suspicious of strangers. And locals love the guy." He returned his gaze to Kinney, slowly shaking his head.

Kinney frowned. Something didn't add up here. "Who are you people? Are you really just some corporation? It sounds like you're an intelligence agency. CIA?"

Molton laughed. "Hardly."

"For some other country, then?"

"Let it go, Kinney. You don't need to know."

"Okay. Let me ask you this. Are you providing support in Guyana? I'll need some things." It was clear he needed to pretend to acquiesce. He'd figure out how to handle things later.

"Here's the good part," Molton said, rubbing his hands together. His grin was almost gleeful, which Kinney experienced as extremely creepy. Sure, Kinney had killed a lot of people, but he'd never taken pleasure in either the planning or the implementation. It had been a job that needed doing. That's all.

Molton continued. "The Brigadier will be in the US next week—at a conference near Princeton University."

"Oh, boy. New Jersey."

Chapter 6

Kinney called Barber, burner to burner, from his car after the meeting.

"We could nail him for conspiracy to commit murder," he told his boss after relating the conversation, "but then my family's dead, and the rest of his organization will just carry on."

"That's assuming he's telling the truth." Barber said. "If I were him, I'd say I have a vast organization behind me. And how many times do threats against families really get carried out?"

"How would I know?"

"Well, so far it's only been twice here at the agency."

"That's two too many."

"Of course," Barber agreed. "But at this point we can't know what the real story is. You need to keep digging and see what else you can find out. Maybe talk this brigadier fellow into pretending to be dead. Use your head. You'll come up with something."

"Okay."

In fact, Kinney had already been planning to the degree that he could ahead of time. Reed planted a tracker under Molton's car while he was eating lunch, which allowed him to follow at a distance when Molton left the restaurant before Kinney did.

Reed tracked him back to an office tower in Santa

Clara. He'd exited the elevator on either the ninth or the fourteenth floor. Despite what his business card read, there was no Molton Enterprises in the building, according to both the directory and the semi-comatose security guard behind a counter in the lobby. Reed had slipped him a twenty, which woke him up enough to snare the bill and mumble a few words.

"We need to do some reconnaissance, bro," Reed told Kinney on his burner as he drove away from the office building. "I think we can rule out the three dentists and the modeling agency in the building."

"I never rule out models," Kinney responded. "For one thing, they might be good survey takers. We need a bigger N for our poll."

"You and that N thing. What does that even mean?" Reed asked. Kinney was once again surprised by what Reed didn't know. His partner just hadn't received a decent education.

"It just tells you how big the sample is when you run an experiment or a survey," Kinney told him.

"Gotcha. Anyway, there are eighteen possibilities. How do you want to split them up?"

"I don't care. We each take a floor?"

"We'll need disguises."

Reed always looked forward to disguises. Kinney figured he'd been held back on Halloween as a kid, maybe for safety reasons. Kinney's mother hadn't let him out of the house in order to protect the other children.

"Sure," Kinney agreed. "I'll be the fat guy this time. I'll wear that greasy ball cap—you know, the one advertising Rooter Rangers."

"I think I'll go as the Hassidic guy."

"This isn't Halloween, Reed. How many Hassidic people have you seen around here? You want to blend in, not stand out."

"So what do you suggest?"

"I like you as a hippie." Kinney told him.

"Okay."

Later, the two agents drove to the office building in separate cars—Reed watching for any tails behind Kinney. There weren't any. Previously, they'd checked the cars for trackers and bugs. The undercarriage of Reed's sedan was strangely complex, requiring him to crawl around quite a bit, which he complained about at length.

Kinney liked the building's lobby. The high ceiling with recessed floodlights reminded him of where his father had worked in Fort Worth. The white marble floor was similar, too. On father-son day—once a year—Kinney had been able to invade the inner sanctum of the major accounting firm. Even as an eleven-year-old, he'd felt a kinship with the ruthless CEO.

Reed headed to the fourteenth floor in a paneled, carpeted elevator. Kinney, in his low-end outfit, found the freight elevator, which smelled strongly of stale cigarette smoke and took forever to rise nine floors.

Outside the elevator, Kinney took a look at the list Reed had texted him, and decided that Meriwether Imports was the most likely office to harbor evildoers. It had the vaguest name and started with an M.

Its tall, imposing front door was unlocked, so he strolled into a small, carpeted lobby as if he had a crapload of goods to import. Or maybe export. He'd decided to be a confused fat guy.

Whoever had decorated the room was obviously a fan of mid-century design. Scooped avocado green chairs sat on slim chrome legs along one wall. To Kinney's eyes, they looked as though they'd be easy enough to climb into, but challenging to escape. The carpet was quite thick—not quite a shag—and the attempt to match it with the chair color—or vice versa—was almost successful. The slight clash registered as an uneasy wrongness, like food that smelled slightly spoiled.

All the remaining Scandinavian-looking furniture—a broad desk, two end tables, and a tall bookcase filled with seashells and twisted driftwood—was lacquered maple.

The alarmingly slim young woman behind the tidy desk looked up as he approached, frowned momentarily, and then unleashed a broad, insincere smile. Her wavy red hair and see-through peach-colored blouse caught Kinney's eye, but he decided to lead by commenting on a different feature.

"You have lovely teeth," Kinney told her.

"Er, thank you."

"I worry about your weight, though. Do you have an unhealthy relationship with food?"

She stared at him blankly. This wasn't the way things were supposed to go. She started to ask if she could help this gross-looking, inappropriate guy when he interrupted her.

"Anyway, I guess that's your business. It's just that I had a cousin who got down to seventy-nine pounds before she died.

"Oh, my goodness." She put a hand over her mouth like a giggling Japanese schoolgirl, although her eyes widened in shock at his words.

"Yeah, she was run over by a train. We're all still grieving. Listen, I met this guy who said he worked here and he could help me out, but I can't remember his name. I can't remember much since my accident."

"I'm sorry. A car accident?"

"No, ironically, it was a train like my cousin. What are the odds? So I've got a photo—I take photos of people I meet since I can't remember names. Could you take a look at it?"

Reed had snapped the photo as Molton had exited Casa Lulu's. Kinney hoped the woman was sufficiently off-kilter by now to simply cooperate. From her perspective, the sooner she accommodated this weirdo, the sooner he'd go away.

Kinney held his phone up and showed her Molton's photo.

"Oh, that's Mr. Meriwether—the owner." She was quite happy she was able to help him. "Shall I tell him you're here to see him. He's very busy, but maybe he'll squeeze you in."

Kinney made an unconvincing buzzing noise, told the woman he had to take a call, and strode out of the office.

He called Reed while waiting for the public elevator. He couldn't face the other one. He had to step away from two modelish-looking young women who were discussing the drawbacks of one on one coverage in the NFL. The shorter of the two—a Eurasian beauty—seemed to know much more about football than Kinney did.

"Got him on the first try," he reported to his partner. "How lucky is that?"

"Bummer. I'm really enjoying being a hippie. I think I was born in the wrong decade."

"Reed, I don't think there were too many sociopaths at love-ins."

"You think I'm a sociopath?" His voice reflected both his hurt and his curiosity.

Kinney noticed the anomalous complexity of his response. Usually, Reed was either angry, happy, or sad—when his sociopathy wasn't dictating a spooky absence of normal emotions.

"Well, we've both killed people, right?" Kinney responded. "Do you have any remorse? I don't. I mean, it doesn't feel right to do it now, but it did then."

One of the models pulled the other one's arm as she rushed into the elevator that had just appeared. Kinney worried for a moment that she might've overheard him, but decided she was probably just in a hurry, perhaps to escape proximity to his woefully unattractive appearance.

"What about army snipers?" Reed asked. "Are you saying they're sociopaths, too?"

"Probably a lot of them are. Don't they shoot civilians sometimes? How can you have empathy and a conscience and do that?"

"Did you look all this up somewhere?"

"Yeah, a long time ago," Kinney told him. "I knew I was different from other kids. I wanted to understand myself. The important thing is that we're using who we are for good—for our country."

"So you're saying we're benign sociopaths."

"I think so, Reed." The next elevator finally arrived. "I'll meet you at Eddie's."

Eddie Sullivan was a guy they used when they

needed someone to look into matters without using the agency's resources. He was the younger brother of a guy Kinney had handed over to the ATF years ago for arms smuggling. Rather than holding a grudge, Eddie had been pleased by this since his brother had bullied him mercilessly his whole life.

An agoraphobic, Eddie was always home. An online shopaholic, he was always ready to take on work to fuel his compulsion. As someone with very poor hygiene, he usually smelled like soiled gym clothes, which was considerably more odious than anything a freight elevator could inflict on a passenger.

On the other hand, Eddie's hair was a work of art—a gelled black pompadour worthy of a rockabilly god. Underneath that, his oversized head competed for attention. Unnaturally round, with huge ears thrusting sideways as if to escape their host, only Eddie's eyes redeemed his face. Their dark amber color stood out, and something ineffable about them told the viewer there was someone very bright inside there.

Kinney and Reed let themselves into the rundown ranch house in an even more rundown neighborhood in East San Jose. Stacks of Amazon boxes formed a rough semicircle around Eddie's command center in the middle of his dimly lit living room. Three huge monitors were spread across a long oak table, and several nondescript black boxes with various cables going in and out of them littered the rest of the surface. There was no other furniture or decor, unless you counted the food containers on the floor, some of which seemed to be permanent fixtures. Dark mold had crept across their surfaces.

"Geez," Reed said, looking around. "You haven't

even opened what you bought, Eddie."

"I know what's in them," he answered in his high-pitched voice. "I'll get to them. I've been busy. What have you got for me, guys? Something juicy, I hope."

"This one should be a breeze," Kinney told him. "We'll wait on the porch while you go at it."

"Okay."

Kinney gave him the little they knew about Meriwether. Forty minutes later, after Kinney and Reed had contentiously hashed out the advantages and disadvantages of their "non-mainstream personalities"—Reed's preferred term for sociopaths—Eddie texted he had something for them.

"Meriwether Imports is a subsidiary of a pretty big outfit based in New Zealand," he told them once they'd reentered the malodorous house.

"I thought everyone in New Zealand was nice," Reed said.

"Well, these people aren't. They bought some contiguous sheep stations—that's what they call these huge ranches over there."

"I've never heard of contiguous sheep," Kinney said. "Is that where they stand really close to one another?"

Reed laughed. Eddie shot him a withering look before continuing.

"Anyway, they broke up some of the land into huge lots, built mega-mansions, and they're long-term leasing them to rich creeps from all over the world. You know—as safe havens if there's a world war or something. The government clamped down on foreigners buying property, so Rakena Investments found a way around that."

"Rakena? Are these people Maoris?" Kinney asked, his eyebrows raised.

"I dunno. Lots of names over there are like that."

"That takes mega bucks. Where did it all come from?" Reed asked, shifting his weight off a noisy piece of cellophane.

"I haven't found that out yet. Definitely from outside New Zealand." Eddie nodded to indicate he was sure about that. "So getting back to Meriwether Imports itself, they bring in sweaters and other wool products. I guess Rakena had to do something with all the sheep."

"So they're legit?" Kinney asked.

Eddie shook his big head, which took some work. "I didn't say that. They don't do enough business to exist—not on paper, anyway. Not legally."

"What about Meriwether?" Reed asked.

"He's supposedly from Alexandria, Virginia. His dad owned a chain of motels and his mother did something in the state department. He went to Yale, worked for a while for a real estate developer—malls, mostly—and then he set up his company."

"What do you mean 'supposedly'?" Kinney asked.

"There's something fishy about his bio." His eyes narrowed, and the corners of his mouth turned down. Then he stroked the tall, stiff side of his pompadour, a gesture Kinney was familiar with. Eddie did it when he didn't know something he wished he did.

"I'm going to check it out more," Eddie continued. "Anyway, at first Meriweather imported gray-market cars—you know, the exotic ones you have to fix up before they're legal here? Then he sold the business to Rakena for much more than it was worth. Now it's been sweaters for four years. They're nice sweaters. I'm going to get one. They raise these brown sheep over there so if you want a brown sweater, they don't have to dye the wool. Pretty cool, huh?"

Eddie looked up with gleaming eyes. His shopping addiction had been triggered. This happened at random in Kinney's experience, sometimes derailing the process of receiving the information he needed.

"Sure," Kinney said.

"So that's who Meriweather seems to be on the surface. Like I said, I need to dig into the guy more."

On this occasion, Eddie had stayed on track. Kinney figured that sweaters weren't as alluring to Eddie as the last item that had pulled him away from a conversation—a rowing machine that Kinney knew he'd never use.

"Who are the rich creeps leasing mansions? And how do you know they're creeps?" Reed asked.

"A lot of this is on Auckland news sites," Eddie told him. "You know they've got a big Green movement over there, right? So these activists have been outing people who are buying into the project as a way to discredit Rakena. They came up with a drug lord from Brazil, a Chinese guy who employs kids in his factories, and one of those hedge-fund swindlers the feds have been looking for."

"How come I haven't heard anything about this?" Reed asked petulantly. He seemed ready to call a news outlet to complain.

"Nobody cares what happens over there unless it's good clickbait," Eddie told him. "What the protesters need to do is have some topless women or maybe they could fake some photos of cute kittens being abused by the construction workers."

"They could have both," Reed suggested. "I'm picturing topless women holding cats—under their arms, I mean—not in front of them. That would defeat the purpose, wouldn't it?"

Eddie nodded vigorously. "I'd click on that."

"So you'll keep looking into this?" Kinney asked.

"Sure. At my usual rate."

"We'll be back tomorrow," Kinney told him.

"Okay."

By their cars, standing in cold drizzle, Reed asked why they didn't phone Eddie the next day instead of visiting. "I don't think I can stand the stench again so soon," he told Kinney.

"He's weird on the phone—remember?"

"You mean weirder."

"Yeah."

Chapter 7

Kinney had Brigadier Wilbur Pope's personal phone number, and he gave him a call when he got home to his two-story condo in Scotts Valley, California.

On the ocean side of the Santa Cruz mountains, the commuter town was a collection of homes, condos, and mobile home parks grouped around a couple of streets sporting shopping centers and fast food restaurants. Periodically, the city council launched projects to establish a real town center without success. Santa Cruz was right down the road, and its vibrant, fun downtown drew both locals and hordes of tourists. The Monterey Bay beaches, a boardwalk amusement park, redwood forests, and one of those spots where a mysterious vortex screwed with gravity enticed even more people.

"Kinney! So good to hear from you," Pope told him. "How are you, my friend?"

"Doing fine, Brigadier."

Kinney had enjoyed spending time with him in Guyana after rescuing his son. It was nice to hear Pope's voice, and it reminded him of metemgee—a stew with dumplings—he'd eaten at the Brigadier's home. Kinney had found a restaurant that served it in San Francisco, but his meal there was a pallid imitation of the real thing. He reflected for a moment on how food and drink colored his memories, rendering them more positive or negative.

"How many times do I have to tell you to call me Will?" Pope said.

"Apparently, at least this many." Kinney was focused again.

"Always the funny man. Now tell me why you called. I'm very busy planning to invade Brazil." Pope chuckled.

"Look who's talking, Mr. Comedian."

"I saved that up for when I heard from you again. Pretty good, huh?"

"Excellent," Kinney agreed. "Here's the thing. I've been hired to kill you in Princeton."

"Oh, please don't." Pope wasn't the least bit alarmed.

"Okay, I won't now that you so persuasively pleaded for your life."

"I'm told I have a wonderfully authoritative voice," Pope said.

"You don't seem upset," Kinney pointed out.

"Someone's been trying to kill me for six months now," the brigadier said. "I'm used to it." His tone reflected that time had indeed turned the attempts into mundane events. He could've been talking about becoming accustomed to new shoes.

"Who do you think it is? And why?" Kinney asked.

"We're going to nationalize oil production."

"You have oil?" Kinney's tone reflected his surprise. As far as he knew, Guyana didn't have *anything.*

"There's not much yet. But an outfit from New Zealand discovered some offshore, so we're making a preemptive strike. We don't want the profits siphoned out of the country. We need them badly. Sometimes I think we were better off as a British colony."

"Nationalization is a government thing, right?" Kinney asked. "What does the military have to with it?"

"The president is only the president as long as I say so. You understand?" His voice was steely now. "We had corrupt leaders for decades until I put a stop to it by putting my guy in, and I only keep him in if he stays in line."

"So you think it's the Kiwis who are behind this?"

"The who?"

"The company from New Zealand."

"It seems likely, assuming they know about our plans. It's supposed to be a secret. We expelled them all, but I'm told they're still in the Caribbean somewhere."

"I've always heard good things about New Zealanders," Kinney told him. "Now it's two times in a day I'm hearing bad things."

"Oh, these aren't—what did you call them?— Kiwis? It's a company that got started there, but now it's run by people from up your way—North Americans."

Pope's disdain for the region leaked out of him. Kinney remembered several diatribes he'd endured when he was on the job. The brigadier had even denigrated Kinney's favorite fast food chain, likening its offerings to motor oil.

"Is that Rakena Investments by any chance?" Kinney asked.

"Yes. How did you know that?"

"I'm looking into something, and their name came up."

"What's the something?"

Kinney paused and pursed his lips. "Actually, the whole killing-you thing," he told him. "These people singled me out because they think I have access to you."

"You do, Kinney. You know you're always welcome in our home. My daughter still talks about you all the time."

"Thank you. And you know I'm affiliated with an agency that works behind the scenes?"

"Yes, yes. You're some sort of spy."

"More or less," Kinney admitted. It had been necessary to let Pope in on that, which Kinney had not been happy about. The fewer people who knew, the better.

Kinney heard a siren in the background. When he'd been in Guyana, there had been a remarkable number of emergency vehicles careening through the streets, and an even more remarkable disregard of these by Guyana drivers. In two short weeks, he'd seen three accidents.

"The thing is," Kinney began, "they've threatened my family to get me to assassinate you. It probably didn't occur to them that I'd call and tell you."

"We must do something about this. Family is the most important thing. I imagine you have something in mind?"

"Yes. Let's fake your death. I understand you've been keeping a low profile in Guyana lately?"

"Yes. But my country will destabilize if I'm presumed dead."

"We'll have to figure out something so Rakena thinks you're dead, but the rest of the world just thinks you went home after your conference in New Jersey."

"Okay. I've never been to Princeton. Do you know it?"

"Actually, I do. That'll help."

****

That evening, Kinney lay on his cushy sofa, firmed up his plan, and checked in with Reed, Barber, and Meriwether/Molton on the phone, varying his reports accordingly.

Reed hadn't thought of anything else helpful to do, so he was playing air hockey in an arcade when Kinney called. Barber was onboard with Kinney's plan, although he pressed for more details than Kinney had come up with so far. And Meriwether was pleased that Kinney had contacted Pope and arranged to meet him in New Jersey.

After that, Kinney watched a Golden State Warriors basketball game from his not so cushy armchair, which supposedly matched the sofa. It looked the same, with brown corduroy cushions and dark oak legs, but clearly its insides represented a different species of furniture altogether. He kept meaning to rearrange the furniture so the sofa faced the TV, but he never seemed to get around to it.

That was the story of his condo. After he laid things out when he first moved in several years ago—guessing what would work for him—he never changed anything. He regularly wrote that task on his to do list, only to cross it off when he got sick and tired of seeing it there.

The microwave door clanged against the side of the refrigerator. The toaster regularly threatened to burn through the power cord of the adjacent coffeemaker. And the most commonly used utensils—forks—were sequestered in the hardest to reach section of an inappropriately small drawer.

Kinney had done better in the bathroom. The only glitch there was a framed photo of his sister's family which tended to get drenched if he emerged from the most convenient end of the bathtub after a shower.

Kinney didn't really understand his resistance to making changes. Why would anyone want to stick with things that hadn't worked out when fixing them would be so easy?

The Warriors lost by nine. On the positive side, after a suitable grieving period, Kinney slept much better than usual, and woke up with very little soreness from his most annoying gunshot wound. Neither Cambodia nor that body part—the left cheek of his ass—were on his list of favorite locations these days.

Eddie called after Kinney had finished breakfast, which consisted of two frozen pot pies and a bowl of chocolate ice cream. As far as Kinney was concerned, one of the best perks of being an adult was the ability to defy nutritional guidelines with impunity.

"I pulled an all-nighter," Eddie told him. "and I've got a lot more information. Can you guys get over here so I can crash?"

"Sure. I'll give Reed a call."

The two agents let themselves in forty minutes later. Eddie looked as though he'd pulled three consecutive all-nighters. His pasty skin was stretched tightly across his wide face. Dark, droopy bags sat under his remarkable amber eyes, and he squinted more than usual despite the dim light. His impressive pompadour listed to one side, threatening to topple onto his ear.

"Okay, here goes," Eddie began. "Rakena, as big as they are, are owned by another company based in Sunnyvale—Moonmatic. I've got a friend who—"

"You have friends?" Reed interrupted, his eyebrows raised.

"Sure. I'm very popular online with the gaming community. Let me show you my avatar." Eddie pulled up a realistic graphic of a man who looked a lot like Reed. "That's me."

Kinney and Reed exchanged glances.

"So this friend…" Kinney primed.

"Oh, yeah. He hacks financial and corporate stuff for some outfit in Belarus, and he owes me a favor."

"Why's that?" Reed asked.

Kinney didn't understand why his partner interjected personal questions like these into work interactions. He'd asked him several times, but all he got back was "I want to know things."

Eddie was only too happy to tell him. "I rescued him from an ogre so he could wrest control of Zimbronia from Curtis752. I'm gonna ask him for help. It's just that he's on vacation in Antarctica. I think he's back later this week. I'll check. It's in my email somewhere. Of course, I'll take credit for whatever I find out from him. I read online that's a good business practice."

"What else have you got?" Kinney asked.

"Okay. Moonmatic is basically Ryan Connelly—the billionaire who keeps running for governor."

"He's a nut job," Reed said. "Even if I wanted to return to the Stone Age, I wouldn't put him in charge of anything."

"I looked it up," Eddie said. "Two hundred

thousand Californians disagreed with you in the last election. Anyway, besides everything else I found out, Connelly is probably up to something locally."

"Up to something?"

"Yeah, I'm not sure what. Maybe something political besides running for governor."

"How does that help us?" Kinney asked.

Eddie shrugged. "I dunno. I just find things out."

"Is there more?" Reed asked, leaning forward with his arms crossed.

"Meriwether is a crook," Eddie told them. "It's not his real name. And all those things I told you about him before are bullshit."

"So Molton isn't Molton, and Meriwether isn't Meriwether," Kinney said. "The guy's a set of Russian dolls."

"Say what?" Eddie said, squinting even more, as if the answer to his question might be visible if he only looked hard enough.

"Never mind," Kinney said. "Who is he, and why is he a criminal?"

"He's Aaron Miner, and he's wanted for embezzlement and financial fraud in the UK." Eddie leaned back in his chair, almost toppling. His self-satisfied smirk morphed quickly into mild alarm as he righted himself.

"How in the world did you find that out if he's been successfully dodging law enforcement?" Reed asked.

"Do you think the cops here are hunting for international white collar criminals? No way. They're busy beating up Black people. Fucking pigs." Eddie voice rose as he spoke.

"How did you find out about him?"

Eddie spoke again, calm now. Apparently, voicing his opinion about police let off enough steam to restore him to his desultory, post-all-nighter tone. "I found a marriage certificate online with Meriwether's name on it. The wife's previous name was Miner, so I looked into her and she'd been married to a guy named Miner before that. Guess what? Same guy. He used to have a mustache and different hair and stuff like that, but in photos, side by side, it's definitely Meriwether. So what they did was get married again using his new fake name so they could be legal. Now she's Judy Meriwether."

"What's her story?" Kinney asked.

"She divorced him two years ago. Maybe she'll tell you stuff—you know, if she's still mad at him for screwing her sister or something." Eddie shrugged dramatically, his shoulders raised all the way up beside his ear lobes.

"Where is she?"

Eddie grinned. "About twenty miles from here—in Los Gatos. She hangs out at a country club there—Los Barrancos. I even know she eats lunch there around noon on weekdays."

"That's great," Kinney told him. "You always come through, don't you?" He was tempted to reach out and pat the hacker on the shoulder before Eddie's body odor reminded him of the danger of that. Once, he'd shaken Eddie's hand. Never again.

"I'm the best," Eddie agreed.

"Hang on," Reed said. "I think I've got some gold stars in my wallet. Let me paste one on your forehead."

"Fuck you," Eddie said with no heat. "Look, I gotta sleep. I printed out everything else, and you can check it out later. Okay, guys?"

"Sure," Kinney agreed. "And let me remind you who you're dealing with. You're scared of us, right?"

"I guess." Eddie shrugged again. This wasn't the response Kinney had been shooting for.

"You ought to be," Reed told him. "Do we need to lug in a corpse full of bullet holes next time?"

"Reed, I never know when you're kidding around."

"I'm not," he said, staring intently.

Eddie rolled his chair back and held up a hand like a traffic guard stopping cars at a crosswalk. "Okay, okay. I get it. We've been through this before."

"Just don't forget," Kinney said. "If someone comes around and offers you a million dollars to sell us out, it won't do you much good if you're dead."

"Leave me alone, Kinney," Eddie said, but his heart wasn't in it.

Outside, in the sun on Eddie's walkway, Kinney kept the printout and told Reed he'd let him know if he needed him. "Go play golf," he added. "It's a beautiful day."

"I could try to get on at Los Barrancos."

"Maybe. Let's see how things go."

"I can charm divorcees with one hand tied behind my back, Kinney. Don't forget that polls prove I'm pretty." He struck a pose as if he were a clothing catalog model, his hand on his hip as he gazed into the distance.

"I won't. I promise."

****

Three men approached Kinney on the sidewalk when he returned home. The men had been hiding behind his neighbor's bushes.

The young one taking the lead was scrawny but moved well. He held a fishing knife low in one hand—alongside his thigh. Kinney estimated the threat from him at seven out of ten. The guy's eyes weren't dead like some hitmen Kinney had tangled with; they reflected a cluelessness he was familiar with. Some violent men were a product of low IQ—the inability to make it in the world using legal means.

The knife wielder wore khaki slacks, a white polo shirt, and a black cap with a silver logo on it—basically the uniform of any golfer besides Kinney and Reed. Kinney momentarily pictured him on the first tee at Seaview before remembering that distracting thoughts put him at risk.

The African-American man on Kinney's left towered over the other two and held a hand inside a black windbreaker's pocket. The jacket listed to the right with the weight of a gun. He was a nine. This monolith looked like a defensive lineman. Kinney imagined him in a 49ers uniform. Then he imagined him lying on the ground.

The third, more nondescript man was hard to figure. He could've been anywhere between a four and a ten, depending on what he held behind his back.

Kinney walked toward the men.

"Howdy, gents. What can I—"

He lashed out his foot and took out the big guy with a powerful roundhouse kick under his chin. He went down hard onto the cement, the back of his head landing first.

The guy with the knife lunged at Kinney, who ducked to the side, grabbed the thug's forearm and pulled him forward and down, booting him in the ass en route. The man lay on the ground and watched as the third man scuttled across a stretch of lawn to get behind Kinney. Kinney tried to sweep this man's legs out from under him. The attacker adroitly leapt over Kinney's maneuver and brandished a kid's aluminum baseball bat.

The guy was an eight, Kinney decided. He wasn't holding the bat correctly, but he was quick. Few people saw Kinney's leg sweep in time to evade it.

"Calm down," the bat guy said. "We just want to talk."

He didn't look like a classic villain or thug. He looked like Kinney's high school math teacher—ordinary to a fault. Of course, Mr. Karch had been fired for slapping a disabled student, so it wasn't as though he was actually ordinary.

"Most people use their mouths for talking," Kinney replied.

The knife guy was back, scything sideways at Kinney's hip. Upon closer examination, he was quite ugly, with a squashed nose and bulbous lips on his bony, narrow face. Kinney kicked the knife out of the guy's hand and punched him in the neck. He went down.

"Okay," the bat guy said, stepping farther away. "I get it. You're a badass. I never saw anyone kick like that. They shoulda told us about this. Here's the deal. We're supposed to bring you somewhere. All they said was that you might not want to go, so we should convince you. Then you attacked us before we had a chance to talk to you."

"You might rethink your plan to convince me."

"Yeah, clearly. I mean, I could try to hit you with

this bat, and maybe I could. But maybe I couldn't."

Knife guy tried to get up. Kinney shook his finger at him, and he lay down again. Kinney was surprised the guy had managed to move. Kinney must've been a little off when he targeted the nerve in the guy's neck.

"Why don't you go ahead and give it a try with your club," Kinney said. "It'll be fun."

The man slowly shook his head and then spoke just as slowly. "I don't think I'll do that."

"So you're the one in charge? I thought it might be this loser on the ground who attacked me first."

"Nah, I just like to send him in to find out who we're dealing with." The man shook his head again, faster this time, apparently disappointed in his colleague. "What are you—some kind of kung-fu champion?"

Kinney shook his head. He wanted to be the one asking questions. "Who is the 'they' in the 'they sent me'?"

"Now, it wouldn't be very professional if I told you that."

The man smiled as if he was proud of himself for his loyalty. He tossed the bat back and forth between his hands, which struck Kinney as a very stupid thing to do. All Kinney would need to do was kick him while the bat was in the air.

But he wasn't ready to end the encounter yet—not while there was still more to find out. "Would you be more inclined to tell me if I take that bat away and beat you with it?" he asked.

"You know, I think I would," The man conceded calmly. With his off hand, he pulled a pistol out of what must've been a holster clipped to the back of his belt and aimed it at Kinney. "But it's a moot point now, I think."

Kinney lunged forward and kicked the gun out of his hand before the man knew he'd moved. He followed that up by grabbing the bat, wrenching it sideways to free it, and then slamming it into the man's thigh. He didn't want to break anything—the femur was like concrete—but the man crumpled to the ground, holding his temporarily useless leg.

Kinney was feeling pretty positive about the encounter until he saw that the gun had skittered across the sidewalk to the knife guy. Cradling it in both hands from a safe distance, he told Kinney he liked shooting people.

"Then why'd you bring a knife?" Kinney asked as he raised his hands.

****

Since he would've had the men bring him where they were supposed to anyway, this plan B of having them in charge while they did so could still work. It was just humbling to screw up against amateurs.

Bat guy decided to leave the big guy on the driveway since he hadn't roused. Knife guy didn't like that. Bat guy told him to shut the hell up and get Kinney in the truck.

"What if Dave rats us out?" knife guy complained.

"He won't," bat guy answered. "And if our muscle gets taken out two seconds into things, what use is he? For Chrissakes, he had a gun, too. Dave's useless."

"Yeah, okay. But can't we call an ambulance or something?"

Kinney piped up. "I thought Dave was really scary-looking. You could do worse."

"What? It could take you *two* seconds to disable some other guy?" Bat guy asked.

"Well, yeah. Or I could've started with you instead of him if he hadn't impressed me. Anyway, don't worry about Dave. I'm sure my nosy neighbors have called the cops by now. They'll take care of him."

"Shit," knife guy said. "Let's get out of here."

Kinney certainly didn't want the police involved. The last time he'd been swept up during a mission, Barber had to call in favors from someone he hated. Kinney paid the price, enduring crap assignments for weeks.

In the backseat of an older king cab pick-up, with a paper grocery bag over his head, Kinney noted the distances and turns according to a system he'd been taught. At this point in his career, this was second nature, so he was able to converse with bat guy as the thug drove.

"Why do they want you?" Bat guy asked. "Who are you?"

"Does it matter?"

"Not really. I'm just curious."

"I'm a secret agent planning to assassinate a foreign dignitary," Kinney told him. "Maybe someone doesn't want me to."

"Fine. Don't tell me. But let me ask you this. Where did you learn to fight like that?"

"My dad was a missionary in China. We lived next door to a martial arts academy," Kinney told him. It was a story he'd told more than once. In Turkey, of all places, a witness to one of his non-lethal missions had responded in Mandarin, and Kinney had needed to kick him.

"Really?" Bat guy asked.

"No," Kinney said. "Why should I tell you anything?" His muffled voice sounded odd to his own ears—sort of like he was underwater.

"Why not?" Bat guy asked.

"You *are* in the midst of kidnapping me, aren't you?"

"Oh, I wouldn't call this a kidnapping. Would you, Gary?"

"Hey, don't use my name," Gary said. "And no, it's more like we're escorting a reluctant guy to a business meeting."

"Exactly. He started a fight before we even had a chance to explain things to him." His reasonable tone sought to sell the idea.

"That's right," Gary agreed.

"Don't worry about your name," bat guy said to him. "I don't think this guy's gonna be picking anybody out of a line-up."

"I might," Kinney said.

"Not if you're a criminal yourself—or if you're dead."

"Why aren't you scared?" Gary asked. "You can't see me, but you must know I've got a gun on you, and you heard what *Nick* just said."

"How do you know I'm not scared?" Kinney asked, his light tone implying that his situation was just as mundane to him as the assassination attempts were to the brigadier.

"Are you?" Gary asked.

"No. I've been physically enhanced in a government lab and they cut out the fear part of my brain."

"I don't believe you," Gary said.

"Good for you," Kinney said. "You're not as stupid as you look, I guess."

"I look fine. Fuck you." Like Eddie, his profanity was perfunctory—conversational.

Kinney wondered if Gary had pulled an all-nighter, too. Doing what? Watching cartoons? Maybe he was studying for a night school class—Sidekicks 101.

At that point Nick turned on the radio and they all listened to what passed for country music for the rest of the trip. As far as Kinney was concerned, these days it was just pop music played on twangy instruments. And most of the singers looked like cut-rate versions of Reed wearing cowboy hats.

After twenty-five minutes, the truck turned into a driveway and entered an echoic space. A warehouse? As a steel garage door whined coming down behind them, Gary pulled Kinney's hood off and gestured with the gun for him to get out.

After a moment to focus in the sudden light, Kinney spied two folding chairs facing each other in the middle of a voluminous auto-body shop. In the one facing Kinney was a familiar figure.

Partially dissembled vehicles surrounded and dwarfed the man, simulating the set of a past-apocalyptic movie. All the scene needed was a few mutants and a desert underneath everyone's feet instead of greasy concrete.

"Special Agent Kim," Kinney greeted. "What a nice surprise."

Kim was tall for a Korean-American, with more pronounced Asiatic eyes and darker skin than the other Koreans Kinney had met. He figured that Kim's heritage included some sort of ethnic or indigenous group. He wore a light gray suit with a blue shirt and a thin black tie. His shoes gleamed with recently applied polish.

"Sit down, Kinney. Gary, Nick, stand a good ways behind him and stay alert. You have no idea how dangerous this man is."

"I think we might," Nick told him.

Kim nodded. "Well, three of you left and only two returned. Maybe you do."

Kinney sat, crossed his legs, and leaned back. The folding chair was surprisingly comfortable. The garage was smelly—a mixture of gasoline, oil, and cigarette smoke—no, cigar smoke.

"Since when did the FBI start to use thugs instead of agents to collect people?" Kinney asked.

"Since you're the collectee. As tight as we're stretched these days, I couldn't risk you injuring any of my men. I remember Philadelphia."

"Me too, Kim. How's your arm?" Kinney pointed to it.

The agent flexed his elbow and grimaced. "It's never been the same, but I don't blame you. It was my own damned fault."

"So what do you want?" Kinney asked. "What couldn't get taken care of with a phone call?"

"A little bird told me you might go back to your old ways within our borders. I can't allow that. You're no longer with the agency, so as far as we're concerned, you're just someone like Nick now." Kim tugged at his tie. He could've just tied it too tight, but Kinney figured he was nervous being around him.

"Holy shit!" Gary said. "You're really a spy."

"Shut up, Gary," Kim said offhandedly, as if he'd had to say that so many times that it became rote.

"I suppose that's true," Kinney said, "although I'm probably better at Scrabble than Nick."

"I'm decent," Nick said. "My wife's an English teacher."

"Shut up, Nick," Kim said. "So Kinney, I'm giving you a chance to explain what's going on. I owe that to you after all you've done for our country." He shifted in his chair.

"I'm still committed to not killing anyone," Kinney asserted.

"What about Dave?" Gary asked. "He didn't look so good."

"He'll be fine," Kinney told him. "He'll just need to put a little ice on it."

"Can I believe you?" Kim asked, cocking his head. "Why am I hearing this rumor?"

"I can't tell you that. It's above your pay grade, Kim. Anyway, if I did, I'd be telling these two flunkies too, wouldn't I?"

"Hey," Gary protested. "I'm not a flunky. I'm a private contractor." He puffed out his concave chest as though this was an achievement worthy of an award.

"No benefits, huh?"

"No."

"We're looking into it," Nick said.

"If you two don't shut up," Kim said, "there won't be any more work for you."

"Is that it?" Kinney asked. "Are we done?"

"Why should I believe you?" Kim's tone was belligerent now, but Kinney didn't think it was anything but posturing.

"I don't care if you do. I haven't committed any crimes, and I'm not planning to. What are you going to do—arrest me because someone told you a rumor?"

"No, but I could hold onto you for a while," Kim told him, locking eyes in another effort to look tough.

"Let me ask you this. Are you willing to kill me?"

"Of course not."

"Are those two behind me authorized to use deadly force?" Kinney asked.

"No."

"Then why do you think you can hold me? You know there could be a dozen guys behind me, and I could still leave whenever I wanted—unless someone shot me." Kinney smiled his menacing smile—the one where his mouth and eyes didn't match at all.

Kim stared at him, his brow furrowed and the tip of his tongue poking out the corner of his mouth.

"So I think I'll leave," Kinney continued.

Kim kept staring at him, continuing to assess his options. Finally he said, "Fine. But I've got my eye on you."

Kinney plucked his phone out of his pocket, called a taxi, and gave the dispatcher the address of the shop.

"Hey, how'd you know that?" Gary asked.

"Government enhancement."

Chapter 8

Miner's ex-wife was one of the most disagreeable people Kinney had ever met. He waylaid her in her country club's parking lot after stopping to pick up a few nonperishables at a grocery store. Mature trees divided most of the parking spaces, and redwood flower boxes circled their trunks. All the blooms were shades of red.

"Who the hell are you?" Judy Meriwether asked as he approached her. "You're not a member—not dressed like that."

Her shiny green top gleamed in the sunlight. A scoop neckline revealed odd cleavage—her breasts began their journey into a visible black lace bra from much higher up than normal.

If Kinney were her, he'd wear turtlenecks. He did like her black, form-fitting skirt. Long legs snaked down from it, culminating in heeled leather sandals that revealed turquoise painted toenails. She was probably in her early forties.

"My name's Kinney," he told her. "I'd like to ask you a few questions about your ex. I'd like to put him in jail."

"That's a great idea, but you're not a cop, either," she said.

Her face could've been pretty, but there was no way to tell because of all the makeup obscuring it. Her hair was as perfect as Eddie's pompadour usually was in its own way—a brunette French braid.

"Not exactly. I'm an IRS investigator," Kinney told her.

"Well, hallelujah. Finally."

"Yes, ma'am."

"Do I look like a ma'am? Do I look like your spinster aunt?"

"You certainly don't," Kinney told her. "If I weren't on the job, I'd be putting the moves on you right now." That might've been true at closing time after eight drinks when he was twenty-one.

"I appreciate that. I go to a lot of effort to look my best."

"It's working. The thing is, they make us say 'ma'am.' I had to go to a training session for all the words we're supposed to use."

"Goddamn fascists. Call me Judy. What's your first name, Kinney?"

"I've just got the one." He shrugged.

"How is that possible?"

"My mother was Danish," he told her. That seemed to satisfy her.

"Well, you better come in. Let's have lunch. It's on me. I'll tell Greg your good clothes burned up in a house fire."

"That's right. Why else would I appear in public in these hideous department store jeans and a henley that wasn't designed by someone famous?"

"Exactly. A fire is totally believable. Anyway, Greg's an asshole."

As they walked toward the imposing New England-style clubhouse—dark green shingles and a gabled roof—Judy Meriwether told a story designed to illustrate Greg's assholeness. To Kinney's ears the man's response to a tirade of hers had been restrained. Kinney would've rescinded her membership and relegated her to some lowly club that allowed the horror of minorities in their midst.

The interior was cavernous and clearly made an incongruous attempt to mimic a mountain lodge. Yellow pine beams wider than telephone poles spanned the high ceiling, and these matched the color of the painted trim on the windows and doors. The floor looked to be wide-plank mahogany, which Kinney knew to be expensive as hell.

To the right, through a peaked archway, Kinney spied a bar and restaurant. To the left, a similar portal led to the golf pro shop, which was mostly filled with racks of colorful clothes. Matching furniture ensembles were scattered around the main room. Each burgundy love seat and two matching armchairs were accompanied by a glass-topped cocktail table and an Art Deco floor lamp.

Greg met them just past the towering vestibule and raised his eyebrows. These were impressive—black and bushy like caterpillars. He was a good-looking, well-groomed, middle-aged man wearing a dark green suit and a purple tie.

"Don't give me any crap, Greg," Judy said. "My friend's house burned down."

"I'm sorry to hear that. Would your friend like to borrow a sport jacket?"

"Sure," Kinney answered. "That would be swell."

A few minutes later, they settled into a table overlooking the golf course. The dining room was a small-scale version of the main room, with the addition of a crystal chandelier and a beige and black patterned carpet. To Kinney's eyes, the pattern looked like a stylized version of the shadows the subpoenaed witness had made on his porch a few days earlier. On the other hand, Kinney knew he tended to create connections that weren't there. It had almost gotten him killed once.

The Los Barrancos golf course wasn't particularly impressive, which surprised Kinney. He spied a few bare dirt spots on the first fairway, and the associated tee box was a bit crowned instead of level. Tall eucalyptus trees lined the hole, dropping bark, leaves, and nuts haphazardly.

"So how can I help?" Judy asked after tormenting their nervous young woman server, and then only ordering coffee and a croissant. Kinney ordered a Reuben sandwich and a beer.

"Tell me about Aaron's business."

"Sure. He supposedly imports wooly things from New Zealand these days, but that's just a front. If that's all he reports on his income taxes, you've got him right there. My forensic accountant said he knew Aaron had money hidden somewhere, but he couldn't find it. If you can find it, I'll cut you in for ten percent when I go back to court and get more alimony. You know his real name is Aaron Miner, right?" She widened her eyes and raised her already arched eyebrows.

"Yes. What is his business a front for?" So far, so good, Kinney thought. Judy was motivated by both money and revenge to help all she could.

"I'm not sure," she responded, "but I know it's something criminal. Aaron lies like it's going out of style, and he stole a lot of money in England." Judy played with one of her gold hoop earrings, flicking it back and forth with her index finger.

"Is that where you met?" Kinney asked. Easy to answer questions like this kept things rolling.

"Yes. I was on a trip with my husband at the time—another snake—exploring my roots—and Aaron slipped me a note in our hotel lobby that said he wanted to take me to Paris and screw my brains out in an expensive hotel. I'd already noticed him. So off we went."

"It was good at first?"

"Yes, actually," Judy told him, smiling as she recalled the rendezvous. "It took a while before I found out what he was really like." Her face darkened, and her lips curled into a scowl. "He's a narcissist with no morals at all. The bastard slept with my sister—in our house!"

"Did you find them in bed? Was that a shock?" Kinney's question was motivated by curiosity this time. It was an experience he'd never weathered.

"No, I was in Vegas with this guy who teaches tennis here, but that's not the point. Whose side are you on, Kinney?"

"Sorry." He held his hands in front of him and smiled as innocently as he could. Innocence was a tough one for him. As a teen, he'd practiced all the facial expressions that other people used, but there were a few he still hadn't mastered.

Kinney continued. "If you had to guess, what do you think Aaron's up to—I mean, specifically?"

"It's probably something to do with state politics. Maybe he's bribing somebody. He was always going to Sacramento, and once I overheard him on the phone talking about getting a bill through. I don't know what it was, though."

Judy switched to fondling her other earring. Kinney figured this was a rehearsed attempt to appear seductive. Instead of flicking, now she was stroking, which wasn't easy with a one inch long hoop.

"This is very helpful, Judy. Did he ever mention Rakena?"

"No. What's that?"

"It's the company that currently owns Aaron's business."

"That's news to me." She shook her head and frowned.

"Do you know someone named Chet who works with your ex?"

"No." She licked her lips and wriggled. "Maybe after lunch, you could take a break," she added. "When I want something, I go for it, Kinney."

"And you want me?"

Judy nodded. "You remind me of my cousin."

"Don't tell me. You slept with him, too."

She grinned, reached across the table and placed her hand on Kinney's forearm, stroking it as if it were an entirely different appendage.

That was it for useful information. When Kinney finished eating, he excused himself to use the rest room and never came back. He met Greg at the front door.

"Could you tell Mrs. Meriwether I'm gay?" he asked as he handed back his sports coat.

"Certainly, sir. Would you like my phone number?"

Chapter 9

Kinney and Reed wouldn't need to fly to New Jersey for a few days, so Reed played golf and Kinney attempted to play detective. Online investigation wasn't his strong suit. He decided to take a break from work and call the woman they'd polled on the street— Georgia. She seemed like she might be a stimulating dinner companion—and maybe more.

"Hi," he began. "This is the rugged guy from the street poll. Kinney."

"Yes, I know all about you."

"Really? How's that?"

"I'm an FBI analyst. I analyzed you," she told him matter-of-factly.

That was a surprise. The FBI? An analyst? And why would she do that? Was she so full of herself that she was sure he would call? Kinney was at a loss as to how to respond. "I don't think that's possible in my case," he finally replied. "Walk me through it."

"Sure. I got hold of CCTV footage from a business near where I took your friend's poll, and I ran you through our facial recognition program. You want to know your bio?"

"I'm kinda familiar with it already." Actually, Kinney had trouble remembering everything the agency had concocted.

"The interesting thing is that you're supposed to be

retired from being a consultant because of an inheritance, but there's no record of any estate ever being left to you."

"Is that a question?" Kinney was hoping to put her on the defensive. He didn't need anyone probing into his true identity, date or no date.

"I guess I'd like to know more about that before we talk any further. I presume you're calling to ask me out. I thought you would."

"Yes, I am." Kinney nodded to his phone.

"So?" Georgia asked.

"Maybe my beloved uncle lived in another country where estate records are kept confidential."

"Maybe not," she said, recognizing a deflection when she heard one.

Kinney wished he hadn't started with a "maybe." That was a tip-off. "No, maybe not," he conceded. "Uncle Gus is a stone mason in San Antonio, and Uncle Fred steals cars. Actually, I work for the government, too. It's classified. If you need to know more, ask Special Agent Kim. He's got a mid-level clearance, so he knows a little about it."

"Alan Kim?"

"Yeah. The guy's a jerk, but he can verify what I'm telling you. Don't mention you want to know in order to vet me for a date. I had to break his arm a little once, so he's not a big fan."

"A little?" Georgia asked.

"All right. In three places. But I didn't tell the guy to interfere with my work."

"So you can hurt FBI agents and not be prosecuted for it? I'm thinking you're not a government bean counter."

"No. Didn't you sense that hint of menace in me that drives chicks wild?"

"Chicks?"

"Sorry, it's from the title of an album. The—"

"Fabulous Thunderbirds?"

"Yes!" Kinney was almost elated that Georgia knew this. He wasn't sure why.

"Okay, then yes back at you about a date, assuming Alan vouches for you," Georgia said after a moment. "Anyone who's a Thunderbirds fan can't be too evil."

"That seems like an odd criterion, not that I'm complaining."

"See? You're using the correct version of criterion—the singular. My decision is being validated minute by minute."

"Thank you. Let's turn things around for a minute. You don't come across as an FBI agent. Are you sure you don't write children's books or something?"

"Why's that?" Clearly, Georgia was puzzled by this notion.

"You're breezy and whimsical."

"Is that a problem?"

"No, no. I love it. I'm just saying it doesn't match my experience with the feds." In fact, it was the exact opposite.

"Well, I'm not an agent, Kinney. I'm an analyst. Think of me as the one who figures out what agents need to know before they go out and humorlessly hassle people."

"Gotcha. I've never really thought about what analysts analyze. It's kind of a vague job title, isn't it? So where shall we go and what shall we do?"

"I'm open to suggestions," Georgia said.

"How about a walk somewhere scenic and then dinner if we're not repulsed by one another?"

"That sounds like a possibility." Her voice reflected ambivalence.

"Why don't I meet you on the Guadalupe River path after you get off work today?" Kinney continued, undaunted by her lack of enthusiasm.

"Here's the why not, Kinney. What makes you think I have nothing going on in my life? You think I can say yes to a short notice invitation?"

She didn't sound affronted to Kinney's ears. Her tone was playful.

"*Do* you have plans? It's Wednesday, after all."

"Well, I don't, but that's not the point. It's insulting for you to think I'm not out on fabulous dates every night."

"Sorry. Are you repulsed already?"

"No, but why don't I make the plan. I don't have walking shoes at work, anyway, so your idea won't work."

"That's fine. What do you have in mind?" Kinney asked. It didn't matter much to him. He just wanted to see her again, wherever it was.

"Why don't we meet tonight for drinks at the bar in the Gadsden Hotel—by the convention center in downtown San Jose?"

"Sounds good."

"Five thirty?"

"Sure."

"See you there. Don't be fooled by my work clothes. I'm not my job."

"And don't you be fooled my efforts to fit in at a swanky bar," Kinney responded. "I usually fail miserably in that department."

"Are we talking filthy overalls? A ratty straw hat?"

"Exactly. With a stained wifebeater under the bib and mud-encrusted shitkickers. I like you already, Georgia. You're fun."

"You too. See you soon."

****

In fact, Kinney liked Georgia enough that he became increasingly nervous as the afternoon passed. After he'd tried on several outfits, he was forced to use breathing techniques he'd learned from an instructor at a gun range. He eventually settled on gray corduroy jeans, white running shoes, and a tasteful Hawaiian shirt—a blue band of hibiscus flowers on a white background. What was the point of misrepresenting himself? If Georgia fell in love with an adopted upscale persona, what would happen when she discovered who he really was? And who cared what anyone else in a bar thought?

Both arrived from opposite directions at the front door to the hotel at exactly five thirty, providing each an opportunity watch the other walk for half a block. Georgia's purposeful stride struck Kinney as formidable, as though it was emblematic of inner strength and resources. He wondered what Georgia made of his approach. Could she sense his preternatural physical abilities?

"Hi," they said simultaneously under a dark green canopy and then smiled.

"Same arrival time, same greeting," Kinney commented. "Who knows what else we have in common?"

"Let's find out," she responded.

As they strolled in side by side, Kinney told her she looked great in her work clothes, which he assessed as an approximate female version of what he wore, despite the lack of grooves in her black slacks, the V neck of her navy shirt, and a pair of tan desert boots like the ones Kinney had worn in seventh grade in a futile attempt to impress girls. He didn't see why she couldn't have walked along the river in those. Did she pick a bar instead because she had a drinking problem?

"Thanks," Georgia said." Let's grab a table."

The hotel bar was about what Kinney expected. Light years more tasteful than Los Barrancos Country Club, it still did its best to ostentatiously proclaim its classiness. High-backed, black-upholstered stools roosted in front of the actual bar, and most were filled by men in expensive-looking suits. The dark paneled walls sported vintage paintings of fox hunting, polo players, and Scottish castles. Other than all of these being associated with wealth, Kinney had never understood their appeal.

A diminutive, young Asian server rushed to their table immediately with a drinks menu in hand.

"What's the hurry?" Georgia asked her.

"I'm on probation, so I have to sell enough drinks to keep my job," she reported. "And today's the day my boss will take a count for the last week, and I'm behind."

Her voice didn't match the content of her declaration or anything else about her. It would've befitted a self-confident entrepreneur or someone in a position to boss other people around—not an elfin young woman with body language that proclaimed, "I'm timid. Be kind to me if it's not too much trouble."

"In that case," Kinney told her, "I'll have twelve Amstels."

Left to his own devices, he couldn't have come up with anything more demonstrative of his being kind. Or, technically, more misleading in terms of the real, original Kinney.

"Seriously?" the server asked, her eyes wide.

"Sure."

"And I'll have thirteen screwdrivers," Georgia told her.

"You guys know how much that's going to cost? We charge a lot here, and you're not dressed-up like you're rich."

"It's okay. We're government employees feeding at your tax dollar trough," Kinney told the server.

"Oh, okay. Thanks so much. I can't believe you're doing this."

When she scurried away, Kinney turned to Georgia. "So I guess you're pretty competitive."

"How's that?"

"Thirteen drinks—one more than me?" Kinney cocked an eyebrow, a maneuver he'd practiced in high school. He could roll his tongue and wiggle his ears as well, but these hadn't proved useful as an adult.

"I can out-generous anyone," Georgia asserted, "and whatever you do, don't shoot pool with me if you don't like to lose." She flashed him a devastating smile, her eyes boring into his.

Her sudden intensity intimidated Kinney for a moment before he gathered himself again. "Maybe we'll put that to the test soon," he said.

Georgia wrinkled her nose, highlighting the light dusting of freckles on her nose. "Maybe," she responded, which seemed like a mild yes to Kinney. He knew he wasn't a maestro at decoding things like that, though.

"I'm pretty much great at everything athletic." Kinney regretted this remark as soon as it was out of his mouth.

The corners of Georgia's mouth turned down a bit. "We'll see."

They both paused, and Kinney assumed that Georgia felt the way he did—not that happy at the way the conversation was going. Bragging wasn't sexy. Competitiveness was outright adversarial.

"Let's start over," he suggested. "How are you today? Tell me about yourself. What do you like best about me so far?"

She smiled again, the corners of her eyes crinkling. "I have a literal mind, so I'll answer you in order. I've been quite busy today and my lack of progress on a particular case has been frustrating. I'm thirty-two and I have no pets. My dad is a philosophy professor and my stepmother is a psychotherapist. I've traveled extensively in Mexico, and I'm divorced from a nice but boring man I married when I was too young. What I like or don't like about you is none of your business."

"Fair enough. Since you already know all about me, we can skip that and get right to the nitty gritty."

"Which is?"

"Dogs or cats?" Kinney asked.

"Dogs, of course."

"Which side of the bed?"

"The left," Georgia said.

"And which Marx brother?"

"Harpo," Georgia reported.

"Okay, we're all set." Kinney leaned back and crossed his arms.

"You seem like a Groucho kind of guy, Kinney."

"I used to be. I graduated to Harpo."

"Good for you. What would you have done if I liked cats, slept on the other side of the bed, and—God forbid—I liked Gummo the best?"

"Good question. We'll never know."

They had their server create an army of extra drinks on two nearby empty tables. Then Georgia stood on her chair and announced in a loud voice that the drinks were free to anyone willing to swear they didn't watch Fox News. Half the bar booed this pronouncement, the other half rushed over. The drinks disappeared in thirty seconds.

"There are going to be a lot of drunk liars in here soon," Kinney commented.

"Probably. Upscale hotel bars in Silicon Valley aren't magnets for Honest Abes."

"Except for us."

"Of course. Except for us," Georgia agreed. "I chose here because it helps me evaluate my potential dates by eliminating the variable of multiple venues."

"In other words, this is where you lure all your suitors to run your date experiments?"

"More or less."

Kinney thought that over. "Did you put that server up to what she said about getting fired?" Kinney asked. "Was that a test to see how I'd respond?"

"Just how Machiavellian do you think I am?" Georgia widened her eyes as she bowed her head just a bit in an effort to look innocent. Kinney decided that Georgia's performance was marginally more convincing than his had been, but certainly not believable.

"I think you're just about that much Machiavellian, actually," Kinney told her, grinning.

"Okay, yeah. That's Sylvia, my coworker's daughter. She's an electrical engineering grad student. You're the first one to ever order any extra drinks from her."

Then they just looked at one another for a while. Kinney was already quite fond of her blue eyes and generous mouth—the two features he generally focused on to gauge character. They both projected strength, humor, and sincerity, which was how he'd experienced her conversation so far, as well.

"Is this really what we want to talk about?" Georgia finally asked.

"So far, I guess, since that's what we've done, but I take your point. Mostly, we're getting to know how good each other is at banter instead of who we actually are."

"Exactly." Georgia nodded and then sipped her drink, which she'd been ignoring. "Tell me about yourself—the real story." She leaned forward, her eyes on Kinney's.

"What do you mean by 'real'?" The notion was alarming, especially since for a moment he'd imagined actually doing it.

"An FBI bio—the stuff I come up with for agents—doesn't really get at who someone is—what they've been through and how they've responded to whatever that was."

"I don't know if I can get into that."

"Because that's classified, too?"

"Yes, and it's been so long since it seemed like a good idea to really level with someone that I think my sense of myself is way out of date."

"Try." Her tone was firm. Kinney thought it might be a dealbreaker if he didn't cooperate.

"Okay," he agreed after some thought. Why not? Better to scare her away now than later, anyway. Once they'd made an emotional investment in one another, ending things would be more painful..

"I'm probably a benign version of someone on the sociopathy scale," he began, then cleared his throat. "I don't have a conscience, per se, but I know right and wrong intellectually and I choose right for the most part—not because I'd feel guilty or ashamed if I did wrong, but just because…Well, why be a dick if you have a choice?"

Georgia nodded. "Thus the twelve drinks."

"Exactly. As far as empathy goes, I've developed something similar even though I'm not actually moved much by other people's feelings. For me, it's conceptual again. I understand that acting as though I have lots of empathy is the way to go—what other people deserve—so I try my best. My sister says this is more exemplary than a naturally kind person acting kind, but I disagree. The net effect on other people isn't nearly as positive."

Georgia nodded again. Kinney couldn't read her internal reaction. He very much wished he could.

"So are you ready to run out of the room screaming?" he asked. "Remember, you asked for the real story."

She shook her head. "What are the benefits of being this way?"

"Well, I can do pretty much whatever I decide to do without negative emotional consequences. I might recognize I made a bad choice or what I did hurt someone, and I learn from that, but I never beat myself up. There's real freedom there—no internal taskmaster giving me shit. And I'm not restricted by culture, family, or even myself. I'll break a rule or a social convention without a second thought if I think it's a good idea."

"And you'll break the law, too?"

Kinney took a swig of his beer. "When it's part of my job, yes. Otherwise, no. I could, but I don't. That's enough about me. I imagine whatever else you're going to tell me about yourself is really different, and I'd love to learn more about you."

"My story is different from you, but not much different from a lot of people. I grew up with four sisters and a brother. I was a tomboy. I wanted to do medical research, but we didn't have the money for the kind of degree I'd need, so I drifted into data analysis, first at a bank, then at the FBI. Every now and then my boss sends me out in the field, but it's never anything exciting. I drive a decrepit sports car, I live in a two-bedroom apartment, I like early rhythm and blues, and I love Mexican food."

Kinney took a moment to take all this in, then he asked, "Are you a good kisser?"

"That's what you want to know? Already?" Georgia leaned back. Kinney found her current frown a particularly strong expression of disapproval.

"Sure," Kinney answered. He wasn't sure what else he could say at that point besides doubling down.

"As it happens, I am," Georgia told him. Her frown

dissipated as she hoisted her screwdriver to her lips again. Kinney had been forgiven.

Kinney smiled. "Why don't we go make out in the men's room?"

"Seriously?"

"Sure. Why not?" He immediately realized he hadn't read Georgia's "seriously" accurately.

"Because it's incredibly inappropriate." Georgia leaned back again and held herself unnaturally still. "I'm thinking of walking out," she announced without an ounce of warmth or concern for how her statement might impact Kinney.

"Please don't," Kinney implored, cradling his hands in front of his heart. "I'm sorry I misgauged the situation. It's just that you can tell a lot from a kiss. It's a litmus test."

"First of all, that's not a real apology. When you couple an 'I'm sorry' with a justification for your actions, you're not really taking responsibility."

"Good point." Kinney nodded vigorously. He was in damage control mode.

"Secondly," Georgia continued, "using a scientific metaphor like a litmus test doesn't set a romantic mood."

Kinney glared at her now, irritated at her hypocrisy. "Says the first date experimenter. Says the co-conspirator in manipulating me about buying drinks as a *litmus test*."

"All right, you've got me there. I can see that if we keep dating, we're going to hold each other's feet to the fire."

Once again, Kinney didn't know if Georgia meant it was a problem or something she welcomed. "I kind of like it," he told her. "People don't generally call me on my stuff."

"Why is that?"

"It might be that menacing thing I mentioned earlier. I think they're intimidated."

"I don't experience you that way," Georgia told him. "You said you're a sociopath, but you haven't demonstrated anything along those lines. You don't scare me. I think you just have a weird self-esteem problem."

"Thank you, I guess. I work at acting like everyone else. What about you? How do you feel about the feet to the fire thing?"

"I'm not sure," Georgia replied, cocking her head to consider the question. "A steady diet of it might get old," she told him as she looked into his eyes.

They both paused, sipped their drinks again, and then glanced away. Kinney studied a print of an equestrian jumping over a hedge. Georgia's eyes were aimed over his shoulder.

She returned her gaze first. "Here's another way you've been successful, Kinney. You've distracted me from your offensive suggestion—your men's room version of intimacy."

"That wasn't my intent. If you want to keep talking about it, that's fine."

"Intent doesn't matter. It's all about impact. How was the other person affected by what you did or said? That's what matters."

"You're kind of wise, aren't you?" Kinney was still trying to repair whatever damage he'd inflicted .

"I suppose so. Listen, I've got to go. Let's do this again. Whether or not it works out between us, this has been interesting and fun."

"I agree. I'll call you?" He raised his eyebrows, accentuating his question.

"Or I'll call you."

"Sounds good."

Chapter 10

Kinney lay awake in bed that night recalling how he'd felt when he was with Georgia. The main thing was excitement. He liked the way she looked and how quick her mind was. He loved Georgia's sense of humor, which mirrored his, and it was damned hard to find a kindred spirit in that department.

Kinney was also aware of fear. What if things proceeded and then he did something stupid and lost her? Well, more stupid things, he realized. Did he really want to go through getting dumped again? When one's idea of right and wrong were merely mental constructs, it was easy to misunderstand what was acceptable behavior—like the men's room debacle.

Finally, while was attempting to remember exactly what he'd said when Georgia asked him for the real story about himself, Kinney finally fell asleep.

****

The next day, after collecting a few things from the garage at a safe house, Kinney and Reed flew separately to Newark, rented cars, and drove down to Princeton. The first part of the trip was typical of northern New Jersey—ugly as hell. The elevated turnpike bisected an oil refinery and ran past sad-looking Linden and Elizabeth. Aggressive and incompetent drivers littered the twelve lanes. Kinney figured they needed at least another six. After taking exit nine at New Brunswick and working his way through the stoplights on Route One, Kinney gradually encountered more and more green countryside, culminating in the majestic trees of Princeton.

The brigadier's conference was at an upscale chain hotel outside town. Reed was able to book a room a few miles down the road at an old-fashioned motel. Kinney opted for a colonial inn in the heart of town—across the street from the university.

Pretty much everything was across the street from the university in Princeton. One side of the main drag was like a park, with the university's gothic buildings scattered across it. Every now and then, a wildly incongruous modern structure jarred Kinney's gaze. On the other side of Nassau Street, businesses catering to students and wealthy townies lined the wide sidewalk. Conscious of its colonial heritage, Princeton had enacted stringent zoning and signage laws that eliminated fast food franchises, neon advertising, and any other garish displays.

Kinney had visited a few years earlier, but everything looked much the same as he strolled around the area near his hotel. All of the shops fronting Palmer Square sold expensive things. That was the common denominator, whether the items were cheese, women's clothes, or even socks. One store window was filled with titanium suitcases, another displayed designer baby clothes. Princeton was the kind of town where you had to drive elsewhere to find ordinary things to buy.

Quite a few of the other pedestrians at three in the afternoon were obviously college students. Kinney studied them to see if these young men and women looked smarter than the ones back home, but he couldn't tell any difference. A preference for wearing black T-shirts and hoodies with Princeton emblazoned them in orange letters proclaimed their lofty Ivy League status. To Kinney's eye, wearing that stuff was like a basketball player wearing a sign on the court that stated he was a basketball player. Did they need to distinguish themselves from all the East Arkansas A&M students in town?

For his part, Kinney wore a blue ski cap, sunglasses, and an oversized bandage on his forehead. He hoped that, à la Gil Saunders' strategy, people remembered the bandage, not him.

He'd arranged to meet Pope at Marquand Park, on the road to Trenton. It was far enough out of town that it received very few visitors. In fact, Kinney could see no reason why it was there at all. He figured that some rich guy named Marquand had donated the land.

After hugging in the small parking lot—Pope was a hugger—they strode to a bench overlooking a copse of odd-looking trees. The brigadier's security detail remained in their SUV, a short distance away.

The trees formed almost perfect, towering cones, with each succeeding layer of horizontal branches a smaller diameter as they ascended. To Kinney's eye, three of the five could've been clones.

"So what's the plan?" Pope asked, bringing Kinney back into the moment. "Am I to die in a hail of gunfire? Will you poison me? I've always thought falling from a great height would be interesting."

Will Pope was in his mid-sixties, but his smooth, dark skin belied his years. His features projected solidity, as did his military bearing. His wide mouth sat under a matching wide nose. His forehead extended up to a receding hairline. In a few more years he'd be completely aerodynamic. Kinney pictured him in a wind tunnel, leaning to stay erect while air rushed over his bald head. Kinney had been impressed by the brigadier in Guyana and felt the man's charisma as Pope spoke.

"We need reliable witnesses to your death," Kinney told him.

"You know I'm giving a speech about small army deployment at the conference?"

Kinney considered that as a fly buzzed near his ear. "Do you care if you finish it?"

"No, not really. They paid my expenses if I said I'd do it." Pope smiled.

Kinney remembered that the Brigadier was notoriously thrifty. "Here's my plan, then," he told him after some more thought and two more flies. All he'd needed to do was adapt what he'd already concocted. "I'll pop up and shoot at you a couple of times, and you'll slap blood squibs on your chest so it looks like you've been hit. There'll be lots of credible witnesses."

"I assume you mean you'll shoot blanks?"

"Of course."

"And squibs are what they use in films?"

"Yes."

"My security men will kill you," Pope told him matter-of-factly. Like Kinney, he was no stranger to violent death.

"Not if they're in on it or they're elsewhere—that's up to you. Do you have a big, strong guy on your detail?"

"Huge."

Kinney smiled. "He'll pick you up after my friend

pretends to be a doctor, and then he'll rush you out of there to your room. I presume the conference pays for their speakers to stay on-site?"

"Yes."

Kinney continued. "I'll give you the squibs. You just tape them down under your shirt, pat them when you need to, and you're all set."

"Then what?"

"We'll put out a press release that says you're recovering in a private hospital—that you'll be okay. I'll have an ambulance with some guys I know ferry you away. But my partner will shoot video of you pretending to be dead, and he'll tie up whoever your assistant or number two is—someone recognizable. Reed knows how to fake a lot of bruises and cuts on someone. Your guy will hold up the day's newspaper and reluctantly read from a script, confirming that you're really dead despite the press release. Then Reed will send the video to the guy who threatened me, using my email account."

"And you think this will work? And you trust your partner with your life?" Pope seemed dubious that anyone could be trusted that much.

"Absolutely." Kinney nodded vigorously, then paused before speaking again. "They'd rather I make it look like an accident, but everything I can think of along those lines is too risky. Later, by the time the truth comes out, Reed and I should've wrapped this up. Either that or we'll be dead."

"About that, won't the police hunt you down? Maybe you'll end up rotting in prison before your adversaries have a chance to kill you."

"The police can try. I've been through this before. I

know what to do," Kinney told him. Of course, on the other occasions, he'd fled from actual assassinations.

"When shall I anticipate you attacking me? It's rather unnerving to wonder." Pope's face didn't reflect any concern, but Kinney believed him.

"That's the whole idea. Go ahead and be nervous. After all, this is your first public appearance in months. Then be surprised when you're shot. You won't have to act at all, other than to pat the squibs, fall down, and lie still."

"You have a way for me to sneak back to Guyana? I don't mind hiding out there if it helps you out and keeps real killers off my back—but not forever."

Kinney nodded. "Give me a few weeks, then be healed and return to your regular life. I think you can figure out how to get home. What do you say?"

"If it saves your family, I'm onboard. Turnabout is fair play."

****

Reed scouted the conference location, where he'd need to comb through the badges the attendees would pick up when checking in the next day. He wanted to find two men who were the right age, ethnicity, and general appearance. Reed had tried to impersonate a Navajo once with disastrous results, as well as a great deal of derision from his fellow agents.

After wandering through the hotel and getting his bearings, Reed's next step was to find out where the badges were kept. He figured that would be harder than breaking into whatever room they were in, but he lucked out after several attempts to pump serious-looking men in uniforms for information.

While Reed stood on line behind two Indian men

who were checking in, he overheard them discussing the conference.

"I hope it's better than last year's," the taller of the two said in accented English.

"I'm sure it will be," the other one replied. He was younger and lighter-skinned. "Courvoisier was killed in Sudan a few months ago, so they've got a new organizer. Harris. I've heard good things about him. Anyway, here we are with a free trip to somewhere only an hour away from New York. I don't really care if the speakers are boring again."

"I got paired with a Spaniard with bad breath last year in a breakout group," the other man said. "I could miss that."

"I feel your pain," Reed told him.

The man pivoted and glared at him. "This is a private conversation."

"Really? You guys look like you're at least lieutenants."

The other man laughed. The first one glared harder.

"So who's this Harris guy?" Reed asked.

"Mind your own business," the glarer said.

"Lighten up, Viraj," his companion said. Turning to Reed, he said, "His name is Kennith Harris, and he's supposed to be pretty sharp. He used to be a colonel in the US Marines."

"Thanks. Where are you guys from?" Reed was expecting to hear cities in India.

"Fiji."

"Really? Fiji?"

"You have a problem with that?" the pugnacious soldier said.

"Not at all."

When it was his turn, Reed smiled and walked up to the desk clerk, a young woman who was obviously taken by Reed's looks—something he was accustomed to and only too happy to take advantage of.

A bit overweight, Sandra—her name tag said she was Sandra—had an Irish milkmaid's complexion—porcelain white with rosy cheeks. Her blue eyes were set deep into her face below strawberry blond bangs. She smelled like lemons.

"Hello there," Reed began. "How's your day going?"

"Just fine. Thanks for asking. Haven't I seen you in a movie?"

"Which one were you thinking of?"

"That one about the cowboy lawyer. You know, he gets off the kid who supposedly murdered his teacher?"

"Yes, that's me, but I'm here incognito." He put a finger to his lips and reached out his other arm to touch Sandra's arm. "Can I count on you?"

"Of course." She placed her hand on top of Reed's, pinning it to her forearm and winked. "Now what can I do for you?"

"I need to meet with the conference organizer—Kennith Harris. We have to coordinate my surprise appearance at the wrap-up."

"Do you think they'd let me into that? I'd love to hear you speak."

"Sure. The password to get in will be…Actually, that's one of the things Harris and I need to determine. After I meet with him in his room, I'll come back and tell you."

"Let me give you my phone number in case I'm not here at the desk. Call me anytime." She wrote the number down on the back of a pamphlet on the counter advertising a kayak tour of a nearby canal.

"So if you could let me know Harris's room number," Reed said, "I'll be on my way."

"Sure. Let me check. Here it is. 343. Do you need directions?"

"No, I'm good." Reed extricated his hand and then reached farther across the counter to pat her shoulder. "You're a beautiful girl, Sandra. I won't forget how you helped me."

She blushed and ducked her head as Reed turned and strode away.

Getting into the room wasn't a problem, but sorting through the badges took time. The door opened as he decided he and Kinney would impersonate Italian military aides.

A portly middle-aged man in forest fatigues strode in. "What are you doing here?" he demanded when he spied Reed by the desk in the corner.

Reed now wore faded gray coveralls over his clothes that he'd stolen from a gym locker back in California. The embroidered name on the front was Jesus. The back bore the name Santos Heating and Air Conditioning.

Using his best Mexican accent, he said, "I do my job."

"And pray tell, what is that?"

Reed pivoted and showed the company name on the back of his coveralls.

The man was not appeased. "This is outrageous. You can't just stroll in here while I'm gone. What's your name? You're in trouble." Harris's face was now bright red. Reed wouldn't have been surprised if the man had a heart attack.

Reed turned around again and pointed to his supposed name. "Jesus," he said, forgetting to pronounce it the way you would in Spanish.

"Well, *Jesus*, why don't you get the hell out of here? And if I find anything missing, I know where to come looking—for the whitest Mexican I ever saw."

"Yes, señor. I go now. My parents were albinos."

"I'm sorry to hear that, but if you're looking for sympathy, you won't find it here." Harris crossed his arms and glared.

"Hokay."

****

Kinney bought a fast used motorcycle on Craig's List from a gangly teenager in a nearby town. Lime green, with yellow lightning streaks along its cowl and gas tank, the Kawasaki certainly wouldn't blend into the background anywhere, but it didn't need to.

Then, the next day after lying low, Kinney and his partner arrived at the conference separately—Reed first.

Posing as the same repairman—watching for both Sandra and the conference organizer—he knocked on the Italians' second floor door. The two attachés they were planning to impersonate were rooming together.

"I'm so sorry. I need access to a wall unit for a few minutes," Reed told the beefy young man who answered the door.

The officer wore green plaid pajamas and a pair of bulky black headphones, which he grudgingly took off after shaking his head. Reed repeated himself. The Italian frowned.

His lank blond hair defied Reed's stereotype of Italians, and his brushy, reddish mustache should've

104

been on a Scotsman's face.

"Now is not so good a time," the attaché responded with a strong accent.

"I'll only be a minute," Reed said as he moved past him.

The Italian turned and firmly grasped Reed's shoulder from behind. Reed whirled and sprayed anesthetic into the man's nostrils, gently lowering him to the ground when he immediately lost consciousness.

"*Chi è la?*" the other man asked as he emerged from the bathroom around the corner from Reed.

"I'm sorry to disturb you, sir," Reed said, striding forward in the short hallway to meet him.

They almost collided at the corner, but Reed was able to employ his spray. Then he laid both men on their beds, removed his coveralls, and changed into the ill-fitting uniform of the taller of the two men—a drab cross between khaki and olive green with all sorts of colorful garnishes. Reed liked the epaulettes the least as he gazed at himself in the bathroom mirror. If he was self-conscious about anything, it was his oversized shoulders, which the epaulettes accentuated.

Reed then headed to a storage room on the ground floor just shy of the lobby, where he deposited Kinney's uniform on a shelf beside a row of cleaning products. From there, he proceeded to the check-in desk in the lobby.

When Kinney entered the building ten minutes later via a back door, he changed into the uniform and then strode to the folding table adorned with American flags on a side wall of the capacious lobby. It was manned by two hard-looking men. He joined a short line behind a short, bald guy in an ornate blue uniform with shiny gold studs on its shoulders.

"*Buongiorno*," he said in his best fake Italian accent when his turn came.

"We speak English here," the stone-faced man on the right told him. "This is America."

Ironically, his square jaw and lipless mouth reminded Kinney of Mussolini.

"*Certo*," Kinney replied in Italian.

The guy stared at him, prison yard-style. He was good at it, but Kinney had seen better.

"Let it go, Floyd," the other man said. An older Latino, he smiled at Kinney. "Welcome to the US. Do you speak English?"

"With people who aren't rude," Kinney responded.

"Fair enough. What's your name?"

"Capitano Lorenzo Brambilla." Kinney stood back a bit since, according to Reed, the slightly out of focus photo on the badge didn't look as much like him as it ought to. "I'd rather not give you a cold," Kinney said, sniffling.

"Ah," the friendly guy said after rummaging through the badges that had previously been in alphabetical order before Reed got to them. "Here we are. Okay, you're checked in. Enjoy yourself."

"*Sicuramente*," Kinney answered, taking the badge at arm's length. He locked eyes with the other guy, who scowled.

As Kinney strolled past a group of men in civilian clothes, he heard one of them call out to Reed, who was marching in the other direction toward the bathrooms.

"*Signore, dove tuo colonnello?*"

Reed pulled his phone out of his pocket, held up a finger, and said, "*Pronto*," to his fictitious caller. Then he kept walking.

A few minutes later, Reed grabbed a front row seat for Pope's talk. He'd changed into a blue suit and a red tie—his idea of what a physician would wear to a military conference, although he suspected a doctor wouldn't be caught dead at one. They wanted to save lives, not take them, he figured. In the confusion following the non-shooting, both Kinney and Reed didn't think anything like that would matter.

Then, as others marched in along with him, Kinney secured a seat by an exit near the back of the nondescript meeting room. It was as if the conference center had worked hard to make sure nothing could possibly elicit an opinion about the decor. All the colors were studiously neutral and the walls were bare.

Kinney was armed with a black, nonmetallic pistol he'd smuggled through airport security. He'd wrapped it in lead foil that he'd shaped to resemble a hairdryer. The gun didn't need to be accurate, which was a good thing since it wasn't. All it needed to do was make a loud noise and look like a gun, which it did.

Kinney had also parked the garish motorcycle nearby. The plates were obscured now by what looked like mud but was actually brown paint.

Most of the audience wore uniforms. The conference wasn't sponsored by the US military—a mercenary outfit had organized it. Nonetheless, it appeared as though the multinational attendees considered themselves on duty. Few of them spoke to anyone outside their own contingent, and no one looked happy.

The room was about two-thirds full ten minutes after the appointed hour. Another military leader was concurrently speaking about rations across the hallway. Apparently, food was more interesting to soldiers than Pope's deployment topic. Kinney got that. He'd have been across the hall, too, if he were an actual attendee.

Pope strode in and stood behind a plain wooden podium, notes in his hand. Two bodyguards, one of them gigantic as promised, flanked him with their brawny arms crossed. They wore tight white T-shirts to make sure everyone was fully aware of their brawniness. The light color accentuated their dark skin.

Pope had eschewed his uniform, which Kinney knew to be even more ornate than what anyone else in the room was wearing. Instead, he wore an unbuttoned navy blazer with a white shirt and no tie. Kinney approved his choice, which would highlight the fake blood from the squibs.

As Pope detailed his nation's military history in a loud, clear voice, Kinney realized he was going to be extremely bored. So he stood, shouted, "Sic semper tyrannis!" and fired his gun twice in the brigadier's general direction.

Pope was a beat slow to react, but not unbelievably so. The squibs performed perfectly. Kinney took off before he saw anything else. Two men grabbed him, and he knocked them away. Another one adopted a fighting stance in front of the rear exit. Kinney knew he needed to dispatch the lithe-looking young marine quickly before he was swarmed by a cadre of trained men.

His initial kick caught the guy's shoulder and spun him. As the soldier turned back, Kinney was waiting for him and delivered a fight-ending heel strike to his cheek. Then he sprinted out the door and jammed a wedge under it. He'd cannibalized the hunk of metal from a cross-brace on the motorcycle's luggage rack.

Kinney was free and clear in fifteen seconds, hopping onto the bike and zooming away. On a nearby country road, he turned into a shaded, unused farm driveway, where he'd parked a stolen delivery truck. Using a plank from a lumber yard as a ramp, he maneuvered the bike into the back, where he placed it between the boxes he'd cleared. Then he piled the boxes up, glued them together, and completely hid his getaway vehicle. It would've been simpler to abandon the bike, but he knew if it was found nearby it could lead back to him.

Within minutes, Kinney was on the road again, wearing a delivery uniform, cap, and false teeth. Since Kinney had also done his best to avoid revealing his face to video cameras at the conference center, he felt safe driving toward Boston, and then flying home with Reed.

Kinney was surprised to find a roadblock fifteen miles out of town on a major artery like Route One. Grim-looking state troopers waved all the vehicles to the side of the road for inspection, resulting in a half hour wait. Kinney could only imagine what the wait would be like a few miles behind him.

Alongside his truck, a new housing development had named itself Princeton Meadows despite being located two towns away from the prestigious community. This kind of thing bothered Kinney. He had to admit, though, that North Brunswick Township Meadows didn't have the same ring to it.

The split-level tract homes weren't quite identical. Every other one was reversed, with the attached garages on the opposite side. That didn't do much to make any of them interesting to Kinney's eyes. It was a perfect example of how money-driven decisions were uglifying the planet.

He watched the vehicles directly ahead of him—two older American cars and a battered semi-truck. After a brief conversation with the drivers of the cars, a young trooper let them go. He had the homeless-looking trucker open up his trailer, which was empty. Then it was Kinney's turn.

"Howdy," he said out his window as the cop approached. "What's up?"

"We're looking for someone, sir—about your age. ID, please."

A series of dark moles littered the left side of the cop's triangular face. They almost matched a constellation that Kinney didn't know the name of. It was one of the ones near the big dipper. Otherwise, the man's face was pinched, with early squint lines at the corners of his brown eyes. His too-large blue cap almost covered the tops of his ears.

"Sure," Kinney told him.

Kinney handed him his fake New Jersey license—the one he'd used the last time he'd operated in the state. He was Burt Gleason. Fortunately, years before, the agency had implanted fake identities into the system. The license would check out with no blemishes, and his current disguise mostly matched the photo.

The cop grabbed the microphone clipped to his lapel. "I've got a number for you to run," he told someone. Then he read it off and returned his attention to Kinney.

"Do you own a motorcycle?" the trooper asked.

"Have you seen a motorcycle in the last half hour?"

"You know I used to ride, but my wife made me give it up when we got married. So I notice when I see one. There were two heading the other way back in Lawrenceville."

"Together?"

"No. About five minutes apart. One was a tricked-out Harley with highway pegs. The other one was some kind of green Japanese crotch rocket. It was going too fast to see what kind—maybe ninety or so."

"Where was this exactly?"

"On Twenty-seven, just past that fancy golf course with the Polish name."

"I need to call this in." The man stepped away and spoke into his mike again, returning a minute later.

"What's in the back?" he asked.

"Packages. I deliver packages—well, boxes, mostly. Want to take a look?"

"Yes, sir."

After showing him that there were, indeed, an array of boxes and packages in the back of the oversized van, Kinney asked if he could get going.

"If I get too far behind, I'll catch holy hell for being late to dinner," Kinney said. He figured there weren't too many hen-pecked assassins.

"Just hold on until I hear back about your license. We're a little backed up here."

"What did this guy do, anyway?" Kinney asked. "I've never seen a roadblock out here. It must've been something terrible. A school shooting?"

"No, sir. Someone shot a head of state back in Princeton."

"My God. I sure hope you catch the guy."

"We will."

Kinney heard a crackling sound—a low-fi voice emanating from a device on the trooper's collar.

"Roger that, Ted," he told his mike. He turned to Kinney. "Okay. Have a good day, sir. Thank you for your cooperation."

"Sure."

Chapter 11

Kinney abandoned the van in the back parking lot of a liquor store in a shabby neighborhood in Morristown. He left the motorcycle parked on the street with the key in it. He'd be shocked if it was still there the next day. Then he drove off in a rental car Reed had parked the night before beside a fried chicken franchise. From Morristown, he drove to a motel in Springfield, Massachusetts, to wait for Reed, who'd be arriving by bus the next day.

Kinney called Barber from his clean, tidy room. He especially liked the perfectly turned down sheets. Perhaps the housekeeper had been in the military. Or perhaps Kinney just had the military on his mind from the conference.

"So how did it go?" his boss asked. "And what more do you know now?"

"I don't know how well the plan worked yet. And I haven't learned anything new about the bad guys. But my sister's family is safe."

"For now," Barber said. "Do you think this is the end of it?"

"No. I bought us time, that's all. Don't worry, I won't stop until these people are out of the picture. My niece is only eleven. It's not kosher to bring her into this."

"Of course not. They're coloring outside the lines.

But let me ask you this. They're saying that Pope is just wounded, Kinney. How does that buy you time?"

Kinney explained the scheme without letting Barber know Reed was involved. He hoped his boss would believe that Pope's men could've pulled off Reed's role on their own.

"I see. What's your next step?"

"After I talk to Miner, I'll make a plan, and I'll head back home tomorrow."

"Keep me in the loop, Kinney."

"You got it."

Reed called a half hour later.

"We're cool. The cops wanted to bust in while we were shooting the video, but the bodyguards held them off. As a doctor, obviously I needed a sterile environment to save Pope. I snuck off once Pope's men let them in, then I sent Miner the email from you at my motel."

"And the fake ambulance guys showed up on time? Pope got away?"

"Yeah, they weren't very convincing, but in the confusion I guess they didn't need to be. Where did you find those guys?"

"I had to work with a Triad gang out of New York last time I was in the state," Kinney said.

"What do you mean?"

"You know—the Chinese-American mob."

"These guys were White," Reed told him.

"Oh, shit." Kinney felt his face tighten. "Maybe my guys hired locals." He didn't really believe that. That wasn't the way the Triads did things. "Actually," he continued, "someone probably hijacked the ambulance and got to Pope. I'll call him. If he doesn't answer…"

"Anyway, I get into Springfield around two," Reed told him.

"Sounds good."

Kinney called Pope. "Brigadier, it's Kinney. Are you all right?"

"Just barely. One of the EMTs tried to shove an IV in me for no damned reason, which I refused. Then he pulled a gun out."

"Shit! I'm so sorry."

"Fortunately, I had Troy with me."

"Is Troy the huge bodyguard?"

"Exactly. He took care of things. You'd be surprised how quickly some big men can move, and of course we were in close quarters. We left the driver and the other EMT in a refuse container."

"Alive?" Kinney asked. He hoped they were. Dead bodies meant a more thorough investigation by law enforcement. A couple of thugs tied up somewhere wasn't a high priority.

"No," Pope answered. "I hope that won't be a problem."

"Me, too. Are you at the private airfield?"

"Yes. We take off in a few minutes. Should I be worried about our stops in Dallas and Mexico City?"

Kinney thought things over, and Pope let him. "I don't know. Possibly. I think a leak must've come from one of your men. I don't see how anyone could've known about our plan on our end. Could one of them be working for Rakena?"

"I'll look into it. I did bring a relatively new hire with me. Maybe Troy can keep an eye on him from this point forward. Listen, I've got to go."

"Godspeed," Kinney said, surprised the word had

fallen out of him. He'd never used it before.

Kinney called Miner before he crashed for the night. Missions always took a lot out of him. He needed to remain on high alert for hours on end—like an air-traffic controller. He barely remembered to refer to Miner as Molton.

"I take it you got my email?" Kinney asked.

"Yes," Miner said. "So the world thinks he's wounded, but you killed him."

"Right. It was more of a sure thing than trying to arrange an accident. I'm not that great at those. I usually just shoot people."

"I understand. This isn't ideal, but I don't see how it can be traced back to us, which is what matters."

"How do I get paid?" Kinney asked. He reasoned that if he was sincerely interested in working with Molton, he ought to care about that.

"Oh, I don't think we need to bother with that."

"Really?" Kinney raised his voice. "Let me remind you who you're dealing with, Molton. You've threatened my family, and now you want to stiff me for my fee. No matter who else is involved in this, I'll kill you when I get a chance if you don't pay me."

"Oh, I doubt you'll ever get a chance. My part in this is finished, and I'm taking off. Good luck finding me."

"I'll hunt you down."

"Like I said, good luck. I'll tell you what. Here's a hint. I won't be on another planet. You can rule that out, Kinney." Molton chuckled.

"I appreciate that. I was going to start with Mercury and work my way through the solar system."

Miner laughed. "You're a hoot, Kinney. Bye."

He hung up.

Kinney called Barber back. "Miner told me he's leaving for parts unknown. Can you get some men on it? He might be traveling under the name Meriwether or Miner. He won't be using Molton. I'd guess he's flying to another country. He was pretty cocky about my not being able to find him. Just let me know where he ends up. I'll take it from there. I'll text you his address, plate number, and the frequency for the tracker on his SUV. And I'll send what little I know about this Chet character who works with him." That had also been in the packet Eddie had handed Kinney.

"Okay. I'll get right on it."

****

By the time Kinney and Reed had driven to Boston and flown to San Francisco, they expected Barber to have the information they needed. Then when they cornered and coerced Miner, he'd probably tell them what the agency needed to know about the mole, as well as whatever else his organization was up to.

But as they walked through the SFO long-term parking lot, Barber called to let them know he hadn't had any luck locating Miner. Kinney put his phone on speaker.

"We found his vehicle," Barber said, "but it didn't lead anywhere. It was in the underground garage by his office."

"No flight information on him?"

"No. Not under any of his names. He could've driven somewhere in another vehicle or used yet another identity."

"He has no reason to suspect we know his real name," Kinney said.

"Who'd you put on this?" Reed whispered to Kinney, who passed on the question.

"I mostly worked it myself, but I sent Muñoz and Foster into the field."

"Foster's hopeless," Kinney said. "She let me down in Italy."

"I know, but she's proved herself since then. And would you want one of our top guys on this? They might figure out what's going on with you two. As it is, I think a few agents are suspicious about your dramatic exit."

"Really? We were pretty proud of our performance. Reed said we should try acting as a career."

"You're not good-looking enough, Kinney. Anyway, as usual, you've dragged us off-topic. Here are your orders. Drop it. Take a vacation. I hear Cabo is nice this time of year. I'll find another way to flush out the mole."

"Wait a minute," Kinney said hurriedly, "what about Chet—Miner's henchman? Any luck locating him?"

"We couldn't find Chet Nyland, either, but we did find out he's got a condo up in Tahoe. He's not there, and I doubt he'll be back. It's on the market as of two days ago."

"What's happening at Miner's office? Maybe I should follow up with that."

There was no way Kinney was ready to let the investigation go. Even putting aside his sister's family—which he would never do—Kinney didn't quit missions before they were finished. He never had, and he never would.

"Miner's office has been cleaned out," Barber reported, "and I mean that literally. We couldn't even find any fingerprints. Kinney, we've done a hell of a lot in less than twenty-four hours, but it's a dead end. I'm ordering you to stand down."

"I appreciate the suggestion," Kinney responded.

"It's not a—"

Kinney hung up.

"That was weird," Reed said. "Barber doesn't usually give up on something so soon."

"And with all the resources the agency has, they can't find two amateurs on the move?" Kinney asked.

By now, they'd reached the far corner of the lot where Reed had parked. Kinney had taken an airport shuttle en route to the East Coast so the twosome could leave together.

"Maybe these guys didn't go anywhere," Reed said. "That would explain why the agency couldn't find them. What if they're hunkered down in a safe house across town?"

"Do you think Miner knows we found out who he really is?" Kinney asked. "If he doesn't know, that gives us a huge advantage finding him, wherever he is."

"I have no idea," Reed said. "You're the one who talked to him. What do you think?"

"He's an arrogant son of a bitch. I think he's got that cognitive bias where he thinks better of himself than he ought to."

"And less of other people?" Reed started the car and pulled out of his parking spot in one smooth arc.

"Exactly," Kinney agreed. "So I think he's assuming his exit plan is bulletproof, and that we think he's Molton."

"He wouldn't worry about his ex then, would he?" Reed said.

"Judy Meriwether. You're right," Kinney said. "Let's go talk to her again. She hates the guy."

"You don't need me to keep a low profile anymore?"

"Naw. I'm rogue at this point as far as Barber's concerned, and he may know about you, anyway."

"What if he sends agents after us?" Reed asked, approaching the kiosk with his prepaid receipt in his hand.

"He can't do that without tipping off the mole. And why would he want to?"

****

They arrived at Judy's huge home in Los Gatos about eight in the evening. Faux Tudor with picture windows squeezed between the dark wood framing, it didn't impress Kinney. In fact, it just looked like an assortment of railroad ties and rough stucco, a far cry from the illusion of historic architecture an architect had been shooting for.

Kinney rang the bell beside the double black doors. "By the way, Reed. We need to be a gay couple."

"What?"

Judy opened the door. She wore a black silk robe. Her hair was pinned up, except for a few stray strands that draped down over one of her temples. Her makeup was just as thick as it had been at the country club. Now she wore diamond studs in her ears. Her sizable breasts swayed under the robe.

"You!—the rude queer guy. Thanks a lot for taking off on me. Do you know how humiliating that was? My friends *saw* you. I told them you were gay, but they didn't believe me. Marsha says she has gaydar because her third husband turned out to like men. Well, I don't know if he liked them. He sure fucked a lot of them."

She suddenly noticed Reed. "Oh my god! This is the best-looking man I've seen in years. This is your partner?"

"Yes. I thought if I brought him, you'd feel better about what happened."

"You mean I'd believe you about being gay."

"Yes."

"I don't even care now. You and your delicious boyfriend need to come in right now."

They followed her into a surprisingly modest-sized living room. The room was crammed with antique furniture, most of which looked as though it would crumble into dust if someone sat or even leaned on it. Fortunately the red sofa the men hunkered down onto held up. Judy obviously liked buttoned upholstery and paintings of mountains. Otherwise, there was no theme or pattern to the decor.

"Let's have a drink," Judy suggested after she sat across a wrought iron and glass coffee table from them. Then she hopped up, ran out of the room and returned with a full bottle of Irish whiskey.

"Does he talk?" she asked Kinney, gesturing at Reed.

"When he has something to say. Ask him a question. He'll answer."

"What's your name, big fella?"

"Bubba." Reed employed a thick Southern accent.

"That's the stupidest name I ever heard. Are you a top or a bottom?"

"We take turns," Reed told her, putting his arm

around Kinney and kissing him on the cheek. His partner resisted a strong urge to wriggle away.

"Are you bi? Do I have a chance?" Judy uncrossed and recrossed her legs, flashing a glimpse of pink panties.

"If you did, you just ruined things by propositioning me in front of my beloved," Reed pointed out, stroking Kinney's hair.

Kinney recognized that all this was payback for springing the gay couple impersonation on him at the last minute. Reed didn't like surprises.

"Oh, I'm just teasing, Bubba," Judy said, waving away his concern. She took a big swig out of the bottle and passed it to Kinney.

"You seem like a drink from the glass kind of gal," he told her before pretending to gulp the whiskey, which he then passed to Reed.

"Nobody gets me. It's not just you," Judy said.

"You're complex," Reed said.

"Exactly. Anyway, I assume you're here to talk about Aaron again?"

"Yes," Kinney told her. "He's gone to ground. If we can find him, I think we can pry money out of him for you."

"Why would you do that?"

"You promised me ten percent—remember?"

"Oh yes. Let's make it five if I tell you where I think he is."

"It's a deal." Kinney held out his hand to shake hers, which she didn't notice since she was staring Reed's face and licking her lips.

"He has a condo in Hawaii," Judy said, "in Princeville on Kauai. He's hidden out there before."

"Aaron hasn't flown anywhere," Kinney told her, shaking his head. "We checked with all the airlines and charter companies."

"Oh, I'm sure he has. They probably made a mistake. They're idiots."

"Do you have the address?"

"Yes."

By now the bottle had been passed around twice. Judy must've been drinking before they arrived because she began slurring her words.

"Who the hell are you guys, anyway? How could you get info from all the airlines?"

"We're spies," Reed told her.

"I knew it! You're not gay. You're spies!"

"He's kidding. We work for the IRS—remember?" Kinney said.

"Oh yes, I forgot."

"We have access to a lot of databases," Reed told her.

"About that address?" Kinney said.

Judy rose unsteadily and wandered off. "I'll just be a minute."

Chapter 12

In the car, Kinney googled Princeville, which turned out to be a planned community on the north shore of Kauai. Kinney had never been to Hawaii. Reed had been to the big island on a golf vacation.

"So if Barber told you to take a trip," Reed said, "we could head to Kauai instead of Cabo with his blessing. He'll just think we're doing what he wants. If it turns out Miner isn't there—and actually I don't see how he could've gotten there with the agency on his ass—we'll still be in Hawaii. It'll broaden your horizons, Kinney. You could use some of that aloha spirit."

"That's a real thing?"

"Sure. All for one and one for all."

"It couldn't hurt." Kinney paused and thought about what Reed had said about the agency's efficacy. "You know, all Miner had to do was have another foolproof identity and maybe fly from LA or Seattle. You're giving Barber and the agency too much credit about this. Anyway, I don't know what else there is for us to do here, so what the hell."

They adjourned to a coffeehouse down the street from Miner's ex-wife. Even though there wasn't a college nearby, it was full of young adults typing on their laptops. The lighting was overly bright, and the wooden chairs dug into the two men's lower backs.

"I'm not one to look a gift horse in the mouth," Reed said between sips of an extremely complicated coffee. He'd liked the font they'd used for it on the menu board. "I'm gonna bring my clubs. I've heard there's a great course in Princeville."

"Really? You want to play golf while we're on a mission?"

"Why not? We know Miner plays. If his condo is well-defended, maybe we'll take him on the course."

"How could a condo be well-defended against us?"

"I don't know. Gimme a break, Kinney. I'm doing all this out of the goodness of my heart. I don't go to New Jersey for just anyone."

"Don't you have a vested interest in getting rehired? Isn't that why you're helping?" Kinney knew Reed was at least as addicted as he was to adrenaline—the dangerous variety.

"Well, sure. That's part of it," Reed conceded, nodding his head.

"I guess I haven't really thanked you, though, have I?" Kinney admitted. "You're right about that."

"So?"

"So thank you. I appreciate your help."

"You're welcome."

****

Georgia called Kinney the next morning. He and Reed were booked on a flight to Hawaii for the following morning.

"I'm calling to see if you're available, Kinney. And I want to apologize for overreacting to your kissing suggestion. It was harmless."

"No, that was my fault," Kinney told her. "I need to learn how to act appropriately when it comes to

125

dating. That's kind of a frontier area for me."

"You told me about yourself—quite candidly. So I knew who I was dealing with. Then you said something that was perfectly consistent with how you described yourself, and I interpreted it as something else."

"Okay, thanks."

"Would you like to get together again? We can do that walk you suggested—maybe somewhere more interesting like Santa Cruz."

"I don't see how that would work," Kinney told her. "By the time you get off work, it's going to be rush hour, so it would take you at least an hour and a half to get there."

He didn't want to experience Georgia's work-all-day-and-then-fight-traffic persona if he didn't have to. If things proceeded, he'd discover her suboptimal self soon enough.

"I'll take off work right after lunch," Georgia told him. "That'll give us the whole afternoon."

"You won't get in trouble?"

That was something else Kinney didn't want to deal with. He'd briefly dated a woman who'd played hooky, faced big consequences, and then blamed Kinney—when he'd tried to talk her out of it.

"No worries there," Georgia reported. "Since I won employee of the month, I've been getting a lot of leeway."

"And a big trophy, I hope. Bring it with you."

"It was a fifty dollar gift card at a grocery store. I spent most of it on frozen entrees, but I did splurge on some specialty dill pickles."

"I hope that pickle jar will offer mute testimony to your glory for years to come."

"Good one. They sang 'Happy Employee of the Month' to the tune of 'Happy Birthday.' "

"I'm sorry I missed that. Win it again sometime, and bring me as your plus one."

Georgia met Kinney by the pint-sized lighthouse next to Steamer's Lane in Santa Cruz, a popular surf spot. As usual, even on a weekday afternoon, the bike path and walkway that lined the top of the cliff was crowded.

While Kinney waited for her, he heard several languages he didn't recognize, which was saying something. International tourists to San Francisco often took day trips down to the Santa Cruz coast to take in its bay views, which Kinney would've seen if he'd turned around instead of watching for Georgia.

He moved forward to hug her as she approached him, but her slight flinch stopped him in his tracks. Then she initiated a cursory hug, keeping her bosom from touching him. Kinney figured she'd endured some sort of trauma at a man's hands. Domestic violence?

Her clothes were a bit different from what she'd worn to the Gadsden Hotel bar. Well-worn jeans constituted the main variation, along with red running shoes and a tight white polo shirt that highlighted the outline of the bra that encased her verboten chest.

They began strolling north toward Natural Bridges State Park, dodging bicyclists for the first few blocks before the path cleared out a bit. Sea lions barked in the distance and a basset hound on a long leash howled back at them. The air smelled a bit rank, as though seaweed had rotted on the water's surface. On the other hand, the periodic whiff of tangy salt water was invigorating. The view across the bay to the Monterey peninsula wasn't as clear as some days, but they could still make out the general shape of it, as well as the Santa Lucia mountains behind it. Sailboats skimmed across the water, dodging a few weathered fishing boats that were returning to shore.

"So, Kinney," Georgia began. "What are you up to these days? Why are you free during the day instead of spying on somebody—or whatever the hell you do?"

"I've got a day free before I have to head out."

"To where?"

Kinney shook his head. "You know I can't go into details, Georgia."

"How's it going to work between us if a whole element always has to be left out?"

"You're thinking there might be a 'between us'?" Kinney was surprised.

"You never know. Not many of my dates admit who they are right up front. And rugged is rugged, right?"

"I suppose. But how do you know I'm into you at that level?" He certainly was, but it felt like admitting that after one date branded him as too needy.

"As my mother used to say, 'What's not to like?' " Georgia responded. "I'm clearly a coveted commodity in the dating community." She grinned, which Kinney found bewitching.

"A commodity? Don't sell yourself short. I see you more as superior merchandise—you know, the kind that never goes on sale no matter how long you wait."

"Once an abusive boyfriend called me a convenient receptacle," Georgia told him, apparently more amused at the memory than offended.

"Is this a test?" Kinney asked. "Our conversation

has taken a dark turn. For the record, I find all these terms reprehensible, especially the last one. What an asshole."

Georgia grabbed his arm and turned him toward her. She locked eyes as she spoke. "Kinney, I don't actually expect that everyone I date will be into me, but I do think you are."

"You're right. Sorry. I'm just wary about moving too fast." He smiled. "Why don't we try having a normal conversation. I'm not sure I can hold up my end of that, but I'll try."

"Sure."

As they began strolling side by side again, both shared tidbits about their families, favorite movies, and places they'd traveled to. Georgia was especially interested in the latter, quizzing Kinney about where he'd visited the last few years.

"I never seem to get too far down my travel bucket list," she told him. "Something always comes up. Recently, I was supposed to attend a conference somewhere I've never been. What happened? My sister's appendix ruptured. I mean, it wasn't an exotic spot, but any chance to get away from the office is welcome."

"Where was this?"

"Princeton. You know—in the good part of New Jersey."

The two looked one another in the eye again, even more intensely this time. Kinney decided that Georgia was definitely studying his reaction. Did she know something she shouldn't? If that were the case, why mention Princeton and tip him off? And why be so interested in his reaction? Maybe she was seeking the empathy he'd told her he didn't have after her tale of woe. Even when he told women about his deficit, they usually didn't want to accept it. Unpalatable reality breeds denial.

"What was the conference?" he asked after a few awkward moments.

"Some military deal, actually. My boss says if I'm going to move up to being in the field full-time, I need to know more about weapons and strategy and all that. It didn't make much sense to me, but he's ex-army." She shook her head. "I think he was throwing me an inexpensive bone. Real FBI training is expensive, and I couldn't do my job while I trained. We're already shorthanded. "

"I see."

That didn't really answer the questions in Kinney's mind. All he'd learned was that if Georgia wasn't on the level, she was a damned good liar. He wondered what she'd learned from studying his face, which he'd kept as neutral as he could.

While Georgia talked about her work as an analyst, Kinney pondered this new development. Perhaps when she'd researched him after their encounter in the street, she'd happened onto something connecting him to Brigadier Pope. He doubted that many FBI files contained information about the agency, but Agent Kim certainly knew some things about Kinney himself. And Kinney had sent Georgia to Kim to vouch for him. That had been foolish.

He knew Georgia was fond of tests and experiments, so perhaps that was all it was—a foray into whether Kinney's work was connected to what had happened in Princeton. And if so, would he be honest or hide his role?

After the walk, Kinney told Georgia he'd call her when he was back in town, and she told him he'd better or else he might wind up on the FBI's most wanted list. In the past, Kinney had actually worried he might.

As they split up back in the parking lot near the lighthouse, Kinney wondered if he'd call. He knew he was playing with fire by dating a fed, let alone one who but for the grace of God might've recognized him when he pretended to assassinate Pope.

****

Kinney and Reed flew nonstop from the Oakland Airport to Lihue, Kauai. Both men were accustomed to flying. Kinney read an inaccurate thriller. He found almost everything in that genre to be comically wrong, which kept him entertained. Reed watched animated movies. He'd briefly attended community college as an animation major before dropping out to join an undisclosed branch of the military.

"You don't get to kill anyone when you're making cartoons," he'd explained to Kinney once.

The airport on the island was small and crowded, as two flights had arrived back to back. Reed jockeyed for position at the lone baggage carousel as Kinney tried to beat the rush to the car rental agency to nab a four-wheel drive Jeep. Reed lost a prime spot to an aggressive Hawaiian grandmother wielding a huge purse. Kinney came in second in his race to the rental counter. He figured there was no shame in that since the winner wore expensive running shoes and wasn't even breathing hard.

As it was, Kinney sweated profusely in the heat and humidity. It may have been a better idea to stroll to the shuttle bus and stand in line at the rental agency without drenched armpits. The difference between the tropical sun and shade was almost as drastic as in the Middle East, where Kinney had spent much more time than he'd liked.

Princeville was almost on the opposite side of the island from the airport, but even so, it was only a forty-five-minute drive through a variety of landscapes—all of them very green. To Kinney's eye, several scenarios mimicked the corner of Cambodia he'd traveled to on his life-changing mission. Abrupt, steep hills sprouted out of the reddish ground. Completely covered in lush vegetation, they formed shapes along their spines. Once again, Kinney saw a naked woman lying down. He needed to get laid.

The road periodically ran alongside beaches, cliffs, orchards, and fields of indeterminate crops. The small towns they passed through were, predictably, full of restaurants, gift shops, and places to rent bikes, surfboards, and snorkel gear.

Everything was on a smaller scale than Kinney expected, both size-wise and in terms of the modest, elderly buildings. Where were the towering resorts and mansions?

When he mentioned this to Reed, his partner told him that no self-respecting resort would be caught dead being right on the main road. "Also,' he added, "they made a law that nobody could build anything higher than a coconut palm tree."

"Really? That sounds like something you made up."

"I swear it's true. When I make up shit, it's better than that. Remember when I convinced you I'd gotten married to a circus acrobat? If you doubt me, look around, Kinney. Have we passed any high buildings?"

"No, we haven't."

Miner's condo overlooked the golf course in Princeville, and beyond that, the ocean. Because the entire town had been built on a high cliff above the water, the shore wasn't visible. The layout of Miner's first floor unit was identical to the one Kinney had seen for sale online—two bedroom suites and a large living room fronting the exterior, with a kitchen and dining room against the interior wall. For 1.8 million dollars, Kinney would've expected more than 1,400 square feet. On the other hand, who wouldn't salivate over the location?

The street side of the complex was unimpressive—four Hawaiian-style two-story buildings, a parking lot, and out of control tropical landscaping. Clearly, a gardener's job on Kauai wasn't to grow anything. It was to keep things from growing.

A low, reddish lava rock wall rimmed the pavement and held back a profusion of otherworldly flowers that threatened to displace the cars in the lot if only that damned wall wasn't there. And Kinney could've sworn that one of the tall flower stalks had been featured in a Star Trek episode. It looked like a red rocket taking off from a hollow yellow tube.

"This doesn't look like a problem," Reed said as they sat in their Jeep with the windows down. All sorts of floral fragrances wafted in. "Are we sure Miner's there?"

"Well, somebody is. The woman in the unit above his heard music as of yesterday. Smooth jazz."

"I hate smooth jazz. It's so…" Reed hunted for the

right word.

"Smooth?"

"Exactly."

"How'd you get her to talk about her neighbor?" Reed asked as he turned to face his partner.

"After Eddie found out who was there and what her phone number was, I called and told her I was a new member of the condo board and we were thinking of adding soundproofing."

"You called Eddie on the phone? What was that like?"

"He disguised his voice by trying to sound like he was Chinese, and he played loud rap music in the background."

"Anyway, what did Miner's neighbor say about the soundproofing?" Reed asked.

"She voted no. She hears her downstairs neighbor's music sometimes, but it doesn't bother her. We had a nice chat about the weather after that. And goose poop. You know the geese you see everywhere around here?"

"Those are chickens, Kinney. They got loose in Hurricane Iniki, and they've gone nuts screwing each other ever since. I read about it in that magazine on the plane."

"I know the difference. The geese are called nenes. They're the state bird, and they're endangered so you can't do anything to them. This lady in the condo picks off the chickens with a BB gun, and she wishes she could ace the geese, too. She's anti-poop."

"Lovely. Maybe Barber should sign her up." Reed paused. "Here's my thinking," he finally said. "We go knock on Miner's door."

"That's it? That's your plan?"

"Yes."

"This is why you don't do the planning, Reed, but for once that sounds fine."

****

They weren't armed, but that didn't matter. A blonde woman in her thirties answered the door. Tall with a slight paunch, her baseline expression seemed to be a scowl. At least she was scowling with no discernible effort for no discernible reason. She wore pink khaki shorts and a yellow T-shirt that proclaimed she loved Chicago. She had once been pretty in a cheerleadery kind of way. Now her lined face reflected too much time in the sun and too many cigarettes.

"Is the man of the house home?" Kinney asked. He didn't know which name Miner was using.

"The man of the house? Are you for real? This isn't the 1950s, and you're not door to door salesmen."

Her mellifluous voice was impressive. She could've been a newscaster on a network show. Well, if her belly could be hidden behind a desk and she could learn how to smile.

"We could be salesmen," Reed asserted unconvincingly.

"Like hell. I know who you are."

"Who's that?"

"I don't have to prove what I know. Fuck you." She spit out the words, her face twisted in anger.

"You remind me of Judy Meriwether," Kinney told her.

"I am nothing like that fat bitch." The woman actually spat now on her taupe Berber carpet. "Anyway, Aaron's not here, so buzz off."

"We don't buzz," Reed told her.

She tried to slam the door. Kinney's foot flashed forward and blocked it.

"Ow!" he said. "That's assault. Don't make us bring you in."

"Don't give me that horseshit. You're not cops. You're business rivals, and you want to recruit Aaron. He told you no before, and he means it. And he told me to call him if you showed up."

"This is Aaron Meriwether?" Kinney asked as he strode in. "That's the name he travels under?"

"Of course. We flew out together from San Jose." The woman walked to where her phone sat on an end table by her couch. Reed hustled through the door behind Kinney and grabbed it before she could call.

"Hey!"

"We'd appreciate it if you told us where he is," Kinney said in a low menacing tone. He found that a lower pitch scared people more. "Sit down," he commanded, a few notes lower yet.

She sank into in an armchair facing a huge TV, crossed her arms, and glared at them.

"How can we convince you to cooperate?" Reed asked as he carried over a chair from the adjacent kitchen and sat in front of her. "We don't want to beat you up or kill your dog or something if we don't have to."

"I don't have a dog."

Kinney suddenly side-kicked a ceramic vase off a nearby table. It shattered, and shards shot across the room, clattering against a sliding glass patio door.

The woman flinched. "You could pay me," she said after recovering from the sudden violence.

"Okay, that sounds good," Reed said. "Let's make

it fifty bucks. What do you think, Mickey. Is that fair? Fifty bucks?"

"Definitely. Especially since we don't need to pay her anything if we don't feel like it."

"Who are you guys, really? The Russian mafia?"

"Do we look Russian?" Reed asked.

"I don't know. You're not HR recruiters. That's for sure."

"You ought to be more scared," Kinney told her. "We're very dangerous men. Sometimes we kill people."

He left the room momentarily to grab a chair as well. Now the two men sat in front of the TV facing the woman.

"I grew up in a nasty cult," she told them. "At least you're not forcing me to have sex when I'm ten. And one of the elders actually did shoot my dog once."

"Ah, that explains it," Kinney said. "Let's make it a thousand dollars."

She shook her head. "Aaron spends that on me for dinner and a show when we're in New York."

"So you're his girlfriend?" Reed asked.

"I hate that word. I'm not a girl, am I? Anyway, we got married in Costa Rico last year. See?" She held up her hand and displayed a gold wedding band.

"What would happen if Aaron goes to prison?" Kinney asked.

"For what? What did he do?" She wasn't nearly as alarmed as Kinney would've thought.

He answered her. "He hired me to kill someone."

"Bullshit. Aaron's an asshole, but he wouldn't do that."

He spoke to the woman again in a softer voice.

"I'm trying to find out if it's in your best interest if your husband goes away. Would you have access to his money?"

"Our money."

Reed spoke up. "He seems like the kind of guy who didn't share his toys with the other kids, let alone his money with you."

"Yeah, okay. You got me there." She wrinkled her forehead and squinted.

"So? Can you answer my question?" Kinney said.

The woman paused, glancing down at her bare feet. "I guess I'd still be able to live pretty well if he were in prison, but I'd be a lot better off if Aaron was dead." She looked up and stared Kinney in the eyes.

That hung in the air for a few moments.

"Okay," Kinney said. "Instead of us giving you a thousand, you give us ten thousand and we'll take care of that. Plus, you tell us where Aaron is."

"Done."

"You've been thinking about this for a while, haven't you?" Reed asked.

"Yes. Aaron's an asshole like I said. I didn't find out until after we got married."

"So where is he?" Kinney asked.

"On the course—in his stupid custom golf cart. It looks like a '57 Chevy in the front. How ridiculous is that? He had an eleven o'clock tee time, so he's somewhere on the back nine by now."

"You play?" Reed asked.

"Badly. Aaron's been teaching me, but he doesn't have much patience."

"So you know the course?" Kinney gestured out the window at the green expanse beyond the condo's lanai.

"Sure."

"What hole is that out your window?" Reed asked.

"The fifteenth."

"Is he part of a foursome or what?" Kinney asked.

"He goes out as a single, even if he has to pay extra—except when his dopey nephew's with him. He says other golfers nauseate him." The woman shook her head and curled her lips.

Kinney had heard enough. "I'm afraid we're going to have to keep your phone, tie you up, and gag you."

"That's okay. That's how Aaron likes sex, anyway."

"Ugh," Reed said, scrunching his face in disgust. "I've never understood that."

"It's all about control," Kinney told him. He'd read about it for a college class. "Dominance and submission."

"Exactly," the woman said. "Aaron always wants to be in charge, even when he doesn't know what the hell he's doing."

Reed cut strips from a bath towel and secured the woman to a chair. Kinney found duct tape in a junk drawer in the kitchen and gagged her. He positioned the chair in the living room so she'd have a nice view. Why be a dick? As he'd explained to Georgia, that was one of his mottos.

"We'll be in contact later for our fee," Reed told her.

She nodded her head.

On Miner's lanai, while lying on a comfortable chaise lounge, Kinney thought he saw a whale spouting a few hundred yards off the shore. When he pointed it out to Reed, his partner peered through a stand of coconut palms and told him it was just water splashing against a rock. Just then, the whale breached a few yards away from where they'd both been looking. Almost vertical, halfway out of the ocean, the whale's splashdown was awe-inspiring as well.

Kinney and Reed exclaimed, "Wow," at almost exactly the same moment.

"That made the trip worth it right there," Reed said.

"Yeah."

"The current Mrs. Meriweather is a piece of work, isn't she?" Reed commented once the men had given up their scrutiny of the water's surface.

"She certainly is," Kinney agreed. "Where does Miner find these women?"

"I dunno. Maybe there's a dating website called Raging She-Devils dot com."

Three chickens strolled by, followed by a pair of geese. One of the geese pooped.

"Did you catch that bit about the name Miner's using to fly?" Reed asked.

"Sure. If she's telling the truth about that—and why would she lie?—then somebody at the agency is fucking with us. It's easy enough to spot the name Meriwether on a flight list."

"Who were the agents assigned to that again?" Reed asked.

"Barbara Foster and Luis Muñoz."

"So one of those is probably our mole."

"That's what I'm thinking," Kinney said.

"I've never liked Foster," Reed commented.

"Me neither. She's full of herself, isn't she?"

"Yeah, and she told me once I was a sexist pig. Just

out of the blue." Reed frowned and shook his head.

Kinney raised his eyebrows and cocked his head.

"Okay, I might be sexist—you know, from a woman's perspective."

"What were you doing at the time?"

"I was staring at her butt, but she couldn't see me."

"They feel that, Reed. It's a psychic thing."

Reed waved his hand dismissively. "What about Muñoz?" he asked.

"I like Muñoz. I went on a mission with him in Jordan once," Kinney responded. "He had my back."

"Okay, so when we find out what we can from Miner, we find Foster," Reed said. "Agreed?"

"Yeah," Kinney replied.

"How do you want to deal with Miner?"

"Why waste time? He's going to be coming around soon. He's probably on the twelfth hole by now. Why don't we enjoy the weather and the view for a little while, and then sneak up and hide behind Miner's golf cart while he's on the fifteenth green over there."

"Then what?" Reed asked.

"We scare the hell out of him," Kinney said

Another goose landed awkwardly nearby, furiously flapping its wings, and a rooster chased a diminutive hen just beyond that, crowing at the top of his lungs. The hen pooped.

"I'm starting to understand the lady upstairs with the BB gun," Reed said. "I think I'm anti-poop, too."

Chapter 13

Kinney fell asleep. Reed jostled him when he spied Miner's baby blue golf cart on the fourteenth green.

"There he is. He'll be on the fifteenth in a few minutes. Let's go."

Kinney had learned the hard way how to fully wake up in seconds. The knife scar on his hip served as a reminder.

The course was almost impossibly green—putting Seaview Golf Course to shame—with long undulating elevation changes, and a few trees and shrubs scattered along its borders. A foursome—a family—in matching tan shorts and white golf shirts departed the nearby green as Kinney and Reed approached it.

"How about that?" the father asked boisterously. "Who had a birdie? Me!"

"You're the best," his adolescent son answered woodenly. From his tone, Kinney figured the boy would rather have been anywhere else.

"You had a so-called birdie once you improved your lie, Tom," the wife said.

"Mom!" the twenty-something daughter implored. "Be nice. Don't crap on Dad's achievement."

"Don't say crap," the father said.

"You just did," she responded.

Then they were mercifully out of hearing range.

"There but for the grace of God," Reed

commented.

"I hear you," Kinney said. "Shoot me if I have kids."

The plan, such as it was, worked fine until the two men left their posts behind their respective just-wide-enough trees and tried to hide behind Miner's golf cart while he walked to the rough on the far side of the green. Kinney and Reed discovered that the only way they could both remain out of sight was to lie on top of one another.

While Miner got ready to chip onto the green, they rock, scissor, and papered their way into Reed being on the bottom.

"I told Judy Meriwether we take turns," he whispered.

"Next time, you can be on top, which isn't so great, either, Reed."

"God, I hope there isn't a next time."

Kinney peeked over the floorboard of the cart as he lay on Reed's backside. Miner wore the same outfit he had when they'd met him at Seaview, except his khaki pants were now khaki shorts and his white polo shirt exhibited substantial sweat stains below his armpits. His oval face was pinched in concentration as he surveyed the green in front of him.

Miner's chip was decent. Kinney narrated this to Reed in the hushed tones of a TV golf announcer. Then, from only eight feet away, Miner three-putted and threw his club on the ground, damaging the green.

"That's reason enough to beat him up," Reed whispered.

"Quiet," Kinney whispered. "He's heading this way."

When Miner neared the cart, nine iron and putter in hand, Kinney realized two flaws in his plan. The clubs could serve as weapons, and clambering to his feet took longer than he thought, due to the ground underneath him not being ground.

Miner dropped his putter and charged Kinney, waving his other club in the air. Kinney scuttled around the back of the cart and pulled a random club out of his quarry's bag. Reed scrambled around the front of the cart and circled behind Miner.

Kinney, of course, could've kicked the nine iron out of Miner's hand as it swung at his head. He could've ducked, too. For that matter, he could've backed up and let Reed take down the older man from behind. Instead, for fun, he wielded his five iron like a sword and deflected Miner's.

"Touché," he called.

"Bad move," Miner said. "I was on the fencing team in college."

"Me, too," Kinney lied.

"Which event?" Miner asked as he feinted toward Kinney's midsection.

"Uh, the one with that long, skinny sword with the thingy on the end. You know, the one you throw at your opponent when you know you're outclassed."

He hurled the club at Miner, who parried with his nine iron. The flying iron clanged to the side of the two men and bounced against the golf cart's fender, ending up beside Kinney's foot.

"This is great," Reed said. "Physical comedy. Do one of those Three Stooges routines."

"Oh, hell," Kinney said, leaping forward and lashing out with his foot while suspended in mid-air. He

144

hit the spot on Miner's wrist that triggered a reflexive action. His opponent's hand opened and he dropped the club.

"Oops," Reed said. "Quick-kick strikes again. Don't move, Miner."

The man froze in place, still in shock at how quickly Kinney had disarmed him. Miner's captain of industry facade evaporated. Now his broad, formerly handsome face was an immobile caricature. Perhaps a communist era USSR poster would've used Miner's current countenance to denigrate capitalism. Kinney was struck by how different someone could look from one minute to the next.

"What next?" Kinney asked Reed.

"We could tie him to the front of the cart and ram into a tree," Reed suggested.

"That might be fun," Kinney conceded, "but I was thinking we could lay him down on the path and run over his legs. Then if he didn't tell us what we want, we could try his crotch. What do you think?"

Miner's face went white, and he cleared his throat. "Fellas, I was just doing my job."

"I think he's a Nazi, Kinney. That's what Nazis say."

"No, no. I'm a Republican."

"Worse yet, " Kinney said. "We're so far on the left, we want to treat poor people decently and tax the rich more."

"Don't hurt me," Miner said, holding up his hands.

Then he took off running, heading for a group of tall ferns in front of a neighboring resort. Reed caught up with him in just a few strides and kicked his legs out from under him. Miner sprawled onto the turf face first.

"Okay, okay," Miner said, climbing unsteadily to his feet. "I'll tell you whatever you want to know."

"That was too easy," Reed said to Kinney. "Where's the fun when they capitulate right away?"

"I know what you mean. Telling people what you're going to do is so much less fun than actually doing it."

"You guys are psychopaths," Miner said.

"Don't forget that," Kinney told him.

In Kinney's experience, casual banter terrified captives, implying that the whole ordeal was a mundane event to the likes of their captors. Once again, it clashed with expectations.

Reed stood Miner up in the back of the cart alongside his golf bag, strapped him in, and told him he'd cut off one of his fingers if he tried to escape again.

Kinney drove the cart toward Miner's condo as the next group of golfers approached.

"What's going on here?" one of them called.

Reed reached behind him and gripped Miner's elbow, applying just enough pressure on a nerve to remind him of what else he could do if he didn't remain silent.

"He's got standitis," Kinney called back. "We're rushing him to the hospital."

"I'm a doctor," the man said. "There's no such thing."

"I meant diabetes," Kinney called as they got out of earshot.

"Diabetes?" Reed said.

"I could've done better," Kinney agreed.

"You two are crazy," Miner told them.

"We're crazy psychopaths. Is that what you're saying?" Reed asked.

"Not if it makes you angry."

"Naw. I kinda like the sound of it," Kinney told him.

He dropped Reed and Miner at the condo and parked the ostentatious cart in the far corner of the complex's parking lot, partially hidden by the low-hanging branches of a fragrant fruit tree. Kinney pulled a few nearby fern fronds over the cart's hood as well, tucking them under the plexiglass windshield. All in all, this did little to hide the cart.

When he returned to the condo, Reed had already tied Miner to a chair next to his wife, who was squirming and grunting. Miner himself had regained some of his poise.

"What's that? You want to hear all about your husband's criminal activity?" Reed asked Miner's wife. "Sure. We can do that. Right, Miner?"

"My name's not Miner."

"You're going to start with a lie? Do you think that's wise?" Reed asked.

"Okay, okay. I used to be Miner."

Kinney stared at him steadily.

"I *am* Miner."

"Good. Now let's hear about what you've been up to. We already know quite a bit or we couldn't have found you, so we'll know if you're lying."

"I wouldn't lie to the two of you."

"You just did about thirty seconds ago, you asshole," Reed reminded him.

"It's just a habit. It didn't mean anything." He shook his head, which he only managed with some effort. His poise was gone again. His mind couldn't successfully command his body now.

"Tell us how you knew about us," Kinney prompted.

"Someone in my organization texted me."

"That's it? That's your answer?"

"Yes. It's all I know." He tried to shrug, but he was tied too tightly to the chair to manage it. He'd lost his white golf cap somewhere and his khaki shorts and shirt exhibited streaks of grass stains. "We were looking for a way to get to Pope, and I got a text," Miner continued.

"Why Pope?"

"Oil."

"Okay, we know about that part. So who was the text from?"

"I don't know. My tech guy couldn't track it down. But it must've been someone at Rakena—you know about Rakena?"

Kinney nodded.

"No one else has that phone number," Miner said, "and why would anyone else want to help?" Once again, a futile shrug pulled at the strips holding him down. He frowned at this minor irritation.

"Good question," Reed said. "So first you were directed to kill Pope, and then later you were steered to us to do it?"

"Not exactly. Molton Imports is a like an action agency for Rakena and its parent company sometimes—Moonmatic."

"By action, you mean the illegal side of things?" Kinney asked.

"Yes, mostly. But we rarely carry out operations ourselves. *We* certainly weren't going to kill Pope. I contract out activities as necessary and clean up messes. I only approached you personally because of time pressure, and because I couldn't afford to let someone else fuck up again."

"You mean the unsuccessful attempts on Pope's life."

Miner nodded.

"Do you know who the mole in our organization is?" Reed asked.

"No. I'd tell you if I did." Miner flashed his salesman smile. He was vacillating between attempts to project sincerity and the stark fear he was actually feeling. "You're still at the agency?"

Kinney answered. "Yes. We faked leaving, Miner. You're kind of a moron, aren't you? So what can you do for us?"

"How can you help us identify the mole?" Reed added. "If you can't, we won't have much use for you after this."

"Good motivator, Reed," Kinney said.

"Thanks."

"I don't know," Miner answered. "I could make inquiries—contact my bosses."

"You have multiple bosses?" Reed asked.

"Three."

"My condolences," Kinney said.

"Is one of them Ryan Connelly—the billionaire who owns Moonmatic and Rakena?" Reed asked.

"Oh, no. He's way above my pay grade."

"Would your bosses get suspicious if you asked them about the text you got?" Kinney asked. "Do you ever do that?"

"Sometimes. I could tell them I needed to contact

our spy in your agency for some reason."

"Okay, let's put that aside for a moment," Kinney said. "Why do you go to Sacramento?"

"I can't tell you. They'll kill me. It's a bigger deal than assassinating Pope. There's billions on the line."

"It's political?"

"Yes."

"Do you think we're going to take no for an answer here?"

Miner thought about his options and then shook his head. "I can't. I wish I could."

"We're crazy psychopaths," Reed reminded him. "Well, I am. I guess Kinney identifies with the wayward cannon demographic—at least he keeps saying that to everyone. What do you think we'll do to you if you don't tell us?"

"I don't want to think about it." Miner closed his eyes as though that might make the whole thing go away. Once again his face froze.

"Maybe we can compromise," Kinney suggested, winking at Reed.

Miner opened his eyes. There was a glimmer of hope there. He leaned forward. "What do you mean?"

"Tell us enough so we can find out on our own. Then it won't get back to you, assuming we let you live and any of this matters."

Miner gulped, and then paused. "Okay. I've been spreading money around to state legislators."

"Who, specifically?"

"Well, there's Hattori and—"

Miner tumbled to the ground in his chair, his face nothing more than an exit wound. Kinney and Reed hit the deck as the crack of the gunshot reached their ears.

As he went down, Kinney knocked Miner's wife's chair over. He could hear her muffled screams.

Blood and brains splattered the two agents. Kinney wiped his face on his sleeve. He watched Reed do the same. "You missed a spot," he told him, pointing to the corresponding spot on his own cheek.

"Thanks." Reed smeared blood across that side of his face. "If we stay down, we're safe," he said. "There aren't any vantage points high enough to get the right angle."

"What'll we do with her?" Kinney asked, gesturing at the woman on her side, who was still screaming into her duct tape gag. Mercifully, facing the way she was, she'd been spared Miner's gore. She wouldn't need a shower and a change of clothes unless she'd peed or crapped her pants, which was always a possibility with traumatized civilians.

"Let's ask her," Reed suggested. He crawled over, avoiding the bloody mess on the floor between them as best he could, and pulled her gag off.

Now she stopped screaming and began gasping.

"Hey there," Reed said. "I realize I don't even know your name."

"It's…it's Terry."

"Well, Terry, what do you want to do? What's next for you?"

"I want to get the hell out of here and forget I ever met you two."

"Okay. We'll help you do that, but how do we know you won't tell the police about us?"

"Are you kidding? You're crazy psychopaths. You'd kill me, right?"

"Absolutely," Reed told her.

Chapter 14

After quite a bit of time on the condo's itchy carpet, Kinney decided it was safe to get up, clean up, change into the clothes from their luggage, and then untie Terry. They snacked on some junk food they found in a kitchen cabinet and then drove themselves and Terry south. The return to the Lihue airport entailed a fair amount of sobbing, which Reed attempted to curtail by inexpertly reassuring Terry that Taiwanese men were terrific lovers and she'd be really tall there.

"I thought you'd kill Aaron somewhere else," Terry managed to say as they passed the ruins of the resort where Elvis had filmed *Blue Hawaii*. "I've never seen anything like that. So there's three of you, huh?"

"No, that wasn't us," Reed told her. "You're off the hook for the ten grand. See? There's a silver lining to everything."

Terry nodded, briefly smiled, and then returned to crying, more quietly now.

At the airport, they put Terry on a plane to Honolulu en route to Taipei. Reed remembered that Taiwan didn't have an extradition treaty with the US. The two agents needed to get the hell off the island as soon as possible, too. Any flight to the mainland would do.

An hour and a half later, Kinney and Reed sat in an air-conditioned waiting room filled with anxious tourists. The flight to San Fransisco had been delayed due to "unspecified mechanical problems," which was why the agents had been able to join the others. Another hour later, they were in the air.

****

The two agents split up back on the mainland after Kinney texted Barber to fill him in and ask him to investigate Barbara Foster.

In the morning, he and Reed would drive the two and a half hours to Sacramento, where the state legislature was in session. Jerome Hattori—a state senator—had office hours for his constituents from one to two o'clock. He represented a sparsely populated northeastern district. Chances were, Kinney and Reed would be his only visitors.

Kinney decided not to call Georgia. He didn't have time to see her, and he didn't need any distractions at this point. He still wasn't sure if she was acting as a federal agent or a date, anyway.

On the way up to the state capitol in the morning in Reed's car, the two men discussed the case, eventually devolving into sharing unlikely theories about it. Kinney suggested that Miner had been murdered by yet another banshee wife. Reed speculated that Foster and Hattori could be having an affair, and the legislator had coerced her into cooperating.

Senator Hattori's waiting room was standing room only. Apparently, something was going on back home. It was a homely space, with a worn, faded Persian carpet, and photos of what must've been landscapes from his district on the walls. The best the senator could come up with were some bare mountains and a small lake surrounded by stunted trees. There was no receptionist, nor would there have been room for one.

Kinney asked a pregnant young woman seated near the door why she was there. Like the others, she wore what looked like her Sunday best, albeit with a billowing waistline on her violet dress. She appeared to have indigenous roots, with high cheekbones, straight, black hair, and light brown skin. On the other hand, most people in California who looked like her turned out to be Mexican-American. Someone had told Kinney once that most people in Mexico were at least partly indigenous, which explained the phenomenon.

"Hattori's got a bill to merge us into a new state with a corner of Oregon," the woman explained with a slight, appealing lisp. "We're here to stop him."

"I've read about that," Kinney said. "They want to call it Jefferson, right?"

She nodded. "They've tried before and it came to nothing, but he's got a petition or whatever they call it with twenty-seven senators and even more assembly people on it this time."

"I thought everybody up your way was onboard with this. You have much more in common with each other than the rest of California, right?"

The woman nodded again. "Sure. We're totally underrepresented. But without money from the state, we won't have the services we need. Poor people would starve to death. Our area doesn't have much industry anymore or a decent property tax base. There used to be lumber to cut and a state prison, but not anymore."

"I can see you've thought this through," Kinney said.

"Wait a minute," she said. "If you're not from our district, what are you doing here?"

"We were thinking of beating up the senator for taking bribes," Kinney told her.

"You go first," someone eavesdropping said.

"Yes, by all means," someone else added.

"Okay, we will," Reed agreed.

Precisely at one, Hattori emerged and showed Kinney and Reed into his office, which was much classier than his waiting room. Unlike Barber's office, Hattori's color scheme was all earth tones, with ochre walls, tan carpeting, and brown furniture.

As he strolled around his desk to sit, Hattori gestured to the two vinyl stack chairs facing it. A floor to ceiling stained pine bookcase full of hardback books sat beside a window behind the desk. A lower set of matching shelves lined the sidewall to Kinney and Reed's left.

"Sit, sit. Call me Jerome. And you are? You've got the look of Modoc county residents. Ranchers?"

Hattori was a stocky Japanese-American, with thinning hair and eyes that belonged on livestock. In short, he looked stupid. He wore a shiny blue suit, a black shirt, and a white tie. Kinney associated this outfit with East Coast mobsters.

"Our names don't matter," Reed said. "And we don't live in your district."

"I'm afraid there's been a misunderstanding. This hour is reserved for my constituents. I understand there are quite a few of them here to see me today."

"They suggested we meet with you first."

"Why is that?"

"We said we might beat you up."

Hattori reached for his phone. Kinney leapt to his feet and kicked it out of his hand. It bounced off the window behind him, cracking the glass.

"Holy shit!" Hattori said, all semblance of bonhomie gone. "You'll pay for that, and I don't mean by buying me a new window. I know some people."

"Like Meriwether?"

That shut him up.

"Why are you taking bribes from him?" Reed asked.

"He's just contributing to my campaign."

Kinney wanted to wipe the smug look off his face with a quick slap. But he resisted. "You're not running for reelection, though, are you?" he said.

"Who are you guys? Feds? No, you're not feds. Did Abernathy send you? Loomis?"

Kinney figured it was time to unleash his disorienting, inappropriate behavior. They'd play good cop/crazy cop.

He rose again, and Hattori flinched. Then Kinney walked over to a photo of Hattori with Donald Trump that was perched on a shelf. He took it down and tucked it under his arm. "I think I'll keep this as a souvenir."

"My friend collects trophies," Reed told Hattori. "He used to carve notches on his gun handle, but once you get too many, you have to get a new gun."

The senator flinched again before gathering himself. "What do you want?"

"We want to know what your deceased briber wanted from you. What are you supposed to do?"

"Meriwether's dead?"

"Very," Reed told him.

"Did you kill him?"

"Let's just say we were there, and our clothes are in the wash with his blood and brains on them."

"Rakena's supporting my bill," Hattori told them hurriedly, his face turning white.

"The one to secede from California?"

"Yes."

"Why?"

"I don't know."

"Guess."

Kinney swapped Hattori's photo for a brass horse head bookend. "I like this better," he said.

Hattori spoke. "You know Rakena has their finger in a lot of pies, right?"

"That's gross," Kinney said. "Who wants to eat a pie after that? Hey, where did this bookend come from? Malaysia?" He hefted it. "It feels Malaysian."

"I don't know," Hattori responded. "Rakena develops land, they have mines, and they do oil exploration. I don't know what else. It's probably one of those things."

"They want to make money from the new state?" Reed asked.

"Of course. They're a corporation." His tone implied that even a simpleton would already know that.

"Did you know Rakena is owned by Ryan Connelly?" Reed asked.

"No." Hattori paused and cocked his head. "If I did, I would've asked for more money."

Kinney sat back down, cradling the bookend in his arms. "You're an asshole," he told Hattori.

"I'm a politician. You have to operate this way to hold office." He enunciated slowly and carefully as if Kinney and Reed weren't native English speakers. It felt like an insult.

"That makes me sad." Kinney pretended to cry,

lowering his face.

"How do you think getting Jefferson going will help these creeps make more money?" Reed asked. "You think it's oil?"

Hattori shrugged. "Probably not. No one's ever found any up our way before. Maybe they bought the mineral rights for something else. Maybe they think they can run the place as their personal fiefdom."

"Good word," Kinney said. "Fiefdom."

Hattori looked at Reed.

"He's a little different," Kinney's partner told him. "Don't ask. Just try to stay on his good side. Tell me this: if any of those things are the case, why not just exploit them now? Why wait until there's a new state?"

"We've assured them we'll grant them tax exemptions and certain other advantages. That could be it."

"Maybe Connelly still wants to be a governor," Kinney said. "He keeps losing when he runs in California. Up your way, he could afford to pay every voter—or whatever else he needs to do."

"That could be it," Hattori agreed. "It makes sense. I met him at a fundraising dinner once—not mine. He's ruthless. He sent his chicken back three times."

"Ah, the horror," Kinney commented.

"You still haven't told me who you two are," Hattori said. "Am I going to be arrested?"

"Eventually—that would be my guess," Reed told him,

"But not by us," Kinney added. "What will happen with us is that we'll come back and kill you if you talk about this meeting."

"I see. You can count on me."

Kinney believed him. Although Hattori had alternated between arrogance and fear, clearly the latter was what motivated him.

"One more thing," Kinney said. "We sort of promised your constituents out there that we'd beat you up. How would you feel about opening the door doubled over and maybe grunting in pain?"

"That would be fine."

"Thanks, Jerome. You've been a good sport," Kinney said. "As a token of my appreciation, I'm returning your bookend."

He hurled it over Hattori's shoulder. The heavy horse head crashed against the crowded bookcase, scattering books to the floor.

When they emerged from the office, with Hattori doing a credible imitation of having been battered, his constituents cheered. Hattori looked up with a genuine grimace on his face.

****

"So do you think Jerome is more scared of us than he is of Rakena?" Reed asked as they walked to Reed's car in downtown Sacramento.

"I do."

"While we're in town," Reed said, "we could brace some of the other politicians who support Hattori's bill."

"I think it'll be more of the same," Kinney said. "Some of these guys will be sincere—they'll just think it's a good idea. Some will have taken bribes. But I don't see why any of them would know any more than Hattori does. It's his bill, after all."

Pedestrian traffic was light on the sidewalk, in contrast to the line of vehicles on the street beside it. As the duo turned a corner, a woman on an electric bicycle almost ran into them when she jumped the curb to bypass cars. Neither man so much as flinched.

"Okay," Reed said, "but let's keep bracing the other state senators in our back pocket. We need to find out who's up the ladder from Miner," Reed said. "It looks like people below him don't know much about this. That's my takeaway. "

"Why screw around with middlemen?" Kinney said. "Ultimately, all of this has to be coming from Connelly at Moonmatic."

"Do you think we can get access to him?" Reed asked. "And do you think he'll scare as easily?"

"I don't know."

By now they were sitting in Reed's car in a parking lot near the capitol building. The greenhouse heat was stifling. Reed started the car and cranked up the air conditioner.

"Maybe we should deal with Foster first," Kinney suggested, raising his voice to be heard over the car's fan. "After all, that's what Barber wants—to find the mole. And I'm still an active agent, despite what it looks like to the world. It's my duty to protect the agency's interests. The agency's interests are this country's interests, right?"

"Absolutely." Reed agreed, nodding vigorously. "That's why I signed up. I'm not even on the payroll now, but no one can make me disloyal. This country would be a mess if the agency didn't take care of everything the other agencies won't touch. I didn't kill all those people just to see my work go down the drain because of some goddamn traitor."

"Why don't I call Barber and let him decide what

we do next," Kinney suggested. "If we go after Foster when Barber knows she's innocent…Well, he won't like that, will he?"

"No. Go ahead."

Reed pulled out and began driving them through the city as Kinney contacted Barber.

After dressing Kinney down for continuing to investigate, Barber let him provide an update on his activities, including Reed's role in the mission. Then he told Kinney not to bother Foster—that she was on an important local mission. He'd also cleared Muñoz. He had no idea why Meriwether's name hadn't been discovered when he flew to Hawaii.

"I'd like you to confront Connelly," Barber added. "We can't do anything official in regard to someone as powerful as him, but you two are out there on your own, which is perfect. If you don't get satisfying answers, you may need to take him out. It sounds like Connelly's behind all this. At the least, bring him in so I can sort him out."

"We'll see about that," Kinney told him. He knew what "sort him out" meant when Barber said it. "Can you text us info on his whereabouts?"

"Sure. I'll find out on my own to keep this confidential."

"Sounds good."

Kinney and Reed hit horrendous traffic on the trip back home from the state capital. They were still on the road when Barber emailed Kinney three hours later. Connelly lived on an estate in the Santa Cruz mountains—540 ridge-top acres with views of the Monterey Bay to the southeast and as far as San Francisco to the north. His office was in Sunnyvale, but he rarely showed up there. In fact, he rarely showed up anywhere.

"He's a recluse," Kinney told Reed when he'd hung up.

"Isn't that a type of spider? That brown one?"

"I don't know, but he's certainly not brown. This guy is White through and through. If he could throw all the brown people out of the country, he would. What I meant was he doesn't go out much."

"So we need to get into his house?" Reed asked.

"I think so."

"And it's likely to be heavily guarded and alarmed?"

"Yup," Kinney agreed.

"Okay. Let's do it. Can I be the crazy guy this time?" Reed asked, not for the first time.

"You know I'm better at it."

"Yeah, I guess so."

Chapter 15

There were no photographs of Connelly's estate online. That was the power of being obscenely rich. And although it wasn't fenced in the back, severe topography—including a sheer cliff face—made it difficult to sneak in and reconnoiter. When it was time, they'd use climbing gear and whatever else they needed.

"I'm not scaling that cliff behind the place twice," Reed asserted. "I'll get some drones from a safe house for surveillance."

"That's your Achilles' heel," Kinney said. "Your fear of heights."

"Hey, it's not fear. It's common sense. You can't fall to your death while you're standing on the ground."

Later that day, Reed launched the first drone from beside a little used forested trail near the north end of Castle Rock State Park, just south of Connelly's estate. The drone was summarily shot down. He sent the second one, armed with a low light sensor, overhead that night. This time, Kinney and Reed parked down Summit Road from the estate.

The drone showed three houses and a four car garage in a line down a long, paved driveway from Summit Road. The building closest to the garage dwarfed the others. It was at least 12,000 square feet. It was hard to tell with limited light at a high enough altitude not to be heard what the style of architecture was. Clearly, it had a high, flat roof with several large skylights.

"Maybe those are our way in," Reed said as they reviewed the video around midnight in his car outside the park.

"We can't know that yet. The main thing is to see if there are guards or dogs or what."

"There are. Did you spot them?"

"No," Kinney told him.

"Let me back up the video." Reed tinkered with his laptop, reversing the ghostly green images. "There! There's a guy with a dog on a leash at the front right corner of the main house. Hold on, I think I saw another guy later on. There! You can see this one's holding an assault rifle. He's on the roof of the garage. He must've been under a canopy or something before. We only see him when he takes a leak off the back of the building."

"Good eyes, Reed. How come you see these guys better than I do?"

"We used night scopes in Afghanistan."

"You know, that's the first time I've ever heard you talk about your time in the service."

"And the last if I can help it. That chapter's closed," Reed told him.

"You were a sniper? Military intelligence? Some elite unit?"

"What'd I just say, Kinney? I don't ask you about your past."

"Sorry."

"So what's the plan?" Reed asked.

"We hike to the northern boundary of the park in the late afternoon tomorrow—there's a trail, beyond the one we were on, that dead ends at the cliff. Then we climb. It'll be safe to use headband flashlights until the final stretch. Then we'll switch to night googles. You take the lead at that point. I'll practice looking through the goggles ahead of time, but you're always going to be better at that than me. Then we take out the guards."

"How are we going to get up on the garage roof?" Reed asked.

"The same way the guy with the gun did. There must be a ladder or something."

Reed thought for a moment before speaking again. "Aren't they going to be suspicious about the drone they shot down?"

"If I were them, I'd think it was the media. I did some research. Connelly's been in the news lately because he's dating that French movie star—the one in the latest Bond film."

"Rosie Aubert!" Reed almost lost control of the car. "Do you think she'll be at the house? I'd love to meet her."

"Maybe you can play some golf up there while you're at it."

"Don't be mean, Kinney."

Kinney's practice session with the agency's night goggles consisted of gazing at hangers in a closet with the door closed.

"All set," he announced after fifteen minutes.

The hike late that evening was challenging on the rocky, single file trail. Steep drop offs to the pair's left kept them vigilant as their headlamps twisted and turned with numerous switchbacks, producing blind spots.

Kinney's feet hurt since he wore relatively new

hiking boots he thought he'd broken in. Reed kept loudly humming Eric Clapton's solo from the live version of *Crossroads*, which annoyed Kinney, who asked him to stop several times. Reed did, and then the humming would start up again a few minutes later. It wasn't the first time this had happened, and Kinney thought he'd gotten used to it. On this occasion, it was like having a mosquito whizzing around his ear.

The climbing was several degrees of magnitude worse than the hiking, although, mercifully, Reed was too focused on his handholds and footholds to hum. There was a reason the state park was called Castle Rock. What Kinney and Reed scaled was almost as sheer as a castle wall—but substantially higher.

Fortunately, years ago, Barber had sent them both to Colorado to rock climbing school. In fact, that was where the two agents had met. Reed had saved Kinney from a bad fall.

When they finally got to the edge of the overgrown, grassy meadow that stretched behind the estate on top of the ridge, both men lay still, breathing heavily. Kinney's hands ached despite the fingerless leather gloves he'd worn. Reed declared that his knee hurt "like a woman in labor if what they always complain about is true."

"Why are we doing this?" Reed asked after a while. "Besides Barber telling us to, I mean. I don't remember."

"For the agency, we need to talk to Connelly to get evidence against these people and find out why they want to create Jefferson so badly. Maybe there's a laptop we can grab in there. What's the agency supposed to do when all the evidence we have is from a dead conspirator and the word of a crooked politician? You know when we force people to talk, none of that can be used in court."

Kinney continued after a few deep breaths. "For me, I need to keep these assholes from harming my family, or killing us, or getting away with murder. I wouldn't be an agent if I didn't believe in justice—if I let criminals or terrorists keep doing what they do."

"So we're doing what the boss tells us to do and that happens to match what we want to do as individual people, anyway?" Reed asked.

"Exactly. At least that's how it is for me."

"Me, too. What else do I need to know before we talk to Connelly?"

"Barber wants Connelly dead, I think," Kinney said. "I didn't tell you that. But I want him in prison—assuming he's guilty, of course. Barber thinks he is."

"Why is it you don't kill anyone anymore, Kinney? You never really explained that."

"You know I died for a while in Cambodia?"

"How would I know that? It's not like there's an agency newsletter, and you never tell me anything."

"Well, I did the white light thing, and I met this entity that spoke to me in my head without talking. And what it told me made me not want to kill anyone anymore."

"Don't keep me in suspense, bro. What did it say?"

"I don't remember. I just remember the feeling I had afterward."

"Which was? God, it's like pulling teeth with you, Kinney."

"It was a sense of kinship—that we weren't really all separate. So it would be like killing a part of myself."

"That's weird, Kinney. Some angel tells you the meaning of life or something—which I know *I'd* fucking remember—and then that's all you tell me? Of course we're all separate. You're over there, and I'm over here."

"I think we need to focus on the mission now, Reed. Are you ready to roll?"

He sighed melodramatically. "I suppose."

Reed led the twosome in a long, diagonal crawl through the meadow. The three foot tall grasses—which were annoyingly scratchy—pretty much shielded them from being spotted.

Reed's sense of direction served them well. They emerged from the meadow where the redwood forest began beside the array of buildings, not far from the corner of the long, multi-doored garage. Beyond that lay the main house.

Both men hid behind a giant redwood tree and caught their breath again. After a few minutes, Reed whispered to Kinney.

"It's go time, bro."

"Right."

Kinney pulled his goggles off his face, which was a relief. If hiking in too tight boots, listening to the same guitar solo over and over, and crawling for fifteen minutes comprised a collective nine and a half on an unpleasantness scale, the damn goggles were about a seven on their own.

Kinney walked out into the driveway and called, "I think I'm lost. Can anyone direct me to the nearest Starbucks?"

The guard with the dog—a sleek, muscular

Doberman—raced around the far corner of the garage, and floodlights suddenly glared.

The guard on the roof yelled to his partner. "I've got eyes on him, Toto. Be careful. I'm thinking he's mental."

"Toto?" Reed asked as the guard on the ground approached him, pistol in hand, moving warily now. The dog slavered with excitement, holding his tail perfectly still as he pulled hard against his leash.

Chunky, with a fledgling reddish beard and aviator-style glasses, the man wore a navy blue uniform that sported a gold stripe on his sleeve. His baby-shit brown baseball cap listed to the left, giving him an incongruously jaunty air.

"My mother loved all things Oz," Toto explained, and then frowned. "Make a move, and I release Rocco. Mock my name again, and things will get worse." He waved the Smith and Wesson he'd pulled from the holster on his hip—a rookie move.

"What could be worse than Rocco tearing into me?" Kinney asked, pointing at the dog and baring his teeth to mimic it. "And by the way, that's a great name for a guard dog."

"Thank you. Now what are you doing here? How'd you get in?"

"I'm a reporter for *Billionaire Weekly*. The front gate is open."

"No, it isn't."

"Sure it is. What do you think? I climbed a bunch of cliffs at night to get here? Why don't you have Dorothy—or whatever his name is—climb down and check it out?"

"You'd like that, wouldn't you? You're not in

charge here. And there's no need to insult Brad. Yes, he's gay, but his mom wasn't cruel enough to give him a name like mine."

"Oh, I don't know. Brad is pretty much a crap name, too. Every Brad I've known has been a loser. But to answer your question, of course I'd like someone to check the gate. It would constitute validation, and we all need that periodically."

"I heard that," Brad called. "I'm not a loser, and there's no need for that kind of language. We're just doing our jobs here."

"Sorry. You're right. I'm just trying provoke you into doing something stupid."

"Well, stop it."

"Okay."

In the meantime, Reed had circled around the back of the garage and discovered an aluminum ladder leaning up against the wall. He assembled his rifle from the parts in his pack and climbed.

Toto turned to Kinney. "I don't buy your story. The gate is definitely closed—and electrified—and you don't look anything like a reporter. For that matter—"

"What *do* I look like?" Kinney asked. "I'm always open to feedback."

"I dunno. Maybe a football coach or a lumberjack."

"That's disconcerting, but thanks for making the effort. Is Brad single?"

"No," Brad called. "And you're not my type."

"Look," Toto said. "We're getting way off track here. You seem like a nice guy in your own strange way. Why not level with me? I can call the cops and have you arrested, you know. Or I can just escort you out. My boss would prefer that we handle things that way."

Kinney cocked his head until he heard a particular bird call. "I'd like to offer an alternative perspective," he said. "I suggest you tell Rocco to sit and then place your gun on the ground."

"And why in the world would I do that? You really are crazy, aren't you?"

"Do it!" Brad called. "There's another guy up here with a rifle aimed at you. He seems like someone who'd really shoot."

"Shit!"

"It was nice chatting with you," Kinney told Toto.

After Reed escorted a contrite Brad down and they'd zip-tied the two guards to the bumper of a classic Porsche in the garage, it turned out that Rocco had a thing for Reed, who'd remembered to slather on eau de dog-in-heat. Kinney had forgotten.

"If we leave Rocco in here, it would be kind of cruel, wouldn't it?" Kinney said. "He's in love with you."

"He's in love with my pants. I just happen to be wearing them."

Rocco kept humping.

"You could take them off," Kinney suggested.

"And meet my first major movie star looking like a pervert?"

"We don't even know if Rosie Aubert is here, Reed. Maybe Rocco should come with us."

"Are you messing with me, Kinney?"

"Yes. Push him away, close the garage door, and let's get over to the house."

After disabling the alarm system and leaving their weapons behind an umbrella stand at the door, the two agents strolled through the dark, capacious mansion, up a wide winding staircase, down a long carpeted hallway, and then into the doorway of a vast Zen-style bedroom.

Bamboo mats covered the floor and none of the furniture sat higher than two or three feet. Simplicity reigned, right down to the lack of handles or knobs on the black lacquered drawers of the three bureaus. Most of the room was space—the absence of decoration or furniture or lamps or…Anything, really. In such a large room, this looked to Kinney like an unfinished Japanese corporate headquarters.

Ryan Connelly and Rosie Aubert sat up in a king-sized platform bed watching a black and white movie on a surprisingly modest-sized TV.

After taking in the scene, Reed and Kinney sidled in. Reed announced their presence with a cheery "Hi guys!"

"Eek!" a topless Aubert screeched as if she'd seen a mouse.

"I admire your work," Reed told her as the two men stood at the foot of the bed.

"If you're going to kill us, get it over with," Connelly said.

"Eek," Aubert screamed again.

"Calm down," Kinney said. "We just want to talk. Do you want to do that in front of Ms. Aubert, Connelly?"

"Sure. We're engaged."

Rosie held out her hand and displayed an enormous diamond. It was at least ten times bigger than any Kinney had ever seen.

"Congratulations," Reed said to Connelly. "You're

a lucky man."

"Maybe not at this moment in time." He was remarkably poised for a man in his situation.

"No, I suppose not," Reed conceded.

Someone in the movie fired a gun, and a woman screamed. Connelly reached to a bedside table and pressed the mute button on the TV remote. "I don't think that's helping matters," he said.

"We're not armed," Kinney told him. "We don't need to be."

"Are Toto and Brad okay?" Rosie Aubert asked in her very cute French accent..

"Yes," Kinney answered.

"And how is dear Rocco?"

"Rocco's fine, despite a bout of unrequited love," Kinney told her.

She shrugged, which caused her exquisite breasts to rise and fall. "I don't know what you mean."

"Darling," Connelly said. "Why don't you cover up?"

She pulled the sheet up.

Her beauty hinted at a modeling career prior to acting. Like many French women, her small features were grouped a bit more in the middle of her face than a typical American's. And her short, spiky haircut wasn't the sort of thing a cover girl in the US would settle on. Kinney made an effort to keep his eyes above her neck.

The overall effect of the actress's blemish-free skin, large hazel eyes, and slightly pointed chin was startlingly elfin, as if she could appear in a fantasy movie without prosthetics or makeup.

"We hardly ever kill anyone these days," Reed told them in an attempt to reassure them.

"That's not the most comforting declaration I've ever heard," Connelly said. His tone was still steady and even, which impressed Kinney.

Connelly wasn't handsome in a traditional sense—his face was too long and narrow—but his chiseled cheekbones and clear, alert brown eyes could explain how he'd nabbed a film star as a companion—that and fourteen billion dollars.

"Let's get to it," Kinney said. "Why are you promoting the new state of Jefferson?"

Connelly stared at him. "I'm not. I'm committed to stopping it. It's a ridiculous idea."

Kinney and Reed were silent for a few moments. Connelly seemed to be telling the truth.

"Can you prove that?" Kinney asked.

"Sure. Can I show you on my laptop? We're preparing an ad campaign to recall Senator Hattori. We're going to saturate his district. The man is a blight."

"You don't have any economic interests there?" Kinney asked.

"Hell, no. There's nothing there, and I don't need more money. I want to spend the latter part of my life in service. That's why I run for office."

Kinney gestured to Connelly that he was free to retrieve his laptop from the top of a bureau next to the TV, which was silently showing a sneering gangster being arrested.

Connelly wore boxers with hearts on them and white athletic socks. His skinny legs were even whiter than his socks. His hairy barrel chest didn't match the rest of him.

Sure enough, the plans for the ad campaign, a

series of emails, and an editorial Connelly had written, but not published yet, proved he was telling the truth. The billionaire climbed back into bed.

"How did we get this so wrong?" Reed asked. "This is embarrassing."

"What did you think my position was? What could warrant a home invasion?" Connelly asked. He was more puzzled than outraged.

"Our boss sent us to gather information," Kinney told Connelly. "A guy who runs a company that Rakena owns has been murdering and bribing people. He threatened to kill my family. We were told you were behind it all."

"That's horrible," Aubert said. "You know, I was in a film once where a villain threatened my daughter."

"What happened?" Reed asked.

"Ninjas killed him."

"I don't think that's going to happen here," Reed said.

"Oh, I didn't mean that was going to happen with you. I just meant that because my character went through that, I understand what it's like."

"Rosie," Connelly said. "Perhaps it would be better if you let me handle things."

"*D'accord*." She slumped down in the bed and sulked.

"Who is this man?" Connelly asked. "Who's committing the crimes that brought you here?"

"Depending on who you ask, his name was Miner, Meriwether, or Molton," Kinney told him. "Someone shot him. He's dead."

"Those names are clever. That way he doesn't have to change his monogram," Aubert pointed out.

Connelly shot her a look and then shook his head. "Never heard of him. What did you think—that I order bribes and murders?"

"Sorta," Reed admitted. "I mean, how does somebody get so rich if they don't cut some corners?"

"You think major felonies can be described as 'cutting corners'?" Connelly's tone was acerbic.

"Look," Kinney said. "Obviously, we screwed up. Let's not argue about semantics. Our boss aimed us at you, so here we are."

"You do everything he says?" Connelly said. "What German regime does that sound like?"

"We should've checked it out. That's obvious now," Reed said.

"Let's think this through," Kinney said. "Why would someone want to feed Barber information that you're a supervillain?"

"Barber's your boss at some sort of agency? You guys aren't just thugs. I can tell that."

"Forget I said that name."

"Sure," Connelly agreed. "I can think of many reasons to spread disinformation about me—it's not the first time it's happened, believe me. In regards to establishing a new state, it's obviously to get my opposition out of the picture. I haven't gone public with my anti-Jefferson stance yet, which leads me to think that whoever's conspiring here has more accurate information about my plans than you do—inside information."

"So you think it's someone within your organization?" Reed asked.

"I do. And I can think of a few likely candidates. Would you two like to help me flush him out?"

"Seriously?" Kinney asked. "You want to hire us after we showed up in your bedroom at two a.m.?"

"Sure. Why not? I'm a good judge of character. I think I can trust you. Rosie, what do you think?"

"Well, if they got past Toto, Brad, and Rocco, they must be good at their jobs. And the good-looking one is charming, too."

"Thank you," Kinney and Reed said simultaneously.

Connelly laughed.

"You've got a pair on you, Connelly," Reed told him.

"I've been told that."

Chapter 16

Connelly's plan, concocted with Kinney's help over the next hour in his cozy study, seemed sound to all parties. Rosie especially liked it. She'd sat in on their conversation, lounging on a black leather couch wrapped in a cream-colored sheet as she inserted occasional film-related comments into the mix.

"It has everything," she said when the others had finished. "Action, suspense, a nice twist. This would be a wonderful film. Afterward, maybe I'll pitch it to some people I know."

"I could take a stab at the screenplay," Reed said.

"Do you have experience?"

"Well, no, but I've been in lots of these situations. I could bring authenticity to the table."

Driving back in the second car they'd parked between some trees on Summit Road near the house, Reed spoke up. "Well, that was different."

"It certainly was. Do you think we're making a mistake by trusting Connelly?"

"You know, I don't. I kinda like the guy despite his politics." Reed hunched over to adjust the heater.

"I know what you mean. He has charisma," Kinney said. "The positive kind. I don't see him leading a cult."

"He also has a smoking hot fiancé." He fiddled with the car's temperature a second time.

"And you're surprised Barbara Foster doesn't like

you?" Kinney asked, shaking his head.

"Maybe we should talk to her, even though Barber said she was clean."

"Yeah, I was thinking that too. She could've fooled him, and for that matter, she might've been the one to mislead him about Connelly."

"Have you ever known Barber to get fooled by anyone?" Reed asked.

"Well, no. But we've got a couple of days before we get going with flushing out Connelly's traitor, so what the hell. Let's take a day off and then pay her a visit." Kinney reached over and turned down the heat.

"Okay, sounds good." Reed turned the heat back up, glaring at his partner, daring him to try again. "Maybe I can win Foster over by saying feminist stuff while we're talking," he added.

"And what would that be?" Kinney asked, slipping down in his seat. He recognized that they were both exhausted and easily irritated. He was more than willing to abandon a temperature war.

"I dunno," Reed answered. "Men are pigs?"

"Good luck with that." Kinney shook his head.

"How do we find her?" Reed asked.

"I'll ask Henry Cutler," Kinney said. "He dated her for a while."

"Really? Cutler—the tech guy?"

"He owes me a favor."

****

Kinney called Georgia the following morning to see if she was free. She told him she was expensive. He countered by telling her he would pay for time on a pool table and as many beers as she wanted so she could be properly humbled about her boast concerning her prowess. She agreed.

If Georgia was on the level—not investigating him for her agency—he'd probably enjoy a fun evening. If she wasn't, more time with her would help him suss that out. Leaving her as a loose end made Kinney uneasy. He needed to know.

They met after Georgia's work day outside a pool hall in south San Jose. Recreating a vintage atmosphere, à la the film *The Hustler,* Bygone Billiards had atmosphere to spare. The owner, Tony, had even figured out how to create what looked like cigarette smoke. Whatever it was, the pervasive haze was odorless and hung in the air over the vintage oak tables. Their green felt gleamed under long, hooded Tiffany-style lamps. Racks of cues lined the artificially weathered v-board walls.

"Hey, Kinney!" Tony greeted the duo as they walked in. An ancient Latino who squinted through thick glasses, he stood behind a counter that matched the style of the tables. Very short, with a bald head and gray stubble on his cheeks, he continued. "Who's the pretty lady?"

"I'm Georgia," she told him. "I've been here before, Tony. Remember? You tried to ban me, and I had my lawyer write you a letter."

"You! It's you! Kinney, why are you bringing *her* here?"

"She brought herself. Calm down. We're just going to shoot a little pool—me and her."

"That's how it starts." He grudgingly handed them a tray of balls.

"What was that all about? Kinney asked as they headed to the table by the back wall, passing several players.

"Tony's weird. So what are the stakes?" Georgia asked.

"Money is so plebeian," Kinney told her. "What do you think would be more interesting?"

"How about this? If I win, you tell me about what you're working on, secrecy be damned. If you win, name what you want."

"Now or once I win?"

"Whenever."

"It's a deal," Kinney said. "I'll tell you once I win, and it isn't what you think."

"Hold on a minute," Georgia said, turning back toward the door and striding away. A minute later, while Kinney read emails on his phone, she returned with a black cue case under her arm.

"Ah, first you make the bet, *then* you get your custom cue."

"Yup."

Kinney worried about Georgia's motives as he picked a cue off the wall, and then racked the balls for a best out of five eight-ball match. Why did she want to know about his current mission? It might be something benign—innocent curiosity or what she'd mentioned earlier—that secrets could block their intimacy. Or it might be that the FBI wanted to know more about him. He could easily picture Alan Kim directing Georgia to find out what Kinney had refused to tell him.

They lagged balls to see who would break. Kinney won that by the slimmest of margins.

"It's a harbinger," he told Georgia, but despite his powerful break, no balls fell.

By chance, the one ball was hidden behind the

seven ball on a side rail. Since the balls needed to be hit in order, with whoever sunk the eight ball winning, Kinney felt okay about the result. The important thing was to gain access to the table again. If Georgia missed or played a safety inaccurately, he figured he could run the table. There were no other clumps of balls. They were spread out and eminently makeable.

Georgia studied the table and then aimed at a cushion at a right angle to the one ball. She was planning to bank the cue ball around the seven into the edge of the one, skidding it down the rail into a corner pocket. It was a ridiculously difficult shot. If she pulled it off, she could run the table herself. If she missed, the game was probably Kinney's.

Drawing the cue back smoothly, Georgia powered into the cue ball, creating a bit of sidespin to get just the right carom off the rail. The one ball scooted into the hole.

"Holy shit!" Kinney exclaimed.

Georgia smiled.

"Holy shit!" was all he could come up with again.

"Is that all you're going to say?"

"It seems like it. Wanna hear it again?"

"No, that's okay."

She methodically ran the table, leaving herself in position for an easy shot after each make. She knocked the eight ball in one-handed.

"I've been hustled," Kinney said.

"Yup. Do we even need to play the rest of the games?"

"Drink your beer. And then have five more," Kinney suggested.

"I might have to switch to my dominant hand to

beat you if I'm drunk." Georgia ginned and looked at him expectantly.

"You're kidding."

"You're supposed to say 'I'm not left-handed, either.'"

"*The Princess Bride*. You're making a mockery of this competition."

"Rack 'em."

Georgia won the next two games, although Kinney had a chance at least in the third one. He needed to make a bank shot of his own, which he just missed.

After losing, Kinney drove them to a nearby dive bar, where they sat at a small table in a corner, nursing their third beers. Almost everyone else looked like a fall down drunk, it smelled like stale beer, and the ancient jukebox played Nancy Sinatra.

"Why here?" Georgia asked. "Is this punishment for trouncing you?"

"No, I think it goes with the pool hall vibe. It's been around forever, and my cousin owns it. Why do you want to know about my work, anyway?" Kinney asked. "Are you a foreign spy planted here as an infant and recently activated to ferret out secrets from rugged American agents?"

He figured a lighthearted approach was the best way to broach the topic. If Georgia was simply curious, anything that sounded as though he were interrogating or accusing her could ruin things.

"I wish. That sounds much more fun than what I do. No, I told you why I want to know. How can we be close if a big part of your life is closed off to me?"

"I really can't go into a lot of detail, Georgia, bet or no bet."

"I'll take what I can get."

Kinney thought for a while, and Georgia let him. Sharing information was, of course, against agency policy—even with the FBI—but Georgia might reveal herself one way or another by the way she reacted. Would she press for more details than he initially shared? Would she listen more raptly than the information warranted? In Kinney's experience, it was hard to disguise the professional version of interrogation.

"Okay," he began, "there's an organization that's doing several dangerous, illegal things—"

"Like what?" Georgia asked.

"Let me finish. That's who I'm working against."

"Where is this?"

"Here—in the US."

"I thought you guys weren't able to operate domestically."

"You're just not going to let me finish, are you? I'm not CIA. I'm not anything you've ever heard of. We do whatever needs doing—wherever it is."

"So what is this other organization doing?"

Kinney thought again about what he was comfortable sharing. His assessment of Georgia's initial reaction had dissipated some of his earlier concerns. When people pumped someone for information, they didn't interrupt. They wanted the pumpee to continue the flow. And there was something personal and natural about her facial expressions. Kinney couldn't say how he discerned this. His ability to sense things like this arose from years of dealing with a demographic that lied about almost everything.

"Okay," he said, "here's the thing. There's a rogue

element in a multinational corporation that tried to assassinate a foreign leader to get oil, and they also want to establish a new US state. They've tried to kill people."

"Brigadier Pope."

Kinney held his hands up. "I didn't say that."

"That's the conference I missed. Kim said you might have been involved in that, which is why I brought it up earlier. Why didn't you let the FBI deal with these creeps?"

"First of all, that wasn't my call. But it's probably because our agency isn't always interested in bringing evildoers to so called justice. Plus, you may have a mole in your office."

"Oh, I doubt that. The vetting process to join the FBI takes ten months. They check *everything*." Georgia paused and then looked Kinney in the eye. "Are you directly involved in these alternative, unnamed solutions to illegal acts? Did you shoot Pope?"

"I used blanks. He's fine. I don't do anything lethal now."

"Why not?"

Kinney told her about his near-death experience, providing more detail than he had with Reed.

"Fascinating," Georgia responded. "So getting back to your work, are you making progress to stop this corporation?"

"Yes, but to do so, my partner—Pretty Boy Reed— and I had to pretend to quit. There's definitely a mole in *our* agency."

"Ouch! You know, I was curious, but I think you're oversharing. How do you know I won't report this to my supervisor? That could screw up whatever you're doing."

"Will you?"

"No, not unless a damn good reason shows up down the line," Georgia told him.

He was sure she was telling the truth. All the signature elements were evident. "There you go," he said. "That's why I told you."

"You trust your assessments of people that well?"

"What else do I have to go by? The fact that I'm still alive doing things my way says a lot."

"Good point." Georgia smiled. "Maybe we should go to my place and screw like bunnies now."

"Sounds good."

Chapter 17

Barbara Foster lived by herself in a cottage in Palo Alto, near Stanford. The following day, Kinney and Reed waited inside it for her to return home from work. Her locks were crap.

Foster's place was spotless, with everything lined up and equidistant from everything else, including the furniture. Her collection of flowered vases on a shelf in the kitchen were so perfectly spaced they didn't look real.

"It's spooky," Reed commented. "Who could live like this?"

"Either a robot or someone with OCD," Kinney replied.

"That's a real thing? I mean, this version? I thought OCD was when you washed your hands every ten minutes."

"That's just one type. I had a neighbor once who had to check his doorknob about twenty times whenever he went out. There are all kinds of OCD."

"That's rough. I never noticed Foster being like this at work. Did you, Kinney?"

"Sure. Unlike you, Foster lets me near her desk without threatening to call HR on me."

"Ah."

At first, they each hid in a closet. Reed chose the one in Foster's bedroom. Kinney settled into a hall closet amongst a vacuum cleaner, a mop, a broom, and an army of cleaning products, all arranged alphabetically.

After a twenty minutes, he extricated himself and called to his partner. "Come on out. She must've stopped at her gym or something."

"I didn't like the closet idea, anyway," Reed replied after he'd joined Kinney in the immaculate living room. "Let's just watch TV. Why surprise her?"

"I thought it would give us a chance to disarm her," Kinney said.

"You think she'll be armed? I don't. Come on, there's a Warrior's game on."

"Sold."

They sprawled onto a gleaming white upholstered couch that matched everything else in the room. Foster had even found a TV with a white frame.

Halfway through the first quarter, with the Warriors up five, Foster opened her front door.

"Hello? Who's there? I have a gun," she called, having heard the game's announcer.

"I'll bet you don't," Reed called back.

"If you're looking to rob me, you picked the wrong place. If you're looking to rape me, I can kick your ass."

"I thought you said you had a gun," Reed called.

"It's us," Kinney said. "Kinney and Reed Bolt. We got bored waiting for you."

Foster sauntered into the room, put her hands on her hips, and glared at them. "I don't appreciate you clowns breaking in like this. You're civilians now. I could call the police. And turn that stupid game off. It's just a bunch of millionaires running back and forth."

Foster was a tall, slim blonde with a long neck and a modest chest. She wore her hair in a ponytail, giving the impression she was younger than thirty-five. Her severely snub nose spoiled her looks to Kinney's eyes, but she was still attractive enough to seduce most foreign agents.

"Basketball is a little more nuanced than that," Kinney protested.

"I don't care."

Kinney turned off the TV with the remote on the table next to him. "We just need to ask you a few things. It's important."

She sank into a white armchair perpendicular to the couch. One hand held down the hem of her green skirt. She leaned back and spread her other arm across the back of the armchair. Kinney noticed the mixed messages in her body posture.

"If I answer your questions, then you'll get the hell out of here?"

"Absolutely," Kinney promised.

"Fine. Go ahead. But if you tracked any dirt in here, you'll pay for that."

"Fair enough," Kinney said. "Barber asked you to check the airlines to see if a guy named Meriwether had gone anywhere, right?"

"Yes. So?"

"So did you?"

"Of course." Her tone was dismissive, and she waved away the question with her former hem-holding left hand.

"And…?" Kinney asked.

"He was booked on a flight to Kauai."

"Why didn't you tell Barber?" Kinney asked.

"I did."

"He said you didn't," Reed told her.

"He's lying," she asserted matter-of-factly.

"Why would he lie, Barbara?" Kinney asked.

"I don't know, but he's done it before when he thought it was in the best interests of the agency." She shifted in her chair, leaning forward now, engaged at a different level.

"Like when?" Reed asked.

Foster grimaced. "Actually, one example was when you supposedly killed the wrong man, Reed. You didn't."

"What!" Reed stood and tightened his fists.

"I'm sure he had his reasons," Foster said hurriedly. Even fellow agents became alarmed when Reed was riled. "Barber always has his reasons. Sit down, for chrissake."

"Jesus Christ!" Reed exclaimed as he fell back onto the couch. "That fucker!"

"Have you been feeling guilty?" Foster asked.

"Well, no. That's not really my deal. But I've suffered in my own way."

"Barbara," Kinney said. "Why do you think Barber lied about Reed's Cairo mission?"

"Maybe he wanted a good reason to partner him up with you on American soil—to do the kinds of missions you two do now. Or did, I guess. What did you do to get desk gigs, anyway?"

"Never mind," Reed said.

"What about Meriwether?" Kinney asked. "Why do you think Barber lied about him?"

"I don't know. What are the two of you up to these days? Could it be something Barber doesn't want you involved in?"

"Yeah, that might be it," Kinney said, but he didn't believe it.

"You know I'll have to report this to him," she said.

"We'd be very disappointed if you did that," Reed told her, standing again and staring down at her.

"Reed can be a bit volatile when he gets disappointed," Kinney added. "Plus we could let Barber know that you told us he'd lied about Reed."

Barbara cocked her head and looked to the side for a moment. "Why don't you pay me five thousand dollars?" she suggested. "The information I gave you is worth that, plus you get my silence thrown in."

"How do we know you won't tell Barber anyway after we pay you?" Reed asked. He relaxed and sat.

Foster paused again to consider that. This time her head cocked to the other side, which struck Kinney as odd. Most people had a go-to thinking-it-over move.

"How about this?" Foster said. "You can owe me the money until whatever's going on is over. I don't want to know who this Meriwether is or anything else. That's your problem. This way you can see for yourself that I don't contact Barber. And if you stiff me, I'll kill you."

Both men knew she'd try.

"Five hundred," Reed said.

She shook her head. "I'm not a street vendor in Tijuana. Five thousand."

"Okay," Kinney agreed.

"While we're here," Reed said, "what's the word in the office about us?"

"No one thinks you're traitors. A few guys think

you're heroes for standing up to Barber. Most of us just think you're assholes with authority issues."

"That's us," Kinney agreed.

****

"So there's another surprising thing," Kinney said in the car. "I believe her."

"Me too. I'm getting really sick of surprises. What's Barber up to? Did he know months ago that you and I needed to be caught up in all this? Is that why he came up with that lie about Cairo?"

"I don't see how he could know that back then," Kinney responded. "That would mean he was already aware of Rakena and Miner and all the rest. For that matter, he'd need to know about the mole, too. Can you see him running the agency for months when he knows there's a traitor?"

"No. What about the Meriwether plane deal?"

"I guess he didn't want us finding him. Maybe he already had a mission ready to roll—capturing Miner or whatever. Maybe we messed all that up by getting Miner killed."

"How was that our fault?" Reed raised his eyebrows and tilted his own head to the side.

Kinney knew this was his partner's confused expression. It reminded him of the rescue dog he'd grown up with, who seemed confused by almost everything that wasn't connected to food, going for a walk, or screwing.

"My guess is that someone was keeping an eye on us, and we led them to Miner," Kinney said.

"Yeah, that could be. But maybe Miner's people were watching him, and when we showed up, they silenced him before he could tell us much. I mean,

192

Miner folded right away. They probably knew he was that kind of guy."

"Isn't that still us causing his death?"

"Whatever, Kinney. What's next?"

"It would be nice to get answers from Barber, wouldn't it?"

"Sure, but we're not going to."

"Yeah, I know," Kinney agreed. "I guess we just go along with Connelly and see what happens."

"It's kinda weird not having the agency resources, isn't it? I mean, we could go see Eddie again, but what would we even ask him to research? It's like flying blind—you know, when all the instruments on a plane fail."

"Does that really happen?" Kinney asked.

"I saw it in a movie once."

****

Kinney and Reed were expected at Ryan Connelly's office in Sunnyvale—in the heart of Silicon Valley. A pale supermodel-looking young woman in a skintight black pantsuit told them she was Connelly's assistant when she met them at the security desk in the modern, sterile lobby.

Her full lips seemed to naturally pout. Her green eyes were so big, Kinney wondered if there was some kind of cosmetic surgery that could create that effect. Her skin was as flawless as Rosie's, and her perfectly straight black hair hung down alongside her oval face.

When the woman sashayed ahead of them, Reed hurried to draw abreast.

"My name's Reed," he told her. "What's yours?"

"Natasha. I'm married."

"Good for you. I was married once."

"How did that work out?"

"Well, here I am hitting on you, so I guess you can figure that out," Reed said, grinning.

"A lot of married men hit on me."

"Those pigs!" Reed responded.

She turned to him and smiled. "Nice try, playboy."

By now, they were entering a private elevator, heading for the top floor of the Moonmatic campus's main building.

Reed turned to his partner. "Kinney, why do women keep saying that to me?"

"You're Kinney?" Natasha interrupted.

"Yes."

"I've heard of you. Ryan mentioned that two men were arriving around ten, but he didn't tell me your names. How many people have you killed?"

"I don't do that anymore."

Kinney studied himself in the mirrored rear wall of the elevator. Did he still look like an assassin? Had he ever?

"More than ten? More than twenty?" Natasha asked.

Kinney glanced at Reed, who was frowning at the woman's attention being pulled away from him.

"Natasha, I appreciate your interest, but this isn't appropriate," Kinney told her, trying to get her to stop while remaining civil. In another context, he would've intimidated her into silence.

"Does Ryan want you to kill someone?" Natasha continued. "He's gathered all his companies' CEOs for a meeting this morning. He's never done that before. He said to let you in there when he calls me. How could you pull off a hit with all those witnesses?"

Reed stepped in to help. "No offense, Natasha, but you have bad boundaries," he told her.

"Yeah, I know, but look at me. Does it matter?"

"Good point."

Kinney spoke up. "I don't know how you know what you know, but let's just pretend we're consultants or something, okay?"

"Sure."

"I am one," Reed told her.

"A security consultant? No, let me guess. I'll bet you know all about mineral rights. You've got that look. You were probably a geology major at some podunk college and you wore bolo ties until a date told you you looked geeky."

"That's exactly right! " Reed exclaimed. "That's amazing! I think we're attuned in some special way, don't you?"

Natasha smiled despite herself. "I'm still married."

"You were right about the podunk part," Kinney told her. "His college turns out sheepherders and telemarketers. And he didn't even graduate."

The glass-walled executive suites they strode past were occupied by industrious young men clicking away on desktop computers.

"Everybody looks so young," Reed commented.

"They are. Ryan believes that people's creativity peaks in their mid-twenties and then fades. Plus, these guys work harder and they're cheaper than the old farts I worked for elsewhere."

"Why aren't you modeling?" Reed asked.

"Really? You haven't given up?"

"No, I have. Honest. I'm just curious."

"I used to model—straight out of high school. It's

incredibly boring. And everyone is so vapid." She rolled her eyes.

"Good word," Kinney told her.

"I went to Princeton."

"No shit?" Reed said. "We were just there recently. It's a beautiful area."

Natasha turned and looked at Kinney. "The Guyana guy? That was you?"

They arrived at a luxurious waiting room, with a cappuccino machine and fresh pastries in a corner. Fortunately, Natasha's phone chimed before Kinney had to answer her. He shot Reed a look that said, "You idiot. Who's got the bad boundaries, now?"

"It's time," Natasha announced. "Ryan wants you to go in that door to the right. That brings you to the head of the conference table. He said to stand behind him and cross your arms. He said you'd know what to do after that. If I were you, I wouldn't cross my arms. That sounds pretty controlling. I mean, they're *your* arms, right?"

"Thanks," Kinney told her, glad he didn't have an assistant, however beautiful.

A few moments later, Kinney and Reed flanked Connelly, who sat in a dark green wing-backed chair that wouldn't have looked out of place in an English drawing room. The nine CEOs lined the rim of a long, oval walnut table. Their chairs wouldn't have looked out of place in a rust belt airport. Theirs were also considerably lower than Connelly's—even more so than in Barber's office.

The billionaire's bearing was regal, his head tilted back so he literally looked down his nose at his executives. The pose exaggerated his long, narrow face.

His lips were pressed tightly against each other as he studied the men in front of him.

Directly across the table from Kinney and Reed sat a familiar, currently ashen face—Chet, Miner's associate. He wore an expensive gray suit. He wriggled within it as though escaping his suit would amount to escaping his situation.

Kinney leaned down and whispered in Connelly's ear. "It's the fourth guy from the left. We don't need to enact the rest of the plan."

"Are you sure?"

"Yes."

"Okay," Connelly told the others at the meeting, "we're done. Everyone but Lyle, talk to Natasha on the way out for your return travel arrangements."

"We came all the way for this?" one guy complained.

"You came from Atlanta," another CEO said. "Big deal. I flew from Singapore, Bob."

Lyle—or Chet, or whatever his name was—bolted for the door farthest away from Kinney and Reed.

"Excuse me," Reed said as he raced out of the room.

Kinney strode to the door to watch. As Lyle began to sprint down the hall, Reed tackled him from behind, driving his shoulder into Lyle's thigh. The two went flying, bounced off a side wall, and Reed ended up on top of Lyle.

"Hey," Kinney called. "That counts as your turn on top."

"No, it doesn't."

"Get off me," Lyle grunted.

Reed ignored him.

Natasha and Connelly sidled up. The other CEOs took off down the hall in the other direction. Kinney had never seen old White men run so fast.

"That was exciting," Natasha said.

"N, would you see to the other men?" Connelly asked.

"Sure, Ryan." She walked after the fleeing CEOs.

Reed hauled his quarry to his feet and marched him back into the conference room. He shoved him down onto a chair and stood behind him. Kinney and Connelly sat across the table from them.

If Lyle's canine doppelganger had been an impressive greyhound with x-ray eyes at the golf course, Lyle now resembled a greyhound who'd been slapped around after losing a race. His eyes lost vitality as Kinney watched. In a few moments, it was as though they'd fully disconnected from who was behind them. Lyle hung his head and slumped his shoulders, which tightened his slim fit suit to the point that the bottom button looked as though it might pop.

"You're the CEO of Rakena?" Kinney asked. "Miner worked for you?"

"Miner?" Lyle looked up with a sliver of hope. Perhaps Kinney didn't really what was going on.

"Meriwether. Miner was his real name."

"Was?"

"Was."

The man visibly gulped, assuming he was next on the hit list.

"I'm very disappointed in you, Lyle," Ryan said. "This is how you pay me back?"

Lyle looked up and locked eyes with his boss, defiance on his face now. "I don't know what you're talking about, Ryan. I know these men. They're dangerous, and they have a grudge against me. That's why I took off. You're not safe, either. Call security."

His brown eyes and expression had regained even more vigor as he spoke. He sat up straighter.

"Give it up, Lyle, or should I call you Chet?" Kinney said.

While Lyle repeatedly tried to interrupt him, Kinney told Connelly more about Miner and Lyle's role in the Guyana oil scheme.

"Is this true?" Connelly asked Lyle when he was through.

"Of course not. We're simply doing everything we can to keep your projects moving forward. The development in New Zealand will be finished next year once we finish dealing with the environmentalists, and the oil off the coast of Guyana will be available soon after that. You wanted results. I'm getting results."

"This isn't the time to appeal to my greed, Lyle. Results at the cost of human lives are not results. Anyway, I'm sure you're finding some way to line your pockets in the midst of this."

"Oh no, sir. Never." Lyle shook his head vigorously and attempted to project sincerity, but his underlying fear leaked out, undermining his performance.

Connelly continued. "I instructed Natasha to get our best forensic accountant to immediately investigate whoever didn't walk out of the conference room. I think your antics in the hallway identify you even better. What am I going to find out?"

"You'll see I have quite a bit of money in a new account, but I can explain."

"Please do."

"In my free time, I've been lobbying for a cause I believe in," Lyle said. "The organization I work for has quite a few wealthy donors, and I've been tasked with strategically contributing to various state legislators' campaigns."

"And you have the funds in a personal account?"

"Just temporarily while we set up our non-profit." Lyle leaned forward as though that could boost his credibility.

Kinney spoke up. "Non-profits aren't allowed to promote political agendas."

"And we don't have a forensic accountant, Lyle," Ryan added, smiling grimly.

"I meant we're setting up an LLC. Sorry about that. I'm pretty stressed right now. How would you feel if you were unjustly accused by one of the most powerful men in the world and a couple of hired killers?"

"I'd feel guilty," Reed told him. "Because you are."

"And this cause of yours is…?" Connelly asked. Of course he already knew the answer from what Kinney and Reed had told him. Hearing Lyle's version would help him understand how much truth was coming his way.

"Establishing the free state of Jefferson."

Connelly frowned melodramatically. "You know I'm against that, and you went behind my back, anyway?"

"Why, I had no idea, sir." Lyle looked sheepish as he declared this. Apparently, even he wouldn't have believed himself.

Kinney had to give him credit for trying. The guy

was dogged to a fault.

"That's another lie," Connelly said. "You were at several meetings where we discussed it."

"Sometimes I doze in meetings."

"This is ridiculous," Reed said, losing patience by the minute. "Let me beat all the truth out of him."

Lyle went white and hung his head again.

"No," Ryan said. "I'm enjoying this. Lyle is revealing who he really is." He turned to his employee again. "Here's the deal. I'm going to call the police and let them sort all this out if you don't tell me about the people behind the Jefferson bill. Who makes money on this?"

Lyle thought things over. Kinney verbally nudged him.

"Forget the police. We'll tell our agency about you, and they'll *persuade* you to tell who your source is in the agency, among other things. Then they'll hold you overseas without a trial."

"When he says 'persuade,' " Reed told him, "he means torture, Lyle."

"Okay, okay. I'm sure we can come to some sort of arrangement here." He spread his arms out, which to Kinney looked as though he was showing how big a fish he'd caught.

"Sure," Kinney answered. "After you tell us."

"Here's the thing. There's lithium there—in northeast California. Lots of it." Now he pointed to the rear wall. Kinney wondered if that was actually the right direction.

"Who holds the rights?" Connelly asked.

"We do."

"We?"

"Rakena."

"This is all off the books?" Connelly asked. "My people don't know anything about it?"

"Yes. The idea is that after I had Rakena buy the rights, this dummy corporation I set up would buy them from Rakena for pennies. I'd approve the sale."

"So you've got me buying the mineral rights at market prices and then selling to you for virtually nothing." Connelly's voice dripped with contempt.

"Basically."

"So what does secession politics have to do with this?" Kinney asked. He'd never been clear why there needed to be a new state about any of this.

"Lithium ore mining is controversial. They've got quite a few mines in Australia—out in the middle of nowhere where there's no usable land or water to ruin. There's only one large-scale operation in the US. The antilithium people are worse than those sheep-loving morons in New Zealand. There's absolutely no way California would let anyone mine lithium."

"But Jefferson would?"

"Yes. We're cutting the politicians in the region in on the deal—we're talking billions and billions eventually—plenty to go around—and everybody wins. The world needs lithium for batteries. It's like performing a valuable service."

"Do you believe your own bullshit, Lyle?" Reed asked.

He ignored that and continued. "I'm happy to share the wealth. In fact, I was thinking of bringing all of you in, anyway. Kinney, remember when Meriwether told you we needed men like you? It's true. We do. And Ryan, with your resources, we'd have the capital to get going on mining as soon as we secede."

"Let me get this straight, Lyle," Connelly said sternly. "You've tried to commit murder in my name, you're planning to embezzle millions from my company, you're corrupting government officials, you want to ruin the environment to get rich, and now you have the nerve to pretend you were planning to include me in these crimes, which basically constitute a conspiracy against me?"

"Well, when you put it like that…"

"How else should I put it?" Ryan asked with heat.

"Okay, fine. I'm a piece of shit and you're God. Is that what you want to hear?" His tone was pugnacious now.

"Who's the spy in our agency?" Kinney asked. "Who gave us up and why?"

"You won't believe me." Lyle sounded sure about this.

"Try me."

"Barber. He's in for ten percent, and it's totally worth it. The guy knows everybody in Washington, and he has access to all sorts of privileged information."

"I don't believe you," Kinney said.

"See? I told you you wouldn't."

"Prove it," Reed said.

"Is it okay if I get out my phone?"

"Sure."

Lyle fumbled for it in his jacket pocket, his shaky hands almost dropping it twice. Then he showed them several incriminating encrypted email threads. Kinney recognized Barber's idiosyncratic syntax and hit or miss spelling. When he thought it over, it made sense— it explained a lot.

"What do you think, Reed?"

"I think Barber's been screwing us." His face was set in stone, his eyes fixed on a point in space behind Kinney.

"Why us in particular?" Kinney asked Lyle. "Why did Barber get us involved?"

"Kinney, he said you're the best," Lyle told him, "and he needed a way to get you killing again, even aside from our plans. Plus, like Meriwether told you, you had access to Brigadier Pope, who was really hard to get to. Then you were supposed to take out Ryan or at least bring him in to Barber. With him out of the way, our man could take over Moonmatic operations. Ryan's heirs don't have any interest in the business."

Reed's eyes narrowed as he worked through this information. "Why would Barber want Pope assassinated, anyway?" he asked. "I've never really got that. How does that help you get oil?"

"Pope basically runs the country." Lyle tried to twirl a mustache he didn't currently have, abandoning the maneuver after a few seconds. "He's the one behind the nationalization plan. With him gone, the plan's gone. Then the money from Rakena's oil profits—the offshore wells—can finance the lithium mining operation. Barber has been onboard with this right from the start. In fact, he's the real villain here. He's betraying the trust of his country. I'm just a businessman trying to make a buck."

"What about me?" Reed asked, emphasizing the "me" and aiming both index fingers at himself. "Why mess with my career—sideline me based on bullshit about me killing the wrong guy?"

"I don't know anything about that. Maybe he

thought you'd find out about him if you stayed part of the inner sanctum at the agency. The guy's ruthless and hard to figure, so it could be most anything."

"Who else is in on this?" Ryan asked. "Spencer for one, right?"

"Yes, and Guiliani, Babcock, and Ko."

"Anyone else?"

"No," Lyle answered.

"He's lying," Kinney said.

"How do you know that?" Connelly asked.

Kinney pointed to where Natasha stood in the far doorway, aiming a rather large pistol at them.

Chapter 18

"Everyone," Lyle said cheerily, "meet my wife, Lily. Remember when I recommended her for your assistant's job, Ryan? Did you wonder why I pushed so hard?"

"Any problems in here, hon?" Lily asked.

She held the revolver in two hands in front of her, her legs spread at shoulder width. Her stance was what gun range instructors recommended.

"None. I played along when I was threatened. I wish you'd retrieved the gun sooner, though. Now they know too much. We'll definitely have to kill them." Lyle smirked. He seemed delighted by the prospect.

"No problem," she told him. "Would you like to do the honors or shall I?"

"I vote for Natasha," Kinney said. "It's a sexier death. Can you do it topless?" he asked her, leering like a drunk sailor in an old black and white movie.

"Or bottomless?" Reed suggested.

"You two are disgusting," Lily told them, shaking her head.

Kinney was pleased that words could catalyze her into moving, even if it was only her head at this stage.

"I've got an idea," he said, continuing his usual tactic of responding to danger in an unexpected way. "What if we all went to a nice restaurant, had a yummy last meal, and then you poisoned our dessert. I could use a slice of pie right now. I skipped breakfast."

Lily waved the gun. "That's enough!" Her voice was loud and shrill.

While the gun was momentarily aimed at the picture window, Reed ducked down behind Lyle's chair, and Kinney bolted out the other door. Ryan dropped under the table. A second later, while Lily tried to absorb what had happened, Reed reached around Lyle and applied a chokehold.

"Give it up or your husband dies," he declared.

"You think I care?"

"Yes, I do. You're bluffing."

"Like they say in the movies—try me," she said in an awful Clint Eastwood impersonation.

"I like the 'do you feel lucky?' line better," Reed said. "What do you think, Ryan?"

As Ryan started to answer, Kinney flew through the door beside Lily, kicking the revolver out of her hand. A moment later, he side-kicked her hip and knocked her down. This time he was careful where he sent the gun, retrieving it at his feet.

Reed released Lyle and stood. "Amateurs…" he said, shaking his head.

Kinney gestured with the gun for Lily to sit beside her husband. She limped forward, her slender shoulders slumped even more than Lyle's.

"Don't worry, you're not seriously injured," Kinney told her. "And congratulations on the whole quirky assistant act. It was very convincing."

She didn't reply as she fell into her chair. Reed stood behind the two.

"What shall we do with you two?" Ryan asked after he'd clambered to his feet and climbed into his armchair at the head of the table.

The couple was silent. Lyle stared out the window, his eyes unfocused. Lily watched Kinney warily as though he might attack her again.

"We can't have them arrested at this point," Reed said. "That would tip off Barber. We need to nail him, too."

"So what do you suggest?" Ryan asked.

Back online, Lyle spoke up. "I assure you you'll never hear from us again if you let us go. Otherwise, I know a lot about Moonmatic and Rakena, and I'd be happy to tell the authorities about your involvement in all sorts of criminal activities."

"I'm not involved in anything criminal," Ryan declared.

"On paper you are."

"Shut up," Reed said, cuffing him on the ear.

"Obviously, we're not going to let you go," Ryan said. "And I've got batteries of lawyers to deal with any false evidence you produce."

"Lyle is kind of a big fat liar, isn't he?" Reed added. "Who knows if he has anything on you, anyway. I think we need to stash these two for a while. Any ideas, Kinney?"

"Leave that to me," Ryan said.

"You're sure?"

"It won't be a problem. I'll call in some people, and you two can get going on whatever you're going to do about your boss in just a bit." Connelly pulled out his phone and talked to the head of security. "His office is right down the hall," he told Kinney and Reed when he'd finished.

A minute later, Kinney handed over Lily's gun to a

burly, older man, and the two agents took off.

****

As usual, they debriefed—this time in Kinney's car.

"Do we have a chance of holding Barber accountable?" Kinney asked. His tone reflected his skepticism.

"Probably not. Who's going to believe us over him? We're disgraced ex-agents as far as everyone else is concerned. Barber made sure of that."

"There's the email evidence and whatever else Lyle can tell us if we get him to cooperate," Kinney pointed out. "He seems like the kind of guy who'd sell someone out for a reduced sentence."

"Yeah, he does," Reed agreed. "But if we go the legal route, Barber will be in the wind. He's got so many favors to call in from powerful people, let alone whatever he's got on them. Remember when he made that guy in Justice release Staats, even though they had an airtight case against him?"

"Yeah, he's probably got an exit plan in place, too—a villa in some country without an extradition treaty." Kinney grabbed the steering wheel and gripped it so tight, his knuckles were white. In that moment, he pictured Barber getting away with everything.

"So we take him out?" Reed asked.

"We could try siccing the CIA or the NSA on him. That might work. Otherwise, eliminating him might be our only option."

"I'll contact some people I know in the CIA," Reed told him. "If it turns out we need to kill him, I'll do it," Reed told him. "If you do, Barber wins."

"Yeah, that's true."

"If I'm Barber," Reed said. "I'd be taking extra precautions. He knows someone shot Miner, and he has no reason to trust a snake like Lyle."

"It was probably Barber who ordered the Miner hit, Reed."

"Yeah, I guess you're right. I haven't had a chance to update my storyline yet. Do you think he used an agent?" Reed asked.

"I dunno, but that might be a place to start. Whoever it was has got to be close to Barber. We could use the shooter to get to him."

"Barber and Hoff are buddies."

"I didn't know that."

"They went skiing together once," Reed told him. "That's how Barber broke his leg."

"Ah, I wondered. Hoff's tough. Besides you and me, I think he's the best agent. He could definitely be the guy, but if we can't get through to him, he's sure to tell Barber."

"Yeah, but what if we tell him what Barber's been up to? I know he's loyal to our country," Reed said, putting his hand over his heart as if he were pledging allegiance. "The guy was probably born in a red, white, and blue birthday suit. Once in the break room, he told me he'd rather die by torture than live in another country, and this was right after he'd been to a conference in Toronto. What's so bad about Canada? It's like a colder, more polite US, right?"

"How in the world did that come up?" Kinney asked.

"I don't remember. I know it started because somebody's yogurt went bad in the fridge."

"That probably makes sense in some alternate

universe, Reed."

****

A couple of days later, after Reed had sufficiently surveilled their quarry and Kinney had once again bunnified Georgia, Kinney approached Hoff as he emerged from a grocery store, a bag under each arm. If the agent's response was violent, Hoff would have to get rid of a bag before he made his move.

Hoff was ordinary-looking—a plus in their line of work. His thinning brown hair sat above a pear-shaped face whose main feature was a long, slightly crooked nose. In an interagency boxing tournament, he'd placed second behind a DEA agent who'd fought professionally. Hoff was younger and substantially shorter than Kinney, and he moved gracefully.

Hoff 's baggy, old man jeans looked out of place, as did his gaily patterned guayabera shirt. The cowboys, horses, and cacti that marched across a Southwestern landscape looked like they belonged on a kid attending another kid's birthday party.

To get to Hoff, Kinney had to maneuver around an elderly woman who was trying to simultaneously push a walker and a laden shopping cart. He toyed with the idea of offering help and accosting Hoff later but decided to stick to his plan.

"Hey, Curtis, got a minute?"

Hoff looked up and squinted in irritation. "Not really." He kept striding toward his car. "What do you want, Kinney?"

"I just want to chat," Kinney told him, hurrying to catch up. "It's important."

"I'm on my way home to get ready for my kid's birthday party at my ex's. Some other time."

"That's terrific. How about I ride with you? I'll get back on my own."

Hoff stopped and stared at Kinney. "And if I say no? What happens?"

Kinney leapt in the air and flicked Hoff's eyebrow with a roundhouse kick.

"Holy shit! I didn't see that coming, Kinney. I've heard about your kicks, but I've never seen one in action." Hoff leaned back and surveyed Kinney, perhaps assessing how he'd do in a fight against him.

"I wouldn't really beat you up on your kid's birthday," Kinney said. "I just wanted to remind you who you're dealing with. And I've got back-up." That was a lie, but Hoff knew Reed was his partner.

"Fine," Hoff said. "But I can't help you with Barber. He's done with you, and that's that."

"That's okay. I'm done with him, too," Kinney replied.

Once they were ensconced in Hoff's EV, Kinney asked Hoff how much time they had.

"About fifteen minutes, so get to it." He started the car and silently pulled out of his parking space. "What's so important?"

"Been to Hawaii lately?"

"I've never been, but we're going next year. My wife has a friend on Maui."

"You know, I can check. If I have to come back, it won't be your kid's birthday anymore."

"It's the truth. Why would I lie about where I go on vacation?" Hoff swiveled his head to stare at Kinney for a moment.

"Who does Barber use for off-the-books wet work?" Kinney asked.

"Not me, if that's what you're implying." This time he kept his eyes on the road, which had become more congested.

"Then who?" Kinney asked.

"Let me think." Hoff drove a few blocks before he replied. "I heard Barber talk on the phone to a guy named VanVleet once about doing him what he called 'an unofficial favor.' "

"You think that was something lethal?"

"Well, when I asked him about it, he said as much. I don't remember the details."

"That's a Dutch name, right?"

"I guess so."

"How could I get in touch with this guy?"

"I have no idea, and why would you want to? Are you working for another agency now? Is this sanctioned?"

"Don't worry about it."

"We're almost there," Hoff said.

"That wasn't fifteen minutes."

"Sue me, asshole."

Reed picked Kinney up, who filled his partner in on the conversation. "I'm pretty sure I can trust what he told me," Kinney finished. "He was surprisingly cooperative."

"I know VanVleet," Reed told him. "He's an independent. He's good. He does a lot of work here in the US for a South American cartel. Our paths crossed in New Orleans, so I had the agency find out about him. Now that I think about it, Barber handled that, which surprised me at the time. Anyway, it turned out we were aimed at the same target, so I let VanVleet take him out. Why not? He gets paid by the job. I get a salary regardless—or I used to, anyway."

"Would your knowing him help us?" Kinney asked.

"I'm not sure. He owes me, so he might want to help. He's not such a bad guy. He could've worked for the agency except he likes killing too much. For you and me, it's a job. For VanVleet, it's a calling. I guess that comes to mind because he wore a priest's outfit when I met him. He took out the target in a church—the guy's nephew was getting married. Can you believe it?"

Kinney shook his head. "That seems kind of dumb—all those witnesses."

"His employer wanted it that way to send a message to the target's brother."

"How do you know all this?" It didn't make sense to Kinney that a hitman would spill his guts about a hit.

"I had a few drinks with VanVleet afterward," Reed told him as he drove the duo back north. "We shot darts, and I won."

"Well, that's an important detail."

"Anyway, I know how to find him," Reed said.

"Did he slip you his phone number so you could go on a second date?"

"I tailed him after the mission."

"To?"

"A house in Austin, Texas. He drove there in the biggest pickup truck I ever saw."

"Why'd you tail him?" Kinney asked. He was growing frustrated by Reed's piecemeal approach to divulging information.

"Barber told me to."

"Aha."

"Aha, indeed."

"How often do you think a contractor like VanVleet is home?" Kinney asked.

"He probably makes enough that he only has to work once a month or something. So odds are he's in Austin."

****

They left late the next morning, renting a car at the Austin airport when they arrived. It didn't take long to find VanVleet. He was watering his front lawn when they drove by in the afternoon, planning to just reconnoiter. The black truck in the driveway was even more monstrous than Kinney expected.

The two-story limestone home resembled a small-scale castle, replete with narrow, vertical windows, a two-story turret, and a domed black roof. Green shutters were the only feature that said, "I won't shoot you if you knock on my door to sell Girl Scout cookies."

The lean assassin must've been in his mid-fifties, with weathered skin and the dead eyes of a less than benign sociopath—or, more likely, a psychopath. He wore a straw cowboy hat, which looked odd on him. Maybe it was his perfect, ramrod posture. Kinney associated real cowboys with slouching. VanVleet's well-worn jeans were a bit too short, and his black T-shirt proclaimed he'd eaten "five alarm chili and survived" at the Austin Chili Parlor.

"I think he made us," Reed said. "I should've worn a disguise."

VanVleet calmly strode to the spigot by his front door and shut it off. He carefully rolled up his hose and walked into the house.

"I think you're right," Kinney said. "He only watered half the lawn."

"Let's get in there before he has a chance to get ready for us," Reed said.

Kinney pulled over and ran to the front door. Reed headed around back. Kinney kicked in the door and jumped to the side as a hail of shotgun pellets poured through the doorway. Kinney and Reed weren't armed. They'd planned to acquire guns before they approached VanVleet.

"Fuck off!" VanVleet called. "Tell Barber he can eat shit!" His accent stole some of the impact from his curses.

Reed called through an open window on the back wall of the kitchen. "Hey, we're with you on that. We don't work for him anymore. Come on, man. You know me. It's Reed Bolt. Remember New Orleans?"

"Tell your friend to back off," VanVleet called back, his Dutch accent slightly less pronounced now. "I know you. I don't know him. And that was an expensive door."

"Sure. Hey, Kinney! Let me handle this. I'll meet you at the car."

"Okay."

"That's Kinney?" VanVleet asked.

"Yeah, we used to be partners at the agency."

"He's a legend."

Kinney was still in hearing range. "Why does everybody know about me?" he called back.

VanVleet ignored him as he opened the back door, still holding a sawed-off shotgun.

"Come on in," he said to Reed. "Can I get you anything?"

"Got a beer?"

"Sure," VanVleet said.

216

"Got a reason to keep aiming that gun at me?"

"I guess not," the hitman conceded. He rocked the shotgun barrel down and led Reed to the kitchen, where he placed the gun on the counter and procured two longneck bottles from a decrepit white refrigerator.

The entire kitchen could've used extensive remodeling. Or better yet, somebody ought to tear all of it out and build from scratch, Reed thought. When new, the lime green counters and cabinets wouldn't have looked out of place in a 1950s sitcom. Now they looked like Beaver Cleaver's kitchen after the whole family had become meth addicts. Every surface was filthy. The stained countertops were pitted and chipped. And it looked like a fire had broken out behind the rusty stovetop, burning a few holes in the dingy sheetrock wall.

"If we wanted to kill you, we wouldn't drive by your house," Reed told VanVleet after they sat at the faded yellow kitchen table. A band of tarnished chrome wrapped around the top edge. "You'd just be dead," Reed continued. "Anyway, we've got nothing against you. You were trying to help us out in Hawaii, right? That was you, right?"

"Yeah, I was surprised to hear you two had gotten squeamish. What kind of secret agent needs someone else to do his killing for him?"

Reed had guessed right, based on VanVleet mentioning Barber's name.

"I'm beginning to think we're not so secret," Reed responded, "but I guess that's beside the point. The thing is, Barber lied to you. I can tell by your reaction to seeing us that you don't trust him. You thought we were here because he ordered a hit on you, right?"

"Yeah, at first. But it doesn't add up. So what *are* you doing here?" He took a long swig of his beer.

VanVleet's eyes were less dead than they had been outdoors. Apparently, guests held his attention better than his lawn did. His graying hair was coarse and stood up untidily. It was the haircut of a guy who didn't give a shit how he looked. It matched his housekeeping. The hitman needed a shave to the point it was unclear if he was trying to grow a beard. Several small stubble-free patches on one of his cheeks highlighted oddly circular scars. Cigarette burns?

"We want to get to Barber," Reed told him. "Can you set it up?"

"He won't even see you now?"

Reed shrugged. "I don't think so. And we wouldn't want to do it on his terms. He must know by now that Kinney and I know things about him he doesn't want us to know."

"Maybe you should ask Kinney to come back in. Maybe he doesn't say things like 'I don't think so.' " VanVleet scowled. "Maybe he answers a question with a yes or no." He tilted his beer up and drank. Reed did, too. "I want to meet this guy anyway," the hitman finished.

"Sure."

Reed texted his partner, and Kinney joined them a minute later, marching through the open front door en route to the kitchen. The living room floor was littered with old pizza boxes and most surfaces were covered with fast food wrappers and beer bottles. Visually, it was worse than Eddie's place, but at least it didn't smell as bad.

VanVleet got another beer out and tossed it to

Kinney as the agent entered the small kitchen. "Have a seat. What's the deal with Barber?" he asked.

Kinney sat down at the table, facing the sink. "What did Reed tell you?"

"Never mind that."

"Barber's a traitor," Kinney told him.

"Why do I care about that? I'm Dutch." VanVleet said this proudly as though everyone knew the superiority of his nationality. His accent had strengthened by the time he got to the word "Dutch."

"We want to hold him accountable," Kinney told him. "Will you lose a lot of business if he's gone?"

"Hell, no. I get more work than I can take on, and the asshole doesn't pay me." VanVleet's scowl was back. "He's got proof about one of my hits. I thought about taking him out myself, but the blowback from killing someone in his position would be…let's say, inconvenient. He heads up some big spook agency, right?" He looked at Reed for confirmation.

"Yeah, but he's using his position for evil instead of good," Reed said.

VanVleet laughed. "Like in comic books. But once again, why should I care?"

"You don't have to care," Reed said, "but you owe me a favor. Just set up a meet, and we'll call it square."

VanVleet thought about that. "Two problems. Why would Barber agree to meet me? He always initiates contact from his end. And what happens if you fail? I could be on the hook for setting it up. I don't want a whole agency on my ass."

Kinney answered, his voice steely. He couldn't rely solely on his reputation to impress the hitman. "We don't fail. Ever," he told him. "And surely you can figure out how to entice Barber. You've got to be a resourceful person to do what you do." Kinney's flattery and attempt to instill confidence in his abilities seemed to be effective.

VanVleet leaned back and pursed his lips. "Well, I'd be happy to see Barber go." He looked at Kinney. "And you're Kinney."

"What am I?" Reed asked with mock hurt. "Chopped liver?"

"That's an American idiom?"

Reed nodded.

VanVleet shook his head. "It's a peculiar one."

"So what do you say?" Kinney asked.

"All right," VanVleet agreed. "Let's do it. Where? Back in California, I assume?"

"Yeah. Let Barber pick the location, so he won't think it's a trap. He must know you wish he were dead."

VanVleet nodded thoughtfully. "Yeah, he's had bodyguards with him the few times I've met him in person. How are you going to deal with that?"

"Let us worry about it," Kinney told him.

"I still don't get why you can't arrange a meet yourselves," VanVleet said.

"Look at it from Barber's point of view," Kinney said, improvising to satisfy VanVleet that they needed him. "Going into a meet planning to capture or kill two highly trained people—us—means he'd use a lot more agents than if he's just talking to someone who works for him—even you. We don't want to disable any more of his people than we have to. These were our colleagues—good people doing important jobs."

"Okay, I understand. One last thing," VanVleet

said. "Kinney, will you kick the overhead light? I want to see that. Bruce Lee did it in a movie once."

Kinney obliged, shattering shards of glass onto all of them.

"That didn't happen in the movie," VanVleet said as he picked a hunk of the bulb off his shoulder.

****

The assassin arranged for the duo to meet with Barber late in the evening the next day. "I'm leaving the country tonight under a different name for a while," he told them on the phone. "If I ever see either of you again, I'll kill you."

"Fair enough," Reed told him.

So on a Thursday at eight thirty in the evening, Kinney and Reed sat in a tree a few dozen yards from the gorilla enclosure at the San Francisco Zoo. They whispered to each other while they waited. Both wore heavy, dark sweaters and black ski caps.

"Remind me why we're here so early," Reed asked. "My butt hurts already."

"I know Barber's standard procedure. He puts his people in place an hour and a half before a meet."

"So *we're* here two hours early."

"Right."

"Why do you think Barber picked the zoo?" Reed asked.

"I'm not sure. It could be because after hours there's just that one security guard we had to get past. He looked like one of those old golfers you hate. And it's pretty isolated here. We're at the far end of a commercial neighborhood with the ocean across the street on the other side of us. Maybe it has good places to hide his men, too. After all, we found this tree easily enough."

"Yeah, about that. Do you think there's a more comfortable one?"

"No. Quit complaining. I'm enduring this, too." In fact, Kinney's butt was killing him already. If he hadn't been committed to keeping both his family and his country safe, he'd have hopped down after ten minutes.

"I think you've got a better branch than me. Does yours have bumps and rough spots?" Reed asked.

"That counts as complaining, Reed. Are you clear about the plan?"

"Sure. Where'd you get the tranquilizer dart guns?"

"I broke into the zoo last night to scout and stole them from a vet's office."

With twenty minutes to go before the meeting, after numerous whispered games of Twenty Questions and Ghost, the two men climbed down wearing their night-vision goggles. They split up and headed for where Kinney thought Barber's people would be stationed.

The first agent Kinney encountered was Barbara Foster. In the dim light, he could still see she was dressed entirely in black and had a holstered pistol on her belt. She wore black combat boots. As usual, her blond hair was tied back in a ponytail. Against standard operating procedure, her head was bowed as she studied her phone.

Rather than just shooting Foster with a dart, Kinney took a risk by stowing his goggles in his backpack and approaching her.

"Hey, Barbara. You're on this assignment, too? I was surprised to get called in at the last minute. What did I miss at the briefing?"

"You're back on the job? I'm surprised. At my place, it seemed like you wouldn't touch Barber with a ten foot pole."

"I used an eleven foot one. No, actually it's kind of on a trial basis. Barber said if I behaved myself, he might consider reinstating me as a field agent."

"And Reed?"

"He's a goner. Barber told him he's out for good."

"Well, I can't say I'll miss him."

"So…the briefing?"

"I don't know what Barber told you, but he's meeting someone really dangerous who we're going to take out. I gather he's a foreign national who's not supposed to be operating here. Gil Saunders is taking the lead on this. He's on the roof of the exhibit hall—above the Komodo dragons—with a sniper rifle. We're just backup in case something goes wrong."

"How many of us are there?"

"Let's see…you and me, Saunders, Lou Franklin over by the anteaters, and Grossman somewhere. So that's five, not counting Barber."

"Wow, this is either extreme overkill or the target is incredibly dangerous," Kinney said.

"Yeah, I was thinking the same thing."

"So where exactly is Saunders' line of fire?" Kinney asked. "I don't know the zoo that well, and I certainly don't want to get shot."

"He's over there." Foster pointed to Kinney's left. "And of course Barber's meeting the guy in front of the rhinos. Didn't he tell you where to deploy?"

"Yeah, I'm just double-checking."

Foster peered at him, her suspicion apparent on her face.

"Sorry about this," Kinney told her as he produced the dart gun and fired it into the fleshy part of her thigh. She immediately toppled since the dosage was designed for a larger species. Kinney grabbed her and gently lowered her to the asphalt.

He headed to the centrally located exhibit hall—where Saunders roosted—having put his goggles back on. He'd need to find a decent vantage point and aim the dart gun more accurately at the sniper than it was designed for. Even Kinney couldn't shoot someone from a distance with an air-powered pistol he wasn't familiar with. He was confident Reed would take out the other back-up agents.

The cantilevered roof of the chimpanzee enclosure was adjacent to the exhibit hall. There was no external means of getting up onto it; Kinney needed to break into the zookeeper's area behind the animals. The lock was no problem—not a lot of thieves were interested in animal food or cleaning products.

The chimps, on the other hand, raised a ruckus when they heard him walking across the long room to the stairs behind their enclosure. Kinney could only hope this didn't tip off Saunders that someone was coming.

When he pushed open the trapdoor at the top of the stairs and peered out, he saw the sniper leaning over the parapet at the front of the adjacent building, looking to the right to see why the animals had been stirred up.

Kinney leapt across a narrow chasm to the other roof and sprinted toward Saunders, who couldn't hear him at first because of the chattering and screaming beneath him.

As Kinney drew closer, Saunders whirled and tried

to bring up his rifle. Kinney nailed him with a dart to his gut and then had to lunge and grab Saunders' legs as the agent began to fall backward off the roof. Hauling him up took more effort than Kinney would've thought.

"Thanks, guys," he told the chimpanzees on the way out.

The next task was to get to the rhino enclosure before Barber took off. After jogging to the corner of the walkway behind Barber, Kinney found himself adjacent to the polar bear enclosure. Two of them stared up at him in the dim light as Kinney waited for Reed to show up. Since he didn't remember if bears could be noisy, he shushed them and then immediately realized how ridiculous that was. Fortunately, they didn't seem to care about him, returning to staring at one another a minute later.

Barber's hands were empty, but his black windbreaker could be concealing a small pistol. Barber also wore a black ski cap just like Kinney's, which looked out of place on him. Of course, Kinney had never seen him outside the office. Maybe he always wore one in his free time.

Barber leaned back against the guardrail of the rhino enclosure, his eyes scanning in both directions like a vigilant animal concerned about a nearby predator, which wasn't far from the truth. Other than that, his face was expressionless, as usual. He wasn't wearing his glasses and his white tennis shoes looked even more out of character than his cap.

When Reed appeared at the other end of the walkway beyond Barber, the older man pivoted to confront him. Kinney glided forward behind Barber.

"Hey, Barber," Reed called. "If you're armed, I

suggest you throw your weapon down."

"Now why would I do that?"

"Because Kinney is right behind you."

"Nice try. You've seen too many action movies. I don't know how you got in here, but there's no way both of you could've gotten past all my agents. And in case you don't know, a sniper's got you in his sights."

"No, he doesn't," Kinney said from close behind him.

"Shit," Barber said, whirling to face him. "You got to VanVleet. And you've neutralized my people. I guess I'd better—"

He threw himself to the ground, rolled, and came up with a pistol in his hand.

Kinney kicked him in the temple, rendering Barber unconscious. Then Reed shot a modified dart into his neck. With half the amount of tranquilizer, it would keep him out for an hour or so, according to what Kinney had read online.

They carried Barber back to Reed's car. Reed got stuck with the heavier top half. Kinney held Barber by the ankles.

Reed groaned. "What were you doing to those monkeys?" he asked.

"Saunders was on the roof next door. They were helping by distracting him."

"Did you tell them to do that in sign language?"

Kinney stared at him and didn't bother to reply.

****

They drove a few hundred yards to Ocean Beach, just across a major thoroughfare, and parked in a woefully small lot, which must've frustrated beachgoers. Then they walked across the beach to just shy of where mid-sized waves were lapping the sand. Reed carried Barber in a fireman's hold in case a car came by. There was a rumor in the office that Barber was afraid of water. Kinney and Reed were about to test this.

The waves grew louder as they trudged through the loose sand. Kinney sniffed the sea air, which smelled mildly fishy and quite salty. Only a few cars drove by behind them.

When Barber awakened a while later, naked, he faced Kinney and Reed on hard-packed sand with his back to the Pacific. He was already shivering. His mask of indifference was gone, and despite the dim light, the two agents were able to fully read him for the first time.

Barber's brown eyes seemed to have receded into his head, as though to help him be less present. He was in there somewhere, though, and the rest of his face reflected mild fear and slow-building defiance via raised eyebrows, a widening and tightening of his mouth, and an exaggeration of the etched vertical lines between his eyes.

"So you know the score," he said in strong, calm voice, which impressed Kinney. Barber made no effort to shield their eyes from his substantial paunch and saggy man boobs. The only body language that hinted of distress was his brief attempt to brush sand off his shrunken penis, which Reed had deliberately dragged on the beach after they'd undressed him.

"We know a lot about what you've been up to, but fill us in on the details," Kinney said. He didn't expect Barber to comply, but as his father always said: "You never know."

"Why should I?" Barber replied. "You're just

going to kill me anyway, aren't you?"

"There are a lot of different ways to die," Reed told him. "You know that."

In reality, they'd talked it over in the tree at the zoo and no longer had any intention of killing him, regardless of whether he cooperated. Government-sanctioned targets were one thing. Murdering anyone on their own say so was another. The plan was to turn him over to the CIA, where Reed's friend of a friend agreed to deal with him. There was no love lost between the two agencies.

"We were leaning toward drowning—you know, a terrible accident here at the beach," Kinney told Barber. "I've heard that's really painful, and someone told me you don't like water."

"But if you cooperate," Reed added, "you can pick the method. How about that? How many people get to decide how they die?"

At this point, a wave washed under Barber, whose teeth began to audibly chatter. Like the air, the water temperature was in the high fifties.

Kinney wore Barber's windbreaker to stay a bit warmer. The sleeves reached two-thirds of the way down his forearms. Reed had brought a black fleece hoodie to wear over his sweater. He looked a mad Russian monk who was concurrently pursuing a modeling career.

"Fine," Barber said, barking out the words as though he were in his office. "What do you want to know?"

"Who else in the agency is on Rakena's payroll?"

"No one. I assume you have Franck?"

"Who?"

"Lyle Franck."

"Yes. He spilled his guts because he thought he was talking to dead men. Next question: who in the government have you brought in or corrupted?"

Barber named names, and Reed put them into his phone. Other than Hattori, neither Kinney nor Reed had ever heard of any of them.

"Did you set me up to kill Pope?" Kinney asked.

"Yes—through Miner. When you told me your plan to fake that, I sent two independents to take out your fake ambulance drivers and sub in mine."

"Was this to get the oil off the coast there?" Reed asked Barber.

"Yes. You don't mine lithium with picks and shovels. It costs."

"Why, Barber? Why did you betray your country?" Kinney asked. It still seemed unlikely he would.

"Did you know I have to beg a roomful of ignorant asses for money for the agency every year? And these jokers are trying to shut us down—and probably will. They don't have the guts to let us do what needs doing. So where does that leave me? Living on a government pension? Relegated to some half-assed agency that tippy-toes around terrorists? It's time to get out. This was my exit strategy. There's been very little collateral damage. We kill far more civilians during operations overseas. And overall, how does it hurt our country to have one more state—an economically viable one?"

"You sound like Lyle," Kinney told him. "That's a pile of self-serving crap."

"Let's get this over with," Barber said, his teeth chattering. "I'm freezing, and the tide's coming in."

It was just like Barber to know a random fact like

that, and sure enough, a moment later a wave washed over his legs and torso. Kinncy and Reed scuttled back to stay dry.

"Any last words?" Reed asked.

"Fuck you."

A rifle shot rang out in the night air, and a spray of sand kicked up at Kinney's feet.

"Watch out!" he called to Reed, who was already lunging toward the ocean.

Since there was no cover, Kinney ran and dove into surf along with his partner as another shot sounded. Even rifle bullets lost velocity in saltwater after a few feet. They stayed down as long as their lungs let them, then peeked back toward the beach. Barber was running toward the road, where an SUV was parked under a streetlight. Even in the sand, he moved about as fast as Connelly's CEOs.

"Shit!" Reed said.

A shot hit the water near him, and he dove under again. Kinney followed suit.

Two dives later, Kinney deemed it was safe to swim to shore. There was no sign of the SUV. By now, both men were freezing, their muscles starting to seize up. A few more minutes in the ocean, laden down by their wet clothes, and that would be the end of them.

Their clothes continued to both weigh them down and keep them freezing in the cool night air as they zigzagged up the beach and then circled around to Reed's car.

"Blast the heater," Kinney said as they climbed in, his clothes dripping with seawater

"Roger that," Reed said through his own chattering teeth. "Do you think this will ruin my upholstery?"

"Probably."

"That fucker!" Apparently Barber's transgressions now included responsibility for seat damage. "Are we going to let Barber get away with this?" Reed asked. "We need to keep going with this, don't we?"

"Hell, yes I want to keep going. We're not safe, my sister's family isn't safe—even though I talked to her about disappearing for a while—and the whole deal sticks in my craw. You want to quit after all we've been through?"

"No, no. I was just checking to see where you were at. The US doesn't need some bullshit new state—not run by criminals, anyway. Where does that stop? What if they decide to annex Nebraska or something?"

"Right. Onward, MacDuff."

"Ooh, I know that one from high school English, Kinney. It's actually 'Lead on, MacDuff.' "

"I stand corrected."

Chapter 19

"So what's next?" Reed asked once they'd taken hot showers and changed clothes in the condo in Fremont where he was staying. They sat in the living room in front of a raging fire. Reed's sweatshirt and jeans were a size too large on Kinney, who couldn't have cared less at this point.

The place was decidedly upscale. It actually had two fireplaces, as well as a hot tub on its back patio. An alcove of temperature-controlled wine racks sat beside the voluminous pantry, and original landscape paintings covered a large percentage of the burnt-orange walls. Had the owners gone to the University of Texas? Kinney wondered. Why else would anyone choose that color for their walls?

"I have no idea where we go from here," Kinney said. "Where do you think Barber will go to ground? And who fired the shots?"

"I think we have a better chance of finding whoever the shooter was than we do of finding Barber," Reed said. "Then maybe the shooter'll lead us to him."

"That makes sense. Do we have enough now to take this to the FBI—to get them on it?" Kinney wondered aloud. "If Barber's on the run, that can't spook him anymore." Then he paused. "I guess we don't. Where's our hard evidence? There's just what Lyle and Barber said, and the emails Lyle showed us.

That's it."

"Couldn't the feds dig up more?" Reed asked. "Lyle named other people in Connelly's company they could interrogate, and we witnessed a lot of shit. Plus Barber just named some new conspirators. Why wouldn't the feds give weight to what we tell them? You know that Agent Kim guy, right? Can we trust him?"

Kinney thought about that, scratching his stubbled cheek for a moment. "He hates me, Reed, but I do know someone else there."

"Who's that?"

"Well, I didn't want to tell you about it because it's early on, but I've been seeing a woman who works as an analyst at the FBI."

Reed raised his eyebrows higher than Kinney had seen before. Not much truly surprised his partner these days.

"No shit? That sounds risky. What's she like? And how come you haven't blown it yet?"

"I did, but she forgave me. She's smart and sexy, and we have a lot in common." Saying this made it even more real.

"How'd you meet?"

"By chance." Kinney didn't see the need to go into that.

"Does she know anything about you? Once she finds out, you're a goner, bro."

"I told her a lot early on."

"That's nuts. And she's still hanging around?"

"I think she admired my candor," Kinney said.

"Well, she's not going to admire your body count. She's basically a cop. What were you thinking? And what kind of woman keeps dating someone like us? That's just weird. I never tell my dates anything real about myself. I say I was raised by Presbyterians in Ohio."

"It's all beside the point right now," Kinney said. "Let's stay on topic." He felt the way Barber probably did when Kinney reported to him. "I'm telling you about her because if I approach her, she might be able to get the FBI into play without compromising us."

"Why don't you go home, get some sleep, and we'll talk about this tomorrow? I can hardly think, let alone about something that I'm not sure is a good idea."

"Sure. But we can't afford to wait too long." Kinney checked his phone. "It's already one thirty, so I'll call you around ten."

"Okay."

****

After Kinney met Reed at eleven the next morning at a pancake house, discussing things with fresh, clear minds, Reed came around to Kinney's point of view. It usually worked that way. After making yet another plan, Kinney called Connelly and filled him in on what had happened. "So are you comfortable with us contacting the FBI?" he finished.

"I suppose," Connelly said. "But how can we be assured there isn't a mole in that organization, too? These people have Barber, state legislators, and several of my key employees in their pocket. Why wouldn't they cover their bases and include someone high up in the FBI?"

"I know someone I can trust," Kinney told him.

"What about his boss? Or his boss's boss? If we go this route, you need to be really careful."

"I agree. One reason I'm calling is to see if you have a better idea. You're obviously savvy, you have vast resources, so why not collaborate?"

"Let me think." Connelly took his time. Finally he spoke. "I don't have anything, unless you need me to help track Barber or discover who the beach shooter was."

"Barber is probably impossible to find. We're going to be looking into the shooter. Barber may have had an agent stationed outside the zoo who followed us. All the agents inside would've still been unconscious. If it is an agent, he wouldn't necessarily be part of the conspiracy, though. If you saw the head of your agency being kidnapped, what would you do?"

"I have no idea." Connelly paused to think again. "Why don't you try to ferret out the shooter, and then go to the feds if you need to?"

"Okay." That's what Kinney had planned, anyway. "Just cooperate with the FBI if they contact you. And if your security team can keep sniffing around Lyle's co-conspirators, maybe they'll find something useful."

"Done."

"Say hi to Rosie for me, " Reed chimed in.

"I certainly will not," Connelly told him. "Go find your own film star."

****

Kinney and Reed decided on several likely suspects—field agents who were authorized to kill bad guys, seemed temperamentally capable of shooting fellow colleagues, and were probably in the area. They waylaid the first of these since he was the lowest hanging fruit. Nate Summerson ate lunch each weekday at a Chinese restaurant near the office. He always ordered the same thing and he always sat at the same table, with his back against the rear wall of the dining area.

Kinney and Reed waited in the nearby men's room for him to appear. The one variable in Summerson's routine was when he showed up. Every few minutes, Reed poked his head out the door and checked. They'd be able to approach their quarry without him seeing them.

"He's there," he told Kinney after a few minutes. "Let's go." They came at him from both sides and then abruptly sat down across from him.

Nate Summerson looked a lot like one of the actors who'd played James Bond after Connery but before Daniel Craig. He'd once mentioned to Kinney that this held him back in the field. "I look like a spy, don't I? I mean, what people think we look like because of those stupid movies."

"Hi, guys," Summerson said cheerily. "How's it going?"

"Uh, we're fine," Reed said.

"You're not worried about seeing us?" Kinney asked.

"Why would I?" Summerson said. "You two aren't such pariahs that I can't be seen with you. Now, I mean it. How are you both doing? I've been concerned about you."

"It's been challenging," Kinney told him. "Part of it is that I thought we were way past merely being pariahs these days at the agency."

"Not that I've heard. Maybe Barber will talk about it at the all-hands afternoon meeting—zoom meeting, I mean. He didn't come in this morning."

"Did he say why?" Reed asked.

"I wouldn't know. I was prepping all morning for my next mission with Flowers. You remember Bill? Well, it turns out his daughter and mine know each other from school. What are the odds?"

"That's great, Nate. Did you see Foster or Saunders at work today?"

"Yeah. They were in Barber's office for an hour or so, along with several other agents. I guess the chief was zooming with them." He paused and scanned both of the faces across the table from him. "Why do you want to know all this? What's going on?"

"We miss everybody," Kinney told him. "You guys are like our brothers and sisters."

"And Barber's like Dad," Reed added. "We don't want to lose touch with the people we care about."

"I get that. I've wondered what it would be like to leave the agency and take a civilian job. How much camaraderie can you have poring over paperwork? Putting that aside, you two are full of shit. Don't tell me what's going on if you don't want to, but let's stop playing games."

Summerson's food arrived. The server—an older Asian woman—handed them the laminated menus she'd tucked under her meaty arm.

"I'm sorry," Kinney told her. "We have to go. This isn't James Bond, after all. I think he's in a different Chinese restaurant."

****

"It's not him," Kinney said in the parking lot.

"I agree."

They approached shooter candidate number two by his car after work. Lamar Jackson was a well-built

African-American who'd played football at Penn State. Reed had heard that he once took out six bodyguards with his bare hands en route to a drug lord in the Dominican Republic.

"What do you two clowns want?" he asked, leaning against the hood of his silver sports car with his muscular arms crossed. While not as good-looking as Reed or Summerson, Jackson could've played the second lead in an action movie. Maybe he'd get together with the female lead's best friend.

"Where were you last night?" Kinney asked.

"None of your business."

"Come on, Jackson," Reed said. "Humor us. What's the harm?"

"The harm is that I got stuck with all your chickenshit missions once you took off. You think I signed up to deliver paperwork or bodyguard some idiot whistleblower?"

"I'm sorry about that," Kinney told him, "but that's not really our fault, is it? Barber had the whole agency to pick from for scut duty and he picked you. There's some reason for that, and that's on you."

"Yeah, okay." He uncrossed his arms and grimaced. "You made your point."

"Iceland?" Reed asked. "Is that where you screwed up?"

Jackson nodded. "Will you go away if I answer your question?"

"Let's find out," Kinney suggested. "So about last night…"

"I was at a mini-golf tournament with my son. He came in third."

"And after that?"

"We went out for ice cream. I had coconut-pineapple. My son had mocha fudge. He had a cone. I had a cup. We used a total of three napkins. Happy now?" Jackson glared at Reed even though Kinney had been the one to ask him.

"And after that?"

"Look, when do want to know about?"

"Actually, between eleven and eleven thirty," Kinney told him.

He wasn't sure why Reed wasn't participating in the conversation. When he glanced at him, he looked distracted.

"I was at a bar with some guys I play softball with," Jackson said. "I'd finished my paternal duty so I treated myself to a few rounds."

"Where was this?" Reed finally asked.

"I'll tell you what. I'll text you the name of the bar, the bartender, and a couple of guys that were there. Okay?"

"Sure. That would be great," Reed said. He gave Jackson his number.

"I don't need you two on my case." He turned to Kinney. "You're the one guy I wouldn't want to meet in a dark alley."

"I could miss that with you, too."

Once Jackson drove away, Kinney and Reed talked things over as they stood on the sidewalk in a stiff wind. Both of them were tired of always sitting in a car as they discussed developments.

"I'm sure Jackson's alibi will check out," Kinney said.

"I agree, but I'll call those people later to be sure."

"Sounds good."

"How long is our prime suspect list again?" Reed asked his partner.

"We've got two more names, and then I suppose we could randomly try every agent who's not overseas if that doesn't get us anywhere."

"What if it's not an agent at all?" Reed asked.

"Then we'll definitely need the FBI's help."

The pair walked to Kinney's car and climbed in. Someone tapped the driver's side window. Kinney swiveled and spied the duo who had brought him to see Agent Kim in the auto body shop—Nick and Gary. He wondered how they'd found him. Had they staked out the street outside the agency's office as Kinney and Reed had? He rolled down his window.

"Hey," Nick said. He'd been the one with the baseball bat—the leader. "We're supposed to bring you to see Kim again. What do you say?"

"I say no."

"Come on. Let's be friends. He just wants to talk like last time."

"We're busy," Reed told him. "Fuck off."

"The thing is," Nick said, "I brought more people this time."

Two swarthy men sidled into view in front of the car and three huge ones appeared by the passenger side. Hard-looking, they'd obviously all seen their share of violence.

"We're armed, too," Gary added. "I brought an even bigger gun this time." He held up a Desert Eagle .45.

"Good for you," Kinney told him as he pushed the starter button on the dashboard. A moment later, the bumper scattered the men in front of them and they hurtled down the street.

"What was that all about?" Reed asked.

"That was a group of hired hands flunking an intelligence test again."

Unfortunately, after dropping Reed off at his place, Kinney found himself surrounded by the same crew on the walkway in front of his condo. One man was limping badly. Another held an assault rifle.

"Put that away," Kinney admonished. "If my neighbors see that, they'll call the police. And Kim won't let you kill me, anyway."

Nick nodded to the man, who reluctantly laid it on the ground—gingerly, as if it were an infant.

Once again, Kinney was struck by how much Nick reminded him of his high school teacher. They were both rangy and moved fluidly. And they both looked totally innocuous otherwise.

"So here we are," Nick said. "Do you really think you can take on seven trained fighters?"

"Yup."

"You're kinda full of yourself, aren't you, Kinney?"

"That's Kinney?" the guy with the rifle said. "*The* Kinney?"

"I'm him."

"I'm out of here. Let's go, Carlos. From what I've heard, he could take on twenty guys. My brother fought him in a tournament when he was twenty-two and Kinney was fourteen. Mario can't even hear out of one ear."

The others glanced at each other nervously as the two took off.

"Five to one is still good odds," Nick said.

Kinney slowly shook his head.

Another guy walked away.

"I've got more guys coming," Nick said unconvincingly.

Kinney snap-kicked him the neck, pivoted, and took out Gary with a sidekick to the outside of his knee.

"That might require surgery," he told him.

Nick and Gary lay still.

"Holy shit," one of the remaining men said.

"I'm going to give him a try," another one said as he shuffled forward.

This twenty-something guy was wiry and taller than the others. Ruddy-faced, with curly dirty blond hair, he wore two gold signet rings that would do damage if he landed any decent punches. Kinney could tell by his stance and the particular way he balled his fist with an extended knuckle that the man was an accomplished martial artist. For a moment, Kinney pondered the use of the word "artist" in conjunction with "martial." It suddenly seemed odd to him. Then the man lashed out with a back fist, which Kinney ducked.

He knew there'd be a follow-up and likely a rehearsed maneuver after that. Most fighters learned sequences as opposed to constructing choreography on the fly.

Kinney blocked a roundhouse kick destined for his midsection and then swept the man's lead foot as he planted it to follow up with a straight right punch to Kinney's crotch.

Kinney's opponent stumbled but didn't fall, balancing on his rear foot for a moment. The remaining man attacked Kinney from the rear, so he pivoted and punched him in the throat. That was the end of that threat. There was no defense against extreme quickness.

In the meantime, the first fighter had gathered himself and now launched a series of strikes designed to open up a gap for a coup de grâce kick to Kinney's chin. If Kinney blocked the flurry of punches in a standard manner, it would've worked. His arms would be spread.

Instead, he grabbed the man's fist alongside his head and twisted, throwing the man off-balance. Then he launched a counterattack. On the defensive, the man backed away and ducked his head, which Kinney anticipated. He leapt to his feet, brought his leg up over the man's head, and struck downward with his heel. This was a move he'd invented himself.

The man went down and didn't get up. Nick did, tipping to one side as he struggled to stay on his feet.

"Nick, get these people out of here," Kinney commanded. "Drag them off if you need to. If you don't, you'll be the next one in the hospital."

"Okay, okay." He held up his hands, nodding furiously.

Kinney walked in his condo and texted his neighbors:

—I'm sorry we needed to practice our karate out front this evening. Our dojo is undergoing fumigation. Don't worry about the men who seem to be unconscious. We like to play act to make our sessions more realistic. Thanks for your patience.

Oh, if you called 911, you can call back and tell them it's a false alarm

Kinney—

A policeman knocked on his door ten minutes later,

anyway. He was young, with a 70s-style mustache and a wrinkled uniform. He looked like he'd just finished getting dressed after performing a scene in a vintage porn film.

"Sir, a disturbance was reported at this address."

"Really? A disturbance?"

"Yes, sir. A man driving by reported that someone who fits your description was involved in a physical altercation." He spoke with a slight stammer, pausing before certain words.

"Oh, I know what happened. My friends and I were practicing karate out front. I guess it looked pretty realistic. If you look for blood, you won't find any. I think that tells the story here. You can check with my neighbors if you want. The woman in 108 probably watched us. She sees everything and then tells everyone about it."

"I know what you mean. We have a neighbor like that across the street. It drives my wife crazy. I'll check it out. Sorry to disturb you."

Kinney had been careful not to hit anyone in a manner that was likely to cause bleeding. Mostly, because it was hard to clean up—who needed bloodstains on their clothes? The whole punch in the nose thing was such a cliché, anyway. In real life, if you didn't hit someone just right and drive the cartilage up into the sinus cavity, it just pissed people off and they kept coming.

The cop didn't return. Kinney chugged a beer and replied to an email from his college roommate about a supposedly fun friend of his who was not only single, but "quite ready for a bit of the old in and out." Aldo had spent his senior year abroad in England.

Then Agent Kim called. "Kinney, what's your problem?"

"You are, Kim. Here we are on the phone. Why didn't you just call me this time? Didn't you learn anything from when you tried this before?"

"The first time, they brought you in."

"Because I let them."

"Whatever you say. How about you come down to headquarters and we work this out?"

"Work what out?"

"There have been problematic Kinney sightings lately—at places with gunshots."

"Like where?"

"Ocean Beach up in the city, for one."

"The only person who could've recognized me there was the one who shot at me. Take a good look at your witness."

"To be honest, it was an anonymous tip you just confirmed." Kim's tone was positively smarmy.

"Rats! Outsmarted again! When will I ever learn?"

"Joke all you want. If you're innocent, why wouldn't you want to come in and talk?"

"There's a mole in our agency, and there may be one in yours, Kim. The one in ours might try to frame me, so perhaps a visit to your office would be more permanent than I'd like."

Kim thought that over. "If I wanted to arrest you, I wouldn't have sent those idiots. I don't think you'd attack a squad of federal agents, would you?"

"Probably not," Kinney conceded.

"Well, while I've got you on the phone, can you tell me what the hell is going on?"

Kinney thought for a while about this. Was there

truly an advantage to going through Georgia instead of Kim? He decided there was. It was definitely less risky.

"Well?" Kim asked.

"I'm sorry, it's above your pay grade."

Kim sighed. "I'll find out one way or the other, Kinney. We don't have to be adversaries here. We're all on the same side, aren't we?"

"Certainly. I've told you what I could. Knowing we have a mole and that you might have one too is important, isn't it?"

"Yes. Thank you for that."

Not ten minutes after the digital version of hanging up, Barbara Foster called.

"Get out of there!" she shouted. "Hoff is coming after you. Barber's orders. I tried to stop him."

"Thanks. Bye."

Kinney slipped out his patio door after retrieving a pistol from under a floorboard. It occurred to him that Foster might've been acting on Barber's orders to flush him out into the open, but on balance it seemed more likely that she knew he didn't deserve to die. After all, he was the one who had organized the bowling party for her thirtieth birthday. And at the party, he'd taught her how to play the kazoo. Would someone want to help kill the man who'd introduced her to the wonders of amplified humming?

Kinney still had no urge to eliminate Hoff or anyone else. Avoid him or disable him—sure. But even when someone was trying to kill him, Kinney did not want to kill him back. Gun in hand, he could visualize shooting Hoff in the shoulder. That was it.

Hoff had brought a friend. The man stepped out from behind a tree at the edge of Kinney's tiny yard while his back was momentarily turned.

"Hold it right there, buddy. Drop that gun," the man said. It was too dark to see his face, but it was clear he was huge—power forward huge. Kinney's first thought was that the Warriors could use a guy like that to improve their rebounding. The human monolith held a pistol.

"How do you know my name?" Kinney asked in a squeaky, friendly voice as he tossed his pistol to his feet. "I'm Buddy Gillespie. What's your name?" He strode forward with his hand extended, confusing the man.

Hoff sprinted around the side of the building. "Back away, Jimmy. Let me handle this."

"Sure." The man retreated back to his tree.

Kinney turned to find Hoff aiming a shotgun at him. The light spilling out through the patio doors highlighted his distinctive crooked nose.

"I suppose you've got the kind of load in there that'll cut me in half," Kinney said.

"I sure do." He fondled the gunstock and glowered. "Tell me why I shouldn't kill you where you stand right now."

"Barber's dirty. He's in league with a group that's trying to muscle in on Guyana oil and start a new state to mine lithium."

Kinney was surprised he could sum up the conspiracy in two sentences. Being held at gunpoint—shotgun point, at that—seems to have sharpened Kinney's mind.

Hoff took a few moments to take that in. "You have proof?" His tone demonstrated his skepticism. He knew the same as Kinney did that people will say anything to save themselves.

"Reed knows about it, too," Kinney told him, which was the first thing he could think of. His sharp mind was becoming duller.

"That doesn't mean anything."

"Ryan Connelly knows—and he probably has proof of some of it by now. You know who he is, right?"

"The billionaire?"

Kinney nodded.

"Isn't he dating Rosie Aubert?" Hoff's eyes lit up. He was a fan.

"That's the guy," Kinney told him, smiling now. He was getting traction in the conversation. "We saw her boobs up at his house," he added.

"Really? What did you think?" Hoff asked.

"They're superb. I think Reed fell in love."

"Kinney, you're either a really creative liar or there's something to your story."

Kinney nodded his agreement. "I guess those are the two choices here. Would you really kill me without checking things out? I know Barber sent you, but what I'm telling you is that you can't trust him."

"So what'll we do?"

"I can call Connelly."

"Anyone can say they're him," Hoff pointed out. "That's as useless as your partner lying for you."

Kinney pondered that. He knew he had to come up with something that would pause Hoff in fulfilling his assignment. "We can drive up to his place in the Santa Cruz mountains," he told him. "You can talk to him yourself. Hey, maybe Rosie will be there, too."

"Rosie, huh? You're on a first name basis?"

"Sure. You'll like her. She's a lot of fun."

Kinney could see Hoff trying to make up his mind.

"I've got rope and duct tape in my condo," Kinney added. "I'll let you immobilize me. If I'm bullshitting you, you'll find out soon enough. Just let me call first to make sure this is okay with Connelly."

"Go ahead."

Kinney pulled his phone out and put it on speaker, holding it at arm's length in Hoff's direction. "Ryan? It's Kinney. There's a guy here to kill me on Barber's orders. Can we come up there so you can verify Barber's the bad guy here?"

"Sure."

"Is Rosie there?"

"Yes. What does that matter?"

"I think the guy would appreciate seeing her breasts."

Connelly laughed. "I'm sure he would. See you in a while. Text me when you're at the gate."

"Right."

Trussed like a particularly ornery hog in Hoff's back seat, Kinney endured an uncomfortable drive to Connelly's estate. Hoff left his huge colleague back in Scotts Valley.

The billionaire was waiting for them under the vast portico fronting the main house. Hoff took a minute to compare the photo he had on his phone to the man outside before he disembarked. Connelly's distinctive long face with its chiseled cheeks and alert brown eyes was clearly illuminated under two floodlights.

Their host strode forward. "You must be our would-be assassin. I'm Ryan Connelly." He held his hand out, and Hoff shook it. "Is that our mutual friend tied up back there? Is that really necessary?"

"Not now. Let me get him. By the way, I voted for you. You're a good man."

As soon as Kinney could get to his phone, he called Reed and told him to get out of the condo to somewhere even safer. "I'll call you later," he added.

"Okay."

The threesome trooped into the house, where Rosie greeted them from a modern chrome-framed loveseat in the vast living room. She wore an oversized baby blue terrycloth robe with black cowboy boots. Her hair was whirled on top of her head like a soft-serve ice cream cone.

"Welcome to our home," she said in her cute accent as she stood. "Can I get you some drinks? Who's your friend, Kinney?"

"This is Hoff."

"Another one-name guy, huh?"

"It's Curtis Hoff, actually," the agent told her. "I love your movies."

"Thank you. Which one do you like best?"

"Uh, well. To be honest, it's about having the opportunity to look at you for a couple of hours. So they all worked for me. And you're even more beautiful in person."

Rosie smiled and looked at Connelly. "I like this guy. Are you sure he's a bad person?"

"I'm not," Hoff asserted. "It appears as though there's been a misunderstanding."

Rosie left to get the drinks no one had asked for. Once everyone else seated himself around a glass coffee table, Kinney glanced around the room, curious to see what an unlimited budget could buy.

The walls were vertical maple planks, which Kinney had never seen before. They stretched up seamlessly to a soaring flat ceiling boasting a huge pastel-colored mural à la Diego Rivera. Instead of farmworkers, the somewhat impressionistic figures in the mural were idealized tech workers in oversized cubicles. That is, they weren't nearly as nerdy-looking as the ones Kinney had ever seen.

Otherwise, the room was sumptuous along more conventional lines, with modern furniture here and there, a few marble statues of Greek or Roman gods, an immense tapestry with unicorns in a corral, and colorful cubist paintings along the far wall.

Kinney had no doubt the statues originated from ancient times, the tapestry had been woven in the Middle Ages, and several Picassos were in the mix on the wall.

"So," Connelly began, gazing at Hoff, "I presume Kinney told you that Barber has conspired with others to commit murders and several other major crimes?'

"It's true?"

"Absolutely. Let me show you a few things."

Connelly had been busy wresting information out of the conspirators who worked for him and had also found an electronic trail to present to the FBI if need be. Hoff was convinced after a brief perusal of the material.

"Here you are," Rosie said as she returned with a tray of strange-looking drinks. Each oversized shot glass held three colored layers—red on the bottom, green above it, and then blue on top.

"What are those?" Ryan asked as she sat down next to Connelly.

"I call it *la couleur primaire speciale*. I invented it

myself. Where's that Reed guy, anyway?"

Everyone took a glass from Rosie's tray, took a sip, and then hurriedly put their drink down.

"He's somewhere safe, I hope," Kinney told her.

"I love the whole homoerotic subtext with you two," she said."

Hoff laughed.

Kinney stared at her. "What makes you say that?"

"Oh, don't worry. It's only obvious to someone like me. You have a bromance. It's like one of those buddy cop movies, only you're something else besides cops. Spies, I guess. How about you, Curtis? Are you a spy?"

"More or less."

"Tell me all about it. This is very exciting."

"Rosie," Connelly said. "We're going to need to talk about some other things now."

"Oh, peuh." She jumped to her feet and stalked out.

"I hope we didn't upset her too much," Hoff said, his brow wrinkled. Upsetting a goddess? Not a good idea.

"Don't worry. Rosie's an actress. It's all about entrances and exits with her. She knew she'd need to leave."

The three men plotted and planned for an hour. As Kinney and Hoff got up to leave, Connelly gave Kinney a thumb drive with the evidence his men had discovered. Kinney would call Georgia in the morning and arrange a meeting. It didn't feel safe to send any information electronically. She was probably wondering why she hadn't heard from him, anyway.

Reed would interview the remaining two agents on their suspect list. Armed with the resources of the agency, Hoff would look into Alan Kim. The timing of the agent's intervention was fishy. Why was he suddenly so interested in Kinney again? And using off the books lackeys—twice now—was certainly suspicious.

Hoff drove Kinney to his own house in Los Gatos. "If I'm going to tell Barber I couldn't find you, you need to be somewhere he'd never look. Do you like dogs?"

"No, I love them. Every single one."

"Herbie can be hard to love," Hoff told him.

"Why's that?"

"You'll see."

Chapter 20

Herbie was a handful—a basset hound with canine ADHD. His favorite activity was trying to trip people, and his breath was abominable. On the other hand, he was a dog, not a screaming toddler.

Hoff lived alone in a gaily painted Craftsman house on a quiet residential street that paralleled the main drag in the upscale community just over the mountains from Kinney's place in Scotts Valley.

"I inherited my home and Herbie from my parents," he explained. "Just over a year ago."

"It's lovely."

It probably would've been if the interior hadn't been littered with American flags, military memorabilia, and shelves holding marksmanship trophies. Also, it was cold in the house. Quite cold.

Kinney called Reed and explained what had happened. It occurred to him that he was having to do that a lot lately. And the explanations had grown increasingly unlikely.

"So Hoff's with us now?" Reed asked. "And maybe Foster? She didn't have to call you about him, did she?"

"Yes to Hoff. I'd guess Barbara drew the line at killing me. I don't think we can count on her for any other help. We'll see."

"That's great about Hoff. He ought to be able to

keep us in the loop about agency stuff. Are you sure he isn't in on Barber's deal, though? They're close."

"He would've followed orders and killed me if he was," Kinney told him.

"Maybe he just said that he was supposed to do that, and his real mission was to find out what we know by going undercover with us."

"I suppose that's a possibility—good thinking, Reed— but I read him as a sincere patriot type. You should see all the flags he has at his house. And he trusted Connelly right away because he voted for him."

"That's where you are? At Hoff's house?"

"Yeah."

"So what's next?" Reed asked.

Kinney filled him in on the plans, including Reed's initial role—to vet the two remaining suspicious agents on their list. "We still need to find who was the beach shooter in case that helps us find Barber," he added.

"Gotcha."

"Where are you?" Kinney asked.

"At an undisclosed location."

Kinney frowned. "We're using burner phones, right?"

"You can't be too careful. Barber might have access to the NSA, and God knows what they're capable of."

"Okay, fine. Let's stay in touch."

In Hoff's guest room, which was mercifully free of medals, helmets, and basset hounds, Kinney called Georgia.

"Where the hell have you been?" she asked, raising her voice as she spoke.

"Crazy busy. I'm sorry."

"I left you multiple voicemails, not that I'm desperately lonely or something. It's just that I've got some information for you."

"I switched to another burner phone," Kinney told her. "My last one is sitting at the bottom of the Lexington Reservoir. I tossed it out of my car as I drove down the mountain. So what's up?"

"Alan Kim is on the warpath, and you're in his sights."

"I'm aware of that. Do you know why?"

"He says you left your agency and you're involved in something big—something criminal. He asked me to look into you. He said you're a dangerous sociopath."

Kinney couldn't tell if Georgia was buying this. "I hope you don't believe him," he said.

"Why shouldn't I?"

"Reed and I pretended to quit our agency so we could infiltrate an organization that's ordered several murders and is corrupting state legislators. I told you that before—well, some of it. I'm actually calling to arrange a meeting with you so I can hand over proof about who's involved. It's time for your agency to get on this, and I don't trust Kim or some random agent. I think it's wise to avoid an electronic trail, for that matter."

"This could be a trap. You're asking me to trust an admitted sociopath who just found out an FBI analyst has been tasked with investigating him."

"I am." Kinney didn't know what else to say. Either she would or she wouldn't.

"Okay," Georgia agreed.

"That's it. You'll meet?"

"Sure. I just wanted to see how you'd react if I said

that."

Kinney wasn't angry. Mostly, he was relieved. But he reasoned that a normal person would be pissed, so he injected some intensity into his voice. "I don't play those kinds of games with you, Georgia."

"No, you just withhold information. I'd say we're even."

"Okay, fine," he said curtly. He decided that was enough play acting. "When and where can you meet?" Kinney asked.

"Why don't you come over to my place?"

"Now?"

"Yes. If you can."

"It's late and I'm tired." As Kinney said this, he suddenly felt exactly that. A moment ago, he just hadn't wanted to see her.

"Fine," Georgia agreed, but Kinney could hear the disappointment in her voice. "Come around seven thirty tomorrow and I'll make you breakfast."

"Sounds good. Do you know who to bring our info to—who you can trust?"

"Yes. A friend of mine is actually quite a few rungs up the ladder from me. He's a good guy."

"Does he try to trip people? How's his breath?" Kinney was thinking about Herbie the basset hound, who had waddled into the guest room and was snuffling Kinney's socks at that moment.

"What?"

"Never mind."

****

Hoff took off before Kinney woke up. His note on the interior of the front door said he worked out at his gym before heading to the office, and Kinney should make himself at home and not kick Herbie, however much he was tempted to.

Kinney scooped up the basset and went nose to nose with him. "If you can stand me, I can stand you," he told him, weathering the foul odor.

Herbie tried to wriggle free, so Kinney lowered him before he plunged onto the polished oak floor. Herbie immediately tried to trip him.

When Kinney left the house after a long, hot shower, with the thumb drive Connelly had given him, he realized his car was back at his condo. Fortunately, there was an Uber driver only five minutes away, so he arrived on time for breakfast at Georgia's. He'd Uber to a rental car office after that. Chances were, his condo and car were being watched.

"Let's eat first," Georgia suggested after kissing him more perfunctorily than he would've liked.

"Sure."

Georgia's oversized green sweater sat above a matching mid-length skirt. Her slippers were fuzzy red boats. Kinney hadn't noticed before how big her feet were, but they were whoppers. Her recently brushed brown hair hung down to her shoulders, and her eyes glittered. Despite the uninspired kiss, she was excited to see him.

"I just need to scramble the eggs," Georgia reported. "Everything else is ready."

True to her word, by the time the eggs were done, the toast was cold, as were the hash browns. Somehow, en route from the frying pan to the table, even the eggs had cooled down. Kinney figured the salsa on top of them had been in the fridge.

Neither of them spoke as they wolfed down the

meal.

"You eat like me," Georgia said when they were through. "Caveman-style."

"I missed some meals yesterday. But yeah, my sister and I used to compete to see who could finish first."

"Why?" Georgia asked.

"Mostly to minimize my dad's oratory."

"Oratory?"

"Pontification. Pedanticism. Stupifying lectures."

"Kind of similar to showing off one's human thesaurus capabilities?"

Kinney smiled. "Exactly."

"So let's head over to my desk and see what you've got."

Kinney followed her there, picturing what was under her clothes as her hips swayed seductively. His internalized feminist chided him, comparing him to Reed, which stopped him in his tracks.

After Georgia had read it all and Kinney elaborated and answered her questions, she asked him why he hadn't just killed Barber at the beach and ended things once and for all.

"You think that's me—a stone cold murderer? I told you I was through with that. It was never our plan to kill Barber. Well, only for a while."

Georgia turned to face him and pushed a stray strand of hair behind her ear. "Kim says you're back in black ops."

"I hate that phrase. It's so racist," Kinney joked in an effort to lighten the mood.

"I think it comes from redacting paperwork," Georgia explained as if he'd been serious.

"I used to do whatever it took to carry out a mission, Georgia. That's true. But like I just told you, I had a near-death experience and now I won't kill anybody. I'm beginning to think you don't listen very closely."

"What about Reed?"

"He's fine with it, but look at who Barber is. Taking him out would be way worse than killing a cop. He keeps US senators on speed dial. And who would be the main suspects if something happened to him? Our lives would be ruined. We pretended we were going to kill Barber to get information from him. That's it. I want to see him rot in prison—one of those nasty ones where gangs run things."

"Well, it looks like you've given me enough for a federal indictment for him, anyway." Her voice was oddly tentative, contrary to her words.

"That's great," Kinney said. Tuned in to her tone, he said this as a default response as he thought about the ambivalence she seemed to be expressing.

Georgia continued, her voice softer now. "You, Reed, and Connelly would have to testify. Would that wreck your career? I mean, you're supposed to keep a low profile, right? How could you do your work if people know who you are?"

"A surprising amount of people have heard of me, actually," Kinney told her. He still didn't understand how that could happen. Was the agency's mole leaking information? "I'm beginning to think it's time for a change, anyway," Kinney added, realizing this for the first time.

"I have a confession," Georgia said. "I heard rumors for years about this super fighter named Kinney.

When I discovered who you might be from facial recognition, it primed me to ignore the whole sociopath thing. I'm glad I did."

Kinney thought about his own early doubts about Georgia—the Princeton reference. He decided not to mention this. Why jeopardize anything by sharing a potentially insulting perspective?

"Say, could you show me a few kicks?" Georgia asked. "I'd love to see you in action."

"Here? Now?"

"Yes."

"Are any of your knickknacks expendable?"

Georgia looked around her home office. "Well, that little wooden cat—"

Kinney lashed out a foot and blasted the cat into orbit. When it bounced off the ceiling, he kicked it with his other foot into the hallway as it fell.

Georgia gasped. "I can't believe I just saw that. It happened so fast."

The cat sat unbroken on its haunches on the carpet outside the door, peering at them.

"It's a sturdy little fella," Kinney said, grinning.

"You kept it intact on purpose, didn't you? That's amazing."

"It's too bad I don't get to fight wooden cats out in the world."

"I wish I could've seen that in slow motion," Georgia said.

"I'll give that a try if you want, but I can't guarantee your knickknack's safety."

"No, no. I need to go to work and get going on this. Let's stay in touch."

"Of course."

A passionate goodbye kiss led to a satisfying interlude in Georgia's bed behind the desk. Neither of them bothered to take all their clothes off.

****

After an inordinate amount of time at a busy rental car office, Kinney drove his Korean hatchback to Eddie Sullivan's—their tech guy. En route, he realized he should've revisited him a lot sooner. He could've helped with several aspects of the situation.

Eddie was, of course, parked in front of one of his monitors, a half-opened package of cookies beside his mouse. Since Kinney's last visit, he'd inexpertly assembled a Swedish-looking file cabinet, which squatted next to the long oak table he used as a desk. All its angles were wonky, especially the top, which slanted forward. The immaculate blond surface contrasted sharply with the rest of the room. Kinney gave it a day before it became littered with God knows what, assuming trash didn't simply slide off it.

"Hey," Eddie said, looking up briefly. "Let me just finish bidding on these ski boots."

"You ski?"

"No. I might take it up at some point, though. You never know. Anyway, I made a program that puts in a barely winning bid a half second before the auction closes. I just have to activate it at the right time…There. Done."

Eddie turned to where Kinney stood on a popsicle wrapper which sat on top of a paper bag. His towering pompadour turned with him. The wrapper had been the most appetizing patch of real estate in the room this time.

Eddie nodded, his oversized, round head tilting up

and down on its own like the bobblehead doll Kinney had been given for being one of the first ten thousand fans at a Warriors game. Eddie's amber eyes didn't move with it.

"What can I do for you?" Eddie asked.

"I need you look into an FBI agent—Alan Kim. He operates out of San Jose."

Although he'd tasked Hoff with looking into this, Kinney wanted to see what Eddie could discover as well.

"Anything in particular you want to know about him?"

He ticked off a list on his fingers. "Financials, known associates, life situation, duties within the agency—things like that."

"Okay."

"Also, see if anyone's talking about me online. Lately, I keep running into people who know about me."

"There are a lot of Kinneys in the world," Eddie pointed out. "Do you really not have a first name?"

"I don't think it's anywhere online, but I'll tell you if you promise never to share it with anyone. It's possible it might help you."

"Scout's honor." Eddie held up two fingers of his own, one short of the actual Boy Scout salute.

"You were never a scout, were you?"

"For a week and a half. Then they made us march around like we were in the goddamn army. Fuck that. It's just an expression, Kinney. You can trust me."

"My first name is Clarence."

"Oh, my God. Clarence! That's the worst." Eddie patted the side of his hair as though his loud declaration might've jarred his pompadour out of place.

"Thanks. That's very kind." Kinney wasn't actually hurt by this or pretty much anything. He didn't care what other people thought about him if he wasn't sleeping with them.

"I'm just saying."

"One more thing, Eddie. Look into Georgia Hale. I already know about her work situation. I'm more interested in personal stuff. She's from Shreveport if that helps. You don't need to go too deep with her. I just like to know a little more about who I'm dating than someone's likely to tell me."

"That's creepy, but okay. Is she hot?" Eddie asked, leaning forward and raising his eyebrows.

"Unless your standards are based on upscale porn, yes."

"They are, actually. I only watch the cream of the crop," Eddie told him, pride on his wide face.

"Pun intended?" Kinney asked.

"Huh?"

"Never mind. How long will all that take?"

"You can hang around if you want preliminary stuff," Eddie told him. "Otherwise, I don't know. It depends."

"Okay. I'll be out on your front porch. Text me when you have something worth my enduring the stench in here."

"Don't be ridiculous. It's fine in here."

Kinney relaxed in Eddie's mint condition webbed lawn chair, replete with a matching drink holder and features you just can't find in other inferior brand-name chairs. In a corner of the wide porch, he listened to conjunto music with his earbuds and remembered dancing to Flaco Jimenez with his high school girlfriend at a club outside Richardson, Texas.

Kinney found it odd that just saying his first name out loud to Eddie could take him back all those years. He rarely reminisced. For one thing, because of his work, his past was littered with activities no one would want to remember. And growing up hadn't been a barrel of laughs, either.

Eventually, Eddie texted.

"So what did you find out?" Kinney asked as he stood on the wrapper again.

"Kim checks out. There's nothing weird about the guy himself. But someone was in the FBI site before me, and they played around with it. It'll take me a while to sort that out. So I don't trust what there is to find out about Kim, Georgia Hale, or anyone else there. Whoever messed with the data is a damn good hacker. They covered their tracks about as well as I could. In fact, that probably means it's someone I know. I'll ask around."

"What about me?" This was actually what mattered the most to Kinney at that point. If his identity was blown, he couldn't operate the same way anymore.

"It turns out you're a legend, or maybe a rumor. People all over the world talk about this guy who beat them up, or killed someone they know, or just kicked people faster than anyone's ever seen. Some of them say his name is Kinney, or Kingsley, or McKinley, or whatever. And there's a video of you fighting in a tournament when you were a teenager. Man, I never saw anything like it, and I watch a lot of martial arts movies."

"Just the best ones, I'm guessing."

"Absolutely. There's an obscure Chinese streaming site that's curated by this kung fu master. I can turn you on to it if you want. We'll need to reconfigure your computer."

"That's okay."

"Is all that stuff true, Kinney? I mean you guys talk tough with me sometimes, but you always seemed like a nice guy. Reed can be a dick. I can see him offing people. But you?" He glanced up to where Kinney's face loomed above him.

"Let it go, Eddie. Just be happy we're not enemies."

The hacker nodded. "Will you kick something for me?"

"No."

"Okay. As far as this Georgia woman goes, there's not much out there on her. It's like she's kept a low profile on purpose."

"As I failed to do, apparently."

"The good news about you is that no one knows where you live or anything like that. And you look a lot different than you did in that old video. For that matter, I had to work really hard to find it. Did you try to get rid of it?"

"Our tech guy did."

"I thought *I* was your tech guy, Kinney." Eddie frowned and glared at Kinney.

"I mean at work."

Eddie looked up, interested again, his hurt gone. "You guys have jobs? There's some place that's okay with the shit you pull?"

"We're getting pretty sideways of our focus here, Eddie."

"Yeah, okay. So Georgia was the valedictorian of her high school class in Shreveport, Louisiana. After she graduated, she took a few years off, and I couldn't find out anything about that. Then she went to Rice on a scholarship."

"Academic?" Kinney asked. He could see it. Georgia was truly quick-witted.

"Softball. She could hit the ball a mile. She still holds the home run record there. Then she moved to New Mexico, and I don't know what she did there. The next thing I could find out is that she's in California being an analyst at a bank, and then at the FBI office in San Jose. According to their doctored website and the internal stuff I've been able to access so far, she works in the same department as Kim. But I don't know how accurate that is. Is any of that significant?"

"I already knew most of it, but thanks, Eddie. I appreciate what you do for me."

Eddie beamed and smiled. "Well, that's it for now. I'll text you when I get more."

"Thanks."

"Are you sure you won't kick anything? What about that pile of…Well, I don't know what it is, but it looks soft."

"Nope. Let me write you a check."

"Sure."

Chapter 21

Kinney met Reed at a taqueria in Santa Clara. Since they were the only ones there, Kinney figured it probably wasn't the best dining choice. Reed always ordered fish tacos at taquerias, and then loaded on the hottest salsa available, so it didn't matter much to him what his food originally tasted like. The decor in the taqueria consisted of Day of the Dead paintings and pottery—colorful skulls and skeletons, for the most part. Kinney had a fondness for that genre ever since a vacation in Oaxaca.

"So here's the deal," Reed told Kinney. "We got lucky. It turns out both Kaiser and Hernandez were working together on a mission up this way."

"Those are the two guys left on our shooter list?"

"Yeah, they were supposed to bring in some software guy. I followed them from the office, and their target wasn't where they'd been told—typical, right?—so I climbed into their backseat as they were leaving, and we had a chat."

"They were forthcoming?" Kinney was surprised. He didn't know these two agents well, but why would they share anything with Reed?

"Well, we chatted while I held a gun on them," Kinney's partner told him. "I think my reputation as an indiscriminate shooter preceded me. Kaiser was pretty scared. Hernandez is tougher. I could've had a howitzer, and he wouldn't have flinched."

"What did they have to say for themselves?"

"They both had alibis for when we had Barber on the beach. I checked them out. Neither one shot at us."

"They're airtight alibis?"

Reed nodded.

"On to phase two," Kinney said with a sigh. "I guess you need to try other, less likely agents."

Reed took a bite of his lunch, spilling taco guts all over his bright yellow plate. "Why don't you call Connelly and see if he's found out anything new that might lead us in a different direction."

"Good idea," Kinney agreed, while he tried to cut an enchilada with the edge of his fork. It seemed to squirm to avoid being eaten. He gave up and punched Ryan's number into his phone.

Rosie answered on the second ring. "*Bonjour*."

"Hi, it's Kinney. Is Ryan there?"

"He's in the shower. How are you?"

"Fine. And you?"

"*Très bien*. I got a callback for one of those super-duper films—you know, where everyone flies around and kabooms the bad guys. I'd be the one who can turn people into animals."

"That's great. I can think of some good candidates for that."

"Oh, I don't think I'll get to choose who I do it to. Hey, Kinney, you never told me if you liked my special drink."

"That's true." Kinney racked his brain for something positive to say. "It was very creative. How did you make the layers?"

"It's a secret. Oh, here's my beloved now. Ryan!"

she called. "It's Kinney."

"Say hi for me," Reed told Kinney.

He did. Rosie told him to say hi back. Then Ryan got on the line.

"Kinney, my team says Kim checks out, but there's a guy named Curtis Hoff whose name came up. He looks like trouble. He may be some sort of operative like you—maybe for another agency."

"It's okay. We convinced him to work with us."

"Really?"

"I think we can count on him. If not, I'd be dead by now. Anyway, have you discovered anything else significant?"

"I'm waiting to hear back from my guys, but they think the remaining conspirators have taken off for parts unknown."

"So nothing about the mole in our agency or the shooter on the beach?"

"No, my guys don't have access to the world you live in, Kinney, although one of them said he heard you're an amazing kicker. I presume he wasn't talking about punts or penalty kicks."

"No."

Once Kinney ended the call, he read the text that had come in from Eddie.

—*Come on back*— it read. —*I need to show you something. I know who hacked into the FBI*—

"That was fast," Kinney remarked to Reed, who was busy stuffing the last bite of his last taco into his mouth. Salsa dripped from the corner of his mouth on top of the beans and cheese sludge on his plate. "It's Eddie," Kinney explained.

He texted back, and then Kinney and Reed headed

over to Eddie's after Kinney conquered his slippery, surprisingly tasty meal.

Reed stood by a window he opened in Eddie's living room. Kinney once again braved the dimly lit interior and the popsicle wrapper.

"Look at this," Eddie said. The two men tiptoed around the vast desk. Eddie brought up a completely incomprehensible schematic filled with coding and terms that were unfamiliar to them. "Pretty cool, huh? This is what chromepizza4 came up with. She's radical."

"Eddie, you must know we can't make any sense out of that," Kinney told him. "For that matter, don't bother explaining it. Just tell us who did it." He and Reed retreated to a safe distance in front of Eddie. The odor near the hacker was almost too horrible to endure.

"I did tell you. Chromepizza4."

"And who is that?"

"Ah, that was the hard part. It turns out she's part of a team that's for hire—the Wilder Bunch. I know most of them and scaryfatguy told me her real name's Sue Exeter in exchange for eighty thousand points in Slave Rescue 3. She's the only one capable of this. It's exquisite hacking. I think I'm in love." A dreamy look came into his eyes, and he half smiled like a rockabilly Buddha.

"Can you contact her and see who hired her?" Kinney asked. "We also need to know what the site looked like before she got to it."

"I can do that last part right now. Nothing really disappears online. As far as who she's working for, she wouldn't tell me."

"You talked to her?"

"We texted."

Reed spoke up. "Maybe she'll tell us."

Eddie shook his head and scowled. "After you beat her up or something? No way."

"Mostly, we just scare people," Kinney told him. "And if we explain why we need to know, I'll bet she'd cooperate."

"Where is she?" Reed asked with a bit of menace in his tone.

"I don't know. Yet. But I'm not sure I want to tell you when I find out."

"I asked you nice, Eddie," Reed said.

"You're sure you won't hurt her?"

"Scout's honor," Kinney told him.

"All right, then. When I know…"

"Now let's see the FBI site from a while ago," Kinney requested. "From before Exeter hacked it."

"How far back?"

"I don't know. What do you think, Reed?"

"Maybe three months ago?"

"Sure, let's try that."

Eddie got to work. A few minutes later, he spoke. "This is weird. There's a block on this, too—a really good one. It's probably Sue again, but I can't tell. Give me some time. I'll let you know when I've figured this out."

"Sure."

Kinney and Reed split up, and Kinney returned to Hoff's to catch up on his sleep. Opportunities to rest could be scarce during missions. He'd learned to take rejuvenating naps.

He was startled awake by a phone call after a couple of hours. It was about four in the afternoon.

"*Salut*, this is Rosie Aubert. I want to have dinner with you, Kinney. Meet me at Gallanto's at seven."

"Why?"

"Do you always ask why when a beautiful woman asks you to dinner?"

"It's hard to generalize about something that never happens. Is this Ryan's idea?"

"No, and don't tell him. I found your phone number in his phone when he was busy."

"Is this about my good looks?"

Rosie laughed, a delightful musical sound. "Maybe. You don't hurt my eyes, Kinney. I'll tell you all about why I want to meet when I see you tonight." Then she hung up.

Kinney couldn't imagine what she wanted. It was going to be hard to keep a low profile dining with a movie star, but his curiosity drove his decision to risk exposure.

So he sat at a table reserved in her name at Gallanto's, waiting for her from seven to seven thirty. The decor was authentic upscale Parisian despite the Italian name, replete with servers in starched white shirts, black pants, and black berets. Versailles came to mind when Kinney looked at the walls and ceiling. Ornate to a fault, he hoped no peasants had starved while the restaurant owners had spent their ruling class profits on it. Perhaps the kitchen help would mount a revolution someday.

The elderly maître d' stopped by several times to ask if Rosie was really going to show. If anyone ever looked like a penguin in his tux, this would be the guy. He was shaped so much like a bottom-heavy bird that Kinney had a hard time refraining from envisioning him in a documentary he'd seen about emperor penguins.

"We had a couple of problematic customers in here last week," the maître d' explained. "We allotted them a good table on short notice because they said they were meeting Neil Young. They didn't."

"She'll be here," he assured the man.

Shortly after that, Rosie's entrance captured everyone's attention. She wore a daring red gown with a deep V neckline that revealed most of her bosom. A high slit up the side created suspense. Would she move in such a way that everyone would find out if she was wearing underwear?

Sashaying over to Kinney's table, she blew kisses to several other diners, and the wait staff applauded. If Kinney didn't watch out, he'd be on tabloid TV— "Major star cheats on billionaire boyfriend with rugged mystery man."

"Kinney!" she gushed. "It's so good to see you. Thank you so much for coming. No, don't get up."

Rosie bent over and kissed him on the cheek, revealing her startlingly pink nipples. She settled across from him. "You like what you see?"

"Of course. But I've seen them before— remember?"

"Oh, yes. That's true. Do you like my dress? I wore it especially for you."

"If you're seeking a romantic partner, Rosie, I need to let you know I'm seeing someone."

"That doesn't matter to me. I love Ryan. I just act like this in public because it's my image. I'm supposed to be a wild woman—someone who has fun with many men, and maybe steals little things sometimes."

"So why are we here?"

Their server sidled up. "Welcome to Gallanto's, Ms. Aubert. My name is Jason. Would you like something to drink?"

"*Bien sûr.*"

"Huh?"

"Of course."

She ordered a Manhattan. Jason ignored Kinney and departed. Then Rosie leaned back and appraised her dinner companion with calculating eyes. She was suddenly a completely different woman. The real Rosie had appeared.

"There you are," he said.

"Yes, here I am. The ditzy persona is fun, but the real me is who needs to be here tonight." Her accent had almost vanished.

"And once again, why is that?"

"Because you need to leave Barber alone. You need to back off. You need to go take a trip somewhere for a few weeks."

"I don't understand." Kinney was having trouble processing her unlikely words.

"Barber introduced me to Ryan. I was offered an obscene amount of money and a role in a Scorsese film. How could I turn that down? I was supposed to be a spy for him, but I really did fall in love." Rosie looked him in the eyes. "Kinney, if you don't let this go, you're going to end up dead, and so will Ryan. I'm your last chance to stay safe. I can't control any of this anymore."

"Where's Barber?"

"I don't know."

"He thinks you're still working for him?"

"Yes," Rosie replied.

"Since I'm not going anywhere, isn't eliminating Barber the next best thing as far as you're concerned?"

Rosie leaned back and frowned. "It's my family back in France. They're all dead if I cross him. And if it comes down to you or Ryan, I'm going to pick Ryan."

"What's to stop me from telling Ryan about you?"

"He won't believe you, and if he does, he'll choose me over you. You can't beat love, Kinney." She placed both her hands on her heart as she said this. The pressure threatened to pop one of her breasts out of her dress.

"What's to stop me from hauling you off somewhere and getting you to talk?" Kinney asked this in an inappropriately casual tone.

"He is."

Rosie pointed to Jason the server, who now stood to the side of Kinney, holding a small caliber revolver under a white cloth napkin.

"Fucking yahoo," Jason muttered.

"This is an interesting development," Kinney said, unfazed by the intrusion. "Congratulations on your stealth, Jason, and who the hell are you?"

"My name is Jason Barber, Kinney. Barber."

"Ah, I should've seen the resemblance. You have that bizarre widow's peak, and you're short with beady eyes. You've managed to become your own man, at least, by adopting that shit-eating grin you're wearing. I think your dad got someone to superglue his facial features in place."

"Fuck you. Rosie? What do you want me to do?"

That was interesting, Kinney thought. Rosie was higher up the hierarchy than even Barber's son.

"Just stay in sight," she instructed, "and tell Henri

and Phillipe to watch the doors."

"Gotcha."

Kinney turned to Rosie once Jason backed away. "So it's not so much of a date as an ambush, huh?"

"Do the right thing and you can walk out of here," she responded.

"Are you aware of my reputation? I could punch you in the head and kill you right now before you even twitch. I could've disarmed Jason in a heartbeat if I wanted to. And I don't care how many men you have on the doors. This was a very stupid plan, Rosie."

She shook her head. "If you could do all that amazing stuff, why didn't you?"

"Because I think we can work together to keep all of us safe and get the bad people behind bars or in their graves. Let me think a minute, and then I'll tell you the parts of our plan you need to know. Just don't mention any of this to Jason or anyone else."

"I can't promise you anything until I hear what you have to say."

"Fair enough." After thinking for a bit, Kinney spent twenty minutes explaining why Rosie didn't need to worry about anyone's safety. Most of it was true. Some of it was designed to get him out of the restaurant without having to hurt anyone.

"That actually makes a lot of sense," she admitted when he was through. "But what about Jason? He's still standing twenty feet away with a gun in his hand."

"Let's figure that out next."

Rosie nodded. When they were through concocting a plan for that, they shook hands. Kinney could see tomorrow's headline: "Aubert strikes multi-million dollar deal with menacing diner."

Chapter 22

Kinney and Rosie never ate dinner. She called Jason over, and they played out the script she'd devised.

"Jason, Kinney has agreed to move to Switzerland if your father pays him half a million. He'll neutralize Reed Bolt first."

"Really?" Jason turned to Kinney, his dark eyebrows raised. "That doesn't sound much like the man I've heard so much about."

"I know when I'm licked," Kinney told him, casting his eyes down in an effort to look defeated. "Rosie has convinced me I can't win. And Reed Bolt cheated at poker once."

"What?"

"I'd rather not say what my real reasons are for getting rid of him," Kinney told him.

"I thought you didn't kill anyone anymore," Jason said. He'd raised his eyebrows in mild disbelief.

"I didn't say I'd kill him," Kinney replied. "There are other ways to get someone out of the picture."

"Like what?"

Kinney was hoping Jason wouldn't ask that. Now he had to go off script. Rosie rescued him.

"I know an Australian movie star who falls for his type," she explained. "Kinney will bring Reed to a party at Ryan's house, and we'll get them together. I guarantee he'll be in Sydney in no time at all. In the meantime, while I set that up, Kinney will lead him on a wild goose chase. He'll send him up to where Jefferson would be to look for your father. It's hours and hours away."

"You expect me to believe all this?" Jason asked. "And why wouldn't my dad want to just go ahead and kill you, Kinney? He'd save half a million, and there'd be no chance you could be any trouble down the line."

"I don't care whether you believe it. I care whether you pass this on to your father, so do it. You don't want to disappoint someone like me. Tell him I've got proof about what he's been doing—proof that's safe with several lawyers. If I stay alive—if he takes my deal—it stays buried."

"I've still got a gun, Kinney." Jason gestured with the napkin-covered weapon, moving it up and down as if it were nodding. "I'm not scared of you, whether you're 'disappointed' with me or not. I could take you out back and shoot you right now."

Kinney snaked his arm out and jabbed his forefinger into a nerve on Jason's bicep. The revolver fell to the carpeted floor. Kinney kicked it under the table. The whole thing took about two seconds.

The two other men across the room took a step toward them. Rosie waved them away and then spoke to Jason again.

"You're here to keep me safe, Jason—and probably spy on me for your father—not to decide anything on behalf of him. I'm in charge tonight."

"Yeah, okay. I'll pass on the message, but don't be surprised if you don't live long enough to get a reply, Kinney. I won't forget what you just did. You made me look like an idiot in front of Rosie and her men."

"I don't think you need any help with that," Kinney told him.

Maurice the maître d' showed up. "We don't bother our celebrity guests," he admonished. "Get back to work, Jason."

"Yes, sir."

When they were alone again, Kinney spoke. "He really works here?"

"That's why I picked this restaurant to meet."

"How do you think we did fooling Jason?" Kinney wasn't as pleased with his performance as he had been when he and Reed had quit the agency.

"It should buy us some time," Rosie responded. "That's all we need," she reminded him. "But as they say, don't quit your day job. I don't think you'd make the cut for a school play, Kinney."

"Fair enough. By the way, what happened to your cute French accent? I kinda miss it."

She reverted to it to answer him. "Unlike you, *I'm* an actor, *mon cheri*. I act."

****

Kinney spied a black sedan three cars back on 880 after he stopped for gas. He was about ten miles from Gallanto's. He'd been driving slowly, pondering the latest events. He took the next exit, and then made two or three random turns and the car stayed with him. It was hard to tail someone with only one car and not be seen. He wondered if whoever was driving wanted that. He decided they were probably just incompetent.

He turned into an indoor parking garage he was familiar with and screamed out of sight after passing through the gate. Either his follower would reveal himself by pursuing him in there or, more likely, wait for him to emerge.

The garage had a little used back exit. When the only other drivers to come into the garage were two young women in a convertible and an old man driving a classic muscle car, Kinney drove out the other exit, circled around, and parked fifty yards behind the sedan. As he strolled down the sidewalk, he saw that whoever was in the car had his eyes fixed ahead, where he expected Kinney to emerge.

Kinney decided to lure his follower out of the car since whoever it was would be less likely to use a gun on the street. This would give Kinney more room to maneuver if he had to fight, too. Of course, all he knew was that he was being followed. It could be the feds or another relatively benign organization.

Duckwalking and then crouching, Kinney used his house key to punch a hole in the sidewall of the car's rear passenger tire. This wasn't an easy feat, but it was made easier because he'd sharpened the tip of the key years before so he always had an edged weapon handy.

He expected a loud noise, but the modern tire just hissed, and then the car tilted back awkwardly on its haunches. Still crouched, Kinney heard but didn't see the driver's door open and close. He coiled himself, ready to spring at whoever showed up around the rear corner of the vehicle.

"Hey, Kinney, that was a new tire."

He pivoted and then uncoiled himself. Barbara Foster had walked around the hood, which for some reason hadn't occurred to Kinney. She wore running clothes, including yellow short shorts, which looked damned good on her. He'd never seen her legs before.

Her blonde hair was down below her shoulders, and it looked as though her face was freshly scrubbed.

Foster appeared to be unarmed, and he remembered her warning him about agents coming to his house to kill him. He rose and asked her, "Why were you following me? And why so inexpertly?"

"I wanted you to make me. I knew you'd approach an incompetent tail at some point. You're in the wind, and I don't have the number of whatever burner you're using. I followed Ms. Aubert to the restaurant on Hoff's last-minute orders—he's been made the de facto chief while Barber's out of the office—and I spotted you. I would've talked to you after you left, but a short guy with pig eyes followed you, so I thought I'd follow him and get him off your tail. Then I found you by using the tracker I put under your car while you were eating."

"That would be Jason Barber you took out."

"Really? The chief's son?"

"So he says. Did you see a resemblance?"

"Not really."

"What did you do with him?"

"He's in his trunk with the warning lights on his car flashing. Some cop'll get him out eventually—he's in a no-parking zone."

"Let's sit in your car and talk," Kinney suggested.

"Good idea."

They settled into her nearly new sedan, which smelled like leather. A garish Christ on a cross pendant dangled from Foster's rearview mirror.

"Didn't I hear you were a Buddhist?" Kinney asked, pointing to the cross.

"My sister's a nun so I put that up there for when I give her rides. She can't drive." Foster reached forward and straightened the crucifix.

"That's one of the rules? I've seen nuns driving."

"She can only see a few feet, Kinney. Is this really what you want to talk about?"

"No. Tell me why Hoff had you tail Rosie."

"After you tell me how you got a date with a major movie star."

"It wasn't a date. How much do you know, and why are you being so pleasant?"

"Curtis Hoff and I have been dating for quite some time. Since it's against departmental policy, we've been keeping it a secret. So I know you've been staying with him, and I know Barber's bent. I suspected it even before Curtis told me."

"Barbara, I find this hard to believe. You and Hoff? There's no sign of any woman ever having been in his house."

"I've got a one word reply—Herbie."

"Ah."

"Anyway," Foster continued, "Curtis had somebody look into Aubert and clearly she's more than some flaky celebrity. In fact, she was in French military intelligence under a different name."

"Really?" he asked mildly. At this point, nothing about Rosie surprised him. "Does he think she's involved in this?"

"I don't know. The point is that he thought she might be up to *something* since she's obviously more than just Ryan's girlfriend."

"I can vouch for that." Kinney filled her in on his non-dinner non-date.

"How can I help?" Foster asked when he was done. She'd turned to face him as he talked. Now she took a breath and then let it out slowly.

"Maybe you could liaison with the FBI about the files I gave them. I'm going to be busy, and I need Barber to think my proposed deal is on the level. Reed will be out of town for a while. Curtis, of course, needs to run the show from the office and keep agents off our asses."

"That ass comment reminds me of Reed. Where is he? What has he been doing?"

"That's a good question. I'll call him."

"Hey, Kinney," Reed answered. "What's up?"

"You go first. By the way, you're on speaker with me and Barbara Foster."

"Really? Foster?"

"She's with us. So what have you been doing?"

"I'm still vetting random agents to see who might be the shooter at the beach, but the pickings are getting slimmer and slimmer. I'm down to Harris and Kawai, and I don't think either of them could hit Shaq from mid-court with a guided rocket launcher."

"No, I can't see how it could be them. Harris only deals with explosive devices, and Kawai is basically a glorified pencil pusher. What do you think, Barbara? You know both of them better than we do."

"I agree. It sounds like it's not someone in the agency. Who then?"

"It's probably a contract killer like VanVleet," Reed said. "I'll bet Barber's got a dozen in his Rolodex."

"He doesn't have a Rolodex, Bolt. Step into the twenty-first century." Foster's caustic tone must've stung.

"Hey," Kinney interjected, "stop that. We're not in

middle school. Reed, you need to go up to where Jefferson is supposed to be and pretend to hunt for Barber. I know that's a wild goose chase, but it gets you out of town like I promised, and you never know."

"Okay."

Kinney filled him in, much as he had Foster. She played a word game on her phone while he did. It looked like a Scrabble rip-off.

"Are you both clear about all of this?" Kinney asked Reed and Barbara when he was through. The others assented. "Barbara, let Curtis know what we've talked about. We've got burners, but I think it's better if I don't contact him directly, and I don't want to wait until I see him. I'll text you who to reach out to at the feds."

"Okay."

"So we're all set?" Kinney asked.

The others agreed, and Reed hung up.

"What about my tire?" Barbara asked.

"I'll help you change it."

"I can do that, thank you very much. I'm not helpless. I mean what about the cost of a new one?"

"Save the receipt," Kinney told her. "That's what I've been doing. Hopefully, when all this over, there will be someone to submit it to."

Chapter 23

Kinney called Georgia once he'd returned to his car, which now sported a parking ticket tucked under its wiper blade. He needed more information to know what he ought to do next.

"Hi, it's Kinney. How are things going?"

"I'm making progress—slowly. Whoever's behind this has hired a world-class hacker to block a lot of avenues of investigation, so we've got our tech guys working on that, and we sent a few people into the field to gather more information the old-fashioned way. Our case needs to be ironclad before we move on someone like Barber—assuming we can find him."

"Slow progress or not, what has the agency found out?" Kinney asked, noticing that he felt more frustration than he thought the situation warranted.

"Barber might be up where the new state would be. That's the biggest thing. A deputy sheriff spotted him—or someone who looks like him—in a grocery store, but we don't know if we can rely on that source yet. In Modoc county, there are only 9,000 residents, so they can't be too picky about who they hire."

"Why would law enforcement up there be on the lookout for him?" Kinney asked.

"You'd have to ask Alan Kim. I guess he knows something we don't."

"Did you look into the bill Hattori is pushing?"

Kinney asked. "We never got around to that. Where exactly would Jefferson be?"

"In California, it's Modoc, Lassen, Siskiyou, Yuba, and Tehama counties, with Yreka as the capitol," Georgia told him. "Then there are some counties in southern Oregon. The southwest corner of Idaho was interested in joining at one point, but the voters in those counties voted it down in a referendum. The new state would end up with a population of about 400,000."

"Here's something I should've wondered about before," Kinney said. "How does passing a bill in the state legislature make this happen? It's got to be the federal government that can create states, right? Like with Alaska and Hawaii."

"I looked into that. It's a first step. It can't go forward unless California allows it to. The Jeffersonians have tried multiple times over the years to convince the legislature. The idea actually goes back to the mid-eighteen-hundreds. According to our guy in Sacramento, this time it's got a lot of momentum."

"I sent Reed up there," Kinney told her.

"To Sacramento?"

"No, to Jefferson. I'll aim him wherever you text me to check out that sighting."

Kinney felt uncomfortable explaining how he'd arrived at the decision to exile his partner since that would entail revealing his meeting with Rosie. For one thing, Georgia might be sensitive about his going out to dinner with someone like her. Also, Rosie had shared two secrets with him, and it felt both risky and kind of creepy to pass them on to anyone. That she was not a bit flighty would certainly impact her career, and that she'd spied on Connelly for Barber put her at risk for prosecution—or worse.

"That's handy," Georgia said. "If there's something to it, you could join Reed up there."

"Sure. Do you miss me?"

"That's a very unKinney-like thing to say. Honestly, I've been too busy to think about you."

"Fair enough."

"I better get back to work," Georgia said. "Kim's been on my ass all morning. I'll text you the store where Barber was spotted in Alturas and the name of the deputy."

"Okay, thanks. Bye."

Kinney called Reed and let him know the wild goose chase he was about to embark on might actually lead to catching a goose.

"Cool. I'll drive straight there. If Alturas is anything like the photos of the other towns I looked at online, it'll be a really a pathetic place, Kinney."

"You're not a tourist, Reed. That doesn't matter."

"I thought I'd pretend to be one, but now I'm having second thoughts. I don't think they get tourists up there. Maybe I could be a tractor salesman."

"Sounds good, as long as you know anything about tractors," Kinney commented. He knew Reed didn't. His partner had a habit of impersonating people he couldn't pull off—like the Hasidic guy he wanted to be when they were looking for Merriwether.

"What's to know?" Reed said. "You turn them on, press the accelerator pedal, and then you tool around farms in them. I guess they drag plows or whatever out in the fields."

"Clearly, you're an expert. Good luck."

"Well, anyway, text me what Georgia sends you

and I'll check it out. I'll start by talking to that deputy."

"Sure."

So now Kinney knew more, but he still felt lost about what his role was at this stage. Was it just coordinating the activities of his colleagues? That was an unsatisfying proposition. On the other hand, it didn't make sense that he should supplant any of them.

Georgia was obviously better at investigating what was going on behind the scenes. She was a professional analyst, after all, and she had the resources of the FBI to draw on. So there was nothing for Kinney to do there. Foster was taking care of officially coordinating their efforts with the FBI, and her relationship with Curtis Hoff meant she could keep tabs on the internal activities back at the office, too. Curtis himself could utilize agency resources to keep an eye out for anything untoward. Reed was perfectly capable of finding Barber if he was really in Alturas. Kinney paused his musing to briefly look up the town online.

Alturas was the Modoc county seat way up in the far northeast corner of California. It would be a long drive for Reed, but if he didn't take his car, he couldn't bring guns, drones, and whatever else they might need. A few thousand people lived in Alturas, with a few hundred more in the surrounding area. When Kinney saw photos, he understood why tourists didn't flock there. The town was remarkably ordinary.

Kinney returned to the frustrating task of sorting through his options. He reasoned that Connelly and his security team could investigate the corrupt executives at Rakena and Moonmatic far better than he could. Eddie was the only guy Kinney knew who could hack a hacker. Until he did, Kinney's hands were tied in that department.

So he decided to just chill out back at Hoff's if Herbie would let him. A little R&R couldn't hurt, and catching up on his reading was an attractive notion. Maybe taking a break would refresh him for whatever came his way tomorrow. Maybe Herbie would drive him crazy.

En route to Los Gatos, Kinney decided to head to Eddie's in the morning. Even if Eddie hadn't found out all he could, Kinney would take any scraps he could get that gave him something to do.

Herbie and Hoff weren't at the house. A note on the kitchen table in Hoff's careful printing stated they were out for the evening. Since Barbara Foster had indicated her strong aversion to the basset hound, Kinney pictured Herbie and Curtis sitting by themselves at a table at Gallanto's before taking in a show at the theater.

Kinney read that evening and then slept well and actually did wake up feeling refreshed. Hoff and Herbie slept in after their big night out. Now Kinney pictured them at a late night rave after watching the ten millionth performance of *Cats*, dancing their brains out while high on ecstasy.

He scrambled three eggs, guiltily ate the last two pieces of toast, and drank more coffee than he should have. He left a note for Hoff.

Thanks again for your hospitality. Herbie ate the last of the toast. I hope you had fun at the rave.

He drove to Eddie's through light early morning traffic. He discovered the hacker asleep at his desk, his face resting on a well-worn black keyboard. He'd cleaned up the room a bit since Kinney was last there, which made it easier to find the light switch and walk over to tap Eddie on the shoulder, who groaned and then gradually awoke.

"Kinney," he said groggily.

"Eddie. Got anything more for me?"

"Yes and no," he said, rubbing his eyes as he stretched. "I couldn't break through the really impressive firewall around the original FBI site. I don't feel good about that. I'm going to keep working on it whether you pay me to or not. But I've been chatting more with Sue Exeter—the one who made the fake site—and she's agreed to meet with you. She works at Apple, so she'll meet you in Cupertino if you buy her lunch at this health food restaurant she likes. She says to order number seven, which seems weird to me.

"Why would a health food place have numbers? That's an Asian restaurant deal—you know, Chinese, Thai, and all those. I think it's because they have weird names for their food. Once I ordered a delivery and I thought it was going to be noodles with chicken and it turned out to be this slimy ocean thing like an octopus without the arms. I got so mad I threw it across the kitchen and nearly hit my monkey."

"You have a monkey?"

"Had. I *had* a monkey. It's too painful to get into, Kinney. Just leave it."

"Sure. So the gist of your rant is that Sue will tell me what I need to know, and maybe she can get into the old FBI site so I can compare it with the doctored one and see what they're hiding?"

"She won't tell *me* anything. That's for sure." Eddie wriggled like a dog shedding water and then stretched again. "It's only after I told her you were a famous spy that she wanted to have lunch with you. I don't actually know if she'll tell you anything at lunch, either—she didn't make any promises. She might just want to ask you stuff. One of the games we play has spies and kung-fu and other things you probably know a lot about. I think she's looking for an edge to get into the championships in Macau next November. Anyway, you said you could be persuasive without hurting someone, right?"

Kinney glowered, his eyes narrowed. "Eddie, we talked about this. Were you supposed to tell anyone about me and Reed?"

Eddie held his hands out in front of him. "It was the only way! I tried everything. And you seemed like you really wanted to know."

"I guess I forgive you. But don't tell Reed. When is this lunch supposed to happen?"

"Today. I was going to call you," Eddie said sheepishly, his eyes downcast.

"But you fell asleep."

"Yeah, sorry." He looked up, his apology freeing him.

"All right. Text me the details."

"Sure."

"Did you find out anything else that might be helpful?" Kinney asked.

"Yeah, I did. Barber has a son named Jason. Rosie Aubert worked for the French military for a couple of years before she got discovered, and Ryan Connelly is a dick."

"Why do you say that? And more importantly, how do you even know I'm interested in those people? I never told you about them." Kinney stared at the hacker. Had Eddie just outed himself as a traitor?

"Reed called me yesterday afternoon." He seemed oblivious of Kinney's suspicions.

"And what's this about Connelly?"

"Dickoid, for sure. Last election he said he wanted to curb online violence like that's why everybody's running around shooting one another. What about gun control? What about getting shrinks for all these crazy people? Plus he gave a shitload of money to this idiotic think tank that keeps coming up with reasons why the military needs even more funding. I think they want to invade Mexico or something. I dunno."

"Did you find out any more about Georgia?"

"The state—where Atlanta is? Was I supposed to look into that?"

"Remember—she's the woman you found out some things about before, but there were a few missing years?" Kinney wondered why Eddie needed prompting about her.

"Oh, yeah. Sorry. I'm still a little out of it. No, I got going on this other thing for somebody else."

"That's all right. You've been a big help, Eddie."

"So what's this all about?" Eddie asked. "Why do you care about these people? Why do you care about the FBI?"

"It's better if I don't tell you any of that. Sorry."

"Aw, man."

****

Kinney headed from Eddie's house to a nearby park. He wondered if the new, upscale SUV that sat down the street was going to follow him, but whoever was behind the wheel didn't. Maybe he was Eddie's other client. The vehicle certainly didn't belong in the hacker's rundown neighborhood.

The park was Kinney's favorite, largely because the fenced-in area for off-leash dogs was always full of happy, playful creatures. Even the dogs' barking and growling struck him as positive. He'd have been equally happy to watch kids cavort on the playground at the other end of the meadow, but these days he'd be taken for a pedophile. As it was, some of the female dog owners glared at him as though they were the ones in his sights.

On a bench under a liquidambar tree, Kinney called Georgia. "I think I know who our hacker is," he told her. "And I think the one you're chasing is likely to be the same one. I'm meeting her for lunch today. I'll see what I can find out."

"That's great. Wait a minute. Her? The one we have our eye on is a guy. Who's yours?" Georgia asked.

"I'd rather not say her name over the phone. I've heard the FBI sometimes monitors its agent's calls." Since Kinney had been told this by the hacker they'd used before Eddie, he wasn't sure it was true. The guy had killed himself.

"Oh, I don't think so," Georgia said, "but I guess it's better to be safe than sorry. I'm curious, though. Where are you having lunch? Should I be jealous about missing out on some great place?"

"Hold on." Kinney checked the text from Eddie to see where the restaurant was. "I don't think it's a good idea to say that on the phone either," he told her, "but it's a hardcore vegetarian place in the heart of the valley."

"I hope it's not the one I got dragged to once. It was dreadful. If they've got numbered menu items, it might be. Don't order number seven. It's totally tasteless."

Kinney smiled. "I'll keep that in mind."

Reed called as Kinney finished checking and then ignoring his emails. The only one that was tempting to respond to was from his niece, who had erroneously sent him school gossip aimed at someone named Camisha.

"Kinney, Barber's definitely up here with some hard-looking guys."

"The deputy found him just like that? That's too easy, Reed. It's probably a trap."

"Yeah, maybe." He sounded dubious.

"Why would anybody even be on the lookout for Barber up there? He's not on a wanted poster, is he?"

"The deputy is a she. That name you sent me with initials for a first name is actually a woman. She said she got a bulletin from the feds. Anyway, she found CC video from the grocery store where she saw him, which showed his license plate. Then she found the Realtor who rented a place to him, too."

"So where's that?"

"They're holed up on an old ranch a few miles south of town that's got a whole lot of nothing around it. No cattle or crops—zilch. There are sight lines up the wazoo."

"Even if we can't get in there without a fight, they've got to get groceries."

"What tipped off the very attractive deputy up here that she should take a look at Barber was the shitload of supplies he was buying at the store."

"Very attractive, huh?"

"Yup."

"All right. It sounds like I need to come up there. Since you drove, I assume you've got guns? I'll bring anything else I can think of that might help us get to Barber. Is there an airport there?"

"Yeah, Alturas Municipal. It's only a few miles outside town. But there aren't any commercial flights from down your way. You'll have get a private plane that's not too big. Or fly through Reno."

"Okay. But I still think it might be a trap. Would Barber be careless enough to let someone spot him? He could've sent one of his men to the store, right?"

"Beats me. Trap or not, get your ass up here. What do you want to do? Ignore the guy we're trying to catch?"

Reed had a point. How could they ignore the news? "Of course not. I'll fly up later today. You probably miss me, anyway, don't you?"

"I've been working with Glinda. She's a lot more fun than you are."

****

The traffic when Kinney entered 85 was ridiculous, given that it wasn't rush hour. Luckily, in just a half mile, Kinney saw why—a three-car accident on the shoulder. Lookie-loos just couldn't help themselves. They had to cruise by at ten miles an hour in case there was any gore to revel in.

Meat Be Damned was in the middle of a newish strip mall. Kinney didn't get why they were still building these. Everybody thought they were a blight— ugly and cheap-looking. The restaurant itself had gone to some trouble to distinguish itself from the dry cleaners and the nail salon that flanked it. A cream-colored exterior wall sported two compact murals:

florets of broccoli dancing with one another and a winged carrot soaring over a turquoise yurt.

When Kinney entered the restaurant, he was surprised to see it looked normal. It could've been a chain coffee shop—and probably had been. Brown faux leather booths lined both sides of the well-lit room, and square wooden tables filled the rest of the space. The only decor that matched the restaurant's funky exterior was the line of overgrown hanging ferns along the back wall. Several dangled down untidily to just above customers' heads.

Kinney scanned the handful of diners and saw a likely-looking Sue. An overweight twenty-something with bad skin gazed back at him. When she waved, he took a step toward her. Then a similarly overweight man pushed past him and waved back to the woman.

"Over here!" someone else called.

Kinney pivoted and spied a slim thirty-ish Asian man who was also waving. Kinney glanced behind him for whoever the wavee might be this time, but no one was there. He pointed at his chest, the somewhat androgynous man nodded, and Kinney strode over to the table alongside the row of windows that fronted the narrow sidewalk.

"You're Kinney, right?"

"Maybe."

"Eddie said you looked like a bad-ass. You fit the bill. I don't see any other tough-looking guys here, do you? I think they're down the street at the Outback Steakhouse."

Kinney lowered himself across the round table from him. "I was expecting a woman named Sue."

"Sit. I used to be her. Call me Max."

"Ah. Sorry." Max was trans, which Eddie hadn't mentioned.

On further inspection, it was clear that Max had started life as a female, despite the fuzz on his upper lip and a buzz haircut. His squarish face, with its wide chin and thick black eyebrows helped project masculinity, but once Kinney knew the story, he could catalogue several feminine features. Max's dark eyes gleamed in the light, and his posture was perfect.

"You're wondering why your hacker friend didn't tell you what to expect," Max said.

"Yes."

"I didn't want him to. I've kept my online handle and my old bio. I can run rings around the likes of Eddie and his ilk, so my secret is safe." He leaned back, a self-satisfied expression on his face.

"Good for you," Kinney told him. "But let's settle something before we go any further."

"Okay."

"Number seven on the menu. What's the deal?"

Max smiled. Their server had noisily sidled over and overheard them. She was a busty woman with purple hair and so many metal bracelets banging against each other that it was hard to see her wrists. She spoke in a deep, resonant voice. Kinney realized she was trans, as well. She must've figured that if you were going to get breasts, you might as well go all out.

"Number seven is a great choice," the server told him. "It's my sister's favorite."

Max watched with a half smile now.

"Does it have a name, too?" Kinney asked.

"Of course. It's called Delightful Surprise."

"Can you tell me what's in it?"

She shook her head. "No. It's supposed to be a surprise. That's the whole idea."

"You have other numbers?"

She handed him a menu, said hi to Max, and then asked Kinney's lunch companion if he wanted the usual. He nodded.

"I give up," Kinney said. "I can't decode your menu. I'll have the number seven."

"Great!" She seemed very happy as she skipped away.

"So what do you want to know?" Max asked.

"Who hired you to screw with the FBI website?"

"Somebody on the phone who used one of those voice-disguising apps. They wired bitcoin into my account, and I got to work."

"With all your hacking expertise, you couldn't trace who it was?"

Max smiled again. Kinney liked his smile, which formed a perfect crescent, revealing a slight overbite.

"I didn't say that," the hacker told Kinney. "Maybe I'll give you a name and maybe I won't. Let's see how this goes."

"All right. What about the details?" Kinney asked. "What exactly did they want you to do?"

"I screwed around with the personnel files."

"You took somebody off of there?"

"No, I made a few alterations," Max told him. "Nothing major. Then I blocked anyone from being able to compare the original site with mine. Harmless stuff." He waved his hand in the air, brushing the idea of harm away as though it were an annoying insect.

"You don't think messing with FBI files could be harmful?" Kinney asked.

"Not in this case. Someone didn't want their personal information to be available, that's all. I support that."

"You're a hacker who values people's privacy?" Kinney asked, his eyebrows raised.

Max grinned. "Yeah, I guess so. Individual people, anyway—not corporations or governments."

A rifle shot rang out, and then another one before Kinney or Max could move. Max slumped in his chair. He'd been hit in the chest and neck. "Call 911!" Kinney shouted as his adrenaline surged, launching him into action.

He leapt to his feet and sprinted toward the kitchen. Two more shots slammed into the wall beside him, and then he raced past several young, very scared cooks into a long, dim hallway beyond the stovetops. A few moments later, he kicked open the back door and launched himself into a low roll onto a paved alley. More shots came from somewhere behind the strip mall, passing harmlessly overhead. He crawled to cover behind a pickup truck.

Then he heard sirens. The restaurant was either right by a police station or a cop had been cruising nearby. Kinney decided to wait until the police arrived at the front door before disappearing. By then, both shooters were likely be gone.

It was a reasonable plan—until Kinney heard soft footsteps approaching the truck. Rather than shoot the guy and lose whatever information he might squeeze out of him, Kinney levered himself into the truck bed and lay flat, hoping he wouldn't be seen.

A light-skinned African-American man came around the back fender, his rifle raised. Kinney recognized him. He was a relatively new agent. Bernard Somebody. Kinney knew all he needed to know now. Barber had sent the men.

Kinney stood and kicked the agent in the ear before the man could move. He crumpled. He'd be out for a while and would have some explaining to do.

Another salvo of shots rang out from the far end of the strip mall—this guy wasn't particularly accurate. Kinney leapt out of the truck and hightailed it through the good-sized parking lot behind the restaurant that served the box store on the next street over. He'd need another car. His rental was untraceable, but for a while it was likely to be part of a crime scene.

At the far end of the lot, he spied an older car with open windows. He hot-wired it and drove away at the speed limit to a nearby golf course. He'd shot eighty-eight there once—a fond memory. Golfers bought nice cars and left them for four or five hours at a time. The owners of the luxury cars closest to the clubhouse would've arrived first, and therefore would be done sooner. The ones farther away would be just starting their round. Golfers were too lazy to park an inch farther away that they had to.

Fifteen minutes later, Kinney parked his gleaming German gas hog—well, someone else's gleaming German gas hog—next to public tennis courts. He needed to think through the ramifications of what had happened. And feel his delayed onset of feelings.

Watching an innocent civilian being slaughtered simply because he'd performed a service for some evil people turned Kinney's stomach. Seeing Miner's face explode at them on Kauai was one thing. During missions overseas, Kinney had seen, and instigated, his share of violent death. But those were players on the geo-political stage. Villains.

Max's smile dominated Kinney's awareness for quite some time as he struggled to absorb the hacker's death and move through his unexpectedly strong emotional reaction. If the feelings endured as he coped with upcoming developments, Kinney would be in trouble. Thinking with one's emotional mind had been the death knell of many an agent.

In succession, Kinney felt his gut tighten, nausea well up, and his head heat up. He also involuntarily tightened his lips and balled his fists. Morphing from physical sensations to outright emotions, Kinney felt disgust, anger, and finally fear. The mission was out of control. Who else would die who didn't deserve to? Could Kinney and Reed really corral Barber and his co-conspirators? Their former boss could tap resources they didn't even know existed.

From feelings, Kinney shifted to thoughts. This was the usual order of things for him—sensations to feelings to thoughts. The next stage was almost always action.

Ostensibly, only Eddie and Georgia had known about his meeting—unless Georgia's line had been tapped. Or if Max had mentioned it to anyone. There was no way to check out that last possibility.

Eddie knew the name of the restaurant. He'd already told Max about Kinney. Would he have done it again with someone else? Eddie had said he had another client. Would he rat out one to another? Maybe under duress.

A mole at the FBI seemed like a more likely candidate to have transmitted information to Barber.

Kinney had given out enough information on an open phone line for someone to put two and two together, or the shooters could've just followed him. With a team of two or three trained agents, Kinney was unlikely to have spotted them taking turns behind him.

All along, Kinney had suspected there was a mole in the local FBI office. Where else would Kim have heard "rumors" that Kinney was supposedly killing again. Barber and Miner knew that—no one else.

If there was a mole, of course he'd want to monitor Georgia's communications. She was the one who'd brought in the files revealing both the Guyana oilfield plot and the one to exploit a new state. The mole might not want the FBI website to show he even existed, so that would explain hiring Max.

What was it that Max said just before he was shot? As far as Kinney could recall—and witnessing a murder from three feet away could muddle your memory— Max had said that he *hadn't* removed something from the FBI's personnel files. Kinney's brief encounter with Max was hardly enough to tell for sure if the hacker had been truthful, but it had seemed like it.

Then a third, less palatable notion floated up. Kinney was surprised it took him so long to get to it. Georgia could be behind the shooting and God knows what else. What was the evidence pro and con about that? He moved on quickly to explore this before he fell back into an emotional reaction to the possibility.

First of all, Kinney and Georgia had met at random when Reed had accosted her on the street. On the other hand, what were the odds that a random person would work at the FBI? Maybe she'd walked by on purpose, planning to initiate something from her end. Kinney thought about that and realized that Miner's office building and the feds' office were only two blocks apart. So it wasn't as unlikely as it could be.

Kinney certainly didn't experience Georgia as villainous, of course. Why would he have slept with her if he had? It was hard to believe she was so cold-hearted that she'd facilitate Kinney's murder. She was smart, funny, savvy, and seemed to care about him. He took a look at that last item on his mental list.

Most women who embodied such desirable qualities didn't want anything to do with Kinney, especially once he told them even slightly real things about himself. Georgia had hung in there when he'd pronounced himself a sociopath, ostensibly because his reputation intrigued her. That had felt strange when she told him, and even stranger in hindsight. Reed had been outright incredulous about it. A co-conspirator would definitely overlook his psych profile in an effort to get close to him.

Then it occurred to Kinney that Max may have placed Georgia *into* the FBI website. Maybe she didn't even work there. He only had her word for that, which didn't mean anything if she was on the other side of the conspiracy.

Whether Georgia actually worked for the feds should be easy enough to check. Kim might be willing to tell him, and if not, how hard could it be to find out? The FBI wasn't a covert agency.

He decided to visit Special Agent Kim to put his mind at rest. There didn't need to be an electronic trail between him and Kim for Barber to find.

Ruling Georgia out would be a great relief. Kim might be able to do that. Alternatively, discovering

Georgia didn't even work for the feds would answer lot of questions. At the least, Kim also had the authority to look into who, if anyone, had monitored Georgia's phone. The only downside to Kinney's plan would be if Georgia and Kim were both bent. Then he'd be royally screwed.

Impulsively, Kinney called Eddie first, who answered this time in a reasonably convincing English accent.

"Sir Reginald's line. How may I help you?"

"It's Kinney. I need a straight answer about something. It's life or death. Did you tell anyone about my meeting Max—I mean Sue?"

"No, of course not," he answered in a deteriorating accent.

"Could anyone have found out somehow? You said you had another client."

"No, I don't see how," Eddie said.

"Are you—"

"Hold it. I went into the kitchen to get some paper towels after my other client—the guy who came in right after you—spilled the soda he brought in. It took me a while to find them since I hardly ever use them. I mean, why bother? Everything just gets dirty again after you clean things. It's a waste of time. Anyway, I suppose he could've seen what I texted you while I was gone. I don't think he did, but he could've."

"Who is this guy? And what did he hire you to do?"

"He said his name was Chase. He wanted to know all about someplace up north. I was supposed to hack into this county assessor's office, where they record deeds and shit."

"Did you?"

"No, I found out what I could legally. That's all. I only break the law for people I know. This guy could've been a cop."

"Did he look like a cop?"

"No, he was an ugly motherfucker, but not big and ugly like cops are," Eddie said.

"Is he short, with beady eyes, and a pronounced widow's peak?"

"What's that?"

"That's when somebody's hairline comes to a point low on his forehead," Kinney told him.

"Yes! That's the guy. You know him?"

"We've met." Chase was Jason Barber. That was who was in the SUV on Eddie's street.

"Oh, I forgot to mention. He said he knew you," Eddie reported, "and he was surprised to see you come out of my house."

"That would've been helpful to know earlier on, Eddie. You could've called me."

"Sorry, man. I'm a computer guy, not a people guy."

"You certainly aren't."

Chapter 24

Kinney thought about what Eddie had told him. The guilty party who'd revealed details about Max and the restaurant was bound to be Jason Barber, which was a great relief. Kinney had never let himself fully entertain the idea that Georgia had betrayed him, and now he could let go of any lingering doubts.

Did that mean he didn't need to see Kim anymore? He tabled making that decision and called about a charter plane flight to Alturas. If there was time to kill before takeoff, he'd head over to the FBI offices. It wouldn't hurt to confirm his assessment.

The outrageously expensive charter flight would be available in two hours. His credit card bill was going to rival the national debt of a small country. He was banking on the agency reimbursing him. If not, maybe Connelly would be willing to foot the bill.

Kinney drove to a municipal parking lot in his stolen car near the FBI office. He skulked his way to the federal building and told the elderly, cheery civilian manning a desk in the sparse, forbidding lobby that he needed to see Senior Agent Kim. The guy called him. Apparently he got reamed out for not supplying a name. When the man winced, even more of his wrinkles stood out. He looked like a human shar-pei, minus the pushed-in nose. The man's schnoz protruded a good three inches.

"I'm Kinney," Kinney told him. "Tell him I'm ready to talk."

The guy passed on the message, put his phone down, and then selected a visitor's badge from an array of badges on the counter beside him. Kinney saw that they came in a variety of colors.

"Why'd you give me the blue one?" He asked. "Are these color coded to reflect someone's status? Am I relegated to the blue demographic because I'm a civilian?"

"No. It matches your shirt. I get bored, so I color them. Want to see the plaid one I did? It wasn't easy."

"Maybe next time."

The guy sent him through a metal detector—Kinney had left his pistol in the car—and then aimed him at the elevator. "Fourth floor. He'll meet you in the lobby up there."

"Thanks."

Kim looked haggard, and his gray suit was wrinkled. He frowned as though he was unhappy to see Kinney, which didn't make much sense. He'd been begging for Kinney to come in for days. The expression somehow made him look even less like a traditional Korean.

"So you finally came to your senses, Kinney. Welcome to the most efficient law enforcement agency in the world." It was hard to tell if he really meant that.

"Thanks. We'll see about that."

"Come on back to my office."

"Sure."

Kinney had never been in the FBI office before. He was surprised that it looked like any other federal office. He'd been to the IRS for an audit and the DEA for work. Not for the first time, he noted how inaccurate his expectations tended to be.

Men and women in dark business attire sat in cubicles in an open area, which was encircled by offices. Half the doors of these were open, showing more government issue furniture and small windows with Venetian blinds. Only men roosted in these more privileged work settings.

Kim's office decor resembled the one Kinney had once sat in to straighten out a problem with his insurance agent, a former lieutenant in the Navy. Everything was in its place, albeit not as perfectly as at Foster's place. The blinds were open, and a shaft of sunlight highlighted a patch of taupe carpet underneath the window sill. The bright light rendered the rest of the room a bit dim despite the two rows of fluorescent light suspended from the cottage cheese ceiling. Three pictures on the wall behind Kim's gray metal desk displayed amateurish efforts to capture moving horses. Maybe Kim had a young daughter who'd painted them.

"So what can you tell me about your recent activities?" Kim asked as he sat.

"First, I need you to answer an important question." Kinney knew he needed to be thorough despite what he knew about Jason Barber.

"Shoot."

"You shouldn't say that to someone like me." Kinney grinned. "Here's my question. Is there an analyst here named Georgia?"

"No. There's only one female analyst. Her name is Brielle."

Kinney went numb. It was a surreal feeling—or not a feeling, actually. That *wasn't* what he expected to hear. "That's a pretty name," he mustered. "I don't think I've heard it before." His voice was wooden.

"You're a bit tangential, aren't you?" Kim asked.

"I guess." Kinney still wasn't ready to face the truth about Georgia.

"Why did you ask about this Georgia person?"

Kinney thought for a moment. "Apparently, she's been impersonating an FBI analyst."

Saying this made it real, and a flood of undifferentiated feelings swept through Kinney. He'd sort them out later, but hurt stood out. He'd never felt that on the job before.

"Do you have a way for us to find her?" Kim asked, leaning forward and staring intensely.

"Yes, I have contact information—her phone number and address," Kinney told him. He paused before continuing, scratching an itch on the side of his nose that didn't exist. He was regressing to old habits again. "You've been in the dark about Barber and all the rest, Kim. I'll tell you about that in a minute, and I brought a hefty file on a thumb drive I'll give to you later. Let me just gather myself for a minute."

"We'll take care of this impersonator. We take that particular felony very seriously. And I'm anxious to hear about your boss."

"Good. Like I said, let me think."

So Kim didn't have the file Kinney had passed on to Georgia. The FBI hadn't been working the case. And Kinney was an idiot.

"Here's what you need to know," Kinney began. He'd decided they needed the feds, and Kim was the only senior agent he knew. He'd just have to take the chance that Kim wasn't working for Barber.

"Wait a minute. I want to record this." Kim reached in a drawer and then placed a phone-sized device on his desk.

Kinney launched into a near-comprehensive explanation of the situation and how it had developed. Kim periodically asked cogent questions. Kinney left out the parts he or Reed could be arrested for and didn't mention Eddie by name. Twenty minutes later, Kim admonished him for having withheld information.

"I could lock you up right now for that. It makes you complicit in the crimes these others have committed." His tone wasn't as stern as his words.

"You could try."

"I won't. If what you've said checks out, we need to get to work on this immediately, and I know your skillset can help. Do you have ideas about how to approach Barber up in Modoc county? Since Waco, we're careful about situations like these." Kim shifted in his chair, demonstrating his discomfort.

"I always have ideas, but I don't know what's going to make the most sense yet."

"You've been involved in similar situations before?" Kim asked.

"Yes."

"And you're heading up to Alturas to join your partner?"

Kinney nodded. "Right after I collect some things and drive to the airport. Your men can be our backup."

"All right. I'll put together a team and make travel arrangements. I'll let you know the details." Kim leaned back. "I'm inclined to believe you about everything you said, although I suspect you left some things out. I'll double check any of this that I can, of course."

"Sure. And I definitely left some things out. But that's all you're getting. Let me text you Georgia's contact information. I don't know if she'll flip when you arrest her, but if she does, she'll know a lot more than we do."

Kim reached out and turned off the recorder. "They have an airport up in Alturas?'

Kinney looked up from texting. "Yes. I imagine there's not much to it, so I'll probably miss out on a cinnamon bun on the concourse."

"Do you know how many calories are in those?"

"Yum. I love calories."

****

Kinney drove south on 880, engrossed in unpleasant thoughts and feelings about Georgia. And himself.

He couldn't bring himself to face the full magnitude of her betrayal, but he was only too aware of his own appalling blunder—trusting and even sleeping with the enemy. He'd been delusional—blinded by his attraction and emotional needs as though he were a teenager with a crush.

When he noticed how he was beating himself up, he refocused on Georgia. She'd been a maestro at playful seduction and equally skilled at out and out lying. Kinney tried but couldn't entertain the idea that she'd actually developed feelings for him as she fulfilled her assignment—à la Rosie Aubert with Ryan Connelly.

That reminded him he needed to check in with Ryan Connelly's fiancée. Plus he needed a distraction. Rosie answered immediately at the burner phone number she'd given him.

"This is Kinney. Can you talk?"

"Yes. I'm just playing with Rocco."

"The guard dog?" He thought that was verboten like with seeing eye dogs. Several blind people had been very cranky when a younger Kinney had petted theirs.

"Yes," Rosie told him. "We have a special relationship."

"Is this part of your ditzy act—special relationships with dogs?"

"Kinney, what do you want?"

"How are things going at your end?"

"We're on track. As far as Barber's concerned, I'm still working with him. He called this morning to hear a report on what Ryan's been up to. I fed him the information we put together. What's happening at your end?"

Rocco barked. Rosie shushed him.

"There's a lot to report," Kinney told her. "We've located Barber up north, and I'm heading there soon. The woman I've been dating has been impersonating an FBI agent and pumping me for information. The feds are working with us now."

"That is a lot. You've been a busy boy."

"Do you have access to Ryan's security team?" Kinney asked.

"Well, I've charmed the bodyguards we use when we go out, which isn't often enough. It's hard to pry Ryan out of the house. Why do you ask?"

"They may come in handy later."

"I see. You're certainly welcome to their help. And I can handle myself, too."

That didn't seem likely to Kinney, no matter what

313

Rosie's background was. In his experience, people with military training tended to develop unfounded confidence about their abilities off the mat. A real fight was just as psychological as it was physical. Amateurs hesitated. Amateurs suppressed their ruthless side. Amateurs lost.

"Are you okay, *mon cher*?" Rosie asked. "An affair of the heart gone wrong…"

"I'm hanging in there. I've never been through something like this—being betrayed by a woman on this scale."

"Not since I tried it at Gallanto's, eh?"

"That was different."

Barbara Foster called ten minutes later while he was absently passing a truck overloaded with logs, nearly striking the corner of its bumper. He'd been planning to call Reed next after taking a break to keep processing his feelings.

"There's a problem with the FBI," Foster told him. "They won't give me access to an ongoing investigation, even when Hoff called and asked for inter-agency cooperation. I think whoever he could get through to had never heard of us."

"I just talked to Special Agent Kim a half hour ago. Don't worry about the FBI."

"Okay, great. I've got to fly to Vegas for a mission, anyway."

"Can't Curtis send someone else?" Kinney asked.

"There's no one as hot as me. This Cuban guy is picky about who he sleeps with."

"Hot, huh? You sound like Reed."

Foster laughed. "I guess I do. Maybe it's having to play the femme fatale with all these creeps that makes me so pissed off when I get toxic masculine crap elsewhere."

"That makes sense. Does Barber still trust you and Hoff?" Kinney asked.

"As far as I know. Curtis thinks so. He's gotten orders from him about you and Reed—to have you both eliminated, I mean. So do what you need to do to stay safe."

"Of course."

"What have you been up to, Kinney? Have you gotten anywhere?"

"Let me tell you about Georgia Hale." Kinney gave Foster a brief summary of his history with her and what he'd found out. He asked her to pass the information on to Hoff.

"That's awful. I can't imagine how I'd feel."

"I can't either. I'm mostly numb about it so far." That had been true a while ago. Kinney wasn't about to share his current feelings with another agent, even though hurt and anger were roiling in him.

"So what are you going to do about this Georgia person?" Foster asked.

"String her along. See what I can find out. There's an advantage to knowing the score when she doesn't know I know."

"Gotcha."

"Listen, I've got to go. Good luck in Nevada."

"Thanks."

****

Kinney couldn't bring himself to call and tell Reed about Georgia's betrayal. Sharing the news with Foster had put him through an emotional wringer. He needed to take a break before reliving the experience again.

He'd tell Reed in person when he landed. He texted Reed his estimated arrival time and left it at that.

Forty-five minutes later, after abandoning the BMW in the San Jose airport parking lot, he called Georgia from a spiffy waiting room in the private terminal. Kinney wanted to stay in better contact now. Seen through the lens of her true allegiance, he might be able to interpret what she said in some useful way.

Georgia told him she'd found out something important. "Barber is definitely at a ranch outside Alturas. Alan Kim found out somehow. We're assembling a team to raid the place, so don't proceed on your own. Kim will crucify you if you mess this up. Can I can count on you?"

"As sure as my name is Kinney." He was struck by how her version of the feds' plan varied from what he'd discussed with Kim. Georgia was trying to keep Reed and him from doing anything. And if Barber planned to lure and trap Kinney and Reed up there, Georgia had just baited the hook a little bit more.

"You mean as sure as you're *Clarence* Kinney, don't you?" Georgia said. "I don't see what's so bad about Clarence, by the way."

Kinney paused. How had she discovered his name? Was this a slip on her part? Even Eddie hadn't been able to find it online. He'd needed Kinney to tell him.

"Well, at least I wasn't named after a Confederate state or an Eastern European country," Kinney replied distractedly.

"You're so defensive. Lighten up."

"Sorry. I got teased a lot as a kid."

"Until you could kick everyone's ass?"

"Well, yeah. Literally. That's why I got into

fighting in the first place."

"I'd have loved to see you demolish a high school kid when you were twelve or something."

"It wasn't pretty. One or two kicks to sensitive areas and the fight was over. And no one ever called me Clarence after I took out the gym teacher."

"I'll bet he was surprised."

"It was a she," Kinney told her, "but in my defense, Ms. Popovich had eight inches and forty pounds on me. She'd rowed crew in college."

"Maybe we should talk about Barber and whoever else is involved."

"Right. How is the overall investigation going? Are you putting a solid case together?" Kinney asked.

"Sure. We're on it."

"All right, then back to the salt mines for me."

"You've got it easy, Kinney. I'm stuck in an office."

"I thought FBI analysts had cubicles."

She paused before responding. "I'm in denial. I call it an office."

"Okay. Ciao for now."

So maybe that was another slip—Georgia saying she had an office.

Kinney felt he'd done a good job of acting normal during his phone call. It hadn't been easy.

Kinney called Eddie next to try to solve the Clarence conundrum. Had Georgia been in contact with him?

Kinney was shocked when there was no answer at Eddie's. He was always home, and he always answered the phone. Kinney called 911, told the dispatcher to send cops to Eddie's house, and then hung up. He expected to find out grim news later. This was why Georgia knew his first name. Eddie had probably been abducted—or worse.

****

The otherwise empty four-seater plane flight to Alturas was uneventful, unless you count enduring really loud engine noise and several bouts of turbulence as events. Kinney knew what to expect. He'd flown on tinier, older planes in Asia. One of them had dripped water from the ceiling, all the seat belts had been inoperable, and the pilot had downed two beers during the flight.

The Alturas airport consisted of one not very long runway and what looked like a converted barn. It had recently been painted chestnut brown. After stepping down from the twin-engine plane and shaking the young pilot's hand, Kinney walked around the makeshift terminal building. He smelled creosote on route. Somebody was waterproofing wood, which seemed superfluous to Kinney as he looked at the bone dry ground beneath his running shoes.

Kinney met Reed by his car, which was parked beside a faded red curb behind a dusty gray pickup truck. The old guy standing by the truck wore denim overalls and a sweat-stained green John Deere baseball cap, completing the rural stereotype. Just beyond him, a sign declared the area was for "Legitimate Passengers Only." Kinney wondered what constituted an illegitimate passenger. Someone with luggage who'd been born out of wedlock?

"Welcome to Nowheresville, Kinney," Reed said.

Kinney scanned the landscape in the dimming light. Brown in every direction despite the recent winter rains in most of the state, flat, scrubby land stretched to a low, rocky mountain range. A strong wind blew from the northwest, kicking up dust from the adjacent dirt parking lot. Five older American cars and three pickup trucks were scattered around the lot.

"It's high desert," Reed told him, "which means they don't have sand dunes, or cactus, or anything else interesting."

"Can they farm around here? It doesn't look like it."

"They've got some hay, wheat, barley, and other crops people don't eat. Not right here. But in the county. Mostly there are ranches and lots of empty land like you see here. I think the wind blows the soil away. Maybe the next county over has it."

"There's not much to ruin if someone were to mine lithium here," Kinney pointed out.

"Yeah, that's true."

As they drove to Alturas, Kinney filled his partner in on what he'd discovered about Georgia at his meeting with Kim, as well as Eddie's abduction—or at least disappearance.

"Shit!" Reed exclaimed when he was through. "We're in trouble, aren't we? Exactly what does Georgia know?"

"Pretty much everything as of yesterday. And I turned over Connelly's information to her, so Barber has that now."

"You've still got copies of the file, right?"

"Sure. I gave one on a thumb drive to Alan Kim, and I've got another drive stashed in a safe place."

"That guy? Didn't you mess him up once?" Reed asked.

"He seems to have forgiven me."

They passed a tractor and then a flatbed truck loaded with shorn sheep, who looked embarrassed to be seen in public as their scrawny selves.

Reed spoke again after he'd managed these maneuvers. "How are you feeling? I don't know how I'd feel if a woman did that to me."

"I don't know how I'd feel, either."

"It hasn't sunk in yet?"

"No, I'm regulating my dosage of reality," Kinney told him. "It's still awful, anyway. It's not so much the literal loss—I mean, I haven't known her very long. The real grief is losing where I thought we were heading. You know, the possibility of a wonderful future together."

"Plus, we're a lot more likely to get killed because of her," Reed pointed out.

"Yes, there's that, too."

****

"Here we are," Reed announced as he pulled into a parking space behind a relatively tall, older building in Alturas. Kinney hadn't been paying attention to the scenery en route, which wasn't like him. He'd have to watch himself or his preoccupation with his feelings would get him killed.

"This is the Myles Hotel, Kinney. It's tied for the most stars online, and it's right downtown."

"Let me guess. Two stars?"

"Yup. It's got a bar and a cafe so we won't have to wander around town and maybe get spotted."

"You're sure no one's seen you already?" Kinney knew that when Reed visited somewhere new, he usually prowled in search of amenable women.

320

"As far as I know. I've taken the usual precautions."

Reed shut off the engine, but the two men remained in the car.

"So tell me more about this deputy—Glinda," Kinney said, still thinking about the hound his partner was.

"It didn't work out between us."

"You already had a beginning, a middle, and an ending?" Kinney's eyebrows shot up. Even for Reed, this was a fast story arc.

"Yeah, but we kinda skipped the middle part. She was a big help while it lasted. We wouldn't have found Barber without her." Reed tried to turn off the ignition again, frowning as he realized he'd already done so.

"Who does she think you are?" Kinney asked.

"I have an FBI shield as Tom Badger."

"Badger?" Kinney wondered why Reed had chosen that name.

"They're cute animals, Kinney."

"No, they're not."

"Sure. They look like little porcupines."

"You're thinking of hedgehogs."

"If that's true—and I'm not saying it is—both names have a 'dge' in the middle, so it's an understandable mistake. Anyway, what does it matter? That's the name I picked, and it worked."

"Right. Why did Glinda dump you?"

"It was mutual," Reed tried.

"No, it wasn't."

"Okay, maybe it wasn't." They disembarked, and Reed hurriedly changed the subject. "Notice the electric car charging stations, Kinney. They're very proud of them here."

Two gleaming blue chargers sat near the back door. It didn't look as though anyone had ever used them. Either that or someone polished them every morning.

"They're lovely," Kinney said, stopping to give them their due.

"I got us a couple of rooms on the second floor."

Reed handed Kinney a key on a brass keychain. Threaded onto it was potato-sized piece of weathered leather that had the outline of the hotel's exterior branded onto it.

"I think they should be proud of their keychains, too," Kinney said.

"Wait until you try to jam it into your pocket."

When they got to Kinney's room, they got to work.

Chapter 25

Kim called while they were attempting to come up with a plan. Kinney put him on speaker. He'd texted to let the fed know where to reach him.

"My team will be there about midmorning tomorrow. They have to fly to Reno and then rent a vehicle. That's how it goes when you're using taxpayer's money. We've got an office in Redding, but I don't trust those bozos for something like this."

"I understand," Kinney told him. "That'll be fine. How many agents are we talking about, and will they be backup like we discussed?"

"Four. Yes, they're there for support. I gave the senior man the name of your hotel and your phone number and told him to follow your lead. You may be an asshole, Kinney, but I learned the hard way years ago that you know what you're doing."

Reed nodded his agreement. Kinney hoped that was for the knowing part, not the asshole part.

"By senior, do you mean the oldest or the best agent?" Kinney asked.

"Don't worry about that," Kim told him. "Jeff Nevitt is the finest we've got. And there's a woman on the team in case that fits into your plans. By the way, what are they?"

"We're working on that now," Reed answered.

"Is that you, Bolt?"

"Yes. What about this Georgia person?" Reed asked. "Do you have her in custody?"

"No luck there." Kim sighed loud enough that Kinney wondered if he'd been holding his breath. "The phone number Kinney gave us originates from our office. Don't ask me how she managed that. And the address is someone else's place."

"I've been there with her," Kinney told him.

"So? Obviously, the great and powerful Kinney was played for a fool, wasn't he?"

Kinney pictured Kim smirking, one of his least favorite expressions. He'd made a point of not learning how to do it when he'd practiced expressions as a teen.

"Hey, " Reed said. "Don't be a dick. How do you think Kinney feels about this?"

"I don't think you two feel anything," Kim responded. "You're psychopaths, aren't you?"

"Sociopaths," Kinney corrected. "There's a big difference. We feel things sometimes."

"And we're benign sociopaths," Reed chimed in. "We work for good, not evil."

"Tell yourself whatever you want," Kim said. "We're only on the same page because of circumstances. I'd arrest you both in a heartbeat if we didn't need you." He paused before speaking again. "Kinney, any guesses about where Georgia might be?"

"She could be up here, I suppose," Kinney answered. "Or Sacramento. They still need to get their bill through the legislature. Maybe she's seducing state senators or something."

"Okay, we'll check into that. And it's good you're up there to spot her in case she's with Barber."

"She might have some role in getting the lithium

mine going," Reed added. "I've looked into that. That's what's going on up here. Rakena bought land about twenty minutes from town, and there's a mining exploration outfit that's set up here in our hotel. Hartshorn Industries."

"We'll look into them," Kim said.

"When were you going to get around to telling me that?" Kinney asked his partner, glaring at him.

"Well, now, obviously."

"I'll leave you two to bicker," Kim said. "Let's stay in touch."

"We're not bickering," Reed said.

"Now you're bickering with me. Goodbye."

After another fruitless session of planning, Kinney and Reed decided to take a break and eat downstairs. The dining room embodied an Old West theme, replete with wooden wagon wheels on the walls and vintage signs banning gambling, spitting, and "tomfoolery."

Once they'd sat in a corner and ordered burgers and fries, Reed provided more details about the premining lithium operation he'd discovered.

"It's a fenced compound that's about eight acres. There's supposed to be some kind of derrick, but not like the oil well kind."

"You haven't been out there yet?"

"No, I waited for you. Glinda said you can't see much from the road, and I figured we'd check out Barber's hideout first thing, anyway."

"I'm thinking we should head out to the mine site with a drone before we tackle the Barber ranch situation. If this is a trap, where Barber is staying is where it'll get sprung, right?"

"Yeah, I suppose so," Reed conceded.

"I think the drilling site—or whatever it is—might be a gateway to getting to Barber."

"Tell me more." Reed played with the salt shaker. Kinney knew his partner often fiddled with whatever was handy, but it didn't interfere with his listening.

"Well, we've been planning for a while," Kinney began, "and so far we haven't figured out a way to get into the ranch—without a lot of bloodshed, I mean. Suppose we find a way to get Barber out?"

"To where the lithium is?"

"Exactly. His being up here has to be connected to that. I mean, that's the whole reason they want to create Jefferson. What if something went wrong there? Or what if they needed him to take a look at something important?"

Reed nodded. "That makes sense. We definitely should head out there and check it out. First thing in the morning?"

"Sure. We need to figure out something before the feds get here to help, so the sooner the better. Any more intel about the site? The topography? The layout? How many men?"

"Nope. It's all pretty hush-hush. We'll need to use the drone to see what's what." He switched to marching the pepper shaker around the perimeter of his placemat. "I only know the compound is there at all because Glinda had to go serve a warrant on a worker who got drunk and punched someone in a bar. This was a few months ago. She said she only got as far as a gate to the dirt road they built. The guy at the gate fetched the puncher, who hit on her in the SUV. That's why she brought it up—so she could complain about men."

They argued over what to watch on TV that

evening, settling on a ridiculous spy movie that neither one was crazy about. It was hard to take any of it seriously when the shrimp of an actor repeatedly beat up giant villains and did totally stupid things like jump a motorcycle onto the top of a train. Reed had once needed to outrun the police on a bike in Ireland. It hadn't been hard since he could squeeze through narrow openings in traffic and the Garda couldn't. The spy in the movie hadn't even researched a route out of town if something went wrong.

One good thing about Alturas was that the day started early there, so Kinney and Reed could get breakfast at six thirty. The same server waited on them as the evening before—a slim teenager with asymmetrical black bangs. Her earrings were bright green feathers that curled inward enough to caress her cheeks when she moved.

"You've got the dinner shift *and* the breakfast shift?" Reed asked her.

"I'm saving for college."

"What are you going to study?"

"Well, it's not classes in the talking-to-you department when I need to get your order and then cover the other tables. So what'll it be?"

"Ouch."

She sniggered.

The omelets were tasty—the morning cook was more skilled than the dinner cook—and the two drove out of town well-fed. Perhaps to compensate for her rudeness, the server had heaped an impressive mound of cottage potatoes onto both their plates.

About a quarter mile from the pint-sized steel derrick that thrust up from bare dirt behind a cyclone fence, an abandoned filling station on the other side of the road sat next to a creaky wooden windmill and a shack with no roof. The station itself wasn't in much better shape. The "Sinclair" sign was missing its "C," and one of the repair bay doors was full of bullet holes where someone had spray-painted a red bullseye. Reed pulled in behind the station.

"I'll send the drone around the perimeter from high up first," he said. "We probably need to find another way in besides the gate Glinda mentioned."

"You brought the quietest one with the most magnification?" Kinney asked.

"Yeah. I don't think anyone will be shooting down a Maverik GR-45 Pro any time soon. It kicks the ass of what I brought to Connelly's place."

"Where'd you get it, anyway? I thought it was military only."

"It was in an unmarked case in the back of a closet in that safe house in Alameda. Apparently the agency has access to all sorts of goodies we don't know about. The thing is supposed to be almost silent. I looked it up."

Once the drone was airborne, Reed opened his laptop and synced up the app. The video was remarkably clear, even as the drone began to reach the limit of its range.

The compound wasn't heavily defended. After all, it wasn't a munitions dump or a terrorist camp. One guard manned the gate. They didn't see a weapon on him, but Reed told Kinney everybody in the area had guns. "It's NRA Central here."

The guard at the gate mostly looked at his phone, only glancing up when an occasional pickup truck tooled by. Away from town, were a lot more of them than there were cars.

Beyond the gate, a couple of green wooden sheds were positioned on wooden pallets facing each other, leaving a space between them that showed deep tire tracks. The dusty structures probably started life in a building supplies warehouse.

Then the property fanned out on the sides, and the tall cyclone fence expanded with it. There was no barbed or razor wire and no indication of electrification.

The derrick sat almost in the center of the compound. To Kinney's eyes, it looked like a junior version of those giant power-line towers you see in the wild, only this one had a long pipe extending down from above the structure to the ground. Did they retrieve core samples with it? Other equipment sat beside the tower. The only thing Kinney recognized was a monstrous generator.

The main building was a good-sized corrugated metal Quonset hut. Several cars and trucks were parked in front of it. Two weathered blue plastic portable toilets sat beside it. Beyond that, a white trailer that had seen better days perched on cinderblocks.

The two men watched closely as the drone drifted past all that, looking for an isolated entry point. Cutting through the cyclone fence wasn't a problem. Doing so out of sight was.

"There!" Kinney said. "Hover it."

An ancient, rusted metal shed hugged the fence at the farthest point from the front gate. It probably predated the current owners.

"No one would see us if we were behind that shed," Kinney said. "Instead of cutting through, we

329

could go over the fence there and come down on the roof of the shed."

"Those buildings are like drums," Reed told him. "Any sound we make on top of it will be amplified."

"I don't see anyone nearby to hear anything. Do you?"

"Let me broaden the field of vision," Reed said. He did so. Unfortunately, two men in blue coveralls leaned against a nearby Jeep behind the trailer, smoking.

"You think they're staying in that trailer?" Kinney asked.

"Either that or it's an office."

"It's still early. Maybe they'll head over to the main building or the derrick to get to work."

"Maybe," Reed replied. "I'll bet this is our best shot, anyway. Let me send our little friend around the rest of the fence line to see. Then I'll hover it high up over the center of the compound. We need to see whoever's in there and what they're doing."

"Right."

The video confirmed that the fence behind the shed was their best entry point. It also showed Kinney and Reed that another security guard in army fatigues was on duty, patrolling the perimeter on foot.

"That's not good," Reed said. "And why would they need that guy? Are they expecting trouble?"

"Let's time the perimeter guy."

"Sure."

The guard made his rounds along the interior of the fence line every ten minutes, walking in front of the shed and rounding off the corners. He seemed about as alert as most security guards tasked with stultifying duty. This guy had a pistol holstered on his military-style webbed belt.

"Ten minutes should give us time to get in there unnoticed," Kinney said.

"Yeah." Reed paused. "I'm still not clear about what we're going to do once we're in to draw Barber to the site, though. And we'll have to deal with that armed guard."

"I think we've seen enough of the layout," Kinney replied. "Let's go figure that out."

Kinney and Reed returned to the Myles Hotel to plot and await the FBI team. By the time the four feds arrived, texting Kinney that they were in the lobby, both men were happy with what they'd come up with.

"Why don't you go down and meet them?" Kinney suggested. "I've got to go find a way to print out our bogus search warrant."

"Sure."

Chapter 26

So it wasn't until Kinney returned from a small office supply store down the street that he was surprised by who the woman on the FBI team was.

Georgia!

Reed didn't seem to recognize her in her navy pantsuit with her hair up, and the senior agent—Jeff Nevitt—introduced her as Brielle Hale, along with the names of the other two agents.

She smiled at Kinney, unaware that he'd believed she was working with Barber. "Nice to see you again," she said in the tone of someone who might've run into him a time or two.

Kinney knew that Hale was Georgia's last name. Was she simply be using a different first name at work—Brielle? He remembered that he had never mentioned her last name to Kim. And the agent had told him there was an analyst named Brielle. For that matter, Georgia's phone had originated in the feds' office. No wonder the FBI hadn't located her. As a separate person, Georgia didn't exist. Georgia was Brielle. Why hadn't Eddie ferreted this out?

All of this raced through his brain as his mouth hung open. Nevitt asked him if he was okay. Georgia/Brielle asked him if he would have a problem working with someone he'd met socially.

"He knows me as Georgia," she explained to the

others. "I use my middle name at work."

"No, no," Kinney replied. "I'm just surprised. Didn't you say you're an analyst? What are you doing out in the field?"

"That was my call," Nevitt said in a sharp tone. "You have a problem with it?"

"No, it's fine. I'm sure she'll be great."

"I hope this isn't sexism," Reed said. "You know how I feel about that." He smiled at Georgia, clearly trying to score points with her at Kinney's expense. "I think I know you from somewhere," he added, cocking his head and studying her face.

"Reed, we need to talk." Kinney pointed to the bathroom.

"Okay." When Kinney closed the door behind them, Reed asked, "So what's up? What was that all about? It was like you were stuck in neutral for a while."

"Didn't you catch the name? That's Georgia. *My* Georgia. She's also the one who said you were pretty on the sidewalk outside the agency's office."

"Really? That's her? She's the one who's been pretending to be a fed?"

"Wait a minute. Let me think about this," Kinney said. "I thought she was impersonating an FBI agent and clearly she's not, but she still could be with Barber. Maybe Nevitt is in on this, too. He brought her when she's hardly ever been in the field before—or so she says. I don't know what to think at this point."

"Didn't you say Kim hadn't received the file that Connelly gave you? You gave it to Georgia to pass along, right?"

"Yes, that's right. You know, why don't I brace her

about all this and see what she says. I don't want to think the worst if I don't have to. I mean, we've been dating and I'm crazy about her—or I was, anyway."

"Okay."

Reed left to fetch Georgia, who met Kinney in the cramped tiled bathroom moments later.

"Kinney, do you know how this looks?" She glared at him. "This is very unprofessional. What's Jeff going to think?"

"I need to ask you a few important questions. They can't wait."

She sighed. "Go ahead."

"Why didn't you give Kim the files I gave you?"

"I brought them to someone higher up. I told you I knew someone—remember? I was concerned that Kim might be compromised. If I were Barber, he's the guy I'd go after. He runs the unit that handles these types of crimes."

"Can you prove you did that?" Kinney asked this in as gentle a tone as he could, but he knew the implication of his words would sting anyway.

Georgia flared her nostrils and bared her teeth like an aggressive guard dog. "Why should I have to? What's this all about?"

Kinney was intimidated. "Bear with me, and please answer my question," he tried.

"Of course I can prove what I shouldn't have to prove, you idiot. Call Assistant Director Dan Forbes in the San Diego office."

"I will. Here's my next question. How did you know my first name?" Kinney asked.

"Really? That's what you want to know? This is ridiculous." Her nostrils flared now in rhythm with her breath, which distracted Kinney for a moment. "But if you must know," Georgia continued, "I have a friend at work who was investigating a hacker who'd penetrated our internal network and tried to get into our personnel files."

"Sue Exeter?"

"No, Eddie something. Apparently my friend already had her eye on him. Anyway, when they hauled him out of his house, he had a panic attack and passed out. In the ambulance, he muttered your name, and Robin knew we were dating so she called me. I went down to the hospital—they thought it might be a heart problem at first—and while he was drugged up, Eddie told me about Clarence. I didn't even ask him. Why would I ask that? I think he wanted to establish he really knew you. He thought that would have some weight with us. Who did you tell this guy you were?"

"I didn't." Kinney thought all this over. "I get the concern about Kim, Georgia, but this Eddie story sounds wildly unlikely. I'm sorry. I'd like to believe you. I really would."

For some reason, Georgia calmed down a bit. "Call him. He's back home. He wouldn't talk, and we haven't been able to get enough on him yet. Now what's this all about, Kinney? You think I'm a mole? A criminal?" Her voice rose as she finished and she bared her teeth again. Mercifully, her nostrils were back to normal.

"Look, I talked to Kim and he said there wasn't a Georgia working with him, and that he hadn't received any files," Kinney told her. He'd backed away involuntarily as he said this. "You should've told me you use a different name at work and that you'd definitely decided you weren't going work with Kim on this. What was I supposed to think?"

Georgia's added narrowed eyes and clenched fists to her medley of nonverbal cues. "So this is my fault?" She glared, and Kinney flinched. He would've preferred to be facing an armed terrorist. "Here's what you were supposed to think," she continued. "You were supposed to care about me—to give me the benefit of the doubt about whatever came along. You were supposed to know who the hell I am by now. You're an asshole, Kinney."

She stomped off, and Reed returned. "Well?" he asked.

"The honeymoon is over."

"She's bad news, you mean—working for Barber?"

"No, I think she's legit. I'm talking about the relationship. I have to make a couple of calls to confirm her story. I jumped to conclusions when Eddie wasn't home, and I didn't look hard enough for alternative explanations about Georgia. I just accused someone I think I'm in love with of being part of a vast criminal conspiracy." Kinney's gut felt tight, and his face heated up.

Reed looked puzzled. "I thought you were just going to ask her some questions."

"Well, she took them as accusations. I would've."

"She did seem really pissed off just now. I wonder how she'll square that with Nevitt. I mean, she goes into a bathroom with some kind of spy, and then she comes out angry. He's got to think that's strange."

"I'm sure she'll find a way to sort it out. She's resourceful."

"So what'll we do?" Reed asked. "Just treat her like any other FBI agent?"

"I guess so—for now."

"Okay."

"I'm going to stay in here and make a couple of calls—just to be sure."

Kinney called Eddie first, who answered immediately, which wasn't like him. Predictably, he acted weird on the phone. In this case, the weirdness was that he sounded normal. He never had before.

"Eddie, I'm glad you're okay. I heard about what happened."

"It was horrible, and I'm sorry I told that lady your first name. I was really scared, and she seemed nice."

"Don't worry about that."

"I thought she'd call you, and you'd help. She said she knew you."

"Really, it's okay. The important thing is that you're safe."

"What do you mean? I'm not safe. The fucking FBI is on my ass."

"Never mind. I gotta go. I'll see what I can do about them."

"Thanks. You've gotta outrank those fuckers, right?"

"Sort of."

Kinney called the FBI's San Diego field office next and asked for Forbes. He managed to get transferred to the assistant director's assistant—Marcy.

"What is this concerning?" she asked in a Boston accent.

"Tell Forbes it's about Georgia Hale—no, make that Brielle Hale."

"Just a minute."

It was a long minute.

"What's this about Brielle?" Forbes asked.

"She told me you could verify something."

"Is this Kinney? You mean the files she sent me?"

"Yes, I'm Kinney. But if I wasn't, you just mentioned my name to a total stranger, didn't you? Is that wise? Do you know who I am?"

His attempt at his usual menace fell flat. He realized he hadn't yet recovered from his confrontation with Georgia.

"I certainly do," Forbes told him. "The delay in talking to you was so I could run your voice through voice recognition software we're testing."

"How in the world do you have my voice on file?"

"Brielle is a very careful person. She recorded one of her phone conversations with you and asked me to run it. It didn't match anything in our database at the time."

"So she was suspicious about me?" Kinney asked. He thought he'd allayed her concerns early on.

"Of course. You told her you were a sociopath, didn't you?"

"Why would she tell you all this? This is alarming."

"Brielle doesn't want people to know, but I'm her uncle. Don't tell her I told you, or there'll be hell to pay."

"Okay. I guess that's it. Thanks for your help."

"Kinney, treat her right, or there'll be a huge, efficient organization that'll have a hard on for you."

"Does accusing her of a criminal conspiracy count as treating her wrong?"

"I'd say so. Wouldn't you?"

Chapter 27

While Kinney had been in the bathroom, someone had rustled up chairs, which were arrayed in a semicircle in the area between the queen bed and the window facing the street. Two agents whose names Kinney had already forgotten sat, while Nevitt, Georgia, and Reed stood facing them.

"I don't know what the hell you think you're doing," Nevitt told him. "Am I going in the bathroom with you next? If you've got something to say, say it to all of us."

"Right. Have a seat, everyone. Let me go through our plan with you." Kinney's tone was brusque—professional. He needed to counteract his idiosyncratic behavior.

Kinney strode in front of the window and took a minute to study the feds. Reed stood next to him. Who were they dealing with here?

Nevitt looked the part of a senior agent. He wore a dark suit with a burgundy knit tie, and black cop shoes with thick soles. His weathered skin spoke to a lot of time in the field—maybe operating from a desert field office like Phoenix. His alert brown eyes were his strongest feature. His bony, stubbled cheeks and jaw were second, reflecting an internal strength to Kinney's eyes.

The agent on Kinney's right was unusually slim

except for bulging biceps visible just below the high sleeves of his tight polo shirt. Clearly, he was proud of his disproportionate muscles. A jutting hawk nose dominated his face, and his puffy red lips reminded Kinney of a girl in high school he'd had a crush on.

The remaining agent could've blended into any crowd. He was so nondescript that once Kinney moved his gaze away, he couldn't remember what he looked like.

When Kinney was through explaining what he and Reed had come up with, Nevitt grudgingly agreed the scheme was likely to work. He didn't like the idea of employing a forged legal document, but he conceded that the FBI had plausible deniability if that should prove to be a problem.

"I understand that whatever agency you're with isn't likely to pursue a legal solution to this conspiracy," Nevitt continued. "That goes against the grain for me, but Alan Kim said to go along with you— that we're just here as backup."

"Well, as you just heard, your team will be more than backup. When you show up with a warrant after Reed and I do our part, that's going to be the coup de grâce. As far as what will happen to Barber, don't worry about it. The guy is too connected for a fair trial. This is one of the most powerful people in the country. I can't tell you more than that."

"Okay. I'm sorry if we got off on the wrong foot, Kinney. We need to work together, and I don't want any enmity—either between you and me or you and Brielle."

"Thanks. I apologize for the time-outs I needed to call." He looked Georgia in the eye for the first time since he'd emerged from the bathroom. "Are we okay?" Kinney asked.

She nodded perfunctorily. It was clear to Kinney that if Nevitt hadn't been there, he would've received a very different answer.

"So when do we get going on this?" the puffy-lipped agent asked.

"And you are?" Kinney responded.

"Atkins. Call me Jake."

"Sure. When do you usually serve warrants?"

The remaining fed spoke. Kinney was momentarily distracted by his effort to describe this nondescript man to himself.

"Rousting perps out of bed early in the morning works best. There's less resistance to our searches and usually they're wearing—or not wearing—something that makes them feel vulnerable. Any edge helps."

"And you are…?" Kinney asked.

"I'm Hannover. Is it so hard to remember a few names?"

Reed spoke up before Hannover could continue. "Kinney is a flawed individual like all the rest of us. We're a messy, bumbling species, aren't we?"

This was a quote he'd memorized to excuse his sometimes boorish behavior. Everyone ignored him.

"Will early morning work here?" Nevitt asked Kinney. "I assume you scouted the site."

"Yes. I think just before sunrise is a great idea. There's almost no cover for Reed and I to approach the fence in daylight. I wasn't looking forward to crawling a few hundred yards holding a tumble weed over my head."

Agent Atkins spoke up. "Kinney, you don't sound

much like a sociopath. You're supposed to be one, right? I think it's important we know who we're working with."

Reed answered. "A successful sociopath knows how to act as though he isn't one."

"I don't think Kinney's actually a sociopath," Georgia said. "I think he just has an eccentric version of low self-esteem."

"That's enough," Nevitt said sternly. "What shall we do the rest of the day?"

"Hartshorn Industries has a couple of rooms upstairs," Reed told him. "I think it might be their base of operations."

"So maybe Reed and I ought to 'talk' to one of those guys," Kinney added.

"And the air quotes around the word 'talk' means something I don't want to know?" Nevitt asked.

"Reed and I can be very convincing without resorting to anything overtly illegal."

"Yeah? Like what do you do?" Hannover asked, clearly skeptical.

Kinney walked over and stood inappropriately close to the agent, his eyes darting back and forth, his fists clenched. "You smell like Jupiter. Are you from Jupiter? I hate people from Jupiter. Tell me your most embarrassing middle school memory or I'll eat all the pizza."

"Okay, I get it. You'll act crazy. That's a little scary, I've got to admit."

Kinney started to walk away, then whirled and kicked Hannover's earlobe.

"Holy shit!" Nevitt exclaimed. Hannover crouched into a fighting stance. "Leave it, John," his boss told him.

Hannover stood down, his brow furrowed and his head shoved forward like a snapping turtle preparing to snap.

"If that doesn't work," Reed said, "I sing Christmas carols while Kinney does the hula."

"You guys really *are* crazy," Jake said.

"You'll get no argument from me," Georgia told him.

"If that doesn't work," Nevitt said, "let us know. Our badges loosen a lot of tongues."

"I don't think we want them knowing you're here," Kinney said. "I think you four should just lie low today."

"Good point. We'll do that."

Kinney turned to Reed. "Shall we?"

"Shall we what?"

"Go find a likely interrogatee from the mining company."

"That's not a word," Reed said.

You know what I mean, though, don't you?"

"Maybe."

"Let's not fight in front of the children, Reed."

****

Culling the young woman they'd selected from the group of five mining engineers in the hotel turned out to be more complicated than Kinney and Reed anticipated. All their potential prey trundled down for lunch en masse. Reed was waiting in the elevator, having been alerted by Kinney, who watched their doors from the end of the hallway.

Observing them as they talked about how unhappy they were to be in Alturas, it was clear to Reed that

Patty—who didn't look anything like a Patty—was the one who was most unhappy. Unhappy people were more likely to yield up what they weren't supposed to. And women tended to be more vulnerable to physical intimidation.

Patty was built like a human tank, complete with a neck that swiveled independently of the rest of her like a turret. When it did, her oversized, squarish head brought intense, dark eyes into play. Her very black hair—dyed, Reed thought—contrasted sharply with her pale skin and deep-set light blue eyes. Reed figured her skin was her best feature, which said something about her overall looks.

Nonetheless, Reed's first thought was to use his film star face and self-proclaimed charm to lure her away from the others. Then one of the men—a geeky looking guy wearing a light green suit—made a crack about her being gay, so that was ruled out. Reed figured they could try something similar with Georgia as the seducer, but why involve anyone else if they didn't have to? Patty could be happily married to another lesbian for all he knew, anyway.

Reed huddled with Kinney on a well-worn couch in the empty lobby after the four men and Patty entered the dining room.

"If we can get this woman's last name, maybe we could have her paged," Kinney suggested after Reed reported what he'd found out.

"Do hotels still do that? I think you've seen too many 1930s movies."

"Yeah, maybe so. Maybe they'd send a bellman to find her."

"Same deal, Kinney. Have you seen any bellmen?"

"Well, no."

"You seem to be off your game. Is the Georgia thing still bothering you?"

"Yeah. I'm not used to my personal life leaking into my work life."

"I know what you mean. Once on the job I ran into a guy I knew from my gym. What a mess."

Kinney thought for moment. "If we get this Patty's phone number, I'm sure we could call and lure her away from the others," he said.

"That's true."

"Let me see if I can get her name from the front desk," Kinney said. "Then the feds can rustle up her number for us, right?"

"I'm sure they can. It's not like she's a spy or on the run or something. That's Wanda over there. I've already established a rapport with her. Leave it to me."

As the two looked across the modest, old-fashioned lobby, they saw the willowy young blonde who'd been manning the hotel's reception leave, replaced by an older man.

"That's a bummer," Reed said. "I'm pretty sure Wanda's bribable."

"This guy might be even more bribable. Who knows?" Kinney said. "Let me try. Wanda looked too young to have had her ideals crushed yet, anyway."

"How much money do you have on you?" Reed asked.

"Let me see…Eighty-five bucks. That ought to be more than enough. Why don't you go have lunch and keep an eye on the mining people. I'll join you when I can. If Patty goes to the bathroom or steps out to take a call, let me know. For that matter, if one of the men does, we can always switch targets."

"Sounds good."

Kinney approached the counter.

"Good day, sir," the man said before Kinney even reached it. "What can I do for you?"

The desk clerk must've been in his fifties despite his soft-looking, pink skin. His friendly smile seemed sincere, and his teeth were incredibly white. He wore a threadbare black suit and a brand new-looking red silk tie.

"I hope you can help me," Kinney said. "I'm trying to get in touch with an old friend who's staying in room 405—she's with Hartshorn."

"I know who you mean. I'll ring her room for you." The man reached for the phone to his right.

"She's not there. She's in the dining room," Kinney told him.

"I don't see what the problem is." He wrinkled his brow as if to demonstrate he'd tried hard to understand. "Why don't you simply go there? Do you suffer from social anxiety?"

"How'd you get to that?" Kinney asked him.

"My wife is the therapist in town. I try to be respectful of our guests' issues."

"I always wanted to date a therapist," Kinney told him in an effort to connect on a personal level. "They've got to be better at relationships than other people."

"You'd think so, wouldn't you?" the man said, shaking his head.

"Anyway, I'm not anxious—just embarrassed," Kinney told him. "I don't remember Patty's last name."

"Why would you need to know that to join her for

lunch?"

"It's a long story. Can you help me out?"

"We have a well-adjusted population here in Alturas," the man told him thoughtfully.

"That's interesting." Actually, Kinney had no idea where this was going.

"So my wife's business isn't flourishing."

"Uh-huh."

"And my salary is more minimal than one might expect."

"Ah, I understand." Kinney pulled out two twenties and set them on the counter. "Perhaps this will help," he suggested.

Without looking at them, the man deftly swept the bills off the counter to his feet. The maneuver looked artful enough that Kinney wondered if a lot of bribes came his way.

"Caulkins," the clerk said. "Patricia Caulkins. You have a good day, sir."

Kinney joined Reed in the dining room. His partner had ordered a crab salad for him.

"I didn't know when you'd get here," Reed explained, "so I thought something cold might be a good idea."

"Where do you think the nearest crabs are?" Kinney responded.

"They have refrigerated trucks. Is this any way to act when I was being thoughtful?"

"Have you ever seen me eat a crab?"

"Fine. Order something else."

"I will," Kinney said.

"Fine."

They glared at one another, and then both started

laughing.

"Are we married or what?" Reed said.

"Yeah, sorry. What a ridiculous thing to fight over. I just hate shellfish."

"What'd they ever do to you?" Reed asked.

The server sidled over. Kinney ordered a BLT.

"Do you have homeless people in town?" he asked the young woman, who looked to be Wanda's sister. They had the same lank, dirty blond hair and pug nose.

"Just one. Henry."

"Do you think he'd like this salad?"

"Sure."

"Problem solved," Kinney told Reed.

Chapter 28

Following Kinney's call to Nevitt to research their quarry's phone number, Patty pushed back her chair and headed to the lobby.

"All that for nothing," Kinney said.

"I'll settle the bill. You follow her."

"Okay."

Patty strolled through the lobby to the sidewalk and turned left. Kinney had yet to explore that end of the four block long downtown. He had no idea what might draw her in that direction.

After a block, the woman ducked into a bar—the Broken Spoke. Kinney followed. From a stool at the opposite end of the long wooden bar, he texted Reed, who drove over while Patty downed a beer and then ordered another.

The Broken Spoke's décor looked like something out of a Gene Autry movie. Unlike the Myles Hotel's version of the Wild West, the place was some pinhead's idea of a cowboy bar. Saddles were glued on top of the barstools, but most were English saddles. Kinney didn't figure there were a lot of steeplechase riders in the area. Neon signs behind the bar were shaped like a lasso, a hat, and a set of spurs. These were purple, yellow, and red, respectively.

Kinney had gotten smashed in real cowboy bars in Idaho. The bartenders there didn't sport silver fringes on the sleeves of their black western shirts. And they didn't play Hank Williams on the jukebox. They played Bob Wills or maybe Earnest Tubb. "Fuck that whiny shit," an old timer in Pocatello told him when Kinney had asked him about Hank. "I'll take a Texas tune any day."

"The car's out front," Reed told Kinney when he'd joined him at the bar.

Kinney had ordered him a milk.

"Touche," Reed said. "Nicely played."

"Thanks. This is an ideal set-up, isn't it?"

"Yeah. Let's do what we did in Chicago," Reed suggested.

"Which time?"

"With the bookkeeper."

"Okay."

So when Patty got up to leave, Reed hustled through the door ahead of her, raced to his car, and opened the door to the back seat. Kinney followed Patty and then herded her to the car, shoved her in, and climbed in next to her. The maneuver was over and done with before she could react by screaming.

"Don't worry," Kinney told her as Reed scurried into the driver's seat. "We won't hurt you."

"Are you going to rape me?" Patty asked. Her tone reflected apprehension more than outright fear, which Kinney found odd.

Reed turned in his seat. "Look at me. Do you think I'm hard up for action? Of course we won't. Even my partner back there is rugged enough to get a few dates."

"Shall we take another poll, Harry?" Kinney asked Reed. "About who's better looking?"

"Then what am I doing in here?" Patty asked. "Is

this a kidnapping? It's true that my father owns Hartshorn and there's plenty of assets beyond that, but he's disowned me and doesn't even know I work for his company. You'll never get a red cent. In fact, the bastard would probably be happy if I disappeared off the face of the Earth."

Reed started driving.

"That sounds rough," Kinney said. "Is it because you like women?"

"*A* woman. Marjorie." Patty seemed insulted that Kinney had generalized her orientation.

"I'm so sorry to hear about your father and what's happened to you," Kinney said. "That's not right. Family is family."

"That's the ironic part. He says he's all about family. He even gave a ton of money to that idiot Connelly's campaign. You know, the guy who thinks women should stay in the kitchen and we should lock up all the Mexicans?"

"Oh, Connelly's not that bad when you get to know him," Kinney told her. "You can't judge a man by his politics."

"Sure I can. Wait a minute. You actually know Connelly? A criminal like you?"

"Actually, we're not criminals. And don't worry. This isn't a kidnapping. I'm beginning to think there may be some common ground here."

"What do you mean?" Patty asked.

"Let me ask you this. If you were involved—I mean, if Hartshorn Industries were involved—in a criminal conspiracy, would you want to do something about it?"

"Of course."

"Even if it meant screwing over your father?"

"*Especially* if it did. You have no idea what kind of man he is."

"Did you know there's lithium in the ground here?"

"Of course," Patty said. "I'm a geologist, for chrissake. But it doesn't matter. We can't mine it. We're looking for what you usually find near it—lepidolite. It's a rare gemstone. A big outfit in New Zealand hired us to find it so they can make some new kind of chip core."

"It turns out that's horseshit, Patty. Can I call you Patty?"

"No."

Kinney turned to face Reed's back. They were motoring down the road now that led to the mining site. The only isolated spot they knew about was behind the nearby abandoned service station.

"What do you think, Harry? Should we level with her? I think if she hears what's really going on, she'll be happy to help."

"Yeah, it sounds like it."

Patty's head swiveled between the two of them as they spoke. "I'll cooperate," she said. "Just don't hurt me. I've got a dog."

"That's your bargaining chip?" Reed asked. "A dog?"

"Hey," Kinney said. "We can't very well orphan a dog, can we? It's not like it's a cat."

"I hate cats," Patty said. "They're so full of themselves."

"See?" Kinney said to her. "We already have something in common. We hate cats, too."

So Kinney started telling her the basics of what they were dealing with and finished as Reed parked out of sight of the road.

Patty listened carefully without comment. When Kinney finished, she said, "Holy crap!" and then sat quietly for a few moments. When she spoke again, she'd regained her poise. "I don't think thugs like you guys could concoct a story like that," she continued. "And it matches the weird stuff going down at the site. I believe you."

"So you're willing to help?" Kinney asked.

"Yes. These people need to be stopped. It's incredibly boring around here, but these are decent, hard-working people who deserve better than to be pushed around by the creeps behind all this. But I still don't like Connelly."

"That's fine," Kinney said.

"How do we know you're not just saying all this to wriggle out of your situation?" Reed asked.

"What do you want? A blood oath?" Patty's voice dripped with sarcasm.

"My, aren't you getting spunky for someone sitting in a car with badass abductors," Reed said.

"Oh, give me a break. Badass? My girlfriend could take you both on." She turned to Kinney. "How do you put up with this guy?"

"It's a challenge."

The three of them continued to sit in Reed's car while they made a new plan based on Patty's inside information and her willingness to help.

"What'll I tell my colleagues about where I've been?" Patty asked when they were through.

"They're all men, right?" Kinney said.

"Yes, unfortunately." Patty grimaced.

"Tell them it's woman trouble," Reed suggested. "They'll back off."

"And if they don't? That doesn't sound like me."

"Do whatever you think will work," Kinney said. "Do they know you have a drinking problem? You could use that."

"I don't have a drinking problem," Patty asserted loudly.

"That's what alcoholics always say," Reed told her. "Denial isn't just a river in Egypt."

"I don't appreciate that. I'm not an alcoholic."

"Didn't you just sneak off to drink two beers in the middle of a work day?" Reed asked.

"Fuck you."

On that note, the threesome headed back to town.

Chapter 29

"That was a stroke of luck, wasn't it?" Kinney said to Reed once they were back in his room. "I mean, what are the odds?"

"Slim to none. Are you sure we can trust her?"

"Reasonably sure. What do you think?"

"I'm always suspicious of people who don't like me. After all, I'm extremely likable."

"It takes all kinds, said the lady as she kissed the cow."

"Where do you come up with this stuff, Kinney?"

"I had an Irish babysitter."

Kinney made a long phone call to Rosie, who acquiesced to his request for additional help. Then the duo headed down to Nevitt's room, where they shared their new plan and told the FBI team what their role was. Nevitt wasn't happy about it but agreed again. They'd implement the plan in the morning.

Georgia sidled up to Kinney and suggested they take a walk. For the benefit of whoever was listening, she stated that it was to "catch up after all these years."

"Sure," Kinney replied, his gut tightening, which let him know he cared a lot about what might happen.

Georgia was silent during the elevator ride down and waited until they'd walked awhile before she spoke.

This time, since he wasn't following anyone as

surreptitiously as he could or searching for a copier machine, Kinney looked around. Alturas was a bit homely, but not nearly as bad as Reed claimed. A few storefronts were boarded up and a few others looked the worse for wear, but all in all, downtown Alturas was a real downtown.

A park sat in front of the county courthouse, which was a grandiose Neoclassical building with six white columns in front of a good-sized copper dome. A miniature white gazebo sat in the middle of the park. New wooden benches were spread around the perimeter. A few people sat on them, eating brown-bag lunches. One woman wore turquoise from head to toe. Another wore a UPS uniform.

"I've given it some thought," Georgia finally told him as they passed an elderly Hispanic couple holding hands. "I understand why you jumped to such a nasty conclusion about me. But it hurts, Kinney."

"Yeah, I get that. I hope we can repair things. I don't want to lose you."

"You never had me in the first place. We were just getting to know each other," Georgia corrected.

"You know what I mean. Don't minimize our connection."

She sighed as she dodged a shaggy Airedale on a leash. "I just don't know. On the one hand, it *was* great and maybe it could be again. But to be accused of conspiring to murder multiple people…How would you feel?"

"Shitty."

"I don't think that's an emotion, Kinney."

"You know what I mean by that, though, don't you? Why are you hassling me for using the wrong word?"

"I'm not just hurt, I'm angry, of course, and it's leaking out. See how easy it is to name an actual emotion?"

"Okay, fine. I guess I don't have a right to complain about anything. Just tell me what I need to do to make this right."

"Give me some time. And nail these bastards."

"Agreed." Kinney turned to her and smiled. "We could spend some time together tonight—maybe dinner?"

"I think not. In fact, I'd like to walk back on my own."

"Sure."

After Georgia departed. Kinney wandered around the downtown more, eventually stumbling onto a hardware store, where he bought a few things they might need. When he returned to his room, he discovered a note Reed had shoved under his door.

"I didn't want to interrupt your talk with Georgia by texting, so I went old school. I'm heading down to the hotel bar to check out the talent. I might not be in my room tonight if all goes well. I hope you two lovebirds made up. Georgia seems like she's worth some major apologizing."

Kinney realized he'd failed to apologize during the walk. He'd had his chance, and he'd blown it. After wrestling with whether texting Georgia represented not giving her the time she asked for, he sent a simple text.

—*I'm so sorry. I forgot to tell you that.*—

She wrote back —*Thank you. I know you are.*—

Kinney read a mystery while he watched a Will Ferrel movie and turned in early.

Chapter 30

Patty drove out to the mining site with Kinney in her trunk in the morning. Reed was already in position outside the fence at the back of the property—where they'd scouted with the drone—and the FBI team lurked behind the service station. Kinney had also arranged for more backup in case it proved necessary.

From within the trunk, Kinney heard Patty greet the guard at the front gate, and then once she'd driven through the center of the compound and parked, he heard a gruff-sounding man confront Patty as she clambered out of her compact sedan.

"What are you doing here? You can't be here today."

"Why not? I need to recheck the soil acidity," Patty told him.

"We've got bigwigs coming to inspect our progress—or lack of it, I should say. If you people had done your jobs properly, I wouldn't have to go through this."

Kinney hoped the man was talking about Barber. That would save everyone a lot of trouble.

"You mean Hartshorn executives? Those guys are all idiots. Just throw around a lot of technical terms. They won't want to admit they don't know what you're talking about."

"No, it's state senators—the ones on a committee

I'm not supposed to talk about."

"Why not?"

"That would be talking about it, wouldn't it?" the man said in an annoyed tone. "How long will it take you to do what you need to do?"

"An hour at the most."

"All right, go ahead. But next time call me before you come out on your own. Bruce knows about this. He was supposed to brief the whole team."

When Kinney heard two sets of retreating footsteps, he pulled the cord that unlocked the trunk from the inside and cracked the lid open a few inches. As promised, Patty had backed up in front of the main building, which was only a few feet away. The door was another fifteen feet sideways.

According to Patty, two men were likely to be working in the building at that time of day. One wasn't going to be a problem. He was in a wheelchair. The other one was an ex-military guy who liked to spend his lunch hour shooting at "varmints" through the fence.

Kinney was armed, but the sound of a gunshot would ruin their plan, so it was important to catch the guy with the rifle off guard. Anyway, why shoot some poor slob who was just trying to do his job?

He crawled out of the trunk wearing the coveralls he'd bought at the hardware store the evening before. Reed had added some convincing grime and stains, although there hadn't been time to add a tradesman logo. His stick-on name tag proclaimed he was Clem.

"Hi guys!" he called cheerily as he entered the Quonset hut.

The office within the Quonset hut was unexpectedly office-like. Someone had erected eight foot high sheetrock walls along the perimeter walls. Against the one to the right, a copier, a mini fridge, a microwave, and several filing cabinets paraded back to an open area behind two wooden desks. Small cacti in colorful pots sat on top of each of these. Most of the unfinished space in the back of the hut was littered with what must've been drilling equipment—pipes, spools of steel cable, and the like. The floor was a simple concrete slab that had been painted brown, and several banks of long fluorescent lights hung down from the high, arched ceiling to normal office height.

As promised, a chubby young man in a wheelchair sat in front of an oversized monitor at the desk on the left. He wore a T-shirt proclaiming he was available for free hugs. The other desk was manned by a formidable-looking guy with a Marine-style haircut, a bruiser of a body, and a fierce scowl. His loose workout clothes didn't fit the office setting.

"Who are you?" the wheelchair guy asked. He was simply curious.

"And what the hell are you doing here?" the burly, buzzcut guy asked in a nasty tone as he swiveled his squeaky desk chair to face Kinney.

"Is that any way to treat good ol' Clem?"

"Who?"

"Clem—me. I'm Clem. You see, my mom wanted a girl, and she was going to name her Clementine—you know, because of that song—but then she had me and as you can see, I'm not a girl, so she named me Clem. That's the story."

The two men looked at one another as Kinney drew closer.

"Are you retarded or something?" the big guy

asked.

"We don't use that term anymore," the other man told him.

"Fuck you, Mason."

"No, I'm a loose cannon," Kinney told them. "But some people think I'm batshit crazy."

"Why's that?" Mason asked, his voice gentle now.

"What kind of sane man would walk in here and do this?" He pulled his pistol from his rear waistband and trained it on the big guy, who dove sideways and came up with a Glock in his meaty hand.

Kinney leaped toward him and snap-kicked the air where the man's wrist was a moment ago. The guy was quick; he'd rolled to the side and now attempted to raise his gun again. Kinney launched a roundhouse kick which thudded into the man's bicep. The man switched hands—tossing the Glock across his body.

Who the hell is this guy? Kinney thought. *This isn't a mining employee.*

Kinney had to dive behind Mason—the wheelchair guy.

"Give it up, Kinney," the big guy said. "I should've recognized you first thing. Barber and four more guys are outside."

"You knew I was coming?"

"Yup. That's why I'm here. Barber said you'd show up here sooner or later, and then we found out last night when that would be."

"Fellas," Mason implored. "Why don't you take this outside? I'm uncomfortable sitting here between two gun-wielding maniacs. Bill, what do you say?"

"Mason," Bill replied, "call Rooney. Tell him Kinney's here, and we've got a Mexican standoff."

"That might be racist," Kinney pointed out to Mason. "I wouldn't say that if I were you."

Mason relayed the message, then tossed the phone to Bill. "Rooney wants to talk to you," he told him. Bill's attention was momentarily diverted to catch the phone.

Kinney bolted for the door, gambling that Bill wasn't authorized to shoot him. He knew Barber would want to interrogate him.

He somersaulted through the doorway after shouldering it open and then leapt to the left toward Patty's car.

Two guards sprinted across the dirt parking lot toward him. They both had assault rifles in their hands.

"Hold it right there!" Bill called as he emerged from the building behind Kinney.

Since Kinney wasn't sure he could avoid killing anyone if he engaged in a gunfight, and he preferred not to die himself, he climbed into the trunk of Patty's car and pulled the lid closed. He heard the men's footsteps halt at the back of the car.

"That's weird. What shall we do?" one of them asked.

Bill answered. "Kinney's a nut job, but he can kick like a motherfucker. And he's got a gun. Let's wait for Barber and let him decide. The guy's not going anywhere, is he?"

"No, sir."

"And find the other guy. He's bound to be here somewhere."

"Right."

Kinney considered his options. He knew that unlike in TV shows and movies, bullets had no problem passing through a car's sheet metal. So he could start shooting from within the trunk and probably hit a couple of the men. But then the remaining ones would probably riddle the trunk, no matter what orders Barber had given them. These were hired contractors, not agents. They weren't going to risk their lives beyond a certain point.

Another option was opening the trunk and surrendering. The phone in his pocket was broadcasting to both Reed and the feds, so they knew about his situation. They could probably rescue him. Or maybe not. What if Barber showed up with a dozen more men?

If Kinney stayed in the trunk—and he wondered at that point why he'd had the impulse to climb in in the first place—that would delay whatever happened next. So his team would have more time to make a plan to nab Barber, and, of course, rescue him. He settled on remaining where he was.

Bill had told him that Barber was on the grounds, but his former boss didn't show up for a long twenty-five minutes. Kinney spent part of the time using a tire iron to create a space to crawl into the back seat. For now, he stayed where Barber expected to find him.

"Kinney!" Barber barked. "Get the hell out of there. We need to talk."

His voice indicated he stood a ways away from the car. Not a target.

"I like it in here," Kinney called. "It's cozy."

"That weird shit isn't going to work with me. And you can't stay in there forever."

"You could punch a hole in the trunk lid and send a tube down. I like wheatgrass smoothies the best. And I could pee in the tire well. It's like a tiny house in here, only tinier."

"I've got a proposition," Barber said, his irritation apparent. "A win-win deal for both of us."

"Why should I trust you?" Of course he didn't. Kinney was just curious how Barber would answer.

"Do you have an alternative?" Barber was acknowledging he couldn't make a case for Kinney to trust him.

"Sure. I've got plenty of choices. I could Butch Cassidy and Sundance it, for example—go out in a blaze of glory."

"No, that's not you. And it's only a matter of time before we find that knucklehead partner of yours in case you were counting on him to save you."

"You've had a half hour, and you haven't found him yet. What does that tell you?" The longer Kinney kept Barber talking, the better, Kinney reasoned.

"It tells me my B team is incompetent. I've brought the A team with me. Face it, Kinney. Your situation is hopeless unless you get the hell out of there and talk to me."

"Okay, okay. But you're going to have to open the trunk from out there. I can't find the pull tab in here in the dark."

If Barber gave that a moment's thought, he'd realize how ridiculous it was. Kinney was banking on Barber's eagerness to settle the score.

Kinney crawled through the opening he'd made to the back seat and opened the door a crack as quietly as he could. When the men's attention was on the trunk, he'd slip out and start firing at them from beside the car—just to wound them. From a stationary position, with the men's focus on the back of the car, he felt confident of his aim.

"Barry," Barber commanded, "open the trunk. And Kinney, throw out your gun first thing."

"Why me?" Barry said. "Let Jeff do it."

"Remember what happened at the ranch the last time someone didn't follow my orders?" Barber said.

There was a pause. "Uh, yes sir."

Kinney heard steps approaching the rear of the car. He readied himself.

As the trunk lid opened and someone yelled, "What the fuck!" he slithered out the door, his gun in his hand. Before he could gather himself and aim, a woman behind him called, "Drop it! I've got a shotgun. I can't miss."

Kinney dropped it. In a moment, he was surrounded by five hard-looking men. One of them picked up his pistol and then hurriedly backed away. Kinney turned to see who'd gotten the drop on him.

It was Georgia!

"Jesus Christ," he said. "Make up your mind. Are you a white hat or a black hat? I'm sick of this switching back and forth."

She smiled grimly. "You could say it depends."

"On what?" The adrenaline surging through Kinney delayed any emotional response to what was happening.

"On what my brother tells me to do," Georgia replied.

Kinney was confused. "Barber?" he finally asked.

"Yup."

"Wow, I didn't see that coming."

Georgia smiled. "You're not as smart as you think, Kinney."

Barber strolled over from behind the car. "Stay at least ten feet away, men. You wouldn't believe how this guy can kick."

"I can," Bill said from about fifteen feet away.

Kinney pivoted to face Barber. "I want in," he said. "Five percent of future earnings or my lawyer will release everything I know."

"Nice try. Are you going to behave yourself?"

"Do I ever?"

Barber sighed. "Barry, use the shackles on his ankles. Jeff, handcuff him behind his back."

"Shackles? What is this—the Middle Ages? Where'd you get those—Shackles R Us?"

"Shut up."

Barry pulled Kinney to his feet after they'd incapacitated him. The shackles weren't locked. They weren't even shackles, in fact. They were flat, black nylon horse hobbles, fastened with something like two belt buckles. It would take some time to extricate himself from them, though, including a contortion to bring his handcuffed hands down to his ankles.

"Bring him to the office," Barber ordered.

Kinney could only shuffle. The good news is that no one thought to search him and take his phone. Kinney figured that Barber's minions were probably battle-hardened mercenaries. You didn't bother to take phones away from enemy combatants.

Reed and the feds would've heard where Kinney was headed. So that was good.

Then Kinney realized that if Georgia was on the property, wearing her black—no, obsidian—hat, the FBI team was likely to be out of the picture. She must've killed or incapacitated her colleagues—if they were even colleagues.

The whole team might be impersonating FBI agents, Kinney realized, and the guy Kinney had called in San Diego to confirm Georgia's credentials could've been part of the hoax.

He didn't know hardly anything he needed to know.

In the office, Barber told Georgia and his minions to go find Reed and greet the state senators who were due soon, leaving him alone with a trussed Kinney, who'd been shoved down onto Bill's desk chair. Mason was nowhere in sight.

"So Kinney, here we are."

"Yup." Kinney gulped involuntarily. He'd probably be dead soon.

"What do you have to say for yourself?"

"I didn't know you had a sister."

"Georgia is my half sister," Barber told him. "For years, she's been an asset at the FBI."

"Then why'd you pimp her out?"

"I beg your pardon. I certainly did not." Barber stood up as straight as he could and looked down his nose at Kinney. It was though he were in a bad movie and the director had told him to act affronted.

"We've screwed a lot over the past week, Barber. She's great in bed." Kinney's mind was scheming in overdrive now. If Barber was going to kill him, he'd at least mess with him in the meantime.

"I know you, Kinney. You say a lot of provocative things. Anyway, if she did that, it was of her own free will. You're not going to get under my skin."

"Heaven forbid. We're just making conversation here."

"Do you really think Bolt is going to rescue you, Kinney? You know Georgia took out the other feds, right?"

Kinney wished he could slap the arrogance off Barber's face. "Reed isn't the ninny you think he is," he told him.

"He's enough of a ninny that he'll try to rescue you despite the odds here. So we'll have him in hand too soon enough."

"You think these hired hands of yours can handle a trained agent?"

Barber ignored that. "So what am I going to do with you? I don't suppose you actually want to join me in the multi-millionaire club."

"I don't think so. Anyway, if I said I did, would you believe me?"

"I suppose not." Barber sighed. "It's such a waste. You're a good man, Kinney. I could always count on you—until you got shot in Cambodia, that is. After that you've been strictly damaged goods."

"I think of it as becoming a new, improved version. Kinney 2.0."

"We all would like to think of ourselves as something more than who we are." Barber looked pensive as he continued. "Look at me. Here I am about to murder a government agent who was just doing his job, yet I still consider myself a moral person. Circumstances just pulled out my dark side. It could happen to anyone. Or so I tell myself."

"You're moral, huh? Tell that to all the dead people you've left in your wake."

Barber shrugged. "It couldn't be helped."

"Are you looking for absolution here, Barber?"

Barber tilted his head to the side as he paused. "I guess I am. You're the closest thing I have to a peer. You've killed dozens of people. You understand."

"No, I don't. That was different. And I don't do that anymore."

"Actually, I'd like to know more about that, Kinney. I know you had some sort of near-death experience, and you were told something important. What was it?"

"Once I tell you, you'll kill me." They both knew this.

"That's true, but as you pointed out on Ocean Beach, there are a lot of ways to die. Humor me, and I'll make sure yours is relatively painless."

"Relatively?"

"Well, it's not like I'm toting around a cocktail of hospice meds, is it?"

"A bullet to the head?" Kinney suggested.

"Sounds good. I can do that. So what's the story?"

"It's a long one, Barber."

Kinney knew that inventing a fanciful tale with lots of details would, at the least, give him a few more minutes of life. At best, it gave his rescuers time to show up.

"I doubt it's actually long, but go ahead," Barber replied. "If I get impatient, I'll just go ahead and shoot you somewhere you wouldn't like."

"Fair enough." Kinney paused. "You know, I tell stories better when I'm not tied up."

Barber just stared at him. "Quit stalling."

"Okay, here goes. I was floating above my body, watching the doctors work on me—trying to revive me, I mean. Things were a little blurry, but I could make it

369

all out."

So far, so good, Kinney reasoned. He'd read others' accounts of near-deaths and this seemed common.

"Then something told me to look up," Kinney continued. "It wasn't a voice or anything—it was just something I knew I was supposed to do. I saw that bright light people talk about and—"

Barber interrupted him. "I don't care about all that. What was the message? What changed you?"

"I'm getting to that. It's not going to make sense without context. Suppose I told you the meaning of life was salami. That would sound absurd without an explanation."

"I take it salami wasn't involved?"

"No, it's just an example."

Barber sighed again. "You have a strange brain, Kinney."

"I've been told that."

"Go ahead," Barber said, exhaling loudly.

"I was drawn to the light through a kind of tunnel. It kept getting brighter until I got there—wherever 'there' was. Then I was in a white room, standing in front of three people who were sitting cross-legged on round, blue pillows."

"Zafus," Barber said.

"Geshundheit," Kinney said.

"That's the name of that type of pillow."

"Oh. Anyway, the three people were old and ugly, but they kind of glowed. A man sat in the middle, flanked by two women. They were all bald. The man spoke in a deep, unaccented voice. 'So what do you want to know?' he asked."

"Let me guess," Barber said. "You asked him the meaning of life."

"Yeah, I did." Kinney paused to concoct even more fictitious details. "He told me it's loving connectedness. I said I didn't think 'connectedness' was a word. He called me an asshole and said now I wouldn't get to die—that I had to endure the continued misery of being crammed into a body because of my insolence. One of the women told him to take it easy. 'Kinney's been under a lot of stress lately,' she said. The other one said, 'Kinney, you're one of a kind. Here's something else you ought to know. If you keep killing people, you won't like where you end up.'

" 'Some place without free beer and slutty starlets?' I asked the woman."

"That sounds like you," Barber commented. "Even in death you just can't help yourself."

"Anyway," Kinney continued, pleased that Barber seemed to be buying his story, "This lady laughed, but the man scowled and told me to shut the hell up. The other woman told me I *was* going to stay alive, but not because 'Ralph' decreed it. It was just my destiny.

"I asked Ralph if I was supposed to share what he told me—the loving part. 'You know, spread the good word?'

" 'Oh, everybody knows they're supposed to be loving,' he said.

" 'Yet few manage it consistently,' I said.

" 'That's the truth. Now skedaddle,' he said.

" 'Tell me one more thing before I go,' I said.

" 'No,' he responded.

" 'I will,' the other woman said. 'What do you want to know?'

" 'Who's going to win the World Series this year? I'm planning to put down a sizable bet.'

" 'It's—' "

Reed burst into the room, holding a gun to Georgia's head as he shoved her ahead of him.

"Great story, Kinney," he said. "Compelling and moving. And, of course, a pile of shit."

"I had to give you time to get here, Reed."

"Whatever. Barber, I know this is your sister. Your henchmen are dimwits. And you didn't win any Nobel Prizes when you didn't think to take Kinney's phone. It's been recording the whole time."

"Fuck," Barber said matter-of-factly, still training his pistol on Kinney. "But if you think Georgia is more important to me than unimaginably huge sums, you've misjudged me."

Reed flung Georgia to the side and shot Barber in the torso. He moved forward to deliver the head shot that would make certain Barber was dead.

In the meantime, Georgia pulled a small .22 pistol from her boot and fired at Reed, hitting him in his upper arm. Fortunately it wasn't the one holding the gun. He whirled to dispatch her, but she'd rolled behind a desk. Reed fired at the wooden relic, but the bullet would've had to go through it lengthwise, piercing whatever was in the drawers.

Kinney brought his handcuffed arms under his butt and unfastened the buckles that bound his ankles. He quietly sidled to the front of the room to outflank Georgia. With his legs free, he'd be almost as lethal as Reed's gun.

Georgia poked her hand up and fired toward Reed. The small caliber bullet pinged high off the corrugated metal wall behind him.

"You've got a peashooter," he told her. "I've got a cannon. And there are two of us. I don't want to kill you. Why don't you come out and talk? I'd love to hear your side of the story."

"Kinney's tied up. It's just you and me. And of course you're going to kill me whatever I say."

"No, I only shot your brother because it's unlikely he could be brought to justice. He's got dirt on everyone. *You* can go to prison like he should've."

Unfortunately, Barber wasn't dead. While sprawled on the floor, he managed to pick his gun back up, and shot Reed in the same arm, just a bit lower.

"That's getting old," Reed said as he shot Barber in the head.

Georgia took the opportunity to make a break for the door. She spied Kinney, but not in time. He snap-kicked the gun out of her hand and continued the kick to her temple. She crumpled and lay still.

Kinney kicked her gun away and asked Reed how badly he was hurt.

"Well, there won't be a trio of weird angels telling me anything. But I'll bleed out in a while unless we do something about it. Both bullets went through so there are four holes that need stanching. The exit wounds are going to be the worst, but it was only a .22."

"Not like Montenegro, huh?'

"God, no. I didn't think I'd survive that."

"Let's look for a first aid kit," Kinney said. "They must have one around here somewhere. Why don't you find something to tie around your arm to keep pressure on the wounds in the meantime—maybe Barber's shirt."

"Sounds good."

Georgia had been feigning unconsciousness and once again made a break for the door. This time, she was able to fling it open and run into the bright light. Kinney raced to follow her. A few yards ahead, Patty stood with her arms crossed, watching the building's door. As Georgia sprinted by her, she casually stuck out her leg and tripped her.

Georgia flopped down, face forward, grunting as she landed on the hard-packed dirt. Patty kicked her in the ribs.

"Bitch," she said.

Chapter 31

Kinney marched Georgia across the hard-packed dirt, past the derrick, to where Rosie Aubert and four armed men held Barber's men at gunpoint by the fence. The film star wore a shiny red tracksuit as if she were an uncharacteristically svelte 1970s mafioso, and she'd casually tucked an assault rifle under her arm. Her hair was a bird's nest and one of her cheeks was smeared with dirt. She still looked beautiful.

"Hey, Kinney. How's it going?" she asked, smiling as if she'd just run into him at the grocery store. "Reed called us and said you climbed into a trunk, and he couldn't reach the FBI agents. Why would you do that? Anyway, the copy of the search warrant worked wonders, but I wish you'd also sent me a list of decent places to stay. My neck hurts, and something bit me."

Kinney grunted and shoved Georgia forward to join the others. He was currently out of words. Reed trailed behind, adjusting his makeshift white bandages. Patty strolled up a few steps behind him. Mason, the man in the wheelchair, followed everyone else, and then wheeled himself over to where the Barber's men stood in front of the cyclone fence.

"Get away from there, Mason," Kinney told him. "You're not like them."

"I don't need special treatment." He declared. "I'm not disabled. I'm *other*-abled."

"Fine. Suit yourself."

The faces of Barber's team told a varied tale. Some of the men were obviously scared, some belligerent, while one pretended not to care what was happening. Kinney had an urge to smack Bill but resisted doing so. Georgia bowed her head and looked down. She'd pigeon-toed her feet as if she were trying to snowplow on a ski slope to halt her descent.

"I'll call Glinda," Reed said. "Someone needs to lock these people up, and someone else needs to either rescue or bury the FBI agents behind the gas station."

"Rescue," Georgia mumbled. "They're just tied up."

As Reed dialed, Rosie spoke up. "Glinda? Which witch was she?"

Georgia answered. "The good witch of the north."

"Shut up," Kinney told her. "Just stand there quietly—all of you."

Rosie nodded to one of her men. "Paul, go see what's happening behind that wrecked place we passed. If there are FBI agents there, bring them back."

"Yes, ma'am."

"Hi, honey," Reed said to his phone, the grimaced. "Glinda hung up," he told the others a moment later.

Mason spoke up. "Women don't like to be called 'honey' these days. Treat her with respect, and I'm sure she'll talk to you."

"Shut up, Mason," Kinney said. "I'll call," he told Reed.

When Kinney briefly explained the situation, claiming to be Reed's partner at the FBI, she told him she was nearby and would be there in a few minutes. There'd be a half dozen other deputies arriving in twenty minutes.

Kinney realized things were going to get really awkward if Nevitt and the other authentic agents didn't get to the site soon. How could Kinney and Reed justify their actions to the local authorities?

When Glinda clambered out of her SUV, Kinney and Reed approached her. As advertised, Glinda wasn't hard on the eyes. Her crisp khaki uniform clung to her curvy torso, and her curly black hair hung down onto her shoulders. To Kinney's eyes, Glinda looked like someone who ought to be hawking a miracle product on late night TV.

"This is Kinney?" Glinda asked Reed. "And what's wrong with your arm?"

"That's Kinney," Reed told Glinda. "And I was shot. Twice. It's lucky I'm so brave and manly or I might be rolling around on the ground in pain."

"Cut the crap," Glinda said as she took in the unlikely scenario ahead of her. "Hey!" she said as she strode forward. "Aren't you Rosie Aubert? What are you doing here? Is this a film set? Are you people messing with me?"

"No, absolutely not. My name is Deborah-Ann Maddox," Rosie told her in a passable Southern accent as she crossed her eyes. "I'm flattered, though. Maybe we could have a drink later." She winked.

Glinda blushed. "Er, never mind. Who wants to explain what's going on here?"

"I will," Agent Nevitt called as he got out of Rosie's security man's car, seemingly no worse for wear.

"And who the hell are you?"

Nevitt strode over and showed Glinda his badge.

"I'm the senior agent here—John Nevitt. We appreciate your help."

The other two agents joined him, having pulled up in the feds' rental car.

Glinda nodded her acknowledgement of his authority.

"Before I get into the details of this operation," Nevitt continued, "I'm going to send you off with one of my men who'll fill you in on the general situation. I need to take care of some business here."

"All right."

Nevitt gestured to the nondescript agent—Hannover—who led Glinda back near the Quonset hut. She shot Reed one last glare over her shoulder. When they were out of earshot, Nevitt turned to Kinney.

"Who are these people?"

"Private security."

"Private security outfits don't hire movie stars, Kinney. That is definitely Rosie Aubert. I saw her hold a rifle like that in *Amazon Commando*."

Rosie switched her rifle to her other arm and stuck out her hand. "*Enchanté*," she said. Nevitt shook it vigorously. "That was not one of my best roles," she told him. "I was under contract for three films, and I had to do that one to get free of those bastards."

"That's really you?" Mason said. "I thought you had a big French accent."

"Shut up, Mason," Kinney said again.

Rosie answered Mason in a very thick French accent. "I am definitely me. *I* should know."

"Look," Nevitt said," somebody needs to explain this."

Kinney spoke up. "Private security outfits don't

hire movie stars, but movie stars hire them."

"I see. And some movie stars are foolish enough to work alongside who they hire, I suppose. Barber? Is he dead?"

"Yes. It was self-defense. You'll find a pistol in his hand in the main building." Kinney gestured past the derrick to it.

"I shot him," Reed added. "No regrets. And now I need to get to a hospital. In case anyone forgot, I've been shot. Twice."

"Can you drive?" Nevitt asked.

"Actually, I'm pretty dizzy." His bandages were now stained with fresh blood.

"Kinney," Nevitt said. "Why don't the two of you take off? Use our car. It's better if you're not around as we sort this out."

"You're sure?"

"I talked to Alan Kim on the way over. That's how he wants to play it. For now. He stressed the 'for now' part. So don't think you're entirely off the hook."

"Got it."

"I'll contact him again so he can call and smooth things out for Reed at the hospital."

"Thanks," Kinney's partner said lethargically as he sagged and almost fell.

Kinney hoisted Reed's good arm over his shoulder. "Off we go, big fella."

As Kinney drove through the gate with Reed slumped in the passenger seat, he encountered Jerome Hattori and two other men about to drive in. He averted his face.

"Sorry we're late," Hattori told him through his open window. "Is Barber still here?"

"In a manner of speaking," Kinney told him. "Go right in."

Epilogue

Special Agent Kim's boss's boss reluctantly cleared Kinney and Reed a month after they returned home. Gayle Costello looked like someone's grandmother, defying Kinney's expectations. Red plastic reading glasses dangled from a silver chain around her turkey neck, resting on a gray cable knit cardigan. Her dyed orange hair was permed into a helmet. If she and Eddie ran at one another and bashed the top of their heads together like rutting rams, it would be a tossup as to whether his pompadour or her hair gave way.

One of her blue eyes was milky, and her eyebrows had been shaved and then penciled in to match her hair. A spiderweb of wrinkles started at the corners of her eyes and spread sideways across her temples, contrasting with smooth skin around her thin-lipped mouth. Surprisingly, Costello spoke like a bookie in an old black and white movie—out of the corner of her mouth in a Brooklyn accent.

"I can see that everything you two did was in pursuit of the national interest," she told them in her cozy office on the top floor of the federal building. It looked the way Kinney imagined her living room did, with the addition of a gleaming new metal desk.

"And it all fell under the mandate of your agency— what you'd been authorized to do," Costello continued.

"It's not up to me to judge whether government agents ought to be operating domestically. So go your merry way, gentlemen. But if I ever see you in this office again, you'll be sorry."

"Thank you," Kinney told her. "We appreciate that."

"Have you got any shiny medals we could put on our fridges?" Reed asked. "We kinda saved the FBI's ass, didn't we?

Costello leaned back in her old-fashioned wooden desk chair. "I heard you two could be amusing. You're not making a case for that, Bolt." She smiled nonetheless. "I run an ass-free agency, by the way." She smiled wider, pleased with herself.

"Good one," Kinney said, "but I don't think Reed was kidding, ma'am. He really does like shiny things. He picks up candy wrappers on the street, turns them inside out, and makes quilts out of them."

Reed nodded. "Sometimes I make them into a hat to keep Martians from monitoring my thoughts. It gets pretty hot under there, though."

Costello smiled again. "I've got to admit that in another life we might all enjoy a meal together. Now get out."

The agency Kinney and Reed worked for was disbanded, its agents either let go or reassigned to the CIA, NSA, or DEA. Kinney and Reed were ignored by the powers that be.

Ryan Connelly hired them as part-time security consultants, tripling their salaries. Mostly, they set up scenarios that enabled security guards at various sites to keep people like the two of them out. The work was boring and required some travel but left them time for golf. Kinney continued to fail in his efforts to meet his unrealistic standards on the course.

When Lyle and his wife were released by Connelly's security team—they'd been held at a cabin in Montana—both were immediately picked up and prosecuted. The FBI rounded up the rest of the conspirators in short order, except for one Rakena executive who committed suicide in a novel manner—he rode a ewe off a cliff in New Zealand.

Georgia was charged with a host of crimes and was eventually found guilty of most of them. Kinney never saw her again. Her purported uncle at the FBI's San Diego office was indicted as well, but never convicted.

Jason Barber turned out to be the guy who'd shot at Kinney and Reed on Ocean Beach up in San Francisco. He was convicted of several additional crimes, but he turned state's evidence against a host of codefendants and was only sentenced to three years.

Rosie Aubert took off to film her superhero movie in Costa Rica, postponing her wedding. Connelly managed to keep her name out of the official investigation, although she lobbied him to highlight her participation for publicity purposes.

Connelly also pulled some strings to make sure Foster and Hoff were granted huge promotions when they transferred to the CIA, and along with this carrot, Kinney told Foster he'd force her to go on a date with Reed if she revealed what she knew about them. She was savvy enough to understand that a more serious threat lay beneath that one. It helped that Connelly paid her the five-thousand dollars they owed her for her initial information.

The Jefferson bill never made it out of committee.

The lithium remained in the ground. Glinda bought the mining compound property and started a B&B based on the infamous shootout that had happened there. Her occupancy rate was mediocre.

Patty was fired from Hartshorn and became a barista. Eddie escaped prosecution and ventured out of the house a time or two to meet female game players with similarly misleading avatars. Kim moved up the ladder at the FBI. And VanVleet was nabbed in Amsterdam, but never extradited because of the US's death penalty.

"We did good," Reed said to Kinney in the San Jose federal courthouse hallway after they watched Lyle's sentencing eight months later. The judge handed down the maximum sentence and said he wished he could punish him more.

"Yes, we did."

"Did you have fun?"

"I did," Kinney told him. "Mostly."

"That's not normal, is it?"

"Nope. We're definitely different."

A word about the author…

Verlin Darrow is currently a psychotherapist who lives with his psychotherapist wife in the woods near the Monterey Bay in northern California. They diagnose each other as necessary. Verlin is a former professional volleyball player, country-western singer/songwriter, import store owner, and NCAA coach. Before bowing to the need for higher education, a much younger Verlin ran a punch press in a sheetmetal factory, drove a taxi, worked as a night janitor, shoveled asphalt missed being blown up by Mt. St. Helens by ten minutes, survived the 1985 Mexico City earthquake (8.1), and (so far) has successfully weathered his own internal disasters.